Book One of the Power's Saga

# POWER'S PRICE

## JAMES KIRKHAM

Published by James Kirkham
Printed in the United States of America

Author: James H. Kirkham
Cover Art: Laura Andersen

ISBN: 978-0-9831723-0-7

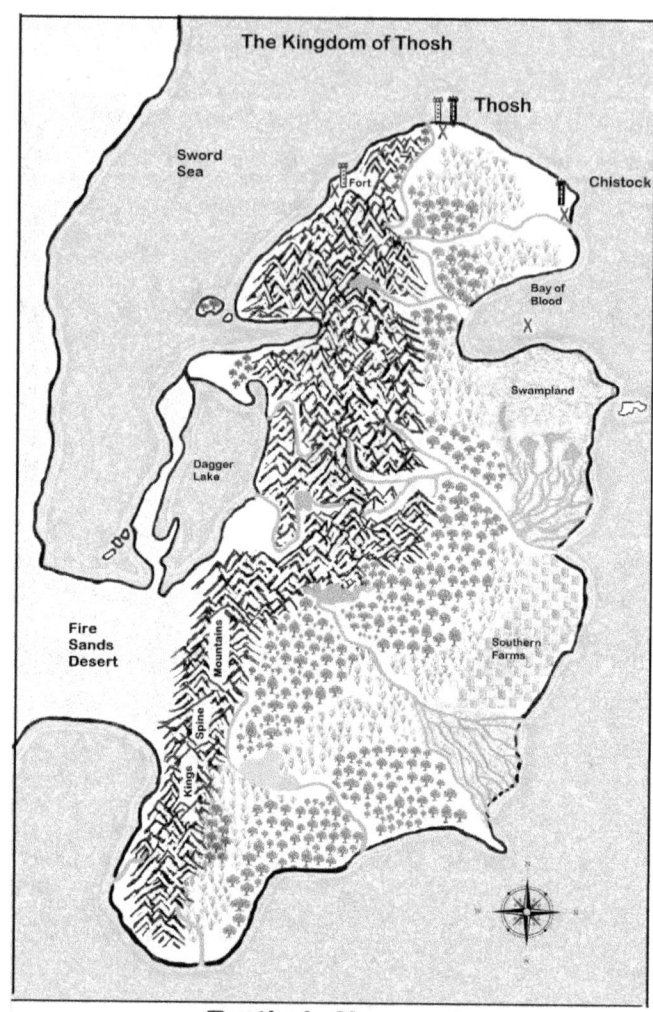

**Zartho's Map**

# Dedicated to:

Jennifer; thanks for the unending support.

Pete; thanks for the unending enthusiasm.

# Preface

Ansyll awoke slowly from the depths of dreamless slumber. Normally he was a heavy sleeper, one who rarely stirred from the time he lay down, until he was forced to get up in the morning. Even then he was slow to rouse and begin the day. If he did wake in the night, he was normally quick to return to the bliss of sleep. This night, however, he became more and more awake. He tried to go back to sleep, but it was a vain effort at best. Finally he gave up and got out of bed in disgust.

"Perhaps if I walk around a bit," he thought to himself, and began pacing his small room. His apartment was small, even for wizards in training. It did boast an incredible view of the ocean though, and that feature above all else was the reason he had chosen this room. He could have chosen any of more than a dozen rooms on this level of the tower, but the single window of this room looked out over several thousand feet of cliff face and over sea's horizon beyond.

The tower had originally been built in conjunction with the nearby fort as a defense for the western shores of the kingdom, but after centuries of neglect and inactivity it had become the last bastion of the failing magic student. Once only the very best had been assigned to this remote shore, now it served to keep the worst of the young wizard students focused on their studies. After all, there wasn't anything else for them to do in this desolate part of the kingdom.

The nearby fort served as a similar place for the young soldiers. They all had to do a six-month duty there at least once in their careers. Though the two groups were each other's only neighbors, they rarely, if ever paid any attention to each other. The soldiers would transfer after their brief tour, but the students in the tower were stuck there for a minimum of two years. If they could bring their abilities up to par in that time they would be allowed to return to the tower in Thosh to continue their studies. If not they may be allowed two more years to try, or they may be summarily dismissed from the study of magic altogether. It depended a lot on their attitude, and whether the keeper of the remote tower, an ancient wizard who hadn't been out of the desolate building in decades, liked them or not.

Ansyll thought of the three months he had been in this place. He had come in the fall with the army during the regularly scheduled transfer. Only one time each year did the keeper of the tower contact the white tower in Thosh using magical means that he didn't understand at all yet, and that had been over a week ago. He imagined that he and the other three students were as cut off from the world as they possibly could be. It would be another year before they would hear any news at all from home. Nearly another year after that before he could visit his home. A brief wave of nostalgia washed over him, and he shook physically to overcome it.

He stood for several minutes gazing out on the moonlit ocean below trying to figure out why he was so awake. He didn't feel the slightest inclination for sleep, and that bothered him for some unknown reason. Maybe there was something going on that he should know about. But then, there was never anything going on in this tower except the silent studies of students on their last chance. Finally he turned away from the window to return to his bed and try to sleep again.

There, less than a foot in front of him was blackness. An oval shaped blackness that hovered in the air between him and his bed. He opened his mouth to cry out, but his voice was silenced as an enormous, taloned hand shot out of the center of the blackness and wrapped around his neck. The only sound was the crushing of his windpipe and the crack of his neck being broken. Then he was yanked off his feet into the blackness. A moment later the dark oval disappeared entirely, and the room was left as empty as the rest of the tower now was.

# Chapter 1

Malak crouched silently in the shadows of the battlements. The top of the tower was dimly lit at best with the waning crescent moon slowly setting behind the mountains to the west. He waited patiently, like the stone at his back: noiseless and unmoving. The guard he had been watching was coming his direction again.

It had taken Malak over an hour to scale the dark-wizard's tower. He had been completely silent and had moved into his attack position without the guard becoming suspicious. His concentration was never totally focused on the target for more than a second or two, just as it was also never fully away from the man. His training and experience kept him alert to everything around him. No matter where he was, his mind never turned it's back on anything. It also never lost sight of the target.

The unwary guard, on the other hand, was thinking about home and the warmth of his bed. He had been walking this post for hours. Normally the dark-wizards in the tower below kept their own guard, but on the spring and fall equinox, they hired the job out to the few soldiers they felt they could trust. He had been working for them like this for several years. There wasn't a lot of money for the one night's work, but it was a welcome little bonus to his normal pay. Though the hours were long in the middle of the night, there had never been any danger. After all, who in their right mind would think of attacking a dark-wizard tower?

The guard slowly made his way towards Malak. He had already come close to him three times before. Each time he had turned and retraced his steps just shy of the assassin's position. This time, however, he took an extra step in his pacing. This time he was close enough. This time was his last.

The edges of the dagger in Malak's hand seemed to glow in the half-light of the waning moon atop the battlements. It was a dirty weapon, made of cheap steel, a knife that could be found and bought easily, and discarded just as quickly. Malak knew well just where to step and how to move to drive the tip into the lung and heart. A quick thrust and a twisting motion, and the guard lay on the ground, blood oozing from his chest. The guard had died before he hit the ground. The only sound of his passing had been the dull thud of the blow, and his low, quick grunt.

Malak slipped quickly back into the shadows and watched the lifeblood leak from the newest corpse to his name. He suddenly wondered why he was here. He seemed to come to himself in a moment. The act of killing had come as a shock to him. He was very good at it, but hated doing it. He thought of the evening, and wondered why he had accepted the job from the fat man at the inn. He had spent the last two years in the port city of Chistock trying to forget his previous life, and the killing. He had worked on the docks, and tried to forget, but now he was back in it. Right now, in fact he was up to his neck in it.

He stood looking at the corpse for a moment longer. This would complicate things a lot. If the body were found before he was finished and gone, there would surely be an alarm and a search of the tower. He didn't think the wizards would look kindly on him for killing their guards and breaking into their home. Especially when they found out what he was there to do. He knew he would talk, everyone talks under torture, and torture was guaranteed at the hands of the black-robes. Not to mention the magical probing his mind would probably also undergo just to make sure they hadn't missed anything, leaving him barely a vegetable.

If he had been attempting to rob a white-robe tower, there might have been a chance for mercy. There were more white-robed wizard's towers than black ones; in fact there were only two black wizard's towers in the entire kingdom. Most students of magic shunned the darker side of their art, and all things involved in the terrible powers of the black-robes. Black-robed wizards weren't known for their mercy. They were known for many things, but not mercy.

Unfortunately, the item Malak was looking for was not to be found in a White tower. The fat man who was paying him to steal it had been emphatic about its location. Now that he thought about it, how did the fat man known so exactly where it was? Why had he been so easily tempted to take the job? Something wasn't right about the whole evening now that he had come to his senses.

In his youth, Malak had been trained as an assassin in the service of the king of Thosh. The training had served him well in the past couple of years since he had slipped quietly away from the king's service in the night. Strangely, the king hadn't tried to find him. Unfortunately, as well as having stealthy reflexes, he also had deadly ones, and now it seemed that they had gotten the better of him.

Malak hadn't meant to kill the guard, he told himself, but he hadn't seen any way to avoid it. The guard had been almost dozing as he walked, and he hadn't been aware of anything around him, let alone Malak's presence. He would have to work quickly now and get out fast. Within moments he had placed a cloth-wrapped grappling hook securely at the top of the tower with its rope hanging down the many stories to the ground below. Then he moved silently to the west side of the tower, scanning the darkness for the trap door the fat man had insisted was to be found there. Supposedly it led inside the tower, and down to the lower levels. Locating it, he pulled the vial of bluish liquid from his tunic, removed the stopper, and poured a thin stream around the door, making sure he was within the circle. Then in a voice just above a whisper, he spoke a few of the magical words that he knew. The Circle flared for a moment, and then turned black. At the same time, there was an almost imperceptible click from within the door. There was also the twinge of sharp pain inside his bowels that he had come to know was part of every minor little spell that he cast.

The fat man had given Malak the spell, and he still wondered where it had come from. He shouldn't have been able to cast spells at all, less than one person in ten could, but in the course of his training as a youth, he was studying magical writings and had, accidentally, performed a small spell. The wizard instructing the class had been astounded and insisted to the king that he receive some training in the art. He had never known who that wizard was. Almost all of his instructors had worn masks, as had his fellow students. This way they were kept from forming any close relationships with their teachers. In fact, he had known only one wizard during his brief magical education and now that man wasn't really a wizard anymore. He had ended Malak's magical training as soon as it was discovered that in spite of his ability, he was wholly unsuited to the practice of most magic. His training had been brief to say the least. He had just enough of it to cast some simple spells that were written, this one was supposed to nullify traps both magical and conventional. Now he would find out if it worked. He reached down carefully, and was about to grasp the ring of the door when he thought better of it. If someone like himself could cast a simple spell, and stop all the dark wizards traps, then something was surely wrong. He quickly retraced his steps to the guard's corpse. Dragging it as quietly as possible to the door, he used his boot to kick the arm of the corpse onto the ring. There was a dim flash of yellow light as the hand fused to the ring and seemed to become steel also.

"Yes," Malak thought, "being paranoid can be a good thing at times." There didn't seem to be an alarm raised, his spell had at least done that much. Malak grasped the tunic of the corpse, now permanently attached to the trapdoor ring, making sure not to touch the skin of the corpse, just in case. He lifted the corpse, door and all, up and out of the way. Carefully he peered over the edge of the hole in the floor. All he could see were stairs descending into the darkness. According to the fat man's instructions, there would be three landings on the way down to the main levels of the tower. He must stop at the first and go no farther. The high wizards quarters were the highest in the tower, and this is where the object was sure to be kept. Providing that

9

the High Wizard was busy with the equinox festivities going on lower in the keep, he should be able to get it and get out before being detected.

Gingerly he began his descent into the darkness. Expecting to set off more traps with every step. He proceeded down for what seemed like about ten feet when he came to the first landing. Feeling along the wall with sweaty hands, he found the door. It was locked, and he quietly went to work picking it. After an indeterminable amount of time, and several heart stopping jumps at the little sounds that are part of most buildings, the lock opened with a deafening click, at least it seemed deafening to his hypersensitive ears. He slipped inside and carefully closed the door behind him.

Inside there was total darkness, worse even than the corridor outside. Working blindly, Malak lit a candle from the bag on his hip, and looked around. The room was semi-circular in shape. At the far end was a large desk, and the wall behind was covered with a large tapestry flanked on either side by shelves of books. To his left was a small, neatly made bed, and on his right was a cold fireplace. There were a few papers on the desk, and a book with a ribbon hanging out of it marking someone's place.

Moving quickly on his tiptoes, Malak crossed the room and went behind the desk to the tapestry. Looking behind it, he counted the stones in the wall behind it. "Three from the left, and four up," is what the fat man had said. Pulling gently on the stone, it slid out with an earthy, grating sound. Malak extended his hand to reach inside the opening, but stopped short. His paranoia was getting the better of him tonight, but with wizards, it was better to be safe than sorry. He looked around the room quickly, fastening his eyes on the fire tongs; he quickly had them and returned to the opening in the wall.

Gently probing the inside of the fissure, he closed the tongs on a solid lump, and started to withdraw it. There was no sound, but the tongs started to vibrate in his hand. He quickly pulled them out and dropped them on the stone floor just as they started to get hot to the touch. A lump of black cloth about the size of a fist fell out of the hole along with a scroll. Malak hesitated in astonishment as the tongs started glowing red with heat. Brighter and brighter they glowed until they were white hot. Finally melting into a couple of odd shaped puddles of steel on the floor before beginning to cool.

Within the folds of the black cloth was a small statue that looked like some kind of winged nightmare. This is what he had come for. He quickly wrapped it back in the cloth, and stuffed it in his belt pouch. On a whim, he also pocketed the scroll for later inspection. He quickly replaced the stone and the tapestry and crossed to the door to make his escape.

He blew out the candle, opened the door, and stepped out onto the landing. Far below, he heard footsteps running up the stairs toward him. "Time to get out fast," he thought to himself as he sprinted noiselessly up the staircase and out into the night air. As he crossed the battlements, and started down the rope dangling from his grappling hook, it dawned on him that the trap in the wall must also have sounded an alarm somewhere. Hopefully, they would search the room before figuring out where he went. He hit the ground harder than he had wanted to, and felt a sharp pain in his right foot. Stifling a grunt, he made his way quickly into the forest, heading east toward the sea, the sounds of the tower behind him becoming more and more alarmed, as they faded into the distance.

As Malak entered the tree line, he turned slightly to the south to reach the ocean close to where his small craft was hidden. The wizards would soon be on his trail, and he needed to make the shore quickly. Behind him he heard in the distance the first sounds of the wizards tracking him. He would have to move even faster now. He knew the black-robes were casting spells to help them find him. He paused in his flight only once, to check a large open clearing before he crossed it.

The field was more of a bog than anything else. Cleared of the dense trees that grew everywhere in this region, it had evidently been abandoned soon after because of the periodic floods that occurred when the tides and rains were just right. Someone in the past had gone to a lot of work for nothing. Malak could see the dark line of the forest all the way around the open area. Most of the sky was covered with thin, high clouds that blocked all but a few stars' light. The air was still, and heavy with the smell of decaying leaves. He looked carefully across the several hundred yards of open area searching for any sign of movement or noise.

After another quick scan of the area, listening more than looking in the dark, Malak took a deep breath and started the long sprint to the other side. He took off at a fast pace, but held back just a little to make sure he would have his wind for the entire distance. He was already breathing deeply from his flight through the forest, and as he ran he forced himself to slow his breath, and speed his legs. About halfway across, he heard again the sounds of pursuit in the forest behind him, and forgot entirely about breathing as adrenalin shot through his body. If they caught him in the open, he would have no chance of escape. His lungs burned from the effort and his legs were starting to feel like they were turning to liquid, but he sprinted on. He practically counted the last fifty steps to the forest edge as if it were approaching too slowly to be real. All the while tingles were running up and down his back as he expected the pain of spells to come slamming into him.

Diving headlong into the underbrush, and rolling back to his feet, he was safely within the cover of the foliage. He slowed his pace to move more silently again, never looking back. Not knowing or caring how close to death he had come. The sounds of pursuit continued in the distance behind him. He still had about a mile to go before he reached the ocean.

Malak ran on through the dense brush and trees sometimes on narrow game trails, sometimes making his own trail. He wasn't worried about leaving tracks, the wizards would track him magically, so speed was more important than caution at this point, he was more worried about tripping and breaking a leg. The forest finally dropped behind him, and he made his way through the tall salt grasses on the beach to where his boat was concealed.

The boat was a small, narrow craft. Built for just one person, it was light, easily portaged, and easily paddled. It was built for simplicity, speed, and stealth across the water. Malak quickly threw off the camouflaging grass, and lifted it onto his shoulder. He made it to the surf in but a moment's time, and threw the boat into the water. Leaping into it, he grabbed the single, double-bladed paddle and went to work. He still had to get out beyond the breakers before his pursuers reached the beach. Once he was beyond the breakers he would be hidden from sight behind the wall of breaking waves.

The spray soaked him as he crested the last breaker, and he shook his head vigorously to clear his vision. As he dropped into the trough behind the wave, a bolt of bright blue light slammed into the water next to his left elbow and exploded violently nearly capsizing Malak and spraying him with steam and hot water.

Malak leaned into the paddle to stay as low as possible. The wizards had been closer than he had thought. This job had been a mistake in more ways than he cared to think about. He paddled hard for another five minutes straight out to sea, and then turned the small craft South toward town. He planned to use the boat to circumvent the city walls and the guards at the gates. After about twenty minutes of constant paddling, Malak slid noiselessly through the breakwater and into Chistock harbor.

Chistock was the third largest port city on the east coast of the known lands. Malak had fled to the city after leaving the service of King Nolan, and had successfully "lost" himself among the rabble of the dockyards. That was two years ago, and he had worked as a day laborer to survive. The work was grueling, but honest. It kept him with enough money to survive, but not much more. Perhaps that is why he had taken the job tonight. The lure of the easy money seemed to haunt him now that he had killed again.

Quietly the small craft slid into the weeds near one of the city's sewer drains and up to the hidden mooring post. Ignoring the smell from the sewer, Malak tied up the boat and stepped into the shin-deep water. Instead of heading back to the Hammer and Anvil Inn, for the payoff, Malak went to his quarters in a run down boarding house near the docks. He wanted to examine the items he had stolen more carefully before he handed them over to his employer. In the darkest hours of the night, the docks of the city were mostly deserted. Malak passed the occasional drunk, but they were ones he had seen before, and of no worry to him. When he arrived at the boarding house, all the windows were dark. All of the tenants were seemingly asleep, and he knew that the old woman who owned the house would not be up to start breakfast for a couple of hours yet.

Malak didn't bother with the door, as the old staircase up to his room creaked. He didn't want to risk waking anyone up. Instead, he went down the side alley that led to the back of the building. There, the bricks had gaps in the mortar, which he could use as finger and toe holds to scale the building to his window. Inside his room, he drew the heavy curtains to make sure no light would escape and lit a candle. Quietly, he sat down on the bed and took out the scroll and lump of cloth in his pouch. He unwrapped the statue first to get a better look at it. "So this ugly thing is worth 500 gold coins," he thought silently. "That's more than a mercenary makes in a good year."

The statue appeared to be made of pure gold, although it didn't seem heavy enough to be solid. The most remarkable thing about it though was the cold feeling that Malak noticed growing in the pit of his stomach as he looked at it. It was a strange creature, apparently someone's imagination of a cross between a dragon and a sea ray of some kind. It had front and rear legs with claws, but no tail. On it's back were a pair of over large and misshapen wings, which made it look almost circular from the top. The mouth was just an open hole with what looked like multiple tongues protruding from it. The longer Malak looked at it, the more he wanted to get rid of it as soon as possible. It was starting to make him feel queasy, like watching someone vomiting.

Quickly he wrapped it again in its cloth, and replaced it in the pouch at his hip. Next he opened the scroll. It was a map of the entire North Country with the locations of the towers of sorcery on it. There were also two small X's drawn on the map in strange locations. One was in some of the roughest country known to exist; the other was in the middle of the Bay of Blood. It looked to be worth less than the parchment it was drawn on. Still, the High Wizard of the black-robes had it in a secret, protected location, so maybe it was worth something to someone. He would hold on to it for any future opportunities that may present themselves.

After replacing the parchment back into the pouch with the statue, Malak blew out the candle, and made his way quietly out the window and down to the street below. There was no one in sight when he returned to the street. He made his way quickly toward the Hammer and Anvil. It was on the other side of the city, and would take him a while to get there.

He had been walking for about ten minutes, when he sensed someone approaching. He quickly ducked into a side alley to wait. Within moments he saw a dark-robe wizard moving quickly down the street in the direction he had just come from. A cold sweat started to trickle down his back, as he realized that the dark wizards were already onto him. He would have to leave town immediately after the sale. "This job," he muttered sarcastically to himself, "is worse than suicidal, it's becoming downright dangerous."

Malak waited listening for anyone else who might be coming down the street. Then instead of going back onto the street he had been on, he went through the alley to the street opposite. He picked up his pace a little, moving on the balls of his feet to be as

15

quiet as possible. Weaving his way through the maze of streets to another alley, he ducked into it and ran to the wall at the back. He quickly scaled the wall, and began moving along its length. This wall had been added onto over the years until it extended for almost a mile west into the heart of the city. Anyone moving along it was impossible to track from the street below. He stayed on the wall almost its entire length. About three blocks from its end, he climbed down in the back of another alley and returned to the streets. The walk on the wall had been quiet and marked only by the sharing of it with a stray cat that had looked at him with baleful eyes before leaping to the ground and disappearing into the night.

Moving much more carefully, Malak finally arrived at the Hammer and Anvil Inn. He entered, took quick stock of the common room, and went to the only occupied table there. The fat man looked up in mild surprise. "You're late," he said in a slightly wheezy voice. "I had almost given you up for dead. King Nolan said you were the best, and I guess this proves it."

Malak almost jumped and ran at the mention of Nolan's name. "You know the King." It was said as a statement, but there remained the slightest hint of a question.

"Of course," said the fat man, "he described you to a tee." "He also said to tell you that he harbored no ill feelings toward you, after all you were most valuable to him once, and you were welcome to whatever retirement you liked."

Malak thought about this for a moment. When King Nolan had discovered that Malak had a talent for magic, he made sure that Malak was trained above any other assassin in his kingdom. He had also used him more than any other. Nolan had been known to be kind to those who served him well though, but Malak didn't know anyone who had retired himself as he had. What were the king's feelings about that? If the fat man was telling the truth, Malak was a very lucky man to have gotten off so easily. Still, King Nolan did have a forgiving streak in him, sometimes. The fat man might just be telling the truth. There had been plenty of opportunity for a trap before now, so Malak thought this might just be his lucky night. And immediately he wondered when the luck would run out.

"You've got the money?" Malak asked quietly.

In response the fat man laid a large bag of gold coins on the table and opened it. "You can count it if you like."

" Why does a man carry such a large sum of money with him unprotected in the city at night?" asked Malak.

"Well," said the fat man, " When you are the High wizard of the true order, you don't fear much by way of robbers."

Malak was mildly taken aback. The man did seem very confident, and he apparently had been sitting in the same seat since they had met earlier in the evening to discuss things. "You're a high wizard of the white-robes?" he asked. "Which tower?"

The fat man took a small sip from the glass in front of him and said softly, "The tower in Thosh."

# Chapter 2

Zartho the Great sat at the head of the high table in the great hall of the dark tower. He was enjoying the spring equinox celebrations for the first time in many years. The task that had seemed unending was finally at an end. He smiled coldly to himself within the hood of his robes. He was tall for a man. Standing almost seven feet above the ground, he tended to use his height as a tool of intimidation, although it was seldom necessary to do so. Those who knew him were very aware of the power at his command, any who would have challenged him had met with unfortunate, and usually violent ends long ago. He felt secure in the respect and fear that all around paid to him as homage.

Normally the equinox celebration would have been carried on without him. Though he gave the impression of being above the activities of the other wizards in the tower, he kept close watch on them through his magic. Tonight though, was different. Tonight the ten years of preparations were finally at an end. By this time next year all of the known lands would be under his total control. The thought of this almost made him chuckle out loud. Only a few dark wizards knew of what was coming, and they had sworn loyalty to him. He knew, as did they that any sign of betrayal would be the last non-agonizing thing they would ever do. They were his to command, like game pieces on a board.

His thin frame was wiry but surprisingly powerful, being a good reflection of the willpower and determination of the man. Since he had come of age and been apprenticed to a wizard, he had worked tirelessly to achieve his goals. All had been achieved with ruthless determination that bordered on obsession, and soon he would achieve his final and ultimate goal, his destiny.

The celebrations were winding down when the mental alarm from the secret alcove in his chamber went off in his mind. He had, against his better judgment, hired mercenaries to guard the tower tonight so that all the wizards could attend the celebration.

It was normal to do so on certain nights of the year, but he had had misgivings about doing it now that he was so close. After arguing with himself, though he had decided to keep with tradition. It would have looked suspicious to other wizards if he changed from the normal course of things. He had decided that perhaps it would be all right if he made sure a few spells were also in place. He had thought that one night would be all right. He cursed himself for the slip in his normal fastidiousness. Though angry, he didn't immediately sound the alarm. Waiting instead for the rush of energy that would hit him as the intruder's life force was burned out and transferred to his body, one of the darkest spells ever to have been created.

Two or three minutes went by, and still there was no rush. Suddenly Zartho leaped to his feet and announced the intruder in the upper levels to the astonished gathering. After a mad dash up many levels, He entered his quarters behind one of the apprentices. He could have led the way but during the final stairs, he allowed several others to pass, feigning weakness. Let the young, eager to impress, rush headlong into the unknown. They would draw the first fire if there were any coming.

Scanning his quarters for signs of danger, he saw that seemingly nothing had been disturbed. He shoved the others out onto the landing and, noticing the open trapdoor above, told them to search the roof. They quickly discovered the dead mercenary, and the grappling hook left behind.

Zartho ordered a full search of the tower and surrounding grounds, ordering the usual tracking spells to aid them in capturing the intruder. "Get after him now!" he screamed, and then slammed his door shut in their faces. Finally alone, he ran quickly to the tapestry and tore it aside. Noticing with pure malice the melted tongs on the ground, he yanked the stone from the wall.

"Now is not the time for foolish anger." Zartho thought, and then cast a spell to detect any traps that may have been laid for him. Sensing nothing, he thrust his hand into the dark, angrily feeling around the empty space. Cursing aloud as he withdrew his hand, he sat down at his desk to wait for the searchers to come back.

Nearly an hour later there was a knock at his door, and Lorban entered. Lorban was shorter by a foot than Zartho, and was more muscular in his build. He carried the scar of a long-forgotten spell gone awry on his right cheek. It extended from his temple to his chin, and many apprentices had imagined its origins while under his instruction. Lorban was especially gifted in the art of summoning demons from other planes. This could easily explain the scar. Lorban was also aware of Zartho's plans. He had been helping him for the past two years.

"The intruder has escaped," he reported to Zartho, and then in a whisper, "Is anything missing?"

"The statue is gone," said Zartho.

"What!" exclaimed Lorban, "How could anyone even know about it?"

"There are ways," Zartho replied coldly. "But I suspect in this case a spy will be found."

There was a brief moment of silence between the two, and then Zartho spoke again, "We must cast a knowing to find the figurine. We must recover it immediately. But first, report to the other wizards that all is well. Set the guard, and return here with Golan and Harnthiston. We will soon have it back, I am sure of it." The last was spoken with such coldness that Lorban grinned inwardly.

It took almost an hour to get the Tower calmed down, set the watch and see that those not on duty were retiring for the night. Zartho had spent the time patiently waiting. He was sure that whoever had the figurine probably didn't even know what it was, and definitely couldn't use it. There was still plenty of time to get it back. The map was another thing altogether, if someone got curious about it...

A knock sounded at the door and Zartho opened it to find Harnthiston, Golan and Lorban lined up to come inside.

Harnthiston was the shortest of the three. He had a solid, almost pudgy build to look at. Beneath the hood of his cloak, his too small blue eyes glowed with a malignant intelligence. His mouth was perpetually pulled down in a scowl of disapproval. The overall effect of his visage was one of sadistic anger cloaked in a thin layer of control.

Golan was next in line entering Zartho's quarters. He was the tallest of the three, standing well over six feet. He stooped slightly to enter the room. His shoulders were straight, with no sign of the hunch that is often present in the very tall. He carried himself with an almost regal bearing, and, in fact, had more power at his command than many kings did. His face would have seemed long if not for the thin black mustache that seemed to divide his face in half. Golan tended to be the silent one. Zartho was sometimes unsure why he had joined with him. When the time came, he would surely be the hardest to control of the three.

Lorban brought up the rear of the group. He, like Harnthiston, was clean-shaven. He stood close to six feet tall, and was built like a swordsman. Solid, but not cumbersome muscles draped his well-proportioned frame. His face would have been handsome, with well-defined features, except being marred by that long scar. His hood was as always thrown back, exposing short blonde hair, and hazel eyes that seemed to take everything in at a glance.

Zartho showed them inside and closed the door behind them. There was a moment of silence as he made the final preparations to cast the knowing spell. The four men stood in a circle in the middle of the room and began the chant. Moments later the image of a room shimmered into existence in the center of the circle. Gradually the image cleared and they could see a man dressed in black looking carefully at the figurine. Subtle changes in the chant brought the image back from the room to the outside of the building. There they saw the name of the street, and the location of a boarding house near the docks.

As the chant ended, Zartho looked at Golan, "Go, and recover our property."

"It will take some time to get there Lord Zartho, the thief may leave before I arrive," Golan hissed in his snake-like voice.

"Then use the traveler," Zartho snapped, "but don't appear too near the boardinghouse. We wouldn't want to make our presence prematurely known to our little thief. And when you return bring him along. I have some questions for him."

"Of course," said Golan as he turned on his heel leaving the room to the others. He went down the stairs past the main levels of the tower. Past the library, and laboratories. His pace slowed and softened as he went by the sleeping quarters. He paused in hidden alcoves twice to wait for the young initiates who served as night sentries to go by and then continued on his way. Past the kitchens and down to the hidden levels below the food cellars to an old door that had no handle and was set flush with the stone corridor. A whispered word and a subtle gesture, and the door swung noiselessly open.

The traveler stood against the far wall of the room. It looked like a full length, oval mirror, the frame of which was carved with runes that seemed to overrun each other. Zartho had found it when he took over as high wizard. At that time, he had methodically checked every part of the ancient structure looking for just this kind of forgotten secret. To Golan's knowledge, only the four confederates knew of its existence, and they knew practically nothing of its true purpose.

Golan closed the door behind him and knelt in the darkness in front of the mirror. He concentrated on a mental image of where he wanted to appear, and began the spell. The location had to be picked carefully. When the traveler opened a portal, there would be a flash of light at the other end. Though invisible after the initial opening at the far end, having someone step out of thin air always drew the attention of on-lookers. The image that began to appear in the traveler was the middle of a back alley a few streets from the boarding house. The alley was deserted just as Golan had hoped.

The Traveler was a powerful tool. It could transport anything from one point to another instantly. It would open a doorway to anyplace that the user could visualize. It was not necessary for the user to have seen the location before, although it did help, a wizard could pick a location in a certain direction and at a certain distance, and a portal would be opened. This could lead to all kinds of dangers. Golan shuddered at the thought of what might happen if the portal were opened in the bottom of the ocean, or perhaps the center of the sun...what would come blasting backwards through the portal would be instant death for anyone near, and many people farther away. The traveler was not to be used by the careless or undisciplined.

Golan could feel the night breeze through the portal. The image was firm and fixed as he stepped forward. A brief moment of disorientation, and he was standing in the alley. He checked to make sure there was no one around as he stepped out of the alley and headed towards the boarding house. In his mind there glowed an image of the portal waiting for his return. If it went out, someone would have closed it from the other side. But it didn't move, it softly glowed in his mind, and reassured him of an easy return to the tower.

As he made his way to the targeted building, Golan failed to notice a pair of eyes watching him from a dark alley. The eyes waited for him to pass, and then quickly went in the opposite direction. If Golan had seen the eyes, he would have known to whom they belonged, and his journey would have been shortened a little. As it was, many things would go wrong tonight, for a lot of people.

Golan was able to slip quietly inside and up the stairs to the second floor with the aid of a little magic without arousing anyone in the house. Quietly, he moved to the door of the room shown in the knowing. He prepared himself mentally for a moment, and then with one hand on the doorknob, he waved his other hand in front of the lock and whispered a word. There was a sharp click as the lock released. Instantly Golan threw open the door and leaped inside, bright flames leaping from the fingers of his hand lit up the room to almost daylight. He leapt quickly from place to place throughout the room, eyes darting into all corners, flames questing, always ready to defend against any attack.

When the room had been cleared to Golan's satisfaction, he searched it vainly for several minutes turning over the bed, pulling the chest of drawers apart looking in all the places where the figurine might possibly be. He suspected the whole time that it was wasted energy, but he had to be sure. In the end, the room was a mess, and he was as empty handed as when he had entered it. In a moment of exasperated rage, flames shot from his fingers engulfing the mess on the floor and instantly setting fire to the room. As the flames rose around him, he pulled the hood of his robes over his head and spoke a few words, again combined with several hand gestures. He could have put out the fire quickly enough, but Golan thought he would let it burn and stay close by, just to see if the thief would return to try and save any belongings. If anyone outside would have been watching the boarding house, they would have seen a black-cloaked figure, ringed in blue light, step carelessly from the flaming building, and move across the street into the shadows. But there was no one to see him, or sound the alarm to wake the sleeping boarders in their final dreams. Luckily, only a few of the rooms were inhabited.

Golan cast a spell of concealment around himself and stood motionless in the shadows across the street. Very soon there was a shout of, "fire!" heard, in the area and the alarm sounded. In true dark robe fashion, he was going to let a bunch of innocent people die in their sleep, because he knew that the thief had left all of his personal belongings in his room, but tonight it seemed everyone would escape. He might return to try and save them if he was still in the area. If not, they would have to find him in other ways. Whoever this thief was, he would soon find life to be full of the worse kind of surprises. Golan quietly chuckled to himself as he thought of the chase that would surely soon follow. But the first concern, of course, was to regain the figurine.

After waiting for about an hour, Golan made his way back through the streets to where he had left the portal. He checked to see that he was unobserved, and stepped through it back into the cellar of the tower. A quick word of command closed the portal with a flash of light, and he left the room. Securing the door behind him and leaving the traveler a dark oval in a darker room, Golan made his way up the flights of steps and through the maze of corridors to report back to his master. As he passed the levels of sleeping quarters, he thought that it would be a long time before he would enjoy a full nights rest. He figured that until the figurine was back in their hands, none of the four would sleep much, if at all. But at the same time, he told himself, "If that is the price I must pay, so be it."

When Golan arrived back in Zartho's quarters, Harnthiston and Lorban were sitting quietly waiting for his return. After making his report to Zartho, he stood silently waiting for further instructions. He did not fear Zartho. Though the wizard was terribly powerful, he knew him to see the entire picture clearly, never forgetting who was on his side, and that the four of them were a team that worked much better together than as a master intimidating his servants. There was silence for several minutes while Zartho sat unmoving seemingly deep in thought. When he did speak, it was in a deep, but controlled voice.

"In spite of the risk of detection, we must perform another knowing." Zartho continued in a slightly quieter voice, "By now the statue will have traded hands at least once. We will deal with the thief later. For now we must get it back. If it is in the hands of wizards, they will probably detect our knowing spell unless it is performed very carefully. Go back to your quarters now and sleep. Wake and perform your normal routine as always. We will meet at midnight tomorrow to perform the knowing. Maybe we can catch them napping. Go now and get some rest," this last was spoken in a hiss as he turned away from them. Zartho knew they would need to be rested if they were going to cast a knowing as sensitive and delicate as was needed. This minor delay would also give the thief time to get rid of the figurine. Thus revealing the people responsible for the theft. The original thief would get away for a little while, but he could be found relatively easily later. Whoever had the tiny statue, come morning, may even get a little careless by the dark wizards seemingly lack of concern over its theft. "Yes," thought Zartho to himself, "a little patience now will serve us better than panic."

"Strange," thought Golan as he left the High Wizard's quarters, "Zartho is still as unpredictable as ever, it seems I will sleep tonight after-all."

Golan's room was two levels below Zartho's. It was long and narrow, widening at the back, as most of the rooms in the upper tower did to fit the tower's general shape. The door was centered on the narrow wall, with his bed on the right side of the room. Across from the bed was a desk, which Golan used for his personal study. On the wall opposite the door were shelves of books and scrolls. To the left of these was a small door leading to a personal laboratory that ran parallel to his quarters, but had no door leading to the main passageway. The upper tower rooms were all arranged after this general pattern.

Golan entered his room, closed the door behind him and spoke a quiet word of command. At its sound, the candles on his desk burst into life. Picking one of them up, he crossed the room to the shelf of scrolls and after a moment selected one off the bottom. He returned to his desk and opened it to make sure that it was the correct one. Then he got ready for bed. Even though he knew its contents intimately, he would study it again before the meeting tomorrow night. He lay down, spoke another quiet word of command, which snuffed the candles out without a trace of smoke. As he drifted off to sleep, he set a mental alarm for sunrise, barely an hour and a half away.

Lorban and Harnthiston made their way down one more level than Golan. In the order of the dark robes Golan outranked them by one level. Lorban didn't like Golan, but didn't broadcast the fact. On his own time, he and Harnthiston would make jokes about Golan's height, referring to him as, "Grow-Long". They were both aware of the power at his command, and were thus always careful of how they spoke whenever he or Zartho was around. They knew that the High Wizard would tolerate no such petty divisiveness in his ranks.

Harnthiston played along with Lorban, as they were close in ability and power. He had no ill feelings toward Golan, and knew the man to be not only powerful, but also potentially dangerous because of his temper. He had seen it on a couple of occasions, and would not soon forget it. At first, he was leery of Golan's occasional fits of rage. They seemed to show weakness and lack of control. But every time Golan had cut loose, it had been the right thing to do ultimately, though it may not have seemed so at the time. Surely that was why Zartho had not said anything about burning the boarding house. Ultimately, it would probably benefit them a great deal.

Harnthiston and Lorban walked quietly to their respective rooms, Harnthiston to bed, and Lorban to study for a while. He was far more driven than Harnthiston, or perhaps, learning and power took more effort for him to gain. He had made himself study at least one more hour per day than anyone else in the tower. It had taken a lot of will power, but it had begun to pay off when Zartho noticed him, and invited him to join the small group. The effort had gotten him this far, and he was determined to continue the practice. Tonight he would be studying a new spell for the first time. By nature it was similar to a fireball, but was far harder to cast, and exponentially more powerful. He had been looking forward to this all day.

# Chapter 3

Malak sat looking at the fat man for almost a minute before he spoke. It had been rumored that King Nolan and the High Wizard of Thosh were close. They shared a love of power, and a mutual respect for each other's abilities and territory. To the best of Malak's knowledge though, they had never been seen together, but that didn't mean anything when wizards were involved. In spite of his brief training in the white tower at Thosh, he had only seen the face of, and had his own face seen by, one wizard. The king made sure that his assassins were virtually unknown and also completely unattached to anyone emotionally, especially their instructors. As a result, Malak could perform most tasks with a mask on, but he also had a deep distrust, if not hatred for the king. For all he cared, the king could take care of his own problems. "So you and the king must be fairly close," Malak finally said in a measured tone.

"The king and I share a mutual respect for each other. I run the magic, and he runs everything else leaving us mostly alone. You were the one exception to that arrangement. That is why; when you left I was quick to advise the King to let you go. I told him that you might be of service to him in the future, and I was right. At any rate, you're smart enough to keep your mouth shut and not pose a threat to him."

"And will there be any other services required of me?" Malak asked sarcastically.

"Just that you finish your disappearing act," replied the fat man with a smile. "It wouldn't do for the black robes to find out that we had stolen their property. It could lead to.... hostilities."

The last word was spoken in a flippant way, but Malak knew it was a ridiculously huge understatement. The last time there were "hostilities" between the white and dark robed wizards, nearly every wizard in the world had been killed. The war had been over five hundred years ago, and there were still ruins of entire cities left from it. There were also rumored to still be demons or worse in the hidden parts of the world that had not been returned to the planes of existence from which they had been summoned. It wouldn't be that easy to disappear entirely, but it was possible. "Why did I agree to this job again?" thought Malak, "Oh yeah, the money."

"If I'm to disappear entirely, I'll have to go into the western lands. I'll need to pack my things, and get some provisions for the trip," said Malak feeling the reality of the situation. There would be spies everywhere. He knew enough about wizards to know that they used more than magic to learn what they wanted; conventional means were a lot less draining, and that meant informers just about everywhere. If the white robes had them, the dark robes did too.

The smug smile that the fat man had been wearing for the last few minutes didn't waver. "I think that you should leave from here. The dark robes, I'm sure, already know where you live and by now they probably know your face as well. If I'm not mistaken, they spied on you when you went home."

"How do you know I went home?"

"I was spying as well, although a lot more carefully than they were."

Malak didn't like where this was going at all. "How am I supposed to disappear if they can spy on me any time they want? I won't make it out of the city!"

"You'll be all right," the fat man said trying to calm Malak. They tracked you because you had their property. Now it is in my possession, and so it is my problem. Here, this is for you in addition to your money." The fat man held out a necklace, and tossed it to Malak. "That is a diffuser, it makes the wearer virtually invisible to magical searches. As long as you are wearing it, they won't be able to find you."

Malak looked carefully at the necklace. It consisted of a small medallion on a finely woven silver chain. The medallion was gold, with a starburst engraved on one side, and wavy, cloud-like lines on the other. He thought about it before he put it on. He thought about the possibilities of the curses that might exist on such an item. Then with nothing really left to lose, he slipped the chain over his head, and tucked the medallion into his tunic.

The smile was gone from the fat man's face now. "You had better leave quickly now. The pack by the door has some food and general supplies for you. Try to be out of the city by sun-up. It doesn't matter where you go as long as it is out of the kingdom. I don't need to tell you not to attract attention to yourself."

Malak still had a lot of questions, but from the look on the fat man's face he could tell the interview was over. He stood up, tucked the bag of coins into his belt pouch, and headed towards the door. Stopping only for a moment to pick up the backpack by the door of the inn, he stepped into the cold dark of early morning.

The door of the inn closed behind him, and Malak stopped to take a breath and check his surroundings. As he did so he noticed a couple of people on the street looking towards the east, towards the docks. Following their gaze, he could see a faint light over the tops of the buildings. It was centered just about where his boarding house should have been. Evidently it was on fire, and had been for some time. He hoped everyone had gotten out all right, but knew that night fires were deadly. He decided not to go back, by the look of the glowing light, the fire would probably be out before he could get there and help anyway.

He took his bearings and turned south, carefully weaving his way towards the city's southern gates. Scanning the streets, he carefully moved in and out of them. He occasionally headed down narrow alleys, and backtracked to shake off anyone that might be following him. There wasn't anyone, at least not anyone that he could detect. Sometimes he would just stop in a shadow and listen for footsteps following him, but again nothing was heard. All of these precautions were slowing him down. By the time he reached the South gate of the city, the sky to his left was very light; the sun would be up in less than half an hour.

Fortunately, the guard was dozing lightly in the pre-dawn quiet, and Malak slipped past him as if on velvet feet.

Outside the city, Malak stayed on the road and broke into a light jog until the road reached the forest. Then he left it and made his way into the woods to find a place to lie down. The last thing he wanted now was to be seen by any travelers. He had been up all night, and he was feeling it. He needed a plan, and there hadn't been time to make one yet. It suddenly dawned on him that he hadn't even checked the contents of his pack yet. "What is going on with me," he thought aloud.

When Malak found a small clearing in the undergrowth that was well concealed, he put his pack down, and opened it. True to the fat man's word, there was a bedroll, and some basic provisions of food, including a water flask, and some traveling supplies. After a brief meal, Malak wrapped himself in the bedroll, rolled under the edge of a nearby bush for additional concealment, and fell asleep. The sun was just above the horizon now, and most of the rest of the world was waking.

---

Dalryms Bok-Salrin sat at the inn's table for a time examining the figurine, and waiting for Malak to get out of the area. He had put the innkeeper to sleep hours ago. The man would awake very refreshed and remember only a pleasant evening's business of the night before. As Dalryms carefully held the small, gold figurine he looked over its every inch. Trying to discover why the High Wizard of the Black Tower, Zartho, held it in such high esteem. He had met Zartho on only a few occasions, but knew him more intimately from second-hand sources. Many of these sources were, however, highly reliable. He knew the man too well to think that the object was a trinket, or merely kept for some sentimental reason.

He quietly muttered a weak knowing spell to see if it would shed some light on the item, and was amazed when the flow of magic seemed to slip around it, almost as if it didn't exist. Dalryms tried again with a more powerful spell this time, only to have the same results again. He gazed into the crystal eyes of the object, "What are you?" he whispered aloud in slight awe. His hand shook involuntarily one time, hard, as if being shocked by lightning, and Dalryms felt POWER! He had experienced magical objects before, but nothing like this. It was like lying at the bottom of the deepest ocean, feeling the pressure of tens of thousands of feet of water squeezing him. A darkness of unbelievable presence engulfed him as though he were the center of some titanic engine.

The sensation was gone as quickly as it had come. Dalryms felt a trickle of sweat run off his forehead. The experience had lasted only a moment, but it had left the High Wizard noticeably shaken. He quickly gathered his things; blew out the lights and left the inn, heading for another one nearby. The memory of the power held by the object in his pocket was fresh in his mind. There was only one comforting thought about it, and he kept that thought running through his mind, at least the massive engine seemed to be idling; for now.

When he reached his quarters at another inn a few blocks away he slipped quietly into his room, drew the shades, and placed the figurine in an enchanted bag to hide its location from anyone trying to find it. He was sure now that the Zartho would definitely want it back. He went quickly to bed to get a few hours sleep. He had told the keeper of this inn that he did not want to be disturbed. It took a while to drift off, as the memory of the sensation kept running through his head.

Somehow he did manage to get a few hours of sleep though, and awoke just in time for lunch. Highly disciplined in many ways, food was the one area where he had trouble denying himself, and this inn was particularly well known for its meals. He looked forward to a hearty lunch, and then it was back to Thosh with his new acquisition.

When he got down to the common room, after shaving and dressing there was already a large crowd gathered for lunch. He took one of the few remaining seats at a small table near a wall,

32

so that he could hear and see what was going on in the room without drawing too much attention to himself. After sitting a few moments, a middle-aged barmaid came up to his table and asked if he wanted to eat. Dalryms recognized her from the day before, and cheerfully asked for a large ale and an even larger plate of food. "Sure thing," she said smiling back at him and hurrying away to other tables. Dalryms realized with a start that he was watching her backside, and turned his attention back to the various conversations in the room.

He soon learned of the boardinghouse fire down by the docks, and that several people had died in it. He also learned that someone had been seen leaving the building by a back window a short time before the fire had started, but the descriptions were vague. The city gates were closed today, while the local law enforcement conducted their investigations into the matter. This action had many of the locals angry. Their shops were without this or that commodity, and some had to close altogether for the day because they were out of fresh foods from the surrounding area farms. There were a lot of angry threats made, and as in any gathering of the like, most were idle. No one expected the gates to be closed for more than a day, and as the winter had been long, the chance for a relaxing day did have its appeal.

He didn't have to wait long before his food arrived. He had picked this particular inn just for the quality and quantity of the meals served. The price was a bit more expensive than most other inns, but the meals more than made up for the difference. Besides, money wasn't a problem for Dalryms. He quickly dug into the roasted beef and potatoes covered in melted cheese. The rest of the room seemed to disappear as he feasted on the spread set before him. He only stopped to look up when every plate was empty and the mug of ale drained. The common room was still buzzing with people. Some new faces had come in, and some previous faces were missing.

As Dalryms got up to join the crowds in the street, he was suddenly aware that someone was watching him from across the room. He looked near the door, and saw a small man staring intently at him from under a dirty, red cap. He stared back at the man, returning gaze for gaze, and the small man seemed to shrink into himself and become even smaller. Then he quickly turned and fled out the door of the inn.

Dalryms thought of following him, but knew the man would have disappeared into the crowded streets before he made the door. From the look on the man's face, he had been looking for something or someone, and had evidently found it. Instead of going into the street he turned and headed up into his room to make sure that his new acquisition was safe. Finding everything there secure, Dalryms thought it would be prudent to make a decoy to throw off the trail.

Carefully, he looked out his window to the street below, checking for anyone who might be watching the inn. He couldn't detect anyone, but there was a lot of the street around the hotel that he couldn't see; at least not with his natural eyes. He left the window and went to the center of the room. Closing his eyes and concentrating, Dalryms started the chant that would create the spell to detect anyone watching the inn. As in most spells, concentration had to be split between performing the spell, to keep the flow of information coming, and sorting through that information looking for spies. Though little exertion would have been evident to anyone watching, Dalryms was wet with perspiration when the spell was over. He had learned that there was one person watching the inn from the backside of the stable, just to the west of the front of the inn, and another person moving away from the hotel quickly, but obviously thinking about it and him.

Dalryms looked around the room for something about the size of the statue. He eventually pulled the ball from the top of one bedpost. Carefully, he removed the figurine from its hiding place. Placing it on the floor next to the bed knob, he began one of the spells that he had studied before leaving Thosh. As he cast the spell, the bed knob appeared to change from iron to gold, the size and shape altered to match that of the little statue exactly. Sweat was now pouring from his forehead and underarms and his breathing was labored, but Dalryms ignored it and continued the casting. The whispered chanting and hand symbols continued for almost half an hour. Occasionally the wizard would reach quickly into one pocket or another and sprinkle a dusty powder over the two objects, or wave an item over the objects. Finally the end came with a gasp of breath and a slumping of the body. Dalryms nearly collapsed from the effort expended. He staggered to the bed to catch his breath.

After relaxing for only a moment, he forced his bulk to get up and finish the job. He quickly placed the fake statue in its hiding place. He noted, as he did so, that it looked exactly the same as the real one. Not only did it look like the real one, but also this fake statue felt the same in his mind. It had that strange ominous feel to it. The real one he placed in a hidden pocket in his cloak. It no longer felt ominous to handle or look at as a result of the spell of hiding placed on it. Next he pulled out of his luggage a small clear glass marble. "Aznul," he said aloud. The marble instantly changed color to a bright sky blue.

At the same time in another inn just a few streets away, a man was eating lunch while casually studying a clear marble, as though he had just found it. Suddenly this marble changed color to sky blue. Quickly the young man placed the marble in his pocket, threw a coin on the table, and walked out of the inn. He casually made his way to the inn where Dalryms was staying. Several times he looked behind him to check his tail. There didn't seem to be anyone paying attention to him, so he took a fairly straight course to the other inn. It took him almost 20 minutes to reach the door to Dalryms room. He gave a strange knock; two quick, one long, and two more quickly. The door opened a few moments later and Dalryms handed him a small bundle.

"Get this to the tower in Thosh." Dalryms said. "And Simon, be careful. Don't fool yourself about this. It is dangerous."

"No problem Dalryms, I'm always careful." With these brief words, Simon turned on his heels and walked down the narrow hall and then downstairs to the common room.

"Of course you are," thought Dalryms. "That is why you are still alive." But as he turned back into his room he knew that this time Simon wasn't going up against a thief's guild, or city's bureaucracy. This time he was delivering against the Black Robes. He didn't really expect Simon to make it back to Thosh. The White tower there had a large private museum and library. Many of the items therein should not have been there, and Simon had helped to "transport" them. Dalryms pushed the feeling of guilt from his mind. He had to give the dark-robes something to go after, and, after all, Simon knew the risks. He had taken them many times before, even if they had never been as great as now.

Back inside his room, Dalryms fought the temptation to lie down on the bed and go to sleep. He thought of the planning he still had to do. He must make his way back to Thosh without arousing any more suspicion than he already had. He had planned to take the figurine back with him overland with a caravan scheduled to leave in the morning. But those plans had changed when he had sensed the power of the object. There was always the chance of finding another, less conspicuous way North, but that would involve hiring a guide and traveling across country, avoiding the major roads and villages. Dalryms was not vain enough to think that this would be an acceptable solution in his current physical shape, there would be nothing but suffering in that route. The only alternative that seemed to present itself with any possibility of success was an ocean voyage. The winds and currents were in his favor heading to the North, and there would be no stops all the way to Thosh. He may even beat Simon back to the tower. He had considered the remote possibility of an ocean voyage when he had been planning this trip, so he knew that there were two ships preparing to depart for Thosh within the next week. He shook off the lethargy that always followed such intense spell casting, splashed his face with some water from the washbasin, changed his clothes to match the street people, gathered anything vital from the room and his luggage, and left the room locking the door behind him. He had only left a few clothes behind. Nothing that was of any value in case those watching the inn tried to search his room. It would look as if he intended to return soon, and should serve to keep them close to the inn.

Dalryms left the inn through the kitchens and a back door, passed through a back alley to the east, and stepped onto the main street from behind two buildings that were several shops away from the inn. He kept moving east towards the docks, checking for pursuit as he went. Occasionally he doubled back across his trail just to make sure it was clear. A couple of times he stopped at a shop along the way to check the street behind him while pretending to be interested in some bauble or trinket. By the time he made it to the docks, the sun had set and the city was bathed in the dim glow preceding dusk. One ship in particular seemed to be making ready to sail.

The name Misty Lady was painted on the transom of the ship in bright green letters that were just beginning to crack and chip a little. The crew was moving about the deck with purpose and energy. A few small packages were still being moved up the gangplank, but all the heavy block and tackle had been cleared from the area. There were a couple of sailors talking to women in the strained tenderness of loving goodbyes amid the sounds of orders being barked from the ship. Everywhere Dalryms looked, there were signs of the ship's impending departure.

He made his way through the crowds and clutter on the dock to the gangplank. After a moments wait at the bottom Dalryms climbed the plank to the gently moving deck above. As he stepped on board, he was challenged immediately by a booming voice from the stern of the ship.

"And just where do ya think you're goin' ya great whale of a lubber?" Said a mass of red hair that appeared to have a nose poking out of it, and perhaps two sunken eyes. It was hard to tell for sure exactly where the features of the face were hidden behind all of the unkempt red hair. The body beneath seemed to be as large and powerful as the voice that boomed from the head. He was striding towards Dalryms, and seemed to be about six feet tall, but incredibly well built and catlike in its movements. He came to stand in front of Dalryms with the easy rolling stride that is natural to those who have spent years walking on rolling decks and climbing in swaying rigging.

"Well?" was the only word spoken by the fiery beard now blocking Dalryms path.

"I am seeking passage to the North, specifically as far as Thosh," said Dalryms meeting the sailor's gaze. He didn't mention his desire to set sail immediately. From the looks of things on deck, he didn't need to. Aside form the fact that the ship was low in the water, obviously laden with cargo of some kind, the crew seemed to be all there and busy at one task or another.

The mass of hair stepped back a couple of feet from Dalryms and eyed him suspiciously. "I don't have time to wait for you to pack. High tide is in less than an hour and we sail with it."

"I am ready to leave now," said Dalryms.

The red hair seemed to consider this for a moment, then, with a slowly inhaled breath, "I'm Captain Jontag, and I can take you to Thosh. It won't be cheap. I hadn't planned on any passengers."

Dalryms started the process of negotiating a price. In spite of his unkempt appearance, Jontag was intelligent enough to realize that Dalryms might be on the run from something. It would be a quick way to increase profits on this trip. And with the time at sea, he might be able to find out why the man was running. This could lead to even more profits later on. The haggling went on for a minute or two. In the end, Dalryms paid less than a desperate man, but more than an honest man. He could have swayed the captain magically, but that wasn't his style. He didn't use his magic to control others unless there was no other way to accomplish his goals. He had used quite a bit on Malak the night before, to be sure he would agree to the theft without any questions, but that spell would be gone by now. This only required a few coins, one way or the other he would be leaving with this ship.

Jontag called one of the crew over to show Dalryms below to his cabin. He would be sharing it with one of the lower ranking deck officers. He dutifully followed the man to his quarters, and stowed his things. He kept the tiny statue with him for fear that his belongings would be searched, and went back on deck to make sure that nothing slowed their departure.

About half an hour later, the ship was hooked up to several small rowboats, and the order to cast off lines was given. The smaller boats towed the ship from the docks and into the current of the ebbing tide. They slid almost noiselessly through the harbor's channel and out to sea amid the clamor on shore of the early evening. Jontag set a course northeast that would take them out to deeper water, while still moving them toward their goal of Thosh.

---

Malak awoke slowly, an uncommon experience for one who had been trained as he had. Normally awake in an instant, this time his mind began moving from an endless black abyss through ever increasing levels of awareness. At first the peace of the abyss was dimly disturbed by noises that felt more like gentle pushes than sounds. Slowly they became more insistent and the blackness lightened into the grayness behind eyelids too long closed. The sounds resolved into birds and leaves gently rustling in the breeze. He lay there for what seemed like an hour or two fading in and out of a light sleep, not thinking at all, but just feeling.

Something tickled the back of his mind, something he should think about, or remember. He tried to bring it closer to his thoughts, but the attempt was futile, and the effort too draining.

After drifting almost back to sleep he wondered idly to himself where he was. The realization that he did not know seemed to accelerate into his mind. It started slowly, barely perceptible, and slammed fully into his mind with enough force to jar him from his mental lethargy into full consciousness.

Malak would have sat bolt upright, but a lifetime of stealth training held him motionless on the ground. He listened intently for several moments to the sounds of birds, insects, and the gentle breeze moving leaves near his head. No other sounds were evident, as he tried desperately to remember what had brought him to this place. Gradually, images of the night before began flickering through his memory until he had pieced things back together. He groaned softly out loud when he remembered that he had broken into a dark-wizard tower, and stolen something obviously valuable to them; not to mention killing a guard in the process! He should have kept the groan silent, but what the hell, he was already a dead man now.

He opened his eyes half expecting to see a dark-wizard or two standing in front of him. All he saw, however, was the leafy green foliage of the bush he was lying under dotted with spots of sunlight that had filtered through the forest canopy. By the angle of the sunlight, Malak figured that it was late in the afternoon, almost evening. Stiffly, he wormed his way out from under the bush and stood up. As he looked around at his surroundings, they became more familiar to him. He picked up the backpack that the fat man had provided for him still wondering why he had taken the job, and how the fat man had known that he would need the pack. In fact, normally he would never have accepted such an item, let alone start a journey with supplies from someone else. Normally, he would have awakened long ago and come to almost instantly.

The thought slowly occurred to Malak that his uncharacteristically rash behavior might not have been his at all. If the fat man had truly been a high wizard, it was possible that Malak had been magically influenced into the activities of the night before. This would explain where he was now and why he had slept so heavily and until so late in the day. It would also explain why he was disoriented and slow to fully wake. He remembered one or two other times he had been the subject of magical use, and the effects were almost the same. It was as if his body and his mind fought the magic the entire time, and were left drained, and slow to rouse.

Still, Malak hated the thought of blaming someone else for his situation. He had spent the last couple of years in Chistok listening to farmers and shopkeepers complain about their problems and blame them all on everything from the government to the weather. There were a few who were happy all of the time and took responsibility for themselves, but these were the exceptions rather than the rule. They were mostly silent, and often ridiculed by the others if they ever offered an opinion. Most of the time they were also the more successful ones, and this fact, coupled with their desire to make do for themselves made them unpopular among the general population of the city.

Malak had always been taught to do for himself, and think out problems by himself. Knowing what assets and resources were available to him and just how to use them were life and death matters. As an assassin, there were few people he could trust or depend on. So it was now. He sat quietly down and concentrated on the immediate problem of staying alive with black robed wizards after him. With his limited knowledge of magic, he didn't know how he had managed to go to sleep and wake up alive. They should have been able to track him down; after all they had probably been responsible for the fire in the docks last night. They had managed to track him that far at least, and they had done it rather quickly too. If the fire wasn't a coincidence, and Malak was not fool enough to think that it was, they were on to him, and wanted him dead. Or worse, they wanted him alive. Either way, they wanted him and it was clear that they were willing to hurt others, to get to him. Malak thought this last while he was looking around in shock as if the answer to the riddle of his continued existence was going to pop out of the forest. It was this shaking of his head that drew his attention to the chain around his neck, and the medallion suspended from it. He gasped suddenly as if noticing it for the first time. It glittered slightly, half hidden by his tunic. He withdrew it slowly from its hiding place and held it up to look at. He remembered receiving it from the fat man last night, but that was all he knew of it.

The light of the sinking sun seemed to slip over it's surface rather than reflect off it, giving it a slightly iridescent look, but tending to make details hazy and unclear. Malak contemplated the medallion in silence for several moments. He had to assume that it was the reason for his survival. He couldn't think of any other rational reason for his luck. He thought very briefly about taking it off to test his theory, but immediately realized that the dark-robes would be searching for him and he didn't want them to even get close to him. He replaced the medallion inside his tunic. It felt neither cold nor hot next to his skin. In fact, it didn't really feel like it was there at all. He would contemplate its mysteries later. For now there were plans to be made.

He quickly took inventory of what he had on him. Thinking all the while that he had to put as much distance as possible between himself and the dark-robes. He would have to run for it. The question was in which direction, and what then? The dark-robes would undoubtedly be watching the roads and trails to the north. Thosh would be the most likely place a thief would try and sell something of magical origins. The numerous small villages would have spies already being notified to be on the lookout for him. To the east was only ocean, an obvious dead end in and of itself, but it could be used as the road to somewhere else. South was a marshy wasteland extending for miles, a good place to hide, but getting there involved a boat or traveling westward through open prairie for miles to get around the Bay of Blood. Then once in the swamps, there was always the question of survival. To the west lay miles of open prairie ending at a mountain range that ran north to south for hundreds of miles.

These mountains would probably also be watched, as there was a remote white-robed wizard's tower west of them, where one might be able to get rid of stolen property, if they were able to get through the mountain passes. As he mulled his options over in his mind, there seemed to be too few options, and all of them were dangerous. It seemed that the marshlands to the south would be the least likely place for a thief to go, and thus he decided to head there.

Malak also had a little bit of knowledge about the swamps available to him. An old friend and mentor by the name of Shial Fonth had spent time in those swamps. In fact, he was probably the best friend Malak had ever had. Shial was, or at least had been a powerful wizard once. King Nolan had "retired" him after several disagreements with the king on how things should be done. Now, he was all but forbidden from performing any magic. He lived northwest of Chistok, and if Malak could reach Shial, he might be able to learn something about surviving in the southern lands. Shial might also be able to shed some light on what was going on. At the very least he would be able to say goodbye to the man who had been the closest thing to family Malak had ever known.

After several minutes of reflection, Malak decided that the best course of action was to go and find Shial. There wasn't any point of running helter-skelter from the black-robes. If they hadn't found him yet, they probably weren't able to. He packed up his meager belongings, dressed up the area to hide any signs that he had been there, and headed west toward the road. He quietly checked for any travelers before he stepped out of the brush. Again checking every direction and listening carefully he crossed the open area and slipped into the brush on the other side of the road.

The trek to Shial's farm took him several hours. The sun had set when he started out, and within an hour he was moving through the forests along game trails that intersected in random places. He would have preferred not using trails at all, but moving over the forest floor would have made more noise than the small trails. Once or twice he had to backtrack to avoid farms and open fields that the trail he was on would come parallel to or cut across. When he had first come to Chistock he had tried to learn all of them, but over the past couple of years one or two had changed. At one point a farm dog sensed him in the nearby woods and started barking. The farmer had come out, and not seeing anything, had scolded the dog and gone back inside. Malak breathed a sigh of relief that the man had not let the dog off its leash. Killing people was one thing, but kill a dog, and someone was going to really start looking. Another problem would be trying to stay concealed while killing an attacking dog. It just wasn't possible. After the first couple of hours, he angled north, making sure to leave plenty of distance between himself and Chistok. When he finally got to Shial's small farm, the lights were out, and it appeared that everyone was already asleep.

# Chapter 4

Malak knocked quietly on the door of Shial's small house. After a few moments with no response, he knocked softly again.

"Who's there?" an angry sounding voice demanded from somewhere within.

"It's Malak, you old coot. Let me in." Malak heard footsteps approach the door, and the sound of two heavy bolts being withdrawn. The door opened slightly to reveal an eye peering out above a thick chain. The door closed again and reopened after the chain had been removed. A smiling, past middle-aged man appeared in the doorway motioning him inside. Malak followed quickly, closing the door behind him.

"What are you doing here at this time of night?" asked Shial while looking Malak over carefully. "Let me guess, you're in some kind of a bind, huh."

"You know me too well Shial, and I resent the implication that I only appear when I'm in trouble."

"Well, it's been several weeks since you came calling, and most social visits don't start in the middle of the night. Now do I get the easy version of you telling me, or do I have to guess it out of you?"

"Dad, is that Malak?" a voice called from behind a door to Malak's left.

"Yes Lena, go back to sleep, dear. Sorry we woke you," Shial called sheepishly toward the door. Lena was Shial's daughter. She was nearly 10 years Malak's junior, and since her mother had died Shial had doted on her to the extreme. She was a bit headstrong, but this trait was tempered by a strong love for her father. If she didn't get her way, she would pout, but was open minded enough to see the wisdom of her father's words and opinions. Shial tended to give Lena a lot of freedom. When he did restrict her, there were good reasons, and she usually complied with his wishes after a token resistance.

The previous spring she had turned 17 and "come of age," but as yet Malak knew of no serious suitors for her hand. This was probably due to her tendency to remain aloof at the social functions in Chistock, combined with the fact that her home was one of the most outlying farms of the region. She had dark, shoulder length hair that hung perfectly straight. Malak had overheard her on occasion wishing for some curl in it like this-or-that other girl she knew. She had light blue eyes, a plain nose, and thin lips that were usually smiling at everyone. Her body was that of a tomboy, developed from the last few years of playing in the woods, and hours of farm labor. Recently she had developed the annoying habit of fidgeting with her hands, at least whenever he was around.

The door on the far side of the room opened and Lena appeared dressed in a red nightgown that looked like it had been hastily thrown on.

"What's up?" Lena asked smiling at Malak but with a hint of concern in her eyes.

"Malak was just about to tell me...weren't you Malak," Shial said casting an affectionate glance at Malak.

Lena looked at Malak and settled herself into a chair.

Malak looked from Lena to Shial and back again. "Shial, I don't know how safe it is for Lena to hear this."

Before Shial could speak, Lena stated coldly, "You're like family to us Malak, and I'm old enough to decide for myself what I will and won't hear, so out with it."

"But..."

"She is of age," interrupted Shial before Malak could even voice his protest.

"Alright," Malak said defeated and knowing it. "But this is serious, and everyone involved needs to be careful. Are you both sure you want to know?"

"Malak, you know the answer to that. You knew the answer before you knocked on the door. That is why you came here. So quit stalling," said Shial. Lena had paled slightly but she nodded her head yes.   Malak had come to them with problems on occasion before, but he had never hesitated like this.

"Don't say I didn't warn you," Malak said as he began his tale.   He told them all of it, showing them the amulet that Dalryms had given to him. He also showed them the map that he had not shown to Dalryms.  He paused only when Shial let a groan escape at the mention and description of Dalryms Bok-Salim, confirming with a look that he was indeed the High Wizard of Thosh.

When he had finished his story, Shial and Lena sat looking at him in silence.  Lena, wide-eyed, as if he had suddenly sprouted horns, Shial as if the room were closing in around him.  Finally Shial took a long breath and started to speak in a quiet, calm voice.

"Malak, the first thing I want to say is this.  Don't take that medallion off for any reason.  Your life depends on it, probably the lives of anyone around you as well.  Yes, it is a powerful obscuring charm.

"Second, as you may have surmised by my reaction to his name and size, Dalryms Bok-Salim is the one responsible for your present situation.  He is and has been the High Wizard of Thosh for many years.  If he has come out of his tower, there must be a good reason for it.  He likes being in his tower and building power.  Believe me, he is very powerful.  You are probably correct in thinking that you were under magical influence when you accepted the job.  Dalryms can be very persuasive."

Shial leaned back in his chair, placed his hands behind his head, and closed his eyes before continuing.

"To tell the truth, I knew that he was coming to see you.  He and I were close friends once, and we manage to keep in contact now and then.  But I didn't know exactly why he was coming. One of the reasons I'm allowed to live away from the tower is to make sure you don't get into trouble.  When King Nolan let you retire, this was one of his conditions.  I assumed he was coming

47

to check up on you. After all, a trained assassin isn't someone you want going nuts in a city. And before you ask, no I don't know what other conditions the king had." Dalryms had checked on Malak more than once, but he had never made contact with him before. It was a little disturbing to Shial that he had done so this time. Something must be wrong for the man to make himself known to Malak.

"As for the figurine that you stole, it could be any number of things. Magically speaking, it could be an energy source, or some kind of focal point for something. From your description it could even be a symbiot, though I doubt that."

"What's a symbiot?" interrupted Malak.

"I forget sometimes that your training and education are not focused in magic," Shial said. "Perhaps if we could have gotten you out of the King's Assassins another way we could have stayed in the tower. You could at least have learned more of the generalities of magic and its history."

Malak thought briefly of the circumstances of his leaving the Kings Assassins. He had been able to do so only because Shial had gone with him. Shial had been one of the head instructors in the white wizards tower at Thosh. He had been one of Malak's teachers there. Early in Malak's education, Shial had befriended him seeing something different in him than in the other students. Already a widower, Shial didn't want to see the youth dead at the hand of assassins, and after carefully questioning the young Malak about what life he wanted, agreed to help him out. The decision ended up with Shial being kicked out of the tower, with the understanding that he would keep an eye on Malak for the king. He and Lena had moved here to farm and live the best they could. The other farmers in the area accepted them, but tended to be aloof. Possibly due to Shial's frequent use of "high language" as they termed it.

"You did show some promise as a wizard, but the council ruled, and I can't teach you," Shial continued. "But I can answer your question, I suppose. Do you remember your lessons on summoning?"

"A little, I never summoned anything bigger than a mite though, and it took me better than 10 minutes to banish it."

"Did you make a circle for protection?"

"Yes, but it wasn't a very powerful one. I made a few errors."

"To be expected of a student," replied Shial. "In the more advanced summoning, where powerful beings are brought into this world a symbiot may be used. It is usually a figurine that closely resembles the entity that it is linked to. It gives the wizard absolute control over the entity. To use it though, a doorway must be opened. The door can be any shape, but it must be symmetrical, and it must be large enough to accommodate the being passing through it. Symbiots are rare, and every one that I'm aware of is nothing like what you've described. It could be a new one, or something found that was hidden long ago. My guess, though, is that it is energy storage of some kind. It is small, easily carried and its shape would allow it to be hidden in plain sight." Shial paused briefly to consider the map.

"So if you use a symbiot to summon something it comes through the circle?" asked Malak.

"Yes, the circle, square or whatever shape you use to define an area. The plane of that area becomes the portal doorway. That is why you need the symbiot to control whatever comes through. Without it, the entity is completely free in this world."

"Now back to this map. What would a dark wizard want with an energy storage and this map?"

"So," interrupted Lena from across the table, "What does Zartho the Great want with this map?"

"Good question." said Shial smiling at his daughter, "Let's not forget who, as well as what, we're dealing with."

"I don't know much about dark wizards," said Malak. "All I know about them is that they tend to be aloof when, and if you see them. The only good they've done in years for anybody that I know of was holding that ship last year in the storm. They kept it from drifting onto the rocks when it's mooring line parted. But, they held it so well that it was nearly swamped by the waves. It couldn't ride up over them. One moment it was up to the gunwales in a wave, the next it was floating in the air as the wave dropped out from under it. It scared the hell out of the dock men that were trying to save the crew. Their rescue boats were nearly smashed against the ship a dozen times."

"Unfortunately," said Shial still looking at the map, "almost any amount of energy could be stored in the figurine. It could be just enough to quickly raise a spells power for a novice, or enough to burn an inexperienced or unwary wizard to a cinder."

"Why would Zartho need a power supply anyway?" asked Malak. "Isn't he powerful enough for just about anything he needs to do?"

"What I know about Zartho can be summed up very quickly. He is indeed powerful," Shial continued. "He is also aloof, as you pointed out before. He also likes acquiring power, or so I have been told. But I know nothing more about him. He may very well be the most powerful dark wizard alive today. There are many rumors that have floated past my ears. I say rumors because I have never heard of an eyewitness to his abilities, at least none alive and willing to talk." Shial corrected himself with a hint of disdain in his voice.

There followed a moment of silence as the three at the table exchanged glances with each other. Each silently considering the implications and the dangers they could all be in. Malak now wished that he hadn't involved them. He knew at the same time that his chances of survival without knowledge were slim at best. He also knew how Shial and Lena would have felt about him if he hadn't come to them for the help that they were both willing and able to give, regardless of personal costs.

As Malak thought of these things, his eyes fell to the map on the table. "So what do you think is so important about this thing?" he asked, nodding toward it.

Shial considered it for a moment. "It is obviously a map of the kingdom. All of the major towns are shown. I don't see anything remarkable about it at all." He slid his chair back smoothly, and stood. Leaning over the map with his hands extended, he muttered some words under his breath. The map glowed blue for a brief moment, then returned to normal.

"There is nothing magical about it that I can detect."

"So it's just a map of the kingdom?" asked Lena.

"What are these little x's?" Malak asked pointing to the two small, thinly drawn marks on the map.

"Once again, I have no idea," answered Shial. "They are about the only thing on the map that's unusual. However, they may be just marks. To the best of my knowledge there isn't anything at those locations. This one is out in the middle of the ocean."

"So why was it kept under such tight security?" asked Lena.

"Again, I have no answer to that, at least not yet," replied Shial. "It may become evident later on though."

"Back to the reason I'm here," said Malak. "I think I should go away for a while. What can you tell me about the swamplands south of the Bay of Blood?"

Lena gasped audibly and looked quickly at her father. "Not There!" she hissed.

"Actually," replied Shial, "that might just be the very place to go, if you can survive, that is." The last was said with a piercing look at Malak.

"Just tell me as much as you can about what to expect and I'll be alright."

"Dad, don't tell him anything, he can't go there!"

"Yes Lena, he can go there. Not only that, but he must go there if he is going to have any chance against the dark-robes," Shial said sternly to his daughter, ending further protests with a quick sweep of his hand.

Lena sat back in her chair with an angry pout on her face. Clearly she didn't like the direction things were moving. She also knew an argument with her father at this time would be pointless. It would be better to remain at the table quietly listening than to be dismissed to her room.

"During the Wizard's War," began Shial, "a lot of things were brought into this world that shouldn't have been. They were mostly conjured by the dark-robes to do their dirty work for them, although white-robes weren't innocent of conjuring them too. Many of these things were sent back to the planes of existence from whence they came during the course of the war. Many more were isolated, captured and sent back after the war in an attempt to clean up the world. Some, though, escaped and went into hiding in isolated places. The southern marshes are home to some of these creatures!

"Malak, you know that in my youth I took part in an expedition into those marshes. We were looking for any possible sites for King Nolan to build outposts that would support colonization. What we found was constant danger, unending wetness, and on many days, death. There are natural dangers as well as the unnatural ones. Roving packs of wolves wander aimlessly through the mists looking for anything that might make a meal. Huge cats stalk from the forest floor to the top of the tree canopy overhead. They tend to be solitary creatures, but very dangerous nonetheless.

"The atmosphere feels oppressive and diseased. You can never escape it. But, worse still are the unnatural denizens of those swamps. Many of them have magical properties as well as their fangs and claws. I can't tell you everything that is in there but I can tell you the obvious. Make as little commotion as possible. They tend to be drawn to violence and struggle.

"What is the most powerful battle spell you know?"

Malak thought for a few moments and said, "I don't really have anything that would be useful in a battle. What with things as they are."

"None at all?"

"You know me Shial, they wouldn't teach me anything of real power."

Shial knew that Malak's magical abilities weren't great. He didn't know all of the details, but he had managed to glean the fact that those responsible for his training were always worried about the consequences of his spell casting. He had never managed to find out exactly what the problem was. All he had known as one of his tutors was that before he could attempt any spell, it had to be cleared with Shial's supervisors. Nothing of any real power was ever allowed. "Well they may not have helped anyway," replied Shial getting up from the table and moving toward a chest buried in the far corner of the room. As he cleared off the chest he continued talking. "You will need something though before you are through."

"I have a small boat with a sail on it that you can use to get to the swamps. It should be safe enough on the open sea for a couple of days." Shial continued talking as he returned to his seat. "I'll tell you where to find it. The roads aren't safe for you to travel now."

"Lena," Shial said without looking up," it's time for you to go...to bed."

"What?" she asked astonished.

Shial looked up with a surprisingly soft expression on his face. "You heard me dear, off you go... to bed."

She stood up stiffly, and went to her room, closing the door softly behind her.

"Don't mind her," said Shial, a tear starting to form in the corner of his eye, "she thinks of you as her brother, a trained killer, but a brother nonetheless. Now where were we...ah yes, the boat. You can't risk the roads or trails as the dark wizards will soon have spies everywhere."

For the next couple of hours, Shial did his best to teach Malak enough about the dangers in the swamps to give him a fighting chance for survival. In the end he had to admit that there was probably more about the swamps that he didn't know than he did.

His final words as Malak left just two hours before daybreak was to be extremely careful, and to be out on the ocean before sunrise.

As soon as Malak had disappeared into the darkness of the forest, Shial closed and bolted the door, blew out the candle and retired to his own room. His concern for Malak and other things weighed on his mind for a while but eventually he drifted off into a fitful sleep.

---

Zartho sat at his desk thinking of ways to torture the thief once he was caught. It wasn't very useful, but there wasn't anything to be done until the appointed midnight hour when his henchmen would arrive to assist with the knowing. He smiled inwardly at his private joke, thinking of them as mere henchmen, for what else were they, really. He used them to save his own strength. Dark-robed wizards were notorious for backstabbing. There were a few wizards who might try to promote themselves if he should appear weak, or unfocused. Like stags in the forest, let the younger ones see weakness and every one of them would be out for his blood. He was already older than most dark-robes ever get, as duels in the lower ranks were common.

Zartho's mind wandered as he attempted to keep it rested in preparation for the upcoming spell. It would not do to let the others see him agitated. Finally the midnight hour arrived. There was a knock on his chamber door, to which Zartho responded softly, "Enter."

The door swung inwards noiselessly and the three accomplices entered the dimly lit room to the sound of their quietly swishing cloaks. As the door swung closed behind them, Zartho arose and showed them into his laboratory. The door closed and locked behind them, and they took their assigned positions around the floor.

Zartho began the spell, speaking only part of the whole. Then having another join in with him and continue as all in turn cast part of the spell. The final part chanted in unison as a large bright orb appeared in front of them. The orb shifted colors several times and then solidified. Finally splitting into two pieces. One globe held steady at eye level, the other disappeared entirely, moving as it was directed by the combined wills of the four men.

As they concentrated on the figurine, they searched the city first and, not finding it there, they sent the now invisible orb on an expanding search path. The Wizards had been in the throws of the spell for a little over two hours when they located the object of their desire in the hands of a man camped north of the city on the road to Thosh. They all made careful mental notes as to the exact location and then called the orb back to join with itself once again. As the orb became single once again, it flashed brightly and then faded into nothingness as the spell died and the wizards relaxed.

Zartho spoke quietly to the others, "Go to the traveler and return with the figurine. I don't care what you do with him. He obviously has no idea what it is or he would be trying to hide a lot better..." he hesitated for a moment, then continued, "on second thought, find out as much as you can from him, and then kill him. But don't leave any evidence behind. We don't want anyone suspecting dark wizards of foul play," he finished with a sneer of contempt.

Lorban, Golan, and Harnthiston filed out of Zartho's quarters as silently as they had come in hours before. When the door was securely locked behind them, Zartho set to work on another spell of knowing. He was sure that somewhere within the walls of the dark tower there was a spy. The thief knew exactly where to look and what he was after, as well as the perfect time to strike. In Zartho's experience there was no such thing as coincidence. Someone had to be responsible for the theft. It may even be one of the three, but Zartho didn't think so. Unknown to them he had looked closely into each ones mind during the spell casting, at least as closely as he dared without arousing their awareness of it. There had been nothing amiss in their thoughts. He had detected no fear or guilt hidden anywhere. An all-out assault on them would have been felt like a battle mace splitting their skulls. An invasion of that kind would have revealed too much of his abilities. No, the traitor was somewhere else in the tower.

Zartho returned to his laboratory and prepared himself for the next spell of the night. Once again he spoke the words to himself and felt the awareness grow around him as his mind reached out, searching...

Golan walked silently behind Lorban and Harnthiston as the three magi quietly passed through corridors and down steps into the bowels of the tower's base. Wordlessly they came to the locked door and entered with only the slightest of pauses to cast aside the locking spells on the door.

When they were secure inside the chamber, Harnthiston spoke out, "I think we should set the portal south of the camp about a hundred yards. We could then approach from within the trees and he wouldn't know anything until we had him trapped."

"Agreed," said Lorban

Golan merely nodded his consent.

Harnthiston stepped to the portal and cast the spell to activate it.

_____

Simon came awake suddenly from a dreamless sleep. He lay perfectly still listening for something that might have woken him. After a few seconds he heard a cricket begin to chirp off to the north. Another soon joined it and several others around him began the chorus. Something had disturbed the insects for quite an area. It dawned on him that the insects south of him were still quiet. Something was either coming or going from that direction. His knowledge of wood lore had saved him before on these missions, and he counted himself lucky tonight to have been such a light sleeper.

Simon quietly moved out of his bedroll, leaving it rumpled enough to appear in the darkness as if he was still in it. Moving silently to the North he slid behind a large tree and waited to see what would appear. He didn't crouch in his hiding place for very long before a flash of yellow light leapt from the trees and struck his bedroll. The bedroll glowed yellow and jerked into the air where it hung, suspended and stiff, as if the blankets were made of wood.

Three figures in black robes slipped from the shadows of the surrounding forest, and approached the bedroll with their hands extended. The sight of them was enough to get Simon moving slowly and silently into the forest. Dalryms had understated the danger somewhat. Being chased by three dark-robes was something out of his worst nightmares.

Harnthiston growled with rage when he realized that the blankets were empty. He spun around looking in all directions at once. Lorban and Golan started searching the night as well, but it was Golan who used magic first to finding the missing thief. He gestured to the blankets and hissed several words of command.

The hovering blankets leapt through the air towards Simon. They slammed into the tree that he had been hiding behind, and was now crawling silently away from. When he heard the bedroll strike the tree behind him, he decided that it was time to sprint, noise be damned. Though he considered himself good in a fight, three black wizards presented odds that he wasn't willing to face with anything less than several hundred warriors on his side.

As Simon sprinted for the next cover available he could hear the three wizards giving chase. He dove for the brush in front of him just as a bolt of lightning slammed into the ground in front, and to the right of him. He dodged left just as another bolt struck him in his hip. Instantly his leg was numb from the hip down and he pitched forward onto his face where he scrambled vainly to drag himself forward. He had moved perhaps a foot when black-robes surrounded him. Soon he was lying frozen on the ground back at his small camp next to the ashes of his fire.

The three wizards began going through his belongings and the clothes he was wearing. They soon found the figurine in his pack. They examined it for a moment and then turned their attention towards him. As they approached, one of them, the shortest one had a look of sadistic glee on his face. The other two faces were hidden in the dark recesses of their hooded cloaks. Simon knew that his illustrious career as a courier was going to end suddenly tonight, but probably not as suddenly as he wished.

In the end, his screams weren't heard by anyone on the lonely road. He told them almost everything that he knew before Golan, tired of the sport that Harnthiston so enjoyed. In mock anger he purposefully overpowered a spell that should have just broken a rib. Instead, the entire chest caved in on itself as if an invisible granite slab had fallen on it. The man who had called himself, "Simon," lay perfectly still on the ground never to scream again.

"You clumsy overgrown fool," Harnthiston hissed in frustration at Golan. "He...he might have been able to tell us more."

"Like how much pain your torture caused?" sneered Golan, kicking the mutilated corpse at his feet.

"He..."

"Let's clean up the mess and get back," interrupted Lorban. "It's close to sunrise now and we can't leave any traces."

Harnthiston snorted and turned away to retrieve the dead man's pack and other scattered belongings. Golan and Lorban placed the corpse, and all it's earthly possessions on the ashes of the small campfire from the night before. Next, the three raised their hands. Fire leapt from their fingers into the pile until everything, including bones and bits of metal had melted or turned to ashes and powder. As they made their way back to the portal a wisp of smoke from the heated ground was all that marked anyone's passing. There was nothing left of Simon except for his small success of having died before they could extract the true name of his employer. He had just made up a name and claimed that some crazy merchant had hired him to take the statue to Thosh.

As the sun was starting to crest the nearby hills, Lorban, Harnthiston, and Golan slipped back through the traveler and the portal closed with a burst of light. The forest began to return too normal as the insects and animals of the night disappeared and were replaced by their daytime counterparts.

The three wizards had to hurry carefully back through the maze of tunnels and passageways underneath the tower. When they re-entered the tower's lower levels, they split up in case any early risers saw them. Golan and Harnthiston took separate routes back to their quarters, while Lorban made his way directly to Zartho's chamber. When he arrived, he had to knock several times before the door was opened and he was allowed entry.

Lorban quietly handed the statue to Zartho, who took it nonchalantly and placed it on his desk. He then turned back to Lorban and asked, "What did you find out?"

"He wasn't the thief," answered Lorban. "In fact, he was only hired by what he thought was a merchant to take it to Thosh."

"Did this merchant have a name?"

"The only name we got out of him was 'Kimo Danton.' Though I think it is probably a false one."

"Why do you say that?" asked Zartho looking intently at him.

"He died before we could completely finish questioning him. Golan was a little angry with the man because of his attempt to escape, I think."

"Regardless," snapped Zartho, "he should have better control. His temper has cost us before. The only thing that makes him useful is his power. It should be controlled better."

Zartho paused for a minute as if he were trying to control his own anger. Finally he looked back at Lorban. "Go to your quarters and rest. We will meet again soon to begin the final arrangements."

After Lorban left and the door was secured, Zartho breathed an audible sigh of relief as he picked the tiny statue up. "All the arrangements in the world would have been for naught without you, eh?" As he tossed the figurine lightly in the air, a flash of reflected candlelight caught his eye. Something about the figurine wasn't quite right. He suspiciously eyed the statue in his hand, and then placed it in the center of his desk.

Four spells and an hour later there wasn't a statue at all on his desk, but a cheap iron bed knob. The spells that disguised it had been both clever and powerful. The real statue was surely in the hands of other wizards. He had feared this from the moment it was stolen. Being methodical had cost him an entire night.

He quickly subdued his emotions and decided to go to bed. There was still time, and the need for secrecy was greater now than before. Already rumors about what could have been taken in the intrusion were circulating. He needed to let things die down. If the other dark-robes in the tower found out about his plans they would surely kill him at their first chance. "Besides," he thought coldly to himself, "we will meet again tonight, and tonight we will not fail."

---

As Malak left Shial Fonth's small cabin, he made his way cautiously to the northwest. He followed game trails, changing direction suddenly and doubling back to check his trail on occasion. Moving as quickly as possible towards where Shial had told him his small boat was hidden in the undergrowth at the mouth of a small stream just north of Chistock.

His path took him fairly close to the dark tower, and he made a conscious effort to stay well away from any of the trails or routes he had used on the previous night. There was always the slight chance that the dark-robes had sent guards to watch the surrounding area. They may have set up listening posts for anyone that might try to slip through, just in case the thief were foolish enough to return to the scene of the crime.

The thought of him returning to the area so soon after so narrowly cheating death almost made him laugh out loud. One of the first rules is to never return to the scene. Necessity pushed him on though in spite of his concerns. He knew that he had to be out on the ocean by daylight if he really wanted to be alive and undetected at the end of another day. He simply didn't have time for any other route.    He had traveled many times through patrolled areas before without being detected, and he managed to do it this time as well.    It took longer than normal, but he balanced his speed with caution to the best of what his abilities and experience would allow.    In the end, after narrowly avoiding a couple of game snares, he finally made it to the ocean about an hour before dawn.    The sky was just beginning to show a little light in the East.

The boat was right where Shial had said it would be, although it was impossible to see.    Malak had to reach inside the bushes to feel it before he was sure that it was there.    He pulled, and it slid gently out from under the thick foliage and into the main current of the stream.    It floated heavily on the water as if loaded with supplies, but it appeared stiff and strong.    Malak wondered for a moment why Shial would have such a craft at the ready like this.    It took him several minutes to get the mast stepped and the boat rigged to sail.    Meanwhile the light in the east was continuing to increase as the new day approached.    When Malak finally had everything arranged the way he wanted it, he paddled out into the stream's mouth and into the ocean.

The boat was about fifteen feet long.    It had a single mast with one sail.    The bow and stern were covered and had closed storage areas with hatches about 15 inches wide on the bulkhead with covers that rotated to lock in place.    Shial had said they contained provisions and a couple of weapons.    The boat was, "just big enough to get me into trouble if the weather turns bad," thought Malak.

As soon as he could, he raised the sail and caught the offshore breeze that was blowing.    It pushed him away from the land, and into the blue water of the deeper ocean.    After about an hour, he changed course to the South, keeping the land just within sight.

In the late morning the wind died out and Malak dozed off and on, lying in the bottom of the boat.    He was awakened occasionally by a trickle of sweat running down his chest. Periodically he would raise his head a little over the gunwales to look around. Having left Chistock behind, with no one in his or her right mind wanting to sail south of the city, there was nothing to be seen on the flat sea.

So Malak dozed, rocked gently on the light swell of the ocean. Now and then he would drink some tepid, stale water from a cask lashed to the stern bulkhead near the tiller. After seemingly hours of bored waiting, a gentle breeze began to blow. He trimmed sail and resumed his course to the southwest again.

As the hours wore on, the swell increased until the little boat was being tossed up and down violently. Malak had been to sea enough to know that this was just the curse of a small boat on open water. The waves weren't big enough to be any real danger, but the trip was definitely not going to be comfortable. He was expecting the queasiness for a while before it finally showed up. It would just take some time to settle his stomach. He was forcing himself to watch the horizon so that his stomach would calm a bit when he suddenly forgot all about being seasick.

From the covered bow compartment there came a banging and shuffling sound. Then the hatch cover began to slowly turn. It jammed, just for a second, and then popped outwards! At the first sound, Malak had crouched low against the bow bulkhead opposite the hatch cover. He sat motionless with his dagger ready to strike the first thing to come out of the hole. But he stopped short as Lena's head and shoulders came fighting their way out of the narrow opening. She struggled through the hatchway, fought to get to the side of the boat, and leaned over the side where she vomited for several minutes into the sea. By the time she was finished, Malak's dagger was back inside his tunic and he had begun to laugh heartily.

"When you're done chumming, you can set a line and catch dinner," he hissed between bouts of laughter.

Lena took a moment to splash her face with seawater before turning around and glaring at him. After waiting a minute to catch her breath, and to let Malak's laughter subside, "Oh, shut-up," was all she could say. This brought on another bout of laughter from Malak. It took several more minutes for him to catch his breath again, meanwhile he just managed to keep the boat on course with his foot on the tiller. Lena leaned against the far side of the boat looking and feeling miserable.

"Lena, what are you doing here?" Malak finally asked.

"Obviously I'm coming with you," she snapped back sarcastically.

"No way, Lena."

"Yes way," she interrupted. "You can't risk going back to Chistock now, and you wouldn't set me ashore somewhere to fend for myself, even though I could do so perfectly well and you know it."

Malak's grin became a glare, knowing that she was right on both counts. He hated it. "Your father is going to kill both of us. You can't come with me."

"My father told me to come." Lena replied softly.

"And just when did he do that?" asked Malak.

"Just before I left the table last night."

"Funny, I was sitting there the entire time and I didn't hear him say a word about you coming."

"Daddy and I have some secret signals we made up just in case of trouble. He knew you would make a fuss if he tried to tell you, so he did it this way. He knew by the time you found out I was with you it would be too late for you to do anything about it. Of course, I was trying to stay hidden a little longer, but I figured it was time to come out or hurl on all of our rations."

Malak sat listening to the rapid discourse thinking carefully. "It's just like Shial to not let me in on something like this," he finally said. "Wizards always hold something back. What else should I know about?"

"He didn't have time to tell me anything else, I left out my window when he sent me, 'to bed'," Lena said. "I think he figures two of us have a better chance in the swamps than one alone."

63

"And just how are you going to help me?" asked Malak feeling trapped and not knowing exactly why.

"Well, I do have some magical talent," said Lena defending herself.

"Where did you learn...no wait, don't tell me, Shial taught you." It was a statement not a question, but Lena nodded affirmatively anyway. "He never really obeyed the wizard's high council before they retired him, why should he change after."

"That's how daddy put it when he started teaching me," said Lena. She was starting to look a little green again.

Malak looked at her a moment then pointed off the bow of the boat. "You see that flat line way off in the distance where the ocean meets the sky?" he asked sarcastically. "That's the horizon. Watch it as much as you can. It's the least moving thing around, and it will tend to settle your stomach."

Lena swallowed hard and turned to look straight ahead. Malak took up his position in the stern at the tiller again thinking quietly. After an hour or so they rounded Point Home and changed course due South, across the entrance of the Bay of Blood.

"This is where life starts to get interesting," Malak said interrupting the silence.

"What do you mean?" asked Lena not bothering to turn around.

"We are now crossing the entrance to the Bay of Blood. If you have any favorite deities, now would be a good time to invoke them."

"What should I pray for?"

"Invisibility. There are several bands of pirates that roam the bay at will. They scavenge anything that they can get their hands on. If they're in a good mood, they'll kill you."

"And what if they're not in a good mood?" Lena asked still staring at the horizon in front of the boat.

"Well, then it takes a while for you to die," Malak said in a low voice as he scanned the ocean all around them.

Lena turned and gave him a sharp look. When she realized that he wasn't joking she went back to looking at the horizon in front of them, as her stomach churned for the thousandth time.

For the next several hours they sailed in silence, bouncing over the waves with the only sound being that of the water sloshing past the hull of the small boat. Malak thought long and hard about his current situation. Shial must have known, or at least suspected more than he let on last night. Lena being on board meant that he wanted her out of the way, but he couldn't figure out what exactly Shial wanted her out of the way of. He didn't have any information, and it was driving him nuts. Finally he decided that if Shial wanted him to protect Lena, then that is exactly what he was going to do. If he had to die doing it, he would. He couldn't think of any better way to go.

The only sign of life they encountered was an occasional sea bird flying low overhead. Every now and then one would even circle above them before wheeling and continuing on it's way into the endless abyss of sea and sky. The sun beat down on them mercilessly. Malak would make them both drink water from time to time. Its brackish taste not quite refreshing, but not bad enough to refuse and endure the thirst that grew throughout the day. As the sun was getting low in the sky, Malak broke the silence and asked what was in the bow compartment to eat.

"How can you think of food while bouncing around like this?" asked Lena incredulously.

"We need to eat now while we can still see." Malak said. "We can't risk even the smallest light at night. They stand out like beacons; it would be seen for miles. Every pirate within twenty miles will know where we are."

Lena grunted her way into the hatch and quickly pulled a bag out, almost without taking her eyes off the horizon. She pushed the bag behind her towards Malak without a word.

Malak opened the sack and looked inside. He pulled out a few objects that were wrapped and sealed to keep out vermin. It took a couple of minutes to break through the wax seal, and then he exclaimed with feigned excitement, "Oh look!"

Lena looked quickly to see what Malak had found. His voice took on a sarcastic ring as he held up his hands.

"Hard tack and salted beef."

Lena groaned loudly as she turned back to the horizon.

"Now Lena," said Malak in a parental voice, "you have to keep your strength up." And then in a softer tone, "I mean it, you need to eat. Take small bites and chew slowly."

"All right," Lena said quietly reaching back without turning around.

Malak leaned forward and placed a small hard biscuit and piece of beef in Lena's outstretched hand. She took the food and started to eat without looking back. Malak ate in silence too while watching the horizon.

They sailed on through the sunset and into the night. Malak steered the small boat by the stars. Lena went into the forward hatch once more and pulled out a pair of blankets as the night chill started to come on. She handed one to Malak without saying anything and went to sleep in the bottom of the boat.

Sometime around midnight Malak woke Lena up to take control of the boat while he slept.

"Keep those stars in front of us," he said pointing out a constellation. "Wake me up if you see anything, or if the wind changes direction."

Lena nodded and mumbled something, and Malak rolled into his blanket and assumed her former position in the bottom of the boat.

Lena got a drink of water from the cask and was glad for the awful taste that made her face contort. "Wow, that'll wake you up," she thought, trying to rub the taste off the roof of her mouth with her tongue. She settled into a slow routine of scanning the horizon from side to side, and checking the stars. Occasionally she would turn and check for anything behind the boat, but she never saw anything. After an hour or so she realized that the nausea she had felt all day was, for the most part, gone. The realization relaxed her mind somewhat and she began to hope that the entire adventure wouldn't be an endless fight to endure hardship. She actually began to enjoy the night a little.

Throughout the dark hours they sailed silently on. Only the sound of the water sliding past the hull and the occasional slap of a wave was to be heard. All around was a void of infinite blackness, as though the boat floated on pure emptiness. The countless stars overhead offered the only relief to straining eyes, like beacons of hope in an abyss of darkness. At times Lena was almost overcome with the eeriness of a night on the water.

# Chapter 5

Dalryms watched as the sun sank into the sea's horizon. He had been up most of the day with a queasy stomach that was just now starting to settle. Of course, he could have cast a spell to help with the seasickness, but he wanted to stay hidden from anyone that might be looking for magical use. Spells being cast flared like a beacon to any other wizards who knew how to look for them, and there was a pretty good chance that someone was looking. On land with many magic users working their spells, it would have been hidden a bit, but in the middle of the ocean, casting a spell would have stood out like the ship's lantern at night. Not many ships carried wizards on board, as there was a tendency for the crew to expect perfect weather and other miracles during the voyage. Besides, whenever wizards traveled, they tried to hide the fact that they were wizards; life was just a lot easier for them that way.

Dalryms had finally been able to eat something at dinner, and although the fare wasn't of any real quality, there had been plenty of it. As the only passenger on the vessel, he was invited to eat at the captain's table. It beat fighting over the Kid for bits of salted beef with the crew. He had also tried to sleep during the daylight hours knowing that if there were going to be trouble, it would most likely come at night. But the endless rolling of the ship had kept him on deck out of the nauseating smells below. The only thing he could do to keep his stomach under some form of control was to stare at the horizon, and try to keep his mind occupied on the puzzle of the object hidden in his pocket. Now, as the light faded from the sky, he found that exhaustion was soon to overtake him. Finally he went below to his small cabin, collapsed onto his bunk, and was lost to dreams and darkness.

---

Zartho again waited in his room for the appearance of his unwitting conspirators. This time they arrived one at a time, within a few minutes of each other. They were all assembled by the appointed hour, and the casting of the knowing commenced immediately. This time the spell took more time to cast, and was more complex. They weren't taking any chances.

The spell was searching for two separate things. Its highest priority was, of course, the figurine. Its second search was for any people with magical knowledge. Zartho would have liked to confine the search to powerful wizards, but the spell would have been impossibly complex and overly specific. It would have been difficult if not impossible to cast, and could have missed the intended target because of some small detail. Zartho thought it better to cast a wide net and sort through the catch, as he didn't yet know any specifics about who they were really looking for.

They spent a couple of hours sorting through Chistock. Carefully they eliminated one person after another until the search expanded outward. They considered Shial Fonth, the defrocked white wizard-turned-farmer who lived nearby, but there was no sign of the statue. Knowing that they could find him again if the rest of the search was fruitless, they moved on. They continued expanding the search outward. To save, time Zartho concentrated the search to the north, as that must surely be the direction the figurine had been taken.

The search was moving faster now. The areas were sparsely populated, and there was little or no knowledge of magic among the farmers in the regions being searched. Zartho's frustration was beginning to build when a spark lit up in their minds way out to sea. "Of course," thought Zartho to himself, "there are often many routes to a goal."

The ship was hard to focus the search on. It seemed that the closer they looked at it, the harder it was to see, as if it was hidden from their spell by some kind of magic. Because of the normal rolling and pitching of a ship, they all had to concentrate even more intently just to keep up with its movements. The ship was heading North towards Thosh though, and that was enough to convince Zartho of it's guilt. After making sure they knew where the ship was, Zartho released the spell so fast that the other three were almost knocked over.

Lorban spoke first, "We'll go and recover the figurine."

"We'll all go," said Zartho. "It will be hard to keep the portal opening centered on a moving ship and I want no mistakes. Lorban, you will remain on this side of the portal, and make sure that we can get off the vessel when we need to. Harnthiston, Golan and I will board her and find the statue. I don't know who we are dealing with yet, and I want all of us if things should start to go badly." He didn't need to remind them to be silent as they moved single-file down the corridors and into the sub-passageways of the tower. The only sound of their passing was the occasional gentle swish of their robes.

Once inside the portal's room, they relaxed a little. Zartho directed them to their places around the magical device.

"Let's be careful. We will open the portal on the stern of the ship, behind the helmsman. Be ready to go through the moment it opens. If we act quickly enough, we may be able to surprise him, and keep him from sounding the alarm too soon. I will go first. Golan, you and Harnthiston follow immediately behind me. Be ready to kill anything you see. We'll search the bodies for the statue and then scuttle the ship. Remember, there is a wizard on board, and he is most likely the one that we seek. Once we have our property, do what you must to get back here, making sure of course, that no one else will ever reach land."

The brief flash of light from the opening portal had the desired affect on the helmsman. He ducked slightly then turned around fast, just in time to see a dark, cloaked form leap out of thin air, bolts of light already exploding from his extended hands. It was the last thing that the helmsman saw in this life. The bolts caught him full in the face, and he was lifted off his feet, thrown over the ship's helm, and down to the main deck. The sickening thud of his corpse impacting the teak deck made enough noise to attract the attention of both the watch forward, and the sailors below.

The forward watch was nearly dozing as he sat with his back to the foremast. He wasn't in the mood to exert too much effort, so he yelled back to the helmsman to be more careful. When there was no response, he decided to find out what had fallen, and help out, as the ship was starting to slowly turn beam-on to the wind. He struggled to his feet, and stepped around the mast in time to see three black figures approaching him, and no one at the helm. With reflexes aided by adrenalin, he screamed the alarm just before lightning from all three wizards tore him to pieces.

Sailors rushed onto the deck from the stern, as well as from the forecastle. Lightning sprayed from the dark wizards' hands into everything from men to ropes to masts and deck. Several fires sprang up and men tried to dodge, fight and put them out at the same time.

Amid this noise and confusion Dalryms stepped onto the deck still trying to shake the sleep from his mind. He was instantly awake though, when he saw the dark wizards in the firelight, and bolts of energy streaking from them into everything in sight. Energy blasted from his own fingers before he even had his hands fully raised. Two of the dark wizards were thrown from their feet, but Dalryms' onslaught missed the third, which turned his full attention on this new threat. Dalryms had to leap behind some barrels, to avoid the missiles streaking from this third dark wizard. He continued rolling his heavy girth across the deck as the barrels exploded into splinters that rained down around him. He came to a bone-jarring halt when he hit the gunwale.

Dalryms looked up to see the two wizards back on their feet, and closing on him with the third. He crawled backwards to try and get his footing, but came up against the stairs that led to the poop deck. He turned to climb them, and was almost knocked over by a blast from the dark wizard coming around the remains of the pile of barrels. As he was spun around, he fired another blast at the wizard. This time his shot struck in the center of the black robe, and the man was flung from his feet. Another blast caught Dalryms high in the shoulder, and slammed him into the

71

staircase.  He fell forward onto the deck on his hands and knees before the other two dark robed wizards.

Just as the dark robes were about to coordinate their attack on him, a sailor leapt onto one of them from behind, driving his knife deep into his back and making him miscast the spell.  The resulting uncontrolled release of power threw everyone to the deck and split the mainmast of the burning vessel.

Dalryms lay writhing on the deck trying to get his vision to focus, and shaking his head.  When he was conscious enough to look up again, the wizard he had blasted in the chest, was already standing, and looking at something on the deck several feet away from him.  The dark-robe made a quick leap and a grab, and Dalryms saw a flash of gold light reflect off something quickly thrust into the wizard's robes.  Dalryms, panic stricken, grabbed the pocket of his own robe where the statue was, only to feel nothing there.  He scrambled to feel his other pockets, with the same result.  Looking up he saw the dark wizards at the top of the stairs on the poop deck.  The one who had been stabbed was slung over the shoulder of one of them.  He fought to get back on his feet and up the stairs only to see the last one disappear into thin air in front of him.

Dalryms stared open-mouthed at the empty space for a brief second when a huge fireball materialized heading straight for his head.  He ducked just in time.  The fireball seemed to arc slowly over the railing and down toward the deck of the ship.  It fell lazily through the open main hatchway and down into the ship's bowels.

White-hot fire, exploded from every hatchway and porthole on the ship.  Anyone that wasn't already on deck simply no longer existed.  Those sailors who were on deck were engulfed in flames.  Some of them made it to the side of the ship and flung themselves into the water.  Most didn't even get three steps before they collapsed.  The ship was an inferno, burning faster every second.

Dalryms had managed to hang onto the poop deck, and now was backing away from the flames. He tried to magically slow the fire, but was too exhausted to put any real power into the spell. The deck below his feet started to smoke, and flames from within were erupting around the sides of the ship. He staggered to the stern rail to throw himself into the sea, and saw one of the ships longboats still hanging off the stern by one davit. It was starting to burn from fire rolling out of the stern windows. Quickly he cut the rope and let the boat fall into the water below. Then he threw himself over the stern railing, striking the icy water mere inches from the swamped longboat.

The shock of cold water forced the air from Dalryms lungs. He fought for the surface as his clothes clung to him slowing his movements and weighing him down. Finally he was able to control his flailing limbs enough to stroke upwards. Using coordinated, powerful strokes he moved upwards through the inky blackness quickly and smacked his head on the longboat. Stars exploded inside his head, and he fought his way upwards again. His lungs burned from the smoke and now aching from the lack of air, screamed for breath. Keeping one hand up to ward off any more debris, he finally broke through the surface of the water just as panic's icy grip started clawing at his mind

Sweet air filled Dalrym's aching lungs bringing instant relief and a promise of continued life. He threw his head back and gulped lungful after lungful, just thankful to be breathing again. He lay out on the water floating and breathing for several seconds. Before he had time to remember the longboat, a strong hand grabbed him roughly by the hair and started yanking him upwards.

Dalryms howled in pain as his head struck the side of the longboat for the second time in so few minutes.

"Shut-up, or I'll leave yeh here to drown, yeh great fat wizard," said a voice Dalryms recognized immediately as that of Captain Jontag. More hands seized him and pulled him over the side of the boat, roughly tossing him into its bottom. He laid there, in several inches of sloshing water for several moments catching his breath. When he finally lifted his head and looked around, he was surprised to find that the captain and two others were the only people in the boat with him. It was hard to believe that only the three of them had hoisted his bulky form into the boat. They were working feverishly to bail the last of the water out of the boat. Without speaking, he started helping them, using his hands, as there was nothing else to use.

When the job was done, Dalryms took a good look around for the first time. The ship had drifted several hundred yards away, and was burning brightly. She was sitting low in the water, and it was obvious to everyone in the boat that she would soon sink. There was nothing to be done about it. Dalryms was too tired from his battle with the dark wizards and his struggle to survive. He knew that no spell he could cast would do anything to change the ship's fate. It would only weaken him more. He sat leaning against the side of the boat watching the ship's final death throes with his three companions. The end came only a few minutes later when the ship suddenly dropped by the stern lifting the bow high out of the water, and slid backwards under the waves with a hissing sound as the fire was finally put out.

After a few moments of silence, Captain Jontag spoke, "Keep a sharp eye for any other survivors."

The two sailors untied the only pair of oars in the boat and fitted them into the oarlocks. They began rowing around in circles, each one larger than the one before in a crude attempt at a search pattern. For the remainder of the night, they searched and called out for survivors with no response. Occasionally the boat would strike something in the water, which was usually a burned piece of wood or other wreckage from the ship. Once however it was the burned, mangled, body of one of the crew. The right side of the body had almost no flesh left. It was impossible to recognize any features of what had once been a face. No one said a word as the body was carefully lowered back over the side of the boat, and left to its watery grave.     Once, Dalryms spoke briefly to Captain Jontag, "Why did you bother saving me when you knew I had destroyed your ship?" he asked.

"There weren't no point in lettin' you drown," came the wry reply. "'sides, you thought 'nough to cut this boat loose, and that saved all our 'ides."

"But I put your ship in danger when I got on board, and your crew is dead now."

"Yeh didn' kill the crew, those black-robed-bastards did it. From what I saw of the fight, yeh were tryin' to kill them, which means you were helpin' the crew. As cap'n, I'm responsible for who I let on board. Don' think I like you. You're the reason they attacked. My only question is this, are they goin' to attack agin?"

"I don't think so, they pretty much got what they were after," said Dalryms after a moments thought. Captain Jontag looked suspiciously at Dalryms for a moment, but decided to let the matter drop. It was clear that the wizard wasn't going to reveal anything more.

The search went on until the morning sun appeared over the watery horizon. Then Captain Jontag turned the boat away from the sun and headed for land. There were no other survivors to be seen. They rigged a small, make-sift sail out of oars and some sailcloth they recovered from a tangled mess of wreckage floating on the ocean. It was a relief to all of them not to have to row anymore, as they had no water, or food on the boat. Rowing all day in the sun would have been pure agony under the circumstances. As it was they were all parched by the time the sun started its descent toward the horizon. By nightfall their thirst was torturous.

The distant shore appeared in the fading light of the sun setting in their eyes. It was still several miles distant, but the wind held true, and by midnight they were almost upon it. The sound of breakers increased as they drew closer to the shore. In the darkness it was impossible to judge either the distance to the shoreline, or the height of the breaking waves. Suddenly the boat leaned forward and accelerated through the water on the face of a breaking wave. The boat's nose buried in the trough of the wave, pitch-poling the boat and throwing everyone into the surf. The four men fought their way to the shore only to collapse for a few moments on the pebbly beach.

Captain Jontag was the first back on his feet. He looked around for a moment, and pointed to their right. "That direction looks as good as any to find a stream that we can drink from, and it takes us in the direction of Thosh. We'll try to rest for a few hours, and then we'll start," he said. As things turned out they didn't start until first light. They were all more tired than they thought, and slept fitfully on the cold, open beach until daylight and discomfort got them on their feet. Within a mile of their starting point, they found a stream of fresh water running into the ocean, and were able to greedily quench their thirst. Then the small party continued north for Thosh.

Zartho and Golan literally threw Harnthiston through the portal and leapt in themselves. Neither one would remember which had actually gone through first. As they dove onto the ground, Lorban was already preparing a fireball spell that he launched back through the portal at the fat wizard who had caused them so much trouble. Then he closed the portal fast. So fast, that he didn't even see if the fireball struck its intended target. Even if it missed, he knew that the crew would probably not survive the resulting firestorm.

Lorban turned to find Zartho already getting to his feet. He was frantically pulling something from his robes. He held the figurine up to the light for a moment admiring its surface. Then quickly putting it away, he turned to Golan who was casting a healing spell to revive Harnthiston, who groaned slightly in his unconscious state.

"Will he live?" asked Zartho.

"Yes," replied Golan, "but he has taken quite a shock." He looked up at Zartho and continued. " I think that was Dalryms."

"Are you sure?" asked Zartho. "He hasn't been very active for years. Mostly he sends underlings to take care of things."

"That's true, but I remember seeing him once in the streets of Thosh when I was an apprentice. His height and girth were the same. I have also heard that when he thinks something is very important, he takes matters into his own hands. The wizard on the ship was powerful enough to have been him."

Zartho thought for several moments. "If you're right about it we need to proceed immediately with our plans. There's no telling how much he knows or guesses."

Just then Harnthiston stirred and tried to sit up. Failing in this effort he slumped back onto the floor unconscious again.

"He'll be alright in a little while," said Golan.

"Good," said Zartho.

Zartho, Golan and Lorban all left the chamber leaving Harnthiston to recover as best he could. When he finally came to and could walk, he made his way to the upper levels and to his assigned duties for the day. His entire body ached and he felt weak and nauseous. These symptoms didn't show at all though. Dark wizards were expected to never be weak, at least not to show it. Any outward show of weakness could prove fatal. During the day, Lorban pulled him aside and told him that they were to make sure and sleep tonight. They would meet again the next night at midnight. Though he didn't show it at all, Harnthiston was greatly relieved that he would be able to rest for a night.

# Chapter 6

The day dawned with Lena still at the tiller. The wind had died once during the night for an hour or so. It had come back in light gusts that sometimes filled the sails, and at other times left them hanging slack, flapping from side to side as the boat rocked on the rhythmic swell.

Malak awoke shortly before the sun crested the horizon. He took the tiller, and the two of them ate a silent breakfast of the same rations as the night before. After washing down the hard biscuit and salty meat with stale water, Lena lay down to rest in the bottom of the boat. Not ten words had passed between them during the course of the morning, Malak choosing to be silent, and Lena not knowing how to warm up to him. She was also beginning to feel the beginnings of homesickness for the farm and her father.

A short time later the breeze strengthened and settled down into a light wind. It moved the small craft steadily through the water toward its unseen goal. The boat was steadier in the water with the wind filling its sails, and Malak used the time to do some small jobs about the boat to keep lines from tangling and other mishaps from occurring.

Lena stirred in the early afternoon and Malak roused her for a bite to eat. During the meal Malak finally interrupted the silence much to Lena's relief.

"We should sight land before nightfall."

Lena looked up slightly startled. "So, are you talking to me now?" she asked with a hint of sarcasm in her voice.

Malak was suddenly aware of the silence that had been between them for almost an entire day now.

"Sorry," he muttered, "I'm not used to having anyone around while I'm in danger. Anyway, we need to plan where we are ultimately going, and what we are going to do." he continued, not giving her a chance to respond. "I still don't know why Shial sent you along. I had intended to disappear for the next several years. That's not going to give you much of a life." He paused then, looking at Lena as if to apologize.

"I'm not sure either," she said hesitantly. "Other than I might be of some help with the magic that I know. Or maybe he wanted me to make sure that you didn't try coming back too soon."

"Or maybe he did want me to come back soon," interjected Malak.

"Yes, that could be it, I guess. He could have also thought that there was more trouble brewing than he let on, and wanted me out of danger,"

"That could be," said Malak. As they were talking he had continued to search the horizon and he suddenly went silent staring intently behind them and slightly to their right. Then he sat up a little higher, straining to get a better look.

"What is it?" Lena asked staring in the direction Malak was looking. She couldn't see anything but sky and ocean.

"It's nothing," said Malak still searching the area. I thought I saw a speck of white. I guess it was a gull or whitecap or something.

"Anyway, when we get to the swamps we will need to be sure we stick close together."

"Alright," Lena agreed. "Which direction are we going to head?"

"The maps I have seen don't give much detail. I think we will have to head South and West. That should take us to higher ground eventually. And we should be able to avoid any pirate camps along the South shore of the Bay of Blood."

"What about the dangers of the swamps?" asked Lena looking doubtful. "I mean, we will be heading into the deepest part of the marshes."

"That's the problem, we know that the pirates inhabit the south shore, and we know that they will kill us if they find us. We don't know exactly what is in the marshes." Malak paused and shrugged his shoulders. "So the choice is to face an extremely dangerous path that you don't know any specifics about, like where the pirates are and what kind of traps or defenses they have set up, or take a completely unknown road."

"Are all the stories about the pirates true?" asked Lena quietly.

"Do you want to find out the hard way?" Malak asked back, not really expecting an answer.

"So, how long will we be in the swamp?" Lena cheerfully asked with a feigned smile.

"I don't have any idea," Malak said mimicking her smile, "but we'll probably have a lot of fun finding out."

"Oh, I just can't wait...what is it?"

Malak had stopped scanning the horizon and stood up in the boat staring behind them again.

"It was a sail," he said simply.

Lena sat silently for several moments staring into the horizon. Then, as they topped a swell, she saw a patch of white in the distance several miles off. Malak saw it too. They both stared at it until it disappeared behind a wave as they dropped into another trough. Malak sat down quickly and adjusted the sail slightly; trying to get every bit of speed he could from the wind.

"Are they pirates?" Lena asked.

"Either that or someone else is looking for us, traders don't go this far south unless they have some kind of death wish," said Malak

"Who would be looking for us?"

"Oh, maybe black-robes."

"Do you think they saw us?"

"Well, we are at water level and we saw them. Our mast is about twenty feet in the air. If there's a lookout on that ships mast, and he isn't blind, he is watching us all the time. Oh, and they seem to be on our same heading so I can only assume they are chasing us."

"No need to get sarcastic,"

"Sorry."

"Can we outrun them?"

"I don't think so," said Malak. "They seemed to be closer than the first time I saw them. Our best chance is to hit the shore before they catch us," said Malak "If they're pirates, they won't venture into the swamps after us, at least I don't think they will. All right, I hope they won't. I've heard they avoid the swamps at all costs."

Lena gave Malak a disbelieving look. It was hard to conceive of him risking both of their lives on a bunch of rumors. Still, they didn't seem to have any other options that wouldn't end up with their deaths before sunset.

They sailed on. Malak pushed the small craft as hard as he could but the sail in the distance appeared more and more frequently, and after an hour it was obvious that the ship was indeed gaining on them. Malak had Lena look in all the covered spaces for anything that they could jettison to lighten their little boat. The only thing they found was the food, some small weapons, a little anchor, and some crude fishing gear. Malak told Lena to dump everything but the weapons, blankets and fishing line. The only food that he kept on board was the half empty cask of drinking water, and a few hard tack biscuits.

After another hour, they saw a wall of fog seemingly rising out of the water in front of them. The wind swirled it around, but didn't seem to be able to break it up. It rose from the water like a white cliff, immoveable and solid.

Malak carefully judged the distance to the mist and considered his speed. He also looked back to the ship, which by now was obviously a pirate vessel, and in constant view. He tried to judge how fast they were being overtaken, but what he came up with didn't fill him with much hope.

"I think we might make it," he said to Lena who had started looking nervous. "But just barely."

The pursuing pirates figured the same thing a few moments later as arrows began to be fired from the ship. They fell far short, but at the rate the ship was gaining, Malak knew they would soon be in range. Half an hour later the occasional arrow was falling mere yards short.

The wall of fog was still another half-hour away. They would beat the ship, but not the ship's arrows.

"You might want to get under the deck where you hid before," said Malak. "The arrows will be landing in the boat soon."

"What are you going to do?" asked Lena, "sit there and become a pin cushion?"

"Well, if you have a better idea, I'm all for it."

"How steady can you hold the boat?" Lena asked.

"About like this, the swell is tossing us pretty good."

Lena stood up in the boat with her feet spread for balance, and her back against the side of the mast.

"Here goes nothing," she said to no one in particular and held up her hands. She began speaking softly words that Malak knew to be magic. He couldn't hear everything she said, but knew that a ruse of some kind was being played.

On board the pirate ship, a yell of triumph went up when they saw their quarry veer suddenly to port to run parallel with the wall of fog that was rapidly approaching.

Malak couldn't believe it when he saw their pursuers suddenly turn hard to port.

"Nice work," he said to Lena, but she was still concentrating on the spell and Malak knew better than to interrupt someone casting spells, especially one that was helping as much as this one seemed to be.

The pirate ship continued on their new course for several minutes when a wave rocked the little boat harder than normal. Lena stumbled and had to grab the small mast with both hands to keep from falling over the side. Immediately the spell was broken and the pirates turned back to their prey, obviously enraged now by the deception.

"I think they're mad at you," said Malak as Lena got back to her feet against the mast.

With a determined look in her eye, she said, "Not as mad as they are going to be." She raised her hands again and began the chant anew.

On board the pirate ship, the crew was in a fury. Every blade aboard was being brandished and the archers were gnashing their teeth at the small boat which had vanished before their eyes only to reappear behind them still heading for the fog. The boat turned away from them and started running with the wind. The captain shouted orders to trim the sails for maximum speed in the run. Within a few minutes they were again gaining on the boat that had been so evasive.

About twenty minutes later, just as the pirate ship was again firing arrows at the small craft, it disappeared entirely leaving the crew baffled and confused. The captain gave orders to set sail away from the fog. It had a long history of strange tales and ghost stories. The crew was only too happy to follow the captain's orders and put back out to sea. The last thing any of them wanted was to be part of one of the ghost stories that were told about the magical fog.

As Malak drove the boat into the wall of fog, Lena collapsed from her post at the mast. She slumped into the bottom of the boat breathing heavily and looking as if she had passed out. Malak tried to help her as he steered the tiny craft, but nothing seemed to arouse her. At one point she stirred momentarily and muttered something about the magic draining her, then rolled over and fell into a deep sleep. Malak kept the boat on course as well as he could, considering the only thing to steer by in the fog was the wind.

Unfortunately, the wind slowed down to a barely perceptible breeze after about an hour. In another hour Malak heard the sound of water lapping a shore somewhere close ahead. Knowing sound can play tricks on you in the fog, he tried to wake Lena again, this time with better results.

Lena stirred and came to almost immediately. She sat up blushing a little and trying to shake the sleep from her head.

"Sorry about that," she said, "but magic always makes me tired. The more powerful the spell, and the longer I do it the more tired I get."

"Don't be sorry for saving our skins, Lena. Thanks," Malak said with sincerity. "I am beginning to see why your father sent you. We might get out of this yet." He paused for a moment to give her time to wake up and him time to listen for the shore again.

The sound seemed closer even though the boat had slowed to a mere crawl through the water. The swell had also changed. The waves were gone, but they hadn't crossed any breakers. Malak wondered at this strange coast and its impossible nature.

"Do you hear the shore?" Lena asked interrupting his thoughts. "Are we close to land?"

"I was wondering if you would notice," replied Malak, "That's why I woke you. I think we are about to enter the marshes."

Moments later the boat hissed into the muddy bottom and slowed to a stop. The faint breeze barely moved the sail now. Carefully they got out of the boat. The water was about mid-calf deep, and the bottom seemed to be a combination of sand and mud so that their feet didn't get stuck, but it was still hard to move. The only sound was that of small waves gently lapping at the shore.

Together they pulled the boat forward past the waters edge and up onto the beach. They lowered the sail, and unpacked the gear they would take with them. Malak insisted they take the rope from the rigging, and they both carried part of it wrapped around their waists. He also insisted that Lena wear a dagger and a short sword just in case. The light was fading quickly around them so they marched inland about a hundred yards and made camp. The ground felt soft and just a little slimy under their feet. There was thick vegetation everywhere they looked. It seemed as if the trees were entombed in moss, and vines. There was almost no sound as they walked. The only sound their steps made was a slight squishing noise, as if they were walking on layers of thick wet cloth.

After their small camp was set up for the night, they ate some of their meager, cold rations and laid out their blankets. Malak took the first watch and settled himself into it. Soon he heard Lena's breathing settle into a deep regular pattern. He knew that magic affected different people in different ways, and the effect of putting the spell caster to sleep wasn't that uncommon, but he had rarely seen anyone as tired from it as Lena was. She was normally talkative, and alert. But after the spell she had cast, which must have been a fairly powerful illusion, she had slept and when awakened she had still seemed lethargic. He wondered quietly to himself when the effects would wear off. She wasn't alert enough now to tramp far through the swamp.

The camp was pitch black. The endless mist and tree canopy blocked out any moonlight or stars. Malak listened carefully to the silence, broken only by insects and an occasional small animal passing through the area. He didn't close his eyes for fear he would fall asleep. His ears were acutely aware of every sound hidden in the darkness. He could tell where Lena was from her breathing. He knew from his training and experience that at night the hearing became more acute because of the eyes being useless. Sounds not heard in the day were clear and meaningful at night. At one point, all of the insects to his left went silent, and he knew that something big was passing by, but there were only a few slight noises to indicate where it was. The creature was so silent in its movements, that he doubted he would have heard it if the insects hadn't tipped him off. He held perfectly still, waiting and listening for any change in Lena's breathing. At last the insects started up again, and he figured that whatever it was had passed harmlessly by.

After what seemed like several hours, (there was no way to measure time in the blackness,) Malak caught himself starting to doze off. He decided to stand for a while to wake up. He wasn't sure if Lena would be awake enough to stand watch. Even a drowsy watch was better than one that was dead asleep. She would have tried to stand her shift if he woke her, he knew that, but when magic had been used, if she needed time to recharge some part of herself, she would fall asleep almost involuntarily. He had seen it once before with one of the other students. Better to let her sleep until she woke up on her own. Then he could be sure she was all right.

The night wore on slowly. Malak's legs were beginning to ache from standing motionless for so long when Lena stirred a little. Malak moved quickly to her side to quiet her if she woke up disoriented in the darkness. She went back to sleep for several moments, and Malak went back to listening and pondering what their next steps would be. It wasn't much longer before Lena stirred again and sat up. Malak leaned in close and whispered a warning for quiet.

"What time is it?" Lena whispered as silently as she could.

"It's nighttime," he said teasing and then thought better of it, "I don't know," answered Malak. "Sometime around 4:00 I think."

"You should have woke me up for my turn on watch."

"I didn't know if you were still under the effects of the spell, and I couldn't have you falling asleep."

"Not that I could see much of anything in this blackness anyway," Lena hissed feeling like Malak had patronized her.

"If you feel up to it, you can take your watch now," Malak replied earnestly. "I am going to need some rest before we get started in the morning."

"All right," Lena agreed. "Where are we going anyway?"

"We'll have to discuss that in the morning. Right now I can't think very straight."

"What is it that I'm watching for anyway?"

Malak thought for a moment before he replied. "In the dark like this, your eyes are useless. Your sense of hearing picks up though to compensate for your eyes not working."

"So I'm supposed to listen, right?"

"Right. Sit by me so you can reach me, and if you hear anything out of the ordinary, quietly shake me. I'll wake up."

"What do you mean by out of the ordinary?" Lena asked knowing their lives depended on her ears.

"Anything that sounds like something approaching," whispered Malak as he laid himself down next to her. "Listen to the insects. If they suddenly go quiet, even if it's only in one area, wake me up."

With these final words of instruction, Malak fell into a deep sleep. Lena sat next to him comforted by his nearness, and the rhythmic sound of his breathing. As she sat listening in the dark, she wondered at Malak's ability to seemingly fall asleep at any time. She had once watched him go to sleep in the middle of the afternoon the same way. There seemed to be almost no transition or relaxation, just awake one moment, and deeply asleep the next. Her father had told her it was part of his training to be able to get as much sleep as possible, whenever possible. He'd said that there were many weapons besides swords.

The thought of a sword was strangely comforting to Lena in the darkness. Malak had taught her a little of the art of the sword when he had visited their farm. The last few years, he had worked on the docks as a laborer, trying to avoid using the deadly skills honed in his youth. He had a strange conscience, a fatal flaw in a hired killer. She knew that he could kill, and that he had killed, but as a youth there were people and places where he refused to do so, even at the peril and threat of his own life. This unpredictability and disregard for orders is one of the reasons the king was willing to let him run away without hunting him down. She knew that he had been very helpful to the king on occasion, and she figured that it was a small gesture of appreciation that the king had let him get away and live.

The sudden noise of an insect taking flight brought Lena back to her duty of listening to the darkness. She thought for a moment that she should make a light. She knew how to do it almost effortlessly using the magic her father had taught her in their secret sessions. He had been forbidden from using magic when he had left the White Tower in Thosh. But he taught her many of the ways of magic, in spite of the possibility of getting caught, and she had learned them well. He had told her that they must be careful, but that he wasn't going to leave her helpless in the world. The only thing that stopped her from making the light was a sudden realization of how much their camp would stand out. Anything and everything in the area that had eyes would know and be drawn to their position. If whatever came to investigate the light didn't kill her, she was pretty sure Malak would when he awoke. Better a little shiver in the dark now and then, than to risk a light.

It seemed to Lena that the sun would never rise. She seemed doomed to spend the rest of her existence in eternal darkness, when suddenly; she thought she could see the outline of trees near her. The growing light silenced the insects that had kept her company during her lonely vigil. Her nerves seemed to settle, and the little noises that the insects did make no longer caused her to jump. The world around her seemed to slowly take shape out of the darkness until all that remained was the forest shrouded in white wispy fog.

Malak awoke about an hour after daylight. He moved from sleep to wakefulness almost instantly. Although Lena thought she could still see the sleepiness in his eyes, his body gave no signs of the usual, post-sleep drowsiness. He was merely asleep one minute, and standing the next.

"How long has it been light?" asked Malak.

"Maybe an hour now," replied Lena mimicking his tone.

Malak seemed to relax a little as he surveyed the campsite. He looked up into the trees but couldn't see the tops of them for the fog. Finally he sat back down next to Lena and opened one of their packs. He handed her half of a biscuit and the small water skin they had to share.

"Enjoy it, we'll have to ration a bit until we can find or kill something to eat," he said with a slight smile. Then he seemed to relax a bit as he looked at her. "Let's look at the map as we eat, and try to figure out what our next move is."

"You mean you don't know already?" asked Lena a little surprised.

"Not entirely, at least not yet. I'm kind of glad to just be here and still alive. Getting here has been enough to worry about so far, after all, I did...irritate... the Dark Robes."

"Irritate?" echoed Lena. "Is that your idea of an understatement?"

"All right, I admit it, I've practically signed my death warrant. And I would blame it all on that fat wizard, but I know that to be under a spell like that, someone has to want to work with it. If I had been fighting it, No one would have been able to make me actually go through with the robbery."

"What are you saying?" Lena asked.

"Just that I think that part of me wanted the adventure. I hate to admit it, but I was getting pretty bored with the dockworker life. The only thing to do for excitement is drink and gamble. I don't drink, and I know the odds of the games. That means I don't gamble either. I think I wanted to get out. The fat man made it easy for me to have to leave. I'm sorry that I drug you and Shial into it too. That's why I've been so quiet. When I got on the boat, and out on the open water, my mind seemed to clear a little and I'm not sure I like what I've done."

"Well there's nothing to do now but continue, is there." said Lena taking a swallow of water.

"Unfortunately, that is correct. There's nothing to do now but continue." Malak replied with a mouth full of half-chewed biscuit. "So let's take another look at that map I stole, and see where our next move is."

They spread out the map in front of them, and knelt side-by-side looking at it.

"Here is our position, by my best guess," said Malak pointing at the map. "If we proceed on foot, our best option would be to head south and west to avoid any pirate camps that may be along the shore. Although the downside to the plan is that we don't know what lives in this marshland. It will take us at least two or three days to get across if we don't get lost."

"What if we get lost?" asked Lena hoping they wouldn't have to answer that question.

"Well," replied Malak, "then it will take longer." As he said this he looked at Lena meaningfully.

"Malak, I'm curious," said Lena, "how do we keep our sense of direction when we can't see where we are going in this?" waving her arm to indicate the mist all around them.

"We can see far enough to not loose our sense of direction," said Malak. "I'll teach you an old trick. It isn't hard, and it should keep us from going in circles. The question is what are we going to do once we reach the plains beyond the swamps. There is at least a good days march to gain the cover of the mountains."

"If we aim a little more westward, then we might come out here," Lena said pointing to another spot on the map. "Then we would be closer to the mountains. But Malak, what are we going to do when we get to the mountains?"

"I'm not sure now," answered Malak. "All I know is that we can't stay here in the swamps for very long. It seems like a good place to hide, but I have heard and read accounts of some of the dangers that live here. We need to get clear as soon as we can. Hopefully, we can pass through unnoticed."

"What if we can't?" asked Lena.

"Then we fight our way through, or die trying to," replied Malak.

Lena was quiet for a moment while the ramifications of those words sank in. "I wish I knew what these funny marks were," she finally said pointing to three marks on the map.

"I've thought about them too," said Malak. "For the life of me they must mean something. They're the only things strange about the map. I mean why would the head dark-robe keep a common map like this hidden and protected unless there was something important about it."

"He wouldn't," replied Lena. "Dark-robes as a group are very tidy. They don't tolerate anything that isn't useful to them. They don't have any use at all for sentimentality, or anything like it. I could cast another small spell to see if there is anything hidden on the map or magical about it."

"Didn't your dad already try that?"

"Yes, but with spells that detect magic, there is always the chance that something will be missed. Something small that wouldn't be seen by one wizard might be by another."

"How much energy would that take?" asked Malak.

"Not much. I used to cast it to find things father had hidden all over the house," said Lena.

"Go ahead," said Malak motioning to the map. "I'm curious about this thing, and it will give me a chance to see how much the spell drains you."

"Thanks a lot," said Lena looking annoyed at Malak's remark she suddenly felt like some kind of animal to be studied.

"Don't get offended," said Malak. "I need to know a little bit about your abilities if I am going to be counting on you in emergencies."

Lena felt the reply was a hidden compliment. Malak had, for the first time since she had known him, shown that he might possibly need someone's help. She cleared her mind and began the spell, which was a combination of words and hand motions over the parchment. When she was done, there was no response at all.

"Is that it?" asked Malak looking at her to see if there was any change.

"That's it," said Lena.

"That didn't tell us much, did it," said Malak.

"On the contrary, it told us one of two things; either we are dealing with a very advanced and powerful concealing spell, or the information that we see is very important to the High Dark Wizard," replied Lena a little smugly.

Malak sat back and rubbed his eyes. He took a deep breath and looked at the map again.

"Didn't Shial say something about geometric shapes?" he asked.

"Well he said that summoning things was done through circles most of the time, and that other shapes could be used for very special ones. "Why?" asked Lena still looking at the map.

"If you connect the small x's with the dark towers and the western white tower, you get an almost perfect pentagon...or pentagram depending on how you connect the points," said Malak tracing patterns on the map.

Lena stared at the map as if seeing it for the first time. She suddenly gasped as if things finally made sense.

"What is it?" asked Malak.

"It doesn't make any sense," Lena began, "This is too huge to be a shape for summoning. I mean, how would you draw the lines across that many miles of ground, and where are the protective runes."

"Let's assume for a moment that they have figured out a way to draw the lines, didn't Shial say the statue might be...some kind of si...sim...sin"

"Symbiot," interrupted Lena. "If the statue is a symbiot, then there wouldn't need to be any protective runes. Whoever held the statue would have control over the thing summoned."

"What do you mean 'thing summoned,'" asked Malak beginning to feel uneasy in his stomach.

"I mean," said Lena beginning to breathe harder, "that whatever the statue represents would come into this world, and would be under the control of whoever held the statue."

"Yea," said Malak dryly. "But why does the portal need to be that big?"

"It doesn't, unless..." Lena drifted off into silence.

"Unless what," said Malak loudly, snapping Lena back to the here and now.

"Unless whatever that statue is connected to needs a door that big to fit through," said Lena still staring at the map.

"But that's impossible," Malak said not sounding too sure of himself.

"I don't know what's possible or not, maybe it is something really big, or millions of small things. Either way whatever comes through is going to destroy…"

"Whatever it wants to," finished Malak.

"Whatever it's told to," whispered Lena looking paler than Malak had ever seen her.

"So how do we stop it?" asked Malak.

"What do you mean?" said Lena in a high-pitched voice. "We don't know for sure that this is what the map is for."

"Lena," Malak said softly, "That is the only logical explanation that we can think of. We need to stop it or some damn dark-robe is going to ruin everyone's lives. How do we stop a summoning like this?"

"If you're right," Lena started hesitantly, "and I don't think that you are. But, if you were right, the best way would be to kill the wizard before he starts the spell. Other than that, you would have to break the line of the pentagram. Destroy one point either before or during the casting of the spell. But you never know what will happen if you break it during the spell. I don't know that much about summoning spells. I only know enough to banish some things already here."

"How easy is it to banish something. Something like this," said Malak.

"The bigger and more powerful an entity is, the harder it is to banish it. I don't think all of the white-robes combined could do it," Lena answered.

"What if we are dealing with the other option, millions of smaller entities?" Malak pressed.

"Then you have to banish one at a time and it just depends on how powerful each individual is," answered Lena shaking her head in disbelief.

"Now think carefully," Malak hesitated before asking the question. "Is it really possible to open a doorway that big?"

"I don't know," said Lena looking exasperated. "I've never summoned anything. Father would never let me. He said it was a hellish practice best left to idiots."

"That sounds like Shial," Malak observed under his breath.

"What?" asked Lena.

"Your father is a good man, Lena. He's helped me more than anyone else in the world would, but when he feels strongly about something, there is no room for discussion. If he doesn't like summoning, he wouldn't teach you anything about it."

Lena nodded her head affirmatively, but didn't say anything.

"If this map is to be used for placing the points of the doorway, whoever made it can make another fairly easily," said Malak. "When will they try to open the portal?"

Lena thought for a few moments before answering. "They will probably try whatever they are planning during the solstice. That's in about three months."

Malak's face went hard as he thought about Lena's words. "That gives us a little bit of time."

"Time for what?" asked Lena.

"Time to figure out how to stop them," replied Malak coldly.

Lena looked at Malak trying to fathom his thoughts. "What are you thinking?" she finally asked realizing he was serious in his intentions.

"We will have to stop them from opening the portal. Their intentions are, I think, nothing less than the domination of the world. At least all of the world that we know." Malak paused for a moment before continuing to look at the map. "The closest point is in the bay of blood, west of here. I think that is our best point of attack."

"But if we attack on the water, won't they see us coming," Lena interrupted.

"True," said Malak, "but the only other point we could hit is on the mountains here to the west. I don't know if we can make it that far and find the right spot in the time we have. We'll have to avoid pirates until then. We'll also have to find enough food to survive until the solstice. Besides maybe we won't have to destroy the ship entirely, maybe just distracting them will be enough."

"I don't think a distraction is going to stop the dark wizards that have planned this," said Lena. "Besides they don't have the statue anymore, so this is all mute."

Malak thought silently about their situation for a few minutes. He carefully weighed the options open to them. If the dark-robes were going to get their hands on the statue again, they would have to do it before it could get to a white tower. They would have to do it soon. If they did get it back, someone would have to stop them from another front. That meant attacking one of the points on the map. They couldn't turn around and go back, the pirates they had played for such fools the day before may still be looking for them, and if not them others were likely to be encountered. If they did make it past pirates and the other dangers of the open ocean, they would be seen coming into Chistock and dark wizards would soon be on their trail. He knew of at least two men who were informants to the Dark Tower. There were probably a lot more spies than those two. They would never survive until the solstice, and if they did, making another attack on the same tower was almost sure to fail. Black-robes were notorious for learning from their mistakes.

"As I see it," Malak began, "Lena, we have two chances of stopping the summoning, or we can hope that the statue is not a symbiot, or that they don't get it back, and move on with our lives the best we can."

"You don't really believe that do you?" asked Lena.

"No, I don't, I think they will try and probably succeed in getting the nasty thing back." replied Malak. "I think that we need to do something to stop a horror from being unleashed on our world. Our best two chances are to stop the spell at one of the two locations on the map that we have already looked at. Both have their difficulties, and their chances of success. If they cast the spell at night, we have a good chance of surprising them at either location. Being that there are only two of us, surprise is an important ally. If they think we are coming we won't stand a chance of success. If they cast the spell during the day, we will be seen as we try to approach on the open ocean. Now, the ship will have a crew that we'll have to get past, or deal with somehow. They will surely slow us down, or maybe even stop us. The ship is the closest to us though, and we stand a much better chance of being in position to attack when the solstice arrives. Provided, of course, that they are going to try and open the portal on the solstice."

"The spot marked on the land is within reach, but barely, if we can find it in the mountains," Malak continued. "We don't have any time to loose while crossing the swamp. If we get lost for long, we won't make it to the mountains in time to search. However, we should be able to approach much closer to whatever is there without being seen. But it will be a long push, and we'll get there pretty worn out. I have no idea what we will face once there. There may only be one or two wizards, as if that weren't bad enough, or there may be a lot of them as well as hired help.

"As I see it, those are our best options. What's your choice between them, and why?"

Lena was a little taken back at this sudden turn in Malak. She had known him to be easy-going and thoughtful at times, but she had never seen the cold efficiency he was now displaying. He had cut the problem down into clear parts. It was almost like watching some kind of machine. There was no fear evident in his face of the dangers before them. The task at hand seemed to be the only concern, and how best to achieve success. She had never seen him as the cold calculating machine that was now before her. A slight shiver ran up her spine as she thought about what he would be like as an enemy. If the truth was known, she didn't know what to say to Malak about which road to take. Either way was uncertain, and full of doubt. Finally she took a deep breath, "I think that our best bet would be to try the ship. It is closer to us, and we stand a better chance of being there for the solstice. I doubt that the spell would be cast in the daytime; dark-robes like to do things of this nature at night. As for the ship's crew, there may be just as many men guarding the site in the mountain as there are on the ship."

"I think that you are right," said Malak slowly. "Let's load the boat, and start up the coast."

They picked up their equipment and headed back to the boat. They had covered most of the distance to the shore when Malak Quickly dropped to the ground, motioning Lena to do the same. He didn't make a sound as he put down the supplies he was carrying, and drew a dagger from the sheath on his hip. He slid through the underbrush with only the slightest rustling of the foliage.

After several minutes, Malak called softly for Lena to join him on the open beach. She pushed through the last feet of underbrush, and stepped into the clear. The beach was deserted as far into the fog, which seemed slightly thinner today than it had been the day before, as she could see. Malak stood a few feet away staring out into the ocean and mist. The boat was nowhere to be seen.

Moving closer to Malak she asked, "Where's the boat?"

"Gone," replied Malak almost carelessly.

"What do you mean, 'gone'?"

"It's not here," he said, "so it's gone."

"Maybe it's up the beach," Lena said hopefully. "I mean in this fog one stretch of muddy sand looks just like the rest. Let's split up and look for it. You go one way and I'll go the other."

"Lena, look at the mud here," Malak said pointing to some impressions in the soft ground. "This is the track made by the boat when we pulled it out of the water. This is where the boat should be."

Lena looked carefully at the mud. She could plainly see the mark the hull had made in it. She could also see the tracks that they had made the day before. There were also some other impressions made by the equipment that hade been moved, and a long strange mark that looked oddly out of place next to the others.

"So what happened to the boat?" she asked.

"It's gone," said Malak turning to look at her.

# Chapter 7

"Please close your mouth," said Malak after almost a minute of Lena staring at him. "You're going to wind up with a bug in it."

Lena closed her mouth with a snap. It opened again immediately, "What do we do now?" she demanded.

Malak thought for a moment then said, "Now we go overland to whatever is in the mountains."

"But what about the boat?" she asked.

"We could spend days looking for it, and never find it. It is probably out on the water now, maybe even at the bottom of the ocean. In that case we would never find it. We don't have time to run around guessing," replied Malak.

"So we give up on our plans?"

"No," said Malak. "We are still going to stop whatever the dark wizards are up to, but now it is going to take a lot more effort. Now we have to do it after a long walk."

"Can't we build a raft, or some kind of boat?" asked Lena.

"Whatever pushed the boat back into the water also made that funny impression in the mud." said Malak indicating the strange indentation Lena had noticed before. "Whatever it was didn't leave a lot of other tracks. It is probably still close by somewhere. Rafts are cumbersome, and slow through the water. A boat would take too long to build, and anything between the two would not be stable enough in the open ocean. Besides anything we could build would take time and make a lot of noise. We would be sitting ducks waiting for whatever is in the swamps to come out and invite us to lunch...as the main course."

"So attacking by sea is definitely out now?" asked Lena.

"No, but we have to go with our best chance of success. I think that now lies in the overland attack," replied Malak. "We can't stay here. I think there's too much danger, and I don't even know what the dangers really are."

"Then how do you expect to get through the swamp?" she asked, her voice sounding a little nervous for the first time.

"We will have to rely on our wits, our skills and talents, and have a little luck," said Malak soothingly. He wasn't enjoying the thought of traveling through the swamps and mist; instinctively he was calming his own emotions as well as hers.

"My father always told me that you didn't believe in luck."

"It's true," replied Malak with a small grin, "I've been trained to make my own luck. But that philosophy only goes so far in the real world. I have studied a lot of wars and battles and peoples lives. By far the most successful ventures in history were planned and carried out with the thought of making their own luck. Even so they also had, at some point in their course a strange set of coincidences that made their success happen. There are always unseen problems that surprise people. Call it what you will, fate usually lends a hand in some way or other. In my earlier studies it seems that those working the hardest to make their own luck will usually have the best luck for some reason."

"So you're saying we should keep trying," Lena said relaxing a little.

"I'm saying that the surest route to failure is to give up."

"Well then we should get going."

"That does appear to be the next step we take," said Malak pulling a length of rope from their supplies. "Tie this end around your waist. I don't know how thick the fog is going to get."

Once they were tied together with about eight feet of rope between them, and they had their packs and weapons on, Malak took his bearing from the shoreline as best he could and started off.

"How do you know we won't wander in circles?" asked Lena.

"There is a woodsman trick for not doing that," answered Malak. "As long as we can see a little way in front of us we should be all right. You just find three objects in front of you that are in a line. Starting at the first, you walk to the second and then pick another beyond the third. You repeat the process always keeping at least two things lined up in front of you and you will travel in a straight line."

"What if you can't see that far ahead?" asked Lena.

"Then you do the best you can and hope you're not wandering in circles."

"That isn't a very comforting thought."

"That's what this is for." said Malak gently tugging the rope. "The mist might get very thick in there, and it will be bad enough traveling without loosing each other. Then our slim chance of success would become a hopeless chance of getting out alive."

The comment brought Lena up short inside. Malak had always talked of their situation in such a positive way that she hadn't thought about the chance of failure. With his last comment, part of her began realizing that their odds might be a lot slimmer than she had assumed they were. As she looked at it now she realized that they were two against many powerful dark wizards and whoever was working for them; just the two of them against the swamp and fog that had defeated groups of explorers and warriors. Their chances of surviving were very slim indeed let alone defeating the wizards that threatened their lands and families.

They entered the tree line with Malak cautioning against noise. "Let's try to get through this swamp making as little noise as possible. If you need to get my attention, tug on the rope. We'll have to whisper when we talk, and try to watch your step. The ground is moist and will hide a lot of noise, but avoid stepping on sticks that will snap if possible, and watch out for sinkholes. We'll probably find them as well as quicksand.

Malak led the way, traveling in a basically straight line. Avoiding the thickest foliage when possible, and using the short sword strapped on his pack to cut through brush when absolutely necessary. Other than the sword, he seemed only to have the daggers on his hip and in his boot as weapons. Though he was supposed to be well trained, Lena was going over the magic she knew in her mind as they walked, trying to figure out which spells would be most useful, and what situations they might run into. In the end, she gave up and decided that the best defense now would be to stay alert to any possible dangers, and face them as they came.

Once when Malak was trying to quietly cut through a patch of thick vegetation, Lena broke the silence between them.

"Aren't you afraid of leaving a trail for something to follow us?"

"The way I see it, there won't be any people following us. The Pirates would have made themselves annoying by now if they dared venture into the jungle. If there is an animal that wants to track us, they won't have any problem following our scent or our trail regardless of how much I chop. I am trying to cut as little as possible, but that's to save on the noise. It's one of life's endless balancing acts. We need to get through the swamp as quickly as possible, but we also need to try and not get noticed by anything too big," said Malak.

They continued on following small trails when they could, and making their own way when there wasn't a trail going theirs. The fog and mist changed little as they walked. In very low places it seemed to be thicker than when they were on seemingly higher ground. The visibility seemed to be stuck at about fifty feet in any direction. Occasionally they would stop and listen for a minute when any small animal would flush from its hiding place near them. Malak would also stop short and listen if they made any sudden noise during their long tramp.

The ground they walked on wasn't as muddy as they had feared at first. It was mostly sand with muddy spots here and there that they had to cross. Most of the time they didn't notice the ground anyway as it was covered in a thick carpet of vegetation, some live and some decaying. The decaying vegetation gave off a thick, heavy smell; like piles of leaves in the fall after a rainstorm. The smell reminded Lena of simpler times and the years she had spent with her father at home storing their crops for the cooler months of winter. She thought of the harvest celebrations and chilly mornings. Cool evenings sitting on the porch with her father watching the sunset and listening to the quiet of the evening. A thousand memories began flooding into her mind.

Lena had to fight back the tears of homesickness that threatened to suddenly overwhelm her. It was a new feeling for her. She had never been separated from her father for more than a day before. When he made trips into the market in Chistok to sell vegetables and buy supplies, she was sometimes left on the farm to keep an eye on things. He was always home by the next sunrise. Usually she made the trip with him. This time was different. This time the separation was definitely going to be several weeks, and perhaps as long as forever.

She was amazed at how thoughts of the smallest things made her heart and head ache with emotion, and her eyes well up with tears. Little things like the way Shial would hum softly as he did household chores like cooking and cleaning; the way that the barn smelled in the cool morning air. She thought longingly of how the sun rose above the trees into a clear blue sky. Now surrounded by the mist and heavy air of the swamp, she fought to control her emotions and not let Malak see her weakness. Even with all of her efforts, she thought he suspected something. He had turned to look at her a couple of times when a particularly poignant memory had made her gasp for breath to keep from sobbing.

Malak had noticed. He was used to listening to the breathing of people to judge their mental state. At first he thought that he was setting too fast a pace, but he had seen Lena run in the woods and hills around her farm too many times to believe that she was that out of shape. It finally dawned on him that the problem with her breathing was emotional instead of physical. He had been alone as long as he could remember. He couldn't remember his parents, and he never had any of his teachers for more than a few months at a time. He tried to consider for a moment what it must be like for Lena to suddenly be away from the only teacher, authority figure, and the closest friend she had ever had. Because Shial was her father, he was much more to her than a friend. Malak understood that fact, but he had never known a true parent-child relationship himself, and so friend was the best, though admittedly inadequate, description of the relationship they shared. He had seen homesickness before, in young people taken from their parents for the first long period of time, and it had always seemed like a sign of weakness to him. Now, though still strange to him, it just seemed like a problem to overcome.

When they finally stopped for lunch, Malak had thought of some things to give Lena to do with her mind. She needed to keep it busy and away from thoughts of her father. This was the only solution for homesickness that he knew. His instructors had always used it to fight the problem in others. As they ate their small rations of bread and jerked meat, and drank water they had collected off some leaves, Malak asked her to listen closely to the sounds around them, and watch for anything seemingly out of the ordinary. He told her outright the extent of most of his fears.

"Whatever moved the boat did so very quietly," he began. "As I have thought about it, I think it has, at least some rudimentary intelligence. If it had been some mindless beast just out to destroy something strange, it would have made a lot of noise tearing it apart. The fact that it was gone without a trace, seems to indicate to me that it didn't want us leaving in it. I may be giving whatever it is too much credit, but if our situations were reversed, I would have done the same thing to control somebody's movements.

"You're saying that whatever moved the boat is smart?" asked Lena incredulously. "Or are you saying that it had to be someone, a person, that moved it?"

"It was probably a person," said Malak in decided manner. "But if someone did, they didn't leave any normal tracks. We also have to wonder if they were traveling alone? And if so, who is crazy enough or dangerous enough to travel alone in the swamps? If there was more than one of them, why didn't they attack us while we slept? Perhaps they couldn't track us at night. Or, maybe, they figured that removing our boat would condemn us to certain destruction in the marshes. Maybe someone else was stranded here, and saw us land. Then they took the boat when it got dark to save themselves."

"Are there any other possibilities that would explain the how the boat disappeared?"

"I can think of only one other plausible one that would also explain the funny track in the sand," answered Malak. "Maybe it wasn't a some*one*, but some*thing*."

"What do you mean?" asked Lena, not sure that she really wanted to hear the answer.

Malak thought for a moment before answering. "Your father told me some of the dangers they faced years ago when the king ordered the swamps explored. You know how deadly the attempt proved to be for most of the expedition. Well, there were a lot of things they had to face, which they expected. Packs of roving wolves took their toll. Lack of proper food and water were a part of it too. They had the usual physical fatigue and exhaustion that you can imagine they would have moving a large body of men through something like this," Malak said waving one arm to indicate the foliage and wetness all around them. "They were plagued by disease and fever all the way through. But, there were other things they had to face as well, things that took their toll on the men's spirits more than any of the mundane trials, or even all of them put together. In the end, only five of the force of five hundred made it out alive."

"What are you talking about, Malak. Don't try to frighten me with ghost stories. If you have something to tell me, out with it," said Lena.

"Malak took a deep breath before beginning again. "Remember the great war of the wizards?" he asked, then continuing after her brief nod. "There were a lot of things brought into our world from other planes. Things conjured to fight dirty battles for both sides. Some of these things escaped the control of the wizards who had conjured them. When this happened, some of them ran amok, destroying everything around them indiscriminately. Without regard for who or what was attacked. These were put down quickly enough, and sent back to the planes they came from. But some of these entities were more intelligent than that. They quickly just ran away and hid. Many were found and banished to their home planes. Some weren't found. Some went into hiding in the swamps and mountains. Feeding off the life forces of whatever they could find to sustain them in this world. They were the biggest danger to the men of the earlier expedition. These beings with intelligence of some level or other were what killed most of the men and left the rest unwilling to talk about the entire affair for years after.

"Your father was successful in banishing several of these entities, but he was sure that there were more of them. One particularly nasty thing was never really even seen. The only way Shial survived was to take the few men left and make a run for the lands beyond the swamps. When the group was small enough and could move quickly and without much noise, they started to survive. Whatever was killing them seemed to attack larger, slower groups. That's why we are going this way. A lone man, or a couple of people might get through unnoticed, but if a large force is following us, they will have a devil of a time.

"So if we move quietly, we should be safe?" asked Lena, feeling a little relieved for the first time. Her father had never told her, or anyone else she had known, about his experiences in the marshes. She had asked him one night a couple years earlier, but he had just said, "There are more pleasant things to talk about."

"That's my plan," said Malak. "There's just one problem. I think we are being followed."

Lena's feeling of relief vanished as quickly as it had come. "Why do you say that?"

"Right now it's just a feeling in my gut," said Malak. "But I've felt this feeling before. We need to watch everything around us. Whoever, or whatever it is will either loose interest in us and go its own way, or it will make itself known when it's ready."

"What do you mean, 'make itself known'," asked Lena.

"I mean it will attack us, or let us see it so it can drive us. Whatever happens, don't panic. Our panic is its best weapon. Just keep your eyes and ears open to what is going on around us. If you see anything, don't get scared. Just tell me in a quiet voice what is going on, and I'll do the same for you."

They packed up their remaining food, and supplies and got ready to leave. Malak checked to make sure his weapons were secure. The short sword and dagger were in place on his hip, and his knife was in his boot as well as other small weapons of one type or another. They picked up their packs, put them on and continued their march.

They had been moving steadily through the terrain for almost three hours when Malak stopped and motioned Lena to come closer to him.

"Wolves," was all he said, as he started to shorten the rope between them.

"How do you know?" asked Lena.

"I've caught a couple glimpses of them. I don't know how many there are, but I know there is more than one. They may attack at any time. Usually they will probe first."

Malak saw the question in Lena's eyes and answered.

"They will send in a pre-attack to see how we respond to it. They're tricky. They will probably attack from the rear, so we'll trade places. Just guide us through the trees like I showed you." He fiddled with the rope and adjusted his sword and dagger in their sheathes, then said, "Let's go."

Lena lined up the trees in her sight the best she could. The middle mark she was aiming for was really just to the side of the middle tree, but there was no help for it. They moved quickly now, making a little more noise than before, but not much. She would look back occasionally, and Malak would smile reassuringly and motion her forward again without a word.

The two of them traveled for several hours this way when the attack finally came. The daylight, what little filtered through the trees and fog to their eyes, had begun to fade. Lena had turned to look at Malak less and less often during the hours of their march, but she just happened to do it at the moment of attack. She looked back at him when a flicker of motion coming at Malak from behind and to the left caught her eye.

Malak saw the shift in her gaze and moved without thinking, just as he had been taught since his earliest memories. He spun away from the direction of her gaze, drawing the dagger and stabbing downward as he did so. The long blade met with furry flesh and bone. Penetrating the eye socket and into the animal's brain. The wolf had come in at an angle to hamstring Malak, but had intentionally been after the leg on the far side. This would have kept it behind Malak when he turned to defend himself, but his training had included dealing with animal attacks of this kind. He had spun the opposite way, and met the attack head-on.

The collision nearly knocked Malak over though, and he had to fight to keep hold of the knife and yank it free. A second wolf came now from the opposite side of the first attack, this one coming in high and at his throat. Malak yanked hard at the dagger, which had lodged in the skull of the first wolf, but it held fast in its new home. He fell backwards and dropped under the leaping wolf at the last moment, striking upward with an open palm, not to really injure the animal, but to let it's momentum carry it over, and away from them. Its teeth missed him by a hairs breadth.

The wolf hit the ground already turning, and was back at Malak instantly. Malak had bought himself just enough time to draw the dagger from the skull of its dead companion, and the next lunge of the wolf met with steel plunging into its heart.

Malak came up from the second attack to see more wolves circling in. He saw the look of fear in Lena's eyes and saw her looking for a direction to run.

"It's no good running from them, they'll have us for sure if we run," he said to her. "Get up in that tree there," he said nodding over her shoulder.

She turned and leaped to the tree only a few feet away. Malak was right behind her and they went up it like two scared cats. The wolves closed in, and within minutes there were over forty of the beasts circling the tree.

"What do we do now?" asked Lena in a shaky voice.

"Now," replied Malak who had been silently watching the movements of the wolves below, "we make ourselves comfortable. Unless you have another trick up your sleeve like with the pirates."

"That spell won't work on animals. I tried once to make some birds leave our crops alone. Their brains aren't like ours. They see things differently than we do. Dad said that all it did was make them see things that didn't make any sense, so they mostly just ignore the illusion."

"Then," said Malak easing himself into the branches a little, "we will be here a while. If you have any ideas I'm open to them, otherwise we'll have to just sit here and think."

"How long will they stay waiting for us," said Lena as she watched several of the animals below lay down, eyes still watching the two in the tree.

"As long as they need to," said Malak. "They know we aren't going anywhere."

The stalemate continued for the rest of the evening and into the night. Malak and Lena ate a quiet dinner of stale rations in relative silence. Lena felt the pangs of despair creeping into her mind more than once. She had always counted on Malak to get her through the ordeal ahead of them. Now he seemed at a loss as to what to do. She began to really doubt that they would live for the first time.

As these hopeless thoughts were running through her mind, she felt Malak put a reassuring hand on her shoulder. She looked up at him, and he could see the pain in her eyes.

"Relax," he said gently, "a solution, however desperate, will always present itself."

"You're not just saying that to keep me from crying, are you?" she asked, forcing a smile onto her lips.

"It always has before for me. I see no reason for this time to be any different," said Malak.

They settled into the branches of the tree to rest for the night. Malak tied them both to keep them from falling in their sleep.

"Shouldn't we keep a watch?" Lena asked as Malak closed his eyes to rest.

"Why bother? We have about forty really good watchdogs working for us tonight. They'll let us know if anything happens, and believe me, they won't let us out of their sight," he said pointing downwards and closing his eyes again.

The night was one Lena would never forget. She could sense the wolves all around them. The darkness amplified sounds until the smallest one seemed to be louder than a shout. Every now and then one of the wolves would move and she would jolt awake at the sound. The tree's branches dug themselves into her without mercy. There was no such thing as a comfortable position. Most of the night was spent trying to find the least agonizing way to endure the situation. Very rarely Malak would adjust his position and that would set the tree in motion, again waking her from the slight doze she had finally managed to drift into. Above all of this were thoughts of near despair about their situation. There didn't appear to be any way out. Sometime before dawn, the wolves settled down and quit moving, allowing Lena to drift into a fitful half-sleep just as the branches started to become visible in the first traces of light.

Sometime later in the morning, Malak awoke with a start. Instinctively he knew something was wrong. It took him a moment to focus his thoughts and pull them from the recesses of deep sleep. He remembered the tree, and finally the wolves at the bottom of it.

The wolves were gone.

Where were they? They should have been there. Were they hiding to trick them into coming down from the tree? Were they that smart? Why would they, when it was obvious that he and Lena weren't going anywhere? These and other questions raged in Malak's mind while he continued to study the ground around the tree. The tracks that he could see from his perch showed that they had left together, almost single-file, all going the same direction. He didn't know what that meant, but they seemed to be gone for good. Why would they do that? Why would a pack of wolves leave a sure meal that only needed to be waited for?

An involuntary shiver ran up Malak's spine as he realized the most likely answer. He shook Lena awake trying not to make any noise as he undid their bindings.

"We have to go. Now!" he whispered.

"What about the wolves?" she asked sleepily.

"Their gone."

"What? Where did they go?" she asked looking at the ground and shaking the sleep from her mind. Malak was moving quickly, not the normal relaxed motion she was used to. It made her nervous.

"That's why we have to go now. They may be back, but I doubt it," he said as he finished putting things away, and started down the tree.

"Malak, what is going on?" Lena asked following his descent.

"Ssshhhh," was all Malak would say until they were on the ground.

Malak quickly checked their direction and headed into the mist.

Lena was about to ask her question again when Malak grabbed her hand and spoke quietly to her.

"Something is coming. Something that a pack of wolves knows they don't stand a chance against. That's why they left so quietly. They didn't want to attract its attention."

"What is it?" asked Lena a little worried.

"I don't want to find out," was all Malak said, and he quickened their pace. He was still holding her hand tightly in his. He didn't want any chance of them becoming separated now.

# Chapter 8

Dalryms sat quietly waiting for the king. The journey back to Thosh hadn't taken as long as he had feared it would. They had traveled as fast as they could manage, and had, he thought, set some kind of record. He really couldn't remember the last time he had eaten, and didn't really care to think about it. His mind was too busy now with the problem of the figurine. Dark wizards had risked a great deal to recover it. What was so important about the little statue that they had openly murdered a ships crew and sunk the ship to recover it?

Dalryms and the surviving sailors had arrived in the city sometime past midnight. He had gone directly to the palace and sought out the king. The guards had known better than to deny him his request, and now he sat waiting for his audience with the monarch. The king had told all palace personnel that the white wizard had access to him day or night regardless of any other circumstances. The wait was short, and Dalryms was quickly shown into an antechamber to the throne room where the king sat behind a desk in his dressing robe. The guard left the room at a wave of the king's hand and closed the door behind him.

"What happened to you, and where have you been?" the king asked, his expression softening at the appearance of his old friend.

"I've been in Chistock using one of our little secrets," replied Dalryms as he slumped into a chair across from the king.

"You contacted Malak? Why did you do that without telling me?"

"I didn't know that I was going to until I got there," Dalryms said trying to pacify the king. "I went there on a tip from Shial Fonth that the dark-robes were up to something."

"And you didn't tell me before you left?" asked Nolan.

"You were in a meeting, and it sounded urgent. Our inside man indicated that there was something bad going on. There were no other details given, so I thought I would check it out personally. Besides, what if it turned out to be of no real importance? It looked like you were with all of your officers, and I didn't want to interrupt something important with something unknown," said Dalryms.

"Not to mention the chance of enjoying some of the local food?" smiled the king, knowing his friends appetites.

"The fare in Chistock is excellent, but we should save that conversation for later, we have a lot of problems, I think, that need dealing with now," replied Dalryms smiling at the king's friendly prod. King Nolan often let Dalryms know that his weight wasn't healthy.

The king got suddenly serious and listened as Dalryms recounted everything that had happened over the past couple of weeks.

King Nolan was quiet for several minutes, as he considered all that his friend was telling him. When he finally did speak, his tone was so serious, that it was almost grave.

"What do you think that little statue is for?" he asked slowly.

"I don't know yet, but I do know that it is very powerful in some way not easily seen. I also know that the dark-robes, or at least some of them want it so badly that they are willing to commit acts of murder and piracy on the high seas to get it back. We weren't supposed to survive the attack. However, I don't really think they ultimately cared one way or the other."

"Which means that they aren't afraid of justice or punishment," the king muttered out loud. Then he looked meaningfully at Dalryms. "Whatever they are going to do, they are going to do soon. And either they won't be where the authorities can get hold of them, or there won't be any authorities left to get hold of them."

"When you left to go to Chistock," King Nolan continued, "I was in a meeting with my generals."

"There was a contingency of troops in the west end of the kingdom. They were attached to the white tower just north of the high plains. When their replacements arrived to relieve the them, they were missing."

"What do you mean, 'missing'," asked Dalryms.

"I mean there was no one there to relieve, or even in the area," said Nolan. "They took charge of the small fort and sent a fast rider back to report."

"Deserters?" asked Dalryms.

"It's possible, but usually there are only one or two deserters in any given situation," answered the king. "Mass desertions rarely occur, but it's not unheard of. This happened a couple of months before you left. I sent another force to man the post and investigate. When they arrived, again there was no one there. Again they took over and sent a rider back to inform me. It was that news which prompted the meeting the day you left."

"I don't know if this has anything to do with your statue," continued the king tiredly, "but I sent a very large force to deal with whatever is happening out there. It will take several weeks, or even months, before we will hear anything. I'm afraid they too will find no one at the post."

"I think we should consider making an attack on the dark tower in Chistock," said Dalryms.

The king looked as if he had been slapped.

"I don't think that is warranted yet," said Nolan. "It would touch off another wizard war, and we haven't recovered from the last one yet. If we move toward them they are going to see it. They will be more than prepared. This city will be a battleground because they will enlist the dark tower here."

"You're not afraid of the dark wizards are you?" asked Dalryms.

"Yes, I am," interjected the king. "And you should be too, just coming off a swimming party arranged by them. It will be a bloody battle."

"Besides," continued the king, "I won't have the men to mount that kind of offensive until the issue in the west is dealt with. I have a defensive force here, but the rest of the army went west."

"I don't think that we have time for the recall of the troops," said Dalryms "We must stop them before they use that figurine."

"It's no use Dalryms, we can't risk that much destruction. The kingdom won't exist anymore," said the king.

"I have my doubts about it existing very long if we don't attack them," said Dalryms with a little more force.

"Old friend," warned the king," remember our agreement. Power is held by each of us, don't think to change my mind. Until I have reason, and that means I'm attacked, we will not wage war on the dark-robes. If you want to start legal proceedings regarding the attack on the ship you may, but this Captain Jontag will probably do that on his own."

"So that's your final word?" asked Dalryms.

"For right now, yes. I'm going back to bed. You should go get some rest too. You look terrible."

With these words King Nolan stood and walked out of the room. The guard outside snapped to attention as he passed.

Dalryms stood as the king left and remained standing for a few minutes thinking about what to do next. Finally he made up his mind and stormed out of the room. If the king would take no action against sure catastrophe, then he would.

He made his way toward the White Tower of Thosh. Moving silently through the deserted streets and alleyways, taking the shortest route he knew. All the while thinking about what he was going to do. His exhausted mind was trying to come up with possibilities and solutions to problems he only half understood. He was already working on the problems he knew about, and yet he realized that there were surely many more he hadn't even thought of that he would need to deal with too. As he finally approached the tower, the first thing he needed was rest. The mind never functioned properly when exhausted, and he felt exhausted clear through to his bones. There was no time for delays, but if he was going to lead an effective assault on the dark-robes, he knew the first thing he needed was rest. He would take a few hours, and then call his most trusted friends in the tower to his aid.

After gaining entrance to the tower past shocked guards, who looked at his appearance with unconcealed amazement, Dalryms went straight to his chambers, and undressed. He cleaned up as best as he could with a cloth and the stale water in his washstand, and then dressed for sleep. As he collapsed onto his bed, he had to force all of his muscles to relax and hold still before he could finally drift off to sleep. He didn't worry about when he would wake up, he just let his body and mind take whatever rest they needed. He knew that after his entrance to the tower, rumors would fly. Taking a long sleep would seem the most natural thing to do, and would be the best thing to calm fears within the lower ranks of the tower.

When Dalryms awoke the sun was sitting low in the afternoon sky. His body reminded him of the abuse it had recently endured with every move he made. It seemed as though every muscle was sore. As he changed into new robes, he kept finding new muscles that would scream out in protest with each use. Finally he was finished and made his way to the dining hall just as the evening meal was being served.

Whispers could be heard as he took his usual place at the head table, and spoke to the wizards around him who he had known for years. He answered their concerns for his welfare by telling them the ship he was on had gone down in a storm, and spoke of the subsequent trip on foot to Thosh. During the course of the meal, he reminded himself not to eat as much as normal. He would need to get himself into better shape, and there really was no time to do it. It would take months to repair the damage done by the previous years' indulgences, but he would have to start somewhere. He also, very quietly asked a few of the more powerful wizards there who he knew and could trust, to join him in his quarters after things quieted down in the tower for the night.

Dalryms went about his normal routine for the rest of the evening, and then went to his chambers to await the other wizards. They slowly filed in one or two at a time until they were all there. These were men whom he had trusted in the past. Wizards of varying degrees of power, more than one of which was possibly the best the world had ever known in their particular field of expertise, who he had known for years and who had helped him before during tough spots. They sat waiting patiently in the few chairs of his office, or standing in mingling groups talking quietly amongst themselves until they had all arrived. Finally Dalryms called them to order and began the meeting.

"Before I start," Dalryms began, " I must ask that everything said tonight be held in the strictest secrecy. What I have to say is very important, and may even be considered treasonous to the king. If any of you have a problem with this, or are uncomfortable with it, you can leave now and I won't think the lesser of you for it." He paused here for several moments to see if anyone would leave the room. None did.

"I have recently been to visit Chistock," he continued. "While I was there, a small statuette came into my possession. It was of some kind of grotesque dragon or something along those lines. I don't know if its shape has any specific importance, but my ship was sunk, and all but three of the crew killed by dark wizards to get it back. Before they did however, I was able to learn something about it."

Dalryms took several minutes to describe the various spells of detection he had used on the object and the results of each of them to the best of his recollection. Finally ending with the discovery of the true amount of power hidden within the object. There were looks of disbelief and unveiled skepticism on most of the faces in the room. Others who knew Dalryms better were silent with wonder.

"I don't know what the true purpose of the figurine is, but I can tell you that in the hands of dark wizards, it can't be any good for us. Or, for that matter, to anyone who enjoys their freedom in the land," he finished.

He thought about the word freedom for a moment while pausing for affect. While it was true that King Nolan did have troops and military forces, they were smaller than most of his predecessors. Secretly he had his squad of assassins. He also collected far fewer taxes from the people than most kings. He had far fewer restrictions on trade and peoples lives in general than most kings and he didn't allow his constables to brutalize the people. Yes, the general population was better off with Nolan as king than they had been for several generations. Dalryms knew this and had, in many cases, assisted the king with his policies knowing what the results would be. Most people wanted to improve their lives and would act accordingly if the ruling power would let them do it, and protect them from thieves and other riff-raff. As a result, the people had a higher regard for the king. Life had improved across the board, and the population in general knew it.

But there were still those who would love to get their hands on the throne and its power. The dark-robes were notorious for their scheming. They were the ones easiest to watch because they were the ones he knew of. They desired power for the sake of power alone. When they had it, they controlled everything and everyone they could. Dalryms grimaced inwardly at his own guilt. He himself had just used Malak in much the same way. The magic involved was far less controlling, but the truth was he had not told Malak everything and given him the chance to decide for himself. There were just things that he couldn't tell anyone, and there hadn't been the time to tell the things he could.

Malak had known little of personal freedom. From his earliest years he had been brought up training to be an assassin for the king. Once someone in bondage tastes freedom for the first time, they hunger for it forever. People who enjoy it all their lives tend to take it for granted, at least most of them do.

"The king has sent most of his forces to deal with whatever is going on in the west right now," Dalryms continued. "He doesn't have enough manpower to deal with this too. He has decided to wait until that problem is solved since most of his forces are already there. I don't think we can wait that long. I don't know when those dark-robes involved will use the statue, but I'm sure that they will use it. They wouldn't have made such a desperate move to recover it if it wasn't needed, and soon. The question is; what are we going to do about it?"

There was a hushed murmuring among those gathered. Finally one spoke up.

"You wouldn't have brought us here if you didn't at least have a plan to suggest, Dalryms. Tell us what you think we should do, and we'll discuss it."

"Well," began Dalryms, "we can't openly attack the dark robes. They haven't actually done anything yet except for the act of piracy on the high seas. Those three responsible for that must be sought out and punished. The regular constables and legal forces of the kingdom will take that on. Although knowing dark robes that process will take some time. They don't seem too cooperative with the law when one of their own is in question. And if we do find out who did it, apprehending them and punishing them is another matter altogether.

"What we need to do, in my opinion is to seem to forget about it. Let them see no outward movement from us. They like to believe that we are passive and weak, so we'll let them. Meanwhile we need to do some research. Someone needs to scour the archives for any information on what the object was, or what it might be for. We also need to perform several knowing spells to see if we can find out who all is involved and what they are up to, what their timeline is, and any weakness they may have. We should also begin preparing our own defenses, which won't be easy, since we don't know the nature of the threat that we are facing."

The group discussed for a while and eventually broke into groups with specific assignments. They all agreed to meet in one week's time to report what had been done and what had been learned. If anything major happened in the mean time, Dalryms would pass the word for an earlier meeting. They broke up and went to their separate quarters in the dead of the night, each with thoughts of foreboding, and mistrust for the dark wizards.

---

Shial Fonth awoke with a start. He hadn't been sleeping well since he sent Lena with Malak. He knew it wasn't the best way to send her, stowing away under the deck, but it was the only way to keep both of them out of the way of the dark-robes until all this was over, whatever 'all this' was. Malak never would have allowed her to go with him if he had known what was up. Besides, she may be useful to him in the swamps. There was danger there too, but the two of them should be able to avoid the worst of it.

His mind had locked onto something and it brought him out of the shadows of sleep into the darkness of the night. He sat for a few minutes willing his mind to figure out what had awakened him. There were no unusual noises outside. The crickets were chirping and there were no noises inside that he could detect. He lay back on his bed to go back to sleep when his brain tugged again at him.

That mental tug could come from one of only two people. One was Dalryms, and the other was inside the dark tower. He knew that if it was the one in the tower, then he was probably a dead man. If Dalryms was trying to contact him then it must be fairly important. The mental link was very slight, and to use it through the veil of sleep was difficult at best. The recipient of the signal would usually never notice it, and he would sleep right through it and awake well rested in the morning with a vague recollection of dreams that never really existed. There was only one way to tell where it was coming from.

121

He got out of bed and slipped on a night robe for warmth, as the nights were still chilly. Making his way into the front of the cabin he lit a candle from the hot coals in the fireplace, and opened the chest on the far side of the room. He withdrew from within it a glass orb and a brass stand in the shape of a coiled snake. He carefully placed these on the center of the table; the stand first followed by the sphere nestled snugly atop. He sat down and focused his thoughts for a moment before he began the spell.

With a few quick passes of his hand over the orb and some brief, muttered words, a misty image began to form above the ball. The girth of the man in the image was enough to identify him before the image was fully focused. Dalryms looked eager to speak to Shial.

"Sorry to wake you," said Dalryms miniature image, "but I thought it would be better in the dead of night than when others might detect the spell. You were right about the statuette. It is very powerful, and of some great importance to someone in the dark tower." He then gave Shial a brief account of the passage north with the statue and of the subsequent events, culminating with the meeting in his quarters which had ended just moments before.

"Our young friend came here the night after he acquired it for you." said Shial. "He is somewhere in the southern swamplands hiding by now. At least I think he made it, thanks to the talisman you gave him."

"Well, I couldn't let the dark robes get hold of him, we may still need him."

"Most noble of you," said Shial with just a hint of disdain for the others tactless remark.

"Oh relax Shial," countered Dalryms, "You knew that using him was the only way to get the king to let one of his assassins out of the business. If we didn't do it once in a while, the king would think we had gone soft. At least one of us has to be tough on the kid, or he would have been dead a long time ago."

"I know," sighed Shial, " you're probably right, of course. It just seems like a waste to use him like that and then have the dark robes get it back so soon. What do you think it is anyway?"

"I'm not sure," said Dalryms thoughtfully. "It could be just a power storage, or any number of things."

"I thought it might be a symbiot for something, but I have no idea what. It doesn't sound like anything I've ever seen or heard of being summoned. Malak came to me after he left Chistock, yes he was wearing the medallion, and I told him to keep wearing it," said Shial, "his description of the figurine just didn't tell me anything for sure."

"Where did you say Malak is now?" asked Dalryms.

"I sent him to hide in the swamps."

"You didn't," gasped Dalryms. "He'll be killed."

"Don't underestimate the lad," said Shial. "He is quite resilient. If he has a little luck, and keeps his wits about him, he should be able to get out alive. Which is more than I can say if the dark-robes catch him."

"That's true," replied Dalryms. "Shial, I think it's time to risk contacting our man on the inside," he said after a moments thought.

"Are you sure we need to do that?" asked Shial. "After the theft they must know that there is a spy somewhere. They will be watching for something."

"You'll just have to be careful, that's all."

"I'll do my best, but I think that I will be endangering both our lives by trying to make contact now," said Shial.

"We can't really prepare for whatever is coming unless we know more specifics about what the threat is," argued Dalryms back. "I understand it is dangerous to you both, but we just don't know enough yet. The power hidden in that little figurine was unreal."

Shial thought quietly for a few moments about what Dalryms had said about the statue. He seemed not only in awe of it, but almost afraid of it. That fact in itself caused Shial to reconsider the need for contacting the spy.

"All right, I'll do it, I'll have to be very careful so it might take a few days," agreed Shial finally.

"Thank you old friend," said Dalryms visibly relieved at Shial's agreeing to the task. "I don't think we have much time, so let me know what you find as soon as you can."

"I'll work as quickly as I can, but if we mark him for the dark robes, he will be dead before he can tell us anything, and I will probably be next."

"Shial, I trust your judgment and abilities. Work as quickly as possible, but try not to get yourself killed," said Dalryms. "We go way back, you and I. I fully intend that you will outlive me."

Shial laughed a bittersweet chuckle at that. "I fully intend to also, Dalryms, I told you when we were students that you had too many aspirations."

"That you did, but I have managed to succeed at most of them." Dalryms said with a smile.

"I'll get back with you as soon as I know anything," said Shial waving his hand over the crystal ball. The image of Dalryms scattered into drifting smoke trails that dissipated into the dark room.

Shial sat silently and thought about how best to contact the spy inside the dark tower. He would have to send a mental "tug" similar to the one Dalryms had used. It would have to be a very short, very weak one so that anyone who might be looking for a spell entering the dark tower wouldn't pick up on it. It would also have to be well timed. Shial figured that the best time for the contact would be in the early morning. The spy would most likely be awake, but any watchers would be pre-occupied with breakfast, or planning the events of the day, or tired from watching all night.

Shial carefully replaced the crystal ball and its stand back in the box. Then he went back to bed to try and get some rest. The spell was not a difficult one per-say, but the level of subtlety that was required was going to require his best effort. He made a mental note of when to wake up so he wouldn't miss his time window. If he overslept, he would have to wait until the next day to send the signal. Since it was unlikely that the spy would recognize such a small mental push on the first try, he may have to repeat the spell several days before he got an answer anyway.

There was too much at stake for Shial to oversleep, and worrying about it kept him from sleeping as soundly as he would have liked. He kept waking up briefly to make sure that the sun wasn't up yet.

At last the sky began to lighten in the east and Shial roused himself and began preparations for the spell. He carefully readied himself for the task at hand. He meditated for several minutes on the communication spell and especially on the limits that he would have to weave into it. The sun was just starting to rise above the distant mountain peaks when Shial decided that it was time to send the signal. It took almost fifteen minutes to cast the spell with all of the necessary shields and a few that probably weren't necessary but thrown in as a precaution anyway.

Shial relaxed, He would have to wait through the day and night to see if there was any response. If there were none, he would recast the spell the next morning. Even if the signal was recognized there was no telling when the spy would be able to answer him. All he could do was wait and listen for a response.

Then a troubling thought occurred to Shial. What if the spy had already been discovered and was dead? They would be wasting time waiting for an answer that was never going to come. There would be no more information available to them about the figurine, and they could be caught without warning of any kind. A complete surprise like that could be the end of the white-robes. No, thought Shial, not the end. Someone was bound to survive the initial attack and be able to counter it, or at least go into hiding if necessary until more favorable times came. Then again, if the dark-robes were in complete control, it may be a very long time before anything was favorable again.

Shial ate a quiet breakfast and went about the daily chores on the small farm. There was nothing to do but wait and try to keep the most horrific of thoughts out of his mind. There was no use worrying about things he had no control of. Worry was just wasted energy, and he knew it. Until he had more information, there was no course of action that could be settled on. Any path might be the right and prudent one, or the most dangerous. There was no way to tell.

# Chapter 9

Malak and Lena had been running for what seemed like hours. Lena had started to stumble now and then, and Malak knew that they couldn't keep this pace up much longer. Finally, he called a rest and they both slumped against the roots of a nearby tree. They sat for a couple of minutes quietly gulping air. When their breathing had slowed to a more resting pace, Lena asked Malak what they were running from.

"I don't know for sure," Malak replied, "but whatever it is, it's bad enough to make a pack of hungry wolves give up a free meal without a fight. I don't want to meet something like that. At least not if I can avoid it."

"You've said all this before," remarked Lena. "You must have some idea about what it could be."

"All I know is what I learned from stories and what Shial told me."

"And, what did he tell you?" asked Lena.

"Shial said," began Malak after a moments pause, "That there were monsters or demons left over from the Wizard War."

"I know that," said Lena, "but what kind?"

Malak hesitated for a minute not knowing how much to tell her of the nightmares they may yet face in the swamps. Up until now they had been lucky. The only real threat they had encountered had been the wolf pack. Shial had warned him about the roving packs of wolves in the area. The one they had faced could have killed them if things had gone differently. The wolves weren't what really made Malak doubt their chances of surviving in the marshes though. Shial had told him of other things far worse.

"Lena," Malak started as he made his decision, "Shial told me about some kind of demon that lives here. It feeds by night. Shial said that during the day they would make as much progress as they could, and at night something would come into camp and kill one or two men."

"What did it look like?" asked Lena.

"That's just it," replied Malak, "no one ever saw it. It would attack whoever was the most vulnerable of the group. If you went just a short distance into the trees to relieve yourself, you could be taken. Even the men on watch could be taken. Anyone left alone for even a minute could disappear. If they took the time to look for the missing one, which they did at first, they would usually find them several hours later, but..."

"But what?" Lena asked.

"But their bodies weren't right. Shial said that they were dried out and decomposed like they had been dead for several months. No one was ever attacked in the daytime, but at night no one was safe. In the end, they left most of their equipment behind and just started running for the coast. They found that if they covered enough ground during the day no one would die at night. Shial said none of his spells did any good. None of them even revealed anything about their attacker. He said it was almost as if whatever was attacking them slept during the day, or hid from the light. Then at night it would try to catch up to them to feed."

"How did he figure that?" Lena interrupted.

"When they were on the run, there were no more killings until the very early hours of the morning, and then only on days that they didn't seem to make enough distance. On days when they didn't know if they had gone far enough some of the men would only sleep about half of the night, and then start fighting their way through the pitch black swamp. On those nights, sometimes the ones who kept resting would be attacked, and sometimes not. The only reason Shial could come up with was the distance traveled during the day. Maybe the thing killing them could have attacked the ones moving at night, but it seemed to just attack the first ones it came upon from behind.

"Shial said that he caught a glimpse of something once during the first days of attacks when he cast a light spell. It was human in shape and size, but he didn't see enough to tell for sure. He said that it was beside a guard, and then after the first light hit it, it took off fast into the swamp. That was the only time they heard it. A few leaves rustled as it ran from the area. Your father said that the guard had his face turned away from it when the light spell burst out. He never even saw it, and it was right next to him. He did jump at the sound of the bushes moving though."

"Did anyone else get to see it?" asked Lena.

"No one that would admit to it. Shial said he just cast the spell randomly and without warning to see if there was anything to see. He said to this day he isn't sure what it was."

"So that's why you're pushing so hard today," said Lena.

"That's why I'm pushing so hard. Maybe the wolves sensed the approach of this thing, or at least something like it, and took off to avoid it. Maybe the sun came up before it could find us and it went wherever it goes during the daylight hours. Maybe we were safe because we were in a tree; maybe something else entirely frightened the wolves away. Maybe they just got bored, although I doubt it."

"So what's the plan now?" Lena asked. "Just keep running until we fall dead from exhaustion? That will help whatever is out there a lot. It can just feed on our corpses."

"That is pretty much the plan, yes," replied Malak ignoring her sarcasm. "By the way, can you cast a light spell?"

"Of course I can."

"Good, we'll sleep in the trees at night, and you'll have to be ready at a moments notice to light up the area as bright as you can. It may not help, but then again it ran from the light before."

They both finished the small meal they were eating and Malak stood, stretched, and helped Lena to her feet. With a nod of his head, they were off, traveling in as straight a line as they could, each knowing that they had unknown days ahead of them before they would be out of the marshes and into fresh air again. The thoughts of danger were always in the front of their minds. Malak would often snap his head around to check behind or to the side of them. Lena always jumped when he did this thinking he had heard or seen something she hadn't. Finally she realized that he was doing it at random just in case there might be something there. He was fishing. It was almost laughable and Lena had to restrain herself. At least he's staying focused she thought to herself.

The running seemed to go on forever. Finally they could tell that the daylight was fading. Malak called a halt to their mad dash through the muck of the swamp, when there was barely enough light to see the trees around them.

"This looks high enough," Malak said to Lena as he approached a much larger tree than the one they had slept in the night before.

Looking up the large trunk, Lena couldn't see how they would get up to the branches. Malak dug into his pack for a minute and pulled out some spikes that he attached to his hands and feet.

"I'll send a rope down when I get to the top. Tie it around your waist and I'll pull you up," Malak said.

After replacing his pack on his shoulders, he scrambled up the tree. Lena lost sight of him in the gathering darkness. Several minutes later, she was startled by the sudden appearance of a rope beside her. She quickly tied the rope to her pack, and tugged on the line. The pack disappeared into the darkness and soon the rope appeared again. This time she tied it to herself and tugged. As she started up the tree, keeping her feet in front of her, she soon noticed that the rope was digging into her back and sides. Hoping that the trip up the tree wouldn't take too long, she gritted her teeth against the pain. She looked down once only to find that she couldn't see the ground below her. Hanging suspended in the darkness with the rope biting into her flesh, she thought the trip up would take forever. When she finally saw the branch Malak was standing on, she was so close that she almost hit her head on it.

Malak pulled her up onto the branch with a final heave. His shoulders and arms were tight from the strain, and his hands burned from the coarse rope. He had to flex them several times to get the blood circulating through them again. When the stinging subsided enough, he and Lena made a loose hammock between some of the branches of the tree. It was difficult work tying knots and checking them in the gathering darkness. Once Lena asked if she could make a little light to help them, but Malak refused, saying that anything close by would see it and be drawn to it.

"Do you really think we're being followed by the same demon my father fled from?" asked Lena.

"I don't know if we're being followed at all," responded Malak. "But there's no point drawing any more attention to ourselves than we need to."

When the hammock was finally done they settled down to eating a few of their rations. Malak was amazed at how tired his muscles were from the day's exertions, and how hungry he was. Life in Chistock had been a little too easy for him. He finished his meager meal long before his stomach said he should have, and washed it down with a few swallows of water. They had been fortunate during their run. They had found a few plants that had collected some rainwater in their leaves. It looked like they would soon have to start filling their water skins from this supply.

Malak thought about Lena. She had somehow managed to keep up with him during the day but now sounded as if she was going to fall asleep in the middle of her meal.

"How are you doing?" he asked quietly.

"I'm alright," she responded in a tired voice. Malak couldn't see her, but thought he heard a small sigh follow the remark.

"I think we're safe enough up here that we can both rest for a few hours. I'll try and watch as best I can after that," he said.

"All right," said Lena not arguing about being able to sleep for a while.

"Tomorrow we won't have to keep up such a terrible pace," Promised Malak. "If you're being followed, the best time to loose them is as soon as possible." Hopefully we did that today."

The encouragement didn't help Lena's sore muscles any, but it did give her hope for tomorrow as she fell into an uncomfortable sleep.

Malak lie down next to her on the hammock and let himself drift off. He hated pushing this hard. It left him nearly useless if a fight were to come their way, and the strain on Lena was beginning to become obvious. They had been running for nearly two days now and they were sure to have at least two more before they could clear the marshes. That was if they hadn't lost their way during their flight.

They both slept for several hours. Malak woke a couple of times when a large insect would run across his body. Once he nearly jumped out of the tree when a large snake chased something across his face. Lena was sleeping so deeply that she didn't seem to notice any of these disturbances. He finally woke up to find that he could just make out the shape of the ropes and branches around him. Lena was still sleeping soundly. The new day was almost upon them.

He carefully worked his way off the hammock to where the packs were tied trying not to wake up Lena. He laid out their breakfast for them so that she wouldn't worry if she awoke while he was gone. Then he began climbing up the tree to see if he could get above the mist and look around.

Working carefully, he made his way past insects and small animals that disappeared instantly upon sighting him. Finally he reached the top of the tree and stuck his head out of the foliage. He couldn't see much of anything in the dim, early morning light. As the sun continued to rise, the light increased gradually until he found that he could a little further than on the ground.

At first the mist was too thick to make anything out, but slowly he started getting glimpses of distant trees as tall as the one he was in. When the sun finally crested the horizon, he could tell where it was although he couldn't see it. The fog and mist were still too thick. Fortunately, it looked as if they were heading away from it so they were still traveling generally in the right direction. He carefully noted the location of the sun and kept track of it as he descended back down into the thicker fog below.

When he reached the hammock, Lena was awake and just finishing her meal. The look on her face was brighter and more cheerful than it had been the previous day.

"Good news," Malak said as he sat down beside her and began to eat. "We are still heading west."

"How much farther do we have to go?" she asked.

"I have no idea," answered Malak honestly. "I couldn't see very far, but I could tell where the sun was. I think we are probably half way through, but don't be mad at me if I'm wrong about that."

Malak finished his meal and they took down the hammock. Using the rope, he lowered Lena down to the ground first and then the packs. He climbed down using the spikes and they began their journey again. Malak kept his promise from the night before, setting a slower pace. His muscles were a little stiff, and he could tell by the way Lena was walking that she was probably in a lot more pain than he was. He didn't say anything to her though. The only cure for the stiffness that he knew was to work the muscles.

They trudged through the muck of the swamp floor, keeping a watchful eye on their unchanging surroundings. They both remembered the wolf pack and how things could catch them unaware if they were not careful. It was a flight that neither could ever remember very clearly. Slowly they moved up and down an endless series of small rises. An endless procession of trees marched into their view, passed them silently, and disappeared behind them, totally unaware of the newcomers passing through their land. The fog thickened and thinned intermittently. It's tendrils now slowly swirling, now hanging low on the ground, and now disappearing completely. The grayness all around them dulled their senses to the point of nonchalance, and finally to near sleepwalking.

Both of them fought it, of course, in their own ways. Malak tried to make out details on the individual trees, and keep alert for any motion between them. He tried to stay aware of the small insects and animals that scurried away from their passing. Aware of his feelings, and intuition, he searched his mind for any twinge that would alert him to unseen dangers. He was also trying to plan the next stage of their journey to the point marked on the map. Without knowing what they would find, he could not get down to specifics and really plan anything. But he tried anyway. Most of his thoughts in that direction were general strategies for moving across the open plains undetected, and finding food along their way, as the rations would not hold out much longer. He didn't have enough information to really plan any tactics or details, and this frustrated his mind to no end. There really were no sure answers to be had until he was on top of situations, and then it would be too late to prepare for them.

Lena tried to keep her mind from being lulled by the mist and monotony by thinking of her father. She wondered what he was doing at any given part of the day, and if he was involved in any of this. Now and then she would catch herself daydreaming about home and the pain of homesickness would wake her and bring her back to the present. Sometimes she would imagine her father walking beside her, commenting on this or that aspect of the landscape they were passing through, bringing to her mind the hours they had walked together in the forest near the farm. These times gave her strength to go on, and kept her mind on the details of the marshes around her. When the day had started, her legs had been sore and stiff. Just walking had taken most of her concentration. The same muscles that had been screaming with pain at the start of the day were now only whimpering tiredly with each step and occasionally moaning as more or less was required of them.

Though traveling slower than the day before, Malak pressed them forward at the fastest pace he dared. He knew that they needed to get clear of the swamps, but they needed to keep their strength up at the same time. Their food supply was getting lower and lower, with no sign of large game to replenish it. He had not seen any fruits or nuts growing naturally, and there were no signs of fish in the shallow ponds they occasionally came across and had to make their way around. The only signs of life were small squirrels and mice. Occasionally he would find a set of rat tracks in the mud, but other than that there seemed nothing bigger. It puzzled him that the wolf pack could survive here. He wondered if they lived solely off the smaller animals, or if they had another source of food that he didn't know about. Of course, he thought to himself, they could just be walking through a desolate part of the marsh. And so the day went.

Again, toward evening they stopped and sought refuge in the branches of a tree. With so much unknown about the land they were passing through, Malak thought that it would be best to stay off the trail at night. He carefully searched for any signs of danger in the trees too, but was never able to see anything specific. For all he knew, the tree branches might be the most dangerous place to sleep. There was no way to know for sure at this point. The only sure thing about their situation was that they needed to sleep. A person could function for quite a while without food, less of a time without water, but even then the will of the person could rule the body for a time. Sleep however was something that would occur fairly regularly with or without the consent of the will. Malak had seen guards fall asleep in their tracks while standing up if they were pushed to go without sleep for more than a couple of days. Sleep could be a weakness to exploit or a weapon that sharpened all other weapons.

The night passed much the same as the previous one had, with only small interruptions in their sleep. Malak checked to make sure they were starting out in the same direction they had been traveling, and they began the day's struggle. The hours went by without much change to the landscape. Both of them were starting to imagine they were seeing things in the fog around them. There were no noises other than small animals that startled

135

as they passed.   They would suddenly jump into motion and scurry for cover away from the two travelers.  Often both of them would jump at this sudden unexpected sound.  Other than these few brief times, the two were alone in the endless shrouds of mist that engulfed them.

Malak started to worry about the missing wolves again.  Why hadn't they shown up on their trail?  Surely, the two travelers would be a blessing for the pack.  The wolves had appeared to be thin and hungry.  Why had they just left, and not ever come back for them?  It was a question that Malak couldn't fathom.  It made no sense to him.  And toward the end of the day he wondered if he would wake from a dream to find Lena and himself back in the tree surrounded by the wolf pack having only dreamed the last three days of endless toil through the mud and muck.  A small chuckle escaped his lips when this thought occurred to him. Lena heard him but didn't have the energy or the interest to ask what was so funny.

Again, just as the last rays of dim sunlight were disappearing, Malak had them up a tree and snuggled into the loose netting he wove between two of the branches.  They ate in virtual silence again.   The only comment was from Malak about how they would have to go on half-rations the next day.

"I thought we already were," was Lena's only reply.  They fell asleep together.

Sometime later Malak awoke.  He didn't know why he was awake at first, all he knew was that he was wide-awake, and something in the back of his mind was screaming danger.  It took him a moment to realize where he was in the pitch-blackness. Then he knew with surety that something had found them.  He reached over and quietly squeezed Lena's shoulder hard.

Lena woke to the pain in her shoulder.  She gasped at its intensity and was about to cry out when Malak cut her off.

"We need light, now." Malak whispered hoarsely.

There was a tone to Malak's voice Lena had never heard before.  It was dark and cold.  It would accept no delays or arguments.   Abruptly the pain in her shoulder eased as he released her.   She had to concentrate for a moment to remember the spell.

It seemed to Malak as if Lena would never cast the spell.   He waited, poised on the net with a short blade in each hand, wondering where the attack would come from.   Turning his head to the left and right to try and catch any sound that would alert him to the location of danger he waited impatiently.   He didn't say anything to Lena as she prepared to cast the spell.   That would only make her loose her concentration.

Light burst suddenly on them from a glowing ball that appeared above their heads.   Instantly there was a snarl of rage and motion on the branch next to Malak.   He brought the closest blade up blindly to ward off the attack.   Fighting to open his eyes against the piercingly bright light, he felt the blade bite deeply into something.

It wasn't human, but it was close.   The creature was roughly human in size and shape.   Its skin was dark blue, almost black.   There was no hair that Malak could see.   He caught an impression of sharp fangs, razor like claws and pointed ears as the fight exploded on the loose net.   Attacks seemed to come from every side, and Malak fought more from defensive reflex than from any strategy.   He just managed to meet each blow with a blade.   Though he parried them reasonably well, he never had time to really get a cutting edge on the thing.

Slashing claws just missed Malak's throat when he rolled under them and got a knife into the torso of the monstrosity.   A second blade arced upward and into the arm that had just missed him as it reversed for a backhand blow.   The thing screamed in pain and frustration.   It leaped backwards nearly pulling the blade from Malak's grip and fell over the edge of the net.

Malak watched it fall about fifty feet to the ground and land flat on it's back.   Through the mist he noticed with some trepidation that the fall hadn't killed it.   Stunned, the creature lay motionless for only a few seconds, and then started crawling away from the base of the tree in full retreat. It got back to its feet just as it was entering the darkness of the surrounding swamp.

Lena stared at Malak. The entire fight had taken less than two seconds. Malak lay on the net breathing hard, and staring down into the forest after the thing. Lena had never seen violence on this level before. The thing had been on Malak instantly when the light flared, but he appeared to be unharmed. She had no clear memory of the fight, just a blur of motion and flashing steel, and it was over.

"Are you all right?" she finally asked a panting Malak.

He rolled over and nodded at her while catching his breath.

"What was that thing?" she asked.

"I don't know," Malak gasped, trying to control the adrenaline that was flowing through him. "I cut it in a couple of places, and stabbed the full length of this blade into it," he said holding up the blade covered in a thick, black blood. "It must have fallen fifty feet, and it got up and ran into the swamp."

"Do you think you killed it?" asked Lena frightened now that the intensity of the moment was over.

"No, I don't think so," said Malak. "It got up too easily after it hit the ground." Looking around them, Malak continued, "How long will that light last?"

"It's a simple spell, it should last an hour or so."

"Good, can you cast it again if we need it?"

"I think so, but I start to fumble spells after about the second time without a break."

"Well, try to sleep. I'll stand guard and watch for the thing," said Malak. "I don't think it will come back tonight, but just in case I'll keep watch."

"Yeah, sure, if not for the magic, there's no way I could sleep now Malak," said Lena.

"Well give it a try. You may need to cast that light spell many more times before we get out of here," said Malak smiling to ease her mind. "I got the impression that the light frightened it more than I did with my knives."

Lena stretched out on the net again and tried to close her eyes against the light over their heads. Although she knew it was almost hopeless to try and sleep now, the small use of magic would help. She new that any rest she could get would do her good. Magic always drained her in this way. And besides, it would be better than looking into the surrounding darkness waiting to be attacked.

Malak sat on the branch and listened to the night. He kept his vision moving, covering every angle around them. There was really no way to know what the creature could do. Its attack had been vicious and deadly, but it had seemed to quit far too easily. Malak had the feeling that the fight had been a probe to test their abilities. It had been watching them and hadn't attacked until the light had caught it off guard. Then it had attacked, but thinking back on the fight it seemed as if it was shying away from the light. Malak decided to try to track it a ways in the morning when it was light enough to see. He might have wounded it more than he thought, the blood trail should be easy to follow, but for now it was time to wait and watch.

The light from the spell slowly dimmed until it was a faint glow. Malak didn't know if Lena was asleep or not. He didn't think that she was. She was pretty restless on the net, and Malak couldn't blame her mind for trying to stay awake. He was about to ask her to cast the spell again, when he realized that there was a very dim light around him. The dawn was coming soon. The creature hadn't found them until the last hours before dawn. He decided to wake Lena in about another hour, or at least let her pretend to sleep for another hour. Then they would see where the thing had gone. It seemed strange to Malak that he hadn't heard any sound of the thing moving through the underbrush just after it disappeared into the darkness. If he hadn't seen it moving into the marsh as well as it did, he would have sworn that it had collapsed and died just a few feet beyond the light.

As the light around Malak increased, he felt less and less worried about the thing coming back to attack them again. Try as he might to remember the demons and other things left in this world from the Wizard War, he couldn't remember anything like what had just attacked them. He knew that the thing was something that shouldn't be in his world. Anything natural to this world would have died from the stab wound. It had moved into the forest like it was gaining strength rather than becoming weaker. Almost as though it was healing right before Malak's eyes. That thought kept coming back to him to keep him awake and on guard.

Much to Lena's surprise she did doze off. Enough that when Malak woke her, she jumped a little. The light of morning quickly set her mind at ease. She was worried about another attack, but at least in the misty light of the swamps, she would be able to see it before it got to her. Remembering how close it had gotten to them the night before unnerved her.

"I can't believe I slept," she said stretching and yawning.

"I'm glad that you did," replied Malak getting breakfast from their packs. "You told me yourself that you have to sleep after casting spells. I think you may need to cast a few more tonight."

"You think it's still alive?" she asked.

"It got up and almost ran into the night. I could tell it was hurt, but not badly enough to make me think it would die, or at least pass back to its home dimension," said Malak.

Lena looked at Malak in a stunned way.

"You think it was a demon?"

"I don't know what it was for sure," Malak explained trying to calm her. "But I'm pretty sure that anything natural to this world would have died from the wounds it received. It ran into the swamp like it was annoyed, not seriously hurt."

Malak handed Lena her breakfast.

"This is all we have left?" she asked.

"No, we have enough for a couple more days. If we only eat this much at each meal." Malak saw a look of worry flash across

Lena's face, and quickly added; "I think that we will be through this mist by then."

"What if we aren't?" asked Lena.

"Then we will have to eat some of the local flora and fauna," he answered matter-of-factly. "But it will be really hard to get a fire going with the soaking wet wood around here. And I'm not really fond of raw snake. So we had better get out of this place soon."

They finished the small meal in silence. Lena thought about having to eat a snake raw and almost felt full. She knew that Malak wasn't kidding. She had heard the tone in his voice before during his visits to her and her father. He was merely stating facts that, though they may be unpleasant, they were the way the world was. Today she would try and walk faster than yesterday. She now had two really good reasons to get out of the swamps.

As soon as breakfast was finished and they were packed and down the tree, Malak started looking for signs of the monster's passing.

"What are you doing?" asked Lena, anxious to be on their way.

"I'm trying to get an idea where the thing went," he answered looking at the ground. "I also want to find out just how badly it was hurt in the fight."

"Right here is where it landed when it fell out of the tree," he said pointing to an impression in the ground. "And here is some of its blood." Malak continued to interpret the marks on the ground out loud, showing where the thing had crawled, and where it had finally gotten to its feet.

"I lost sight of it about here in the darkness, and it went..." Malak's words drifted off into silence as he looked around them carefully. He was looking up as well as down, almost in a panic.

"What's wrong?" asked Lena puzzled at his actions. "Where did it go?"

"It didn't," was all Malak said retracing the tracks on the ground. He continued to go over the trail from the tree outwards two more times before he spoke again. Lena just watched him and waited patiently for him to make sense.

When Malak finally stopped at the end of the tracks, she asked tentatively, "So where did it go?"

"It didn't go anywhere."

"What do you mean?" asked Lena looking around nervously.

"Oh don't worry, it isn't here," said Malak noticing her anxiety. "It just didn't go anywhere. There are no more tracks, and there are no signs of it passing through any of the underbrush past this point. None of the trees have any marks on them that show signs of being climbed," he said. And then thoughtfully added, "Including our tree."

He checked the trail once more to make sure and then grabbed their packs.

"We need to be going now," he said helping Lena on with her pack.

"What's wrong?" asked Lena not sure about the situation. It wasn't often that she had seen Malak this way. In fact thinking about it, she had never seen him this way. He seemed to be nervous, almost afraid.

"We'll talk as we go," Malak said.

"What about needing to be quiet?"

"I don't think that matters now, and I'll explain that too while we are walking."

Malak set off in the same direction that he had been going for the past several days. Lena had to move quickly to keep up with him and she knew that he wasn't going to let up on the pace anytime soon.

"Think back to what your father told me," Malak began as they walked. "He was attacked by something that only attacked by night. It was noiseless, and left only a few tracks to the bodies of its victims. It only attacked if they hadn't gone far enough the day before. Shial told me he didn't know how far that was because it was hard to tell in the mist and fog, but when they were really pushing to cover a lot of ground, they were safe at night. He thought that the thing wanted them out of the swamp. I think that the thing that attacked us was the same thing, or just like the thing that attacked him years ago. I also don't think it wanted them out of the swamp, I think it couldn't keep up with them. It was hunting them."

"That's a lot of thinking Malak," said Lena a little sarcastically. "How do you come to all those conclusions?"

"Look at what we know," said Malak ignoring the sarcasm. "It attacked us last night, but not until almost morning. The same way Shial said it did. If this is what frightened the wolves away, then it must have been almost morning when the wolves left. It didn't have time before daylight to attack us. That day we were moving fast! We hardly stopped at all, and we covered a lot of ground. Yesterday we didn't push as hard. It must have taken that long to catch up with us. It would seem to only be able to move at night."

"I'm still not convinced, Malak," replied Lena. "And I also don't know what it all means."

"Well," continued Malak, "for one thing it means that we don't have to worry about being attacked during the day, except maybe by the wolves, but I think they left for safer food. It also means that if we want to avoid it we need to cover a lot of ground today."

"But why aren't there any tracks?" asked Lena.

"It flies."

"It flies?" repeated Lena.

"It doesn't walk on the ground, and it doesn't move through the trees, so what else is there?" asked Malak. "But it seems not to be able to fly during the day."

"Why do you think that?" pressed Lena. She liked the fact that they were talking. It was somehow comforting to her compared to the days previously spent with hardly a word spoken between them. The topic wasn't her favorite, but it was better than nothing. She could still remember the thing pouncing on Malak in the night.

143

"That's why it doesn't attack until almost morning," Malak continued. "It can't, or won't travel during the daylight hours, so most of the night is spent trying to catch up to us. Evidently it doesn't fly much faster than we walk."

"Why fly at all then," Lena asked. "Last night it seemed to be able to move pretty fast when it wanted to."

"I don't know," said Malak. "For some reason it prefers to fly. It hides during the day, out of the light probably, and then flies, or more likely floats toward its prey hoping to find it soon enough to feed before daylight."

Lena felt a cold pit open in her stomach as she thought of the horror slowly, inexorably hunting them through the black night. The fear inside her spurred her to a new resolve to move as quickly as she could for as long as she could.

"Malak," she said after a few moments, "can it be killed?"

"I don't think so," came the uncertain reply. "At least not easily, and maybe not at all. If it's a left-over from the Wizard War, it can be banished back to its natural plane of existence, but we'll have to hurt it a lot more than I did last night."

Malak didn't say it, but the creature's claws had come dangerously close to him during the fight a couple of times. He was pretty sure that he was alive because the burst of light surprised and confused the thing. It had screamed when the light hit it. It had fought, in Malak's mind, more like it was afraid than it was hurt, or hungry. Why the light affected it so was still a mystery in his mind, but one that he intended to use against it, if he could just figure out how.

In the meantime they almost ran through the mists and swamp. That was the only defense open to them. Malak kept them on course the best that he could. They didn't talk much for the rest of the day, partly because they had to watch where they were going so there wasn't time to talk, and partly because they needed their breath to keep them moving. The only stop they made during the day was to eat a quick lunch and try to gather some water from the leaves around them. The running had depleted

144

their water, and the leaves offered the only trustable supply. They gathered it moving as they went, it slowed them down considerably, and after about half an hour, they gave up and continued at their best speed. They decided to drink on the run if they had to.

When they finally stopped for the night, it was almost too dark to see the tree Malak scaled. Lena thought that she might not make it up, as Malak had to stop and rest twice while raising her. They ate full rations that night. They needed the energy, and would need it the next day too if they were to stay ahead of the thing hunting them.

"Having food in your pack won't help you at all," Malak said, justifying the increased rations, "if you are too dead to eat it."

They both went to sleep, figuring that they were probably safe until at least the middle of the night. Malak promised he would wake her if he even suspected there was danger.

---

The demon had been waiting underground for the light to leave. It hated the light. The smallest amount struck it like a blow, forcing it to take its vulnerable physical form. The strong one with the knife had hurt it, and it hated him. It hated the other one too. The other one had made the light, it was sure of that. It had spent the daylight hours starving for their life force, and it hated them for that.

Summoned long ago, by an ignorant wizard using an ancient text, the llgothi had enjoyed this dimension for centuries. It happily devoured the energy of life from everything it could. It had been tracking the two humans since it came across their trail while it was hunting the wolf pack. It quickly recognized the better of the two meals. The demon didn't like taking the life from wolves, they were too unlike it, but it could survive on their life force and stay in this world. Now, for the first time in decades it had the human prey that it yearned for. In its home dimension the llgothi was one of the weaker beings. It lived in fear most of the time. But on this world, it was at the top of the food chain. The thought of going back someday made it hate the living prey it had missed the night before even more.

As soon as the Ilgothi sensed the swamp was engulfed in darkness it dissolved its form. It became a vaporous cloud and rose from under the ground to join the hunt anew. It could sense the prey's trail and moved to follow it, a misty cloud among endless mists. In this form it was safe from almost any weapon. It would be careful in its approach tonight. Any light would force it back to its physical form where it could be hurt and banished back to its home dimension. Tonight it would feed, it was sure of that.

---

Malak awoke surrounded by darkness. At first he was worried that he had slept too long but a quick feel with his hand confirmed that Lena was still by him and sleeping peacefully. He didn't know what time it was or how long he had slept. It took him a minute to realize that the thing was closing in on them. He could sense it coming. It hadn't caught up to them yet, but it was near, and getting closer. He tried to think of alternatives to using Lena's magic, but he knew there was no way of starting the soaking wood of the swamps on fire. The best you would get is a lot of smoke, and no flames. The last thing they needed was more fog. With no other options, he woke Lena gently.

"What time is it?" she asked groggily.

"Time to make some light," Malak answered.

Lena sat up fast looking around, trying to see through the pitch black of the night. But, of course, she couldn't see anything at all. As she prepared herself to cast the spell, her imagination ran away from her a little bit. She imagined that she could feel the monster from the night before right behind her, just ready to spring at her. The thought of falling into its clutches made her shiver and loose concentration on the spell she was trying to cast. Through sheer will power, she forced herself to wake up and concentrate. Finally, a ball of light burst into existence above their heads.

There was nothing to see but the tree around them.

In the blackness of the night the llgothi moved as fast as it could in its misty form. It knew instinctively that it was closing on the prey. It should have caught up to them by now, but they had gone a long way during the daylight hours. The hunger it felt intensified and it tried to move more quickly. There were still a couple of hours until it had to hide from the light of day, but it didn't know how much farther it would have to go.

Finally, just when the creature thought it was getting close, it felt light. It was still far ahead, and not yet visible, but definitely light. It moved more cautiously now. Closer to the prey until it stopped short. Very dimly through the fog and vapor, it perceived the pinpoint of light. It already felt the first tightening and compressing of its body back to its solid form. It hated light, even more than it hated the prey it sought to devour. It decided to wait and see what would happen. It still had time before the light of day came and forced it to hide. As it watched, it noticed with something like delight that the light wasn't constant. It was slowly, very slowly fading away. It would have to be patient, but there was still a chance to feed this night.

Just as the night before, the light spell wasn't permanent. Malak and Lena sat under the floating orb and kept a silent watch all around them. Malak could sense the thing near, but now it wasn't getting closer. It seemed to be waiting. Malak could not have told Lena how he knew, he just did. It was a trait that had saved him more than once as a youth. As he suspected from Shial's tales and the experiences of the night before, the thing didn't like the light. He didn't dare sleep, because obviously, it could attack in the light, but Malak thought it wouldn't if there was a chance it could be seen coming. They sat silently under the slowly dimming light while they waited for daylight to come.

As the light dimmed, Lena looked more and more sleepy, as if she might go to sleep. Malak spoke to her softly to keep her awake. He didn't know if he could wake her from a sleep after she cast a spell or not. He hadn't been successful at it yet, and he didn't want to try. They both wished that the daylight would hurry and come. They knew that they would only be safe while the sun shone and dimly lit their way through the swamp.

Suddenly Malak became aware of the thing being much closer than it had been a while before. He also noticed how dim the light had become. Looking at Lena who was almost to drift off to sleep, he asked her quietly if she could increase the spells power, or make it last longer.

"I can recast the spell. That will bring it back," she said sleepily. "But it wont last as long the next time, and even less the next."

"Please do what you can," asked Malak. The concern in his voice for both her and their situation was evident, but Lena seemed too tired to notice.

Lena forced herself awake enough to cast the spell again. It took longer this time. Malak was fingering the handles of his knives nervously waiting for the spell to be complete. Again the light ball seemed to explode with intensity. It flooded the surrounding trees and mists with brightness. As it did so they heard the sound of something suddenly falling through the branches of the trees a short distance away from them. It sounded as if it were flailing around as it fell and struck the ground. Then all was silent again.

The llgothi had been close to them again. It had only a few more moments until it could get close enough in its vaporous from for a surprise attack. It had lifted off the ground, and into the trees when the light suddenly came back, forcing it into its physical form and dropping it to the ground like a rock.

Hatred raced through it again more intense than before. The only feeling more potent than its hatred now was its hunger. Hunger for the life of the two who had evaded it for so long. It had been years since it had feasted on humans, and the closeness of these two almost drove it to madness. It was intelligent enough to see the folly in an all-out attack like that. The one with the blades had injured it the night before. They were small injuries, easily healed. But it wouldn't risk another fight if it didn't have to. As yet it didn't have to.

Malak and Lena just looked at each other after the sound had died away. They knew without talking how close the thing had been. Lena started to shake a little, and Malak sat next to her with his arm around her to offer what comfort he could. If the light failed before sunrise...

After only a few minutes, they could both tell that the light was fading as it had before, but definitely quicker.

"I think I can cast it one more time, but it is really wearing me out," said Lena seeing the unspoken question on Malak's face.

"We'll try it if we need to," he answered back. "Sunrise should be pretty soon now."

They sat together for a few minutes longer before Malak sensed the light of day was approaching. It was hard to tell at first because of the light bathing them from above. As the magic light faded, the unnatural light of the fog-shrouded landscape was slowly replacing it. Time almost seemed to stand still to Malak. It seemed like an eternity before he could see the outline of the other trees around them. He appeared calm from the outside, but on the inside he was fidgeting.

Lena was doing everything she could to keep herself awake. Malak saw her pinching herself a couple of times hard enough to bring tears to her eyes. They both knew that they would have to make another run for it today. Malak wondered how Lena would fare if she were already this tired from the use of the magic.

Well before full daylight, they were packing up their things and making their descent from the tree. When they reached the ground, Malak divided the day's rations, giving Lena the largest portion of the food. They ate it quietly, wondering how far they could get today, Lena fighting the sleep that seemed about to overwhelm her, and Malak wondering what they could do to protect themselves if they didn't get far enough.

Finally, Malak stood up and took a last drink of water from his skin. They wouldn't have much time today to gather water, so he didn't drink a lot. He picked up his pack and put it on, adjusting it for the most comfort, then turned to help Lena up.

She was sound asleep. Leaning against the trunk of the tree with the last bite of food still in her hand, and her pack at her side. Malak knew from the past times when she had slept after using magic that there was little chance of waking her now. She would wake up when she could. If he left her, she would die. The analytical part of his mind told him that if they were to stop the dark-robes, it might be necessary. Other parts of his mind that had been awakening since he left the king's service told him that he couldn't face Shial without her again, or at least a better story than, "I left her." After all, she had kept them out of the pirates' hands, and saved them in the night twice. These things aside, he found that the thought of leaving her was creating a new feeling in him that he didn't like. It just wasn't an option he could accept.

Malak carefully rolled Lena onto her stomach and began to put her pack onto her shoulders. When it was on, he rolled her onto her pack and cinched up the waist strap. When that was secure, he squatted down in front of her and got a good grip on the back of her buckskin pants, then stood up lifting her at the same time. Dropping to one knee and quickly ducking under her arm, he draped her across his own pack. Then carefully, he stood and felt the load. It was heavy and the going would be tough and slow, but hopefully she would wake up in only a couple of hours. If so, they might get far enough today.

After carefully checking his course, Malak started off through the mist. He noticed that besides the extra weight, and also because of it, his feet sank much deeper into the muddy ground than before, leaving a trail that a blind man could follow.

# Chapter 10

Malak had carried Lena for several hours before he let himself take a rest. From the brightness of the mists around them, he figured that it must be almost noon. There wasn't much food left, and he allowed himself only a couple of bites for his meal. He would leave enough for Lena and another couple of small meals between them. He hadn't been able to get nearly as far as he had hoped. If he hadn't been carrying her, he could have made much better time. There was no way he would leave her though. They were pretty close friends. Besides, there was no way that he could face Shial again without her. As he thought about how far they had come together in almost total silence through the swamps and fog, he knew that they had to be close to the end of the mists.

If they had gotten lost and traveled in circles, they would never get out. But he knew that it wasn't likely for him to have done that. He had navigated in total darkness for days before in the service of the king. He knew that he had made no mistakes. It was only a matter of time, but at the pace he had made this morning it was doubtful if they would make it before dark. Because of the inherent danger of the swamps, their boundaries were very well marked on the maps. Malak knew they were close to being out, but not quite close enough. He dreaded the thought of spending another night in the blackness. He was sure they were being followed, and that whatever had attacked them twice wouldn't give up the chase. Their only hope was to get out of the total darkness of the swamp's misty nights and into the starlit nights of the open plains beyond.

Malak finished his brief rest, and hefted Lena back onto his shoulders. He hoped that she would wake up soon, but he needed her as rested as possible for the night ahead. After another hour of walking, Lena stirred from her sleep.

"What's going on?" she asked as Malak lowered her gently to the ground. "Where are we?"

"We are still in the swamps," replied Malak with a slight smile. "And I'm very glad that you are awake."

"How long have I been asleep?"

"Several hours now," said Malak still smiling at Lena. "I ate lunch about an hour ago, there is still some food if you're hungry."

Lena nodded her head and began opening the packs. She was still a bit groggy from the magic induced sleep. It made her angry inside that her body reacted to the use of magic in the way that it did. She knew that anyone who used magic paid a price for it in some way or other. Hers just seemed to be a lot more frustrating than any other she had heard of. Most wizards would never disclose what their personal price was. They kept it a secret from everyone. Lena, on the other hand, couldn't hide hers. Not only was everyone around going to know what the magic did to her, the worse part was that using magic left her entirely vulnerable for a period of time. The only encouraging thing about her use of magic was that she seemed to recover more quickly with more experience.

"Lena," said Malak as she started to eat, "I think that we are going to have to spend another night in this swamp. We are really close now to the end of it, but I don't think we will be out by nightfall."

Lena looked at him with a mixture of emotions crossing her face.

"You mean we are going to be out tomorrow?" she asked, her face brightening.

"Yes, we should reach the plains beyond the mists by tomorrow afternoon," replied Malak. "But there is a very good chance that we won't see tomorrow at all."

"You mean that we will have to face that thing again tonight, don't you?"

"Yeah, that's what I mean. I hoped to get much further today than we have. There just wasn't any way to travel faster."

Lena looked at him for a moment knowing full well that his decision to stay with her may have cost him his life. Still, she was glad he hadn't left her.

"Isn't there anything we can do?" she asked hopefully.

"Well, your dad said that they survived by traveling through the night," said Malak. "I don't know of any way to do that without light of some kind. We don't have any torches, so that's out. We could try and make a fire, but the mists soak the wood here. All we would make is smoke. The other alternative is for you to light our way magically. You would, of course, have to keep the light going all night. Do you think that you could do that?"

Lena thought for a minute, and at last shook her head. She wished that she could, but she knew her limitations, and the truth was worth more than her pride.

"No, as much as I wish I could," she said, "there's no way I could make it for more than a couple of hours. Even less if I have to walk at the same time. I'm sorry."

"Don't be," said Malak quickly, "you're the reason we've made it this far. Our only hope then is to repeat what we have been doing the last two nights. I think we should stop an hour earlier than normal to allow us to set up a good defense in the trees. I will also need to get some sleep early on in the night to be ready for the attack that will surely come. Hopefully it will be near dawn again, and we won't need your light too much."

"I'll be as ready as I can be," said Lena mustering her courage.

"Let's get going," said Malak, " we still have several hours of daylight left. Who knows, maybe we'll get lucky and break out of the fog before dark."

"Is there really a chance of that?" asked Lena

"Yes," responded Malak looking into her eyes. "But to be totally honest with you, I don't think we will."

They quickly repacked the food and began walking through the mud and wet sand as fast as they could. They held to this pace for several hours with no discernable change in the fog around them. Though they knew they were close to the end, they couldn't find a break in the mists yet. Finally Malak called a halt to their march. They could have kept going, and maybe broken through, but he knew if they failed to do so, they wouldn't be able to set up any defenses in the dark. He also noticed a place in the branches that would lend itself well to setting up some traps. Tonight would determine whether they lived to make it out of the swamp, or whether they became two more anonymous faces that the fog had swallowed up.

They set to work quickly with Malak showing Lena the basic ideas of fortifying an area. They sharpened stakes and attached them to strategic branches. They cut some branches nearly through so that if stepped on, they would break and fall under the weight. He made her memorize where it was safe to stand, and where it wasn't, just in case she had to move about. When everything was ready to Malak's satisfaction, they ate a quick meal. Then they lay down to get what rest they could before the sky darkened fully into the night's blackness.

As the gathering darkness shrank the world around them, Malak stirred himself for the first watch. He knew Lena would need to be as rested as possible; they both would really, if they were to survive. He didn't think for a minute that they were safe, or that the demon hunting them had given up. He suspected instead that their two escapes had made it more determined than ever. Malak considered Lena's features as they disappeared into the darkness. He had seen death many times and even cheated it on several occasions. He considered himself neutral on the subject. He could have cared less whether people lived or died. At least that was how he had felt before Shial had gotten him out of the king's service. He still didn't know how or why Shial had done it. Now looking at Lena, The thought of her or Shial dying filled him with a pain and sadness that he had never known before.

The llgothi awoke in its underground bed. It dissolved itself and floated out of the mud up into the night. After its battle the night before, it had fled into the darkness of the swamps. In its dim intelligence, it intuitively knew that its prey would be heading for the land beyond the fog where the lights in the sky shown all around, and its form was locked into the solid state, more vulnerable to physical attack. There were also winds outside the swamps. They could be deadly to it too. When in its mist form, a wind would scatter it to pieces, never to be brought together again. It was a dangerous place. It knew it had to catch its prey before they left the swamp.

On leaving the scene of the battle the night before, the llgothi had headed for the border of the marshes. It was trying to get ahead of them to cut the distance it would have to travel during the night. The strategy had worked well. It soon found the trail of its prey. They had passed close to it during the day and not even known of the peril they were putting themselves in. Tonight it would feed well. It was still injured from the battles of the two previous nights. It would not heal fully until it fed. The hunger it felt was increasing to the point of almost madness.

The demon followed Malak and Lena's trail as it had the past several nights, moving as a mist among mists. It sensed several small rodents as it went along and could easily have fed on any of them to help it heal. It often fed on them to survive when it couldn't catch larger prey. But the thought of the feast awaiting it at the end of the trail was all consuming. It hadn't had to fight this hard for centuries to claim its prey. Anger flared within it as it thought of the life force it would soon absorb. Hatred and hunger blended into something indescribably horrific within its vapors.

The smallest of the swamp's creatures fled in fear of its approach. They knew all to well of its presence in their world. They had felt it pass before as it sought preys larger than themselves, and they hid themselves as best they could. All around the demon the swamp's denizens made way for the floating patch of mist and cowered to safer distances. Although the swamp was normally quiet at night, with only the occasional sound of insects or small rodents moving about, there was always a deathly silence surrounding the demon, this night a much larger than normal area around the thing was silent.

---

Malak woke Lena for her turn at watch, and after double-checking the traps he had set he closed his eyes for sleep. It was difficult to relax at first, his nerves being alert for anything out of place, yet he finally dozed knowing that some sleep, however slight, was better than no sleep at all. Lena kept watch trying to feel rested and alert, but she was still sleepy inside her mind. She fought her sleepiness and stared into the long blackness before her. She listened intently to every small sound around her and jumped at many of them.

It must have been sometime in her second hour of watch, as she was just looking forward to waking Malak, when she noticed that everything was silent, that for the last several minutes she hadn't heard anything. Not a sound at all. She reached out to wake Malak and her hand collided with his chest as he sat bolt upright.

Instantly he grabbed her wrist and twisted her between himself and the trunk of the tree.

"It's here," he whispered hoarsely in her ear. "Make a light, fast."

Malak couldn't believe that the thing chasing them had caught up so quickly. True, they had moved slower and covered less ground than the days before, but this was a lot faster than he had expected. He had counted on an hour or two more darkness that they would have to fight through than before, but the night was still relatively young and the thing had already caught up with them.

He could hear Lena whispering the words to the spell. He wished silently that she would hurry it up as he drew a dagger from its place of concealment within his clothes. There was little enough room in the branches to stand, let alone fight and swing a sword. He would need his other hand free for emergencies, and for holding on. The extremely close quarters would also negate the longer blade of the short sword strapped to his back. He knew that any strike he did make with a blade would have to have enough leverage behind it to make it count. The shorter dagger was the wisest choice for a weapon in the conditions they now faced.

Malak squinted against the light from Lena's spell as it erupted all around them. It was almost impossible to see anything in the first moments of brilliance. Malak did see one thing though. In the first flash of light, a particularly dense patch of mist very near them seemed to slam into itself from every direction. Then the black thing was standing there looking almost shocked to be where it was. It didn't stay shocked long though, just long enough to grab the closest branch as it fell.

The branch happened to be one that Malak had rigged, and it gave way with the sudden weight. Underneath the branch were two sharpened spikes that had been lashed in place, and that caught the fiend as it fell, piercing it through the torso in two places. It screamed in agony as it lay face down suspended by the spikes, and trapped by the light. The sound was airy and low, as if it resonated through miles of underground tunnels before escaping its mouth.

Malak watched its back for several moments as it twisted and writhed on the spikes. Then suddenly it got a grip on the spikes and shoved downwards. The tips of the spikes sank down into the things back as it lifted itself up and off of them. Malak started to worry a little more than he had. The thing was going to break free. He had never seen anything as tough and strong as this. It should have been banished back to whatever plane it had come from with the injuries it had already sustained. Instead, it looked like it was going to get up and keep right on fighting. Was there no end to its strength? No, he decided, it had to have its limits.

"Keep the light on, Lena," Malak said and leapt down from his perch onto the back of the thing driving it further onto the spikes than it was before. The black demon screamed again in pain and frustration. Again it started to rise off the spikes, this time with Malak standing on its back. Malak jumped up and down forcing the thing onto the spikes even more. Again it screamed and started flailing its arms behind it in an attempt to reach Malak. It was a hopeless gesture, and Malak knew it. He drove his dagger into its back just to the side of the spine between its shoulder blades, stabbing around where its heart should have been.

Just then there was a sharp cracking sound, and one of the spikes split under the weight and violence of the fight. The creature rotated and spun under Malak and he fell off into the darkness below, wrenching the knife out of the demon thing as he fell. He tumbled headlong into the darkness below, bouncing off one small branch after another. He struck a solid one that knocked the breath out of him. Twisting and groping he managed to hang onto it. He looked up to see the thing rip the broken spike out of its body. Then, slowly it reached behind and to its side. Grabbing another nearby branch, it pulled itself off the final impaling spike. It stared down at Malak with fury in its eyes and then looked up at Lena in the branches above it.

The demon started up toward her moving fast. Malak fought like crazy to climb back up to her. The thing was going for her and the light, and for the first time, he wasn't between them to protect her. Panic screamed into his brain. He hadn't experienced it like this since his childhood, and he fought to control it, breath, and climb at the same time. He had to be careful and avoid all of the traps he had set earlier in the evening, and this forced him to the back of the tree. Twice he smiled grimly to himself as he heard the creature find more of his traps. It stopped both times to remove the impaling spikes, once from an oozing eye socket, and once from its throat. Malak didn't even stop to see the carnage. He had to get back up the tree to Lena.

The demon made its final lunge. There was nothing between it and the source of the light now. It shot toward her, hands outstretched for her throat. She stood entranced by the spell, and only vaguely aware of the thing flying at her. She recoiled in terror inside, but kept the magic light as bright as she could. The thing's grasp was an inch from her throat when a streak of motion exploded from around the tree. A glint of silver slammed into the demon knocking it reeling from the girl and into another set of spikes.

Malak had to fight to keep his balance as he blasted past the entity. His blow had struck the thing between the shoulder and elbow. His arm felt like it was broken, but his fingers still clung tenaciously to the dagger. He fought to slow his momentum and keep from falling out of the tree again. He twisted and danced, avoiding several traps that were still set. Finally, he came to a stop and reversed his direction. He raced back to Lena as the demon was freeing itself from the coils of vine and spikes it had become entangle in.

Lena was deeper in the magic now than she had ever been. The light was brighter than any Malak had seen in days. It was maybe even brighter than the sunlight that never got to this fog enshrouded part of the world. She had become less aware of the fight going on around her as she had steeped herself more deeply into the magic as she tried to intensify the spell. Now she knew almost nothing of her surroundings.

Malak watched the thing untangle itself. It seemed to be having trouble getting clear. Then he saw the reason why. It only had one arm. The arm he had struck in his charging panic had been completely severed just below the shoulder. Still the thing kept coming. It was oozing black liquid from wounds all over its body, several of which should have been fatal. It finally cleared itself from the vines and immediately launched into another attack.

The thing headed straight for Lena. It wanted to destroy the light that kept it trapped in its solid form; trapped in its pain. It knew instinctively that it would succeed quicker and feed easier once it could get rid of the light. Malak stood between the monster and Lena. He tried to move and draw the thing away from her out toward more of the traps still to be sprung, but it didn't work. The thing was intent on Lena and it was determined to get to her. Malak knew that he couldn't move Lena without breaking her concentration, and there were many hours of darkness left before sunrise.

Malak closed the distance to the demon. He wanted to fight it as far as he could from Lena. He doubted that he could delay it for long, but maybe he could take its other arm off too. The thing didn't hesitate at all; it lunged at Malak. Its not that it wanted Malak first, he was just between it and the source of the light that it wanted to destroy. Malak countered by throwing himself at the demon.

He slipped inside its grasp long enough to shove the dagger into its throat, but the blow wasn't as strong as he had intended it to be. His arm throbbed terribly from the earlier battle, and the blade didn't go in nearly as far as he had wanted it to. As a result, he got jammed up trying to leap back, and the thing grabbed him by the front of his tunic.

It wrenched him around and pulled him close to its face. Malak struck blow after blow at the thing. He was almost a blur to watch as he stabbed, hit, kicked, elbowed, and kneed every part of the thing he could reach. It was almost as if the demon were in a dream. It brought Malak close to it, and wrapped itself around him, like a lover. Somehow they stayed upright and didn't fall out of the tree. Darkness began to engulf Malak, a darkness that seemed to travel from him to the llgothi holding him bound.

Malak suddenly felt as if he was being pulled apart from the inside out. Every nerve over his entire body screamed in agony. He felt as if a fire had exploded within him and was engulfing him. Not only the nerves on his skin felt it, but the heat went deep into his core. He tried to scream, but only a hiss escaped past his lips. He seemed to be floating in a sea of pain carried along the current toward the fiend that was devouring him. There wasn't any way he could escape. He fought the current, but it only seemed to speed up the pain and he flowed even faster. At first it seemed that light was all around him, but that light was getting dimmer and dimmer as time passed. He could feel the hatred in the being consuming him and it filled him with horror.

He struggled against the current with all of his might only to regain enough awareness of his surroundings to know he was hopelessly locked in the things embrace, and that Lena stood just a few feet from him, still entranced, still lighting up the night of the swamp. He fought to free an arm enough to drive his thumb into the things only remaining eye. It grunted in pain, and pain again flooded over Malak.

Again he was in the flow. It was stronger this time, and he knew that he didn't have the strength to fight his way back out again. He knew that the thing had at last won the battle. His flowing to the creature sped up as it fed off him. The river he was in was becoming a foul black sludge moving faster and faster to the thing. Malak felt all of the hunger and the hatred of the monster consuming him, and hated it back. The sludge slowed a little with his fighting and hating. He grew angrier and started to swallow up the stream himself. If that was what the thing fed on, then he would feed first, and join its unholy feast. He drank deeply of the filthy stuff. The light around him turned red as blood, and he could tell the things hatred had erupted and exploded toward him.

The llgothi was suddenly filled with a pain beyond its experience. Confusion took over its mind. One moment it had been feasting on the human, and the next the prey had started to feed off of it. This was beyond its experience, and so it fed harder and harder with more anger and hatred at the prey that had defied it so long.

A vicious circle had begun, the two feeding off each other's life force. They each fed and drank faster and faster only to be hungrier and thirstier. Malak's perception of the experience was always to seem like floating in a river of sludge or filth that he was drinking like a man dying of thirst. The more he drank, the thirstier he became until he was trying to drink up the entire river. Using his hatred and anger for the fiend that was killing him, he drank and drank until he thought he should explode, and yet the thirst for more consumed him.

The demon had never felt this kind of pain. He hated the prey that was pulling him apart from the inside. It was like he had shifted into fog inside of a roaring furnace. Its anger and hatred and hunger exploded exponentially and it pulled the life force from Malak's cells with a fury unknown even to it before. Yet the harder it fed, the hungrier it became.

Lena started to come out of the trance that she was in. She had sensed no movement for some time, around her and began to wonder if she had died within her spell. As she did so, she became aware of how tired she was. The light of the spell began to fade a bit as she withdrew from the trance, and exhaustion began to take its toll on her. She became aware of Malak and the thing standing on the branches near her locked in an embrace.

Blue sparks of lightning were jumping back and forth between the two of them. Lena gazed in astonishment at the scene before her. It dawned on her that the thing must be feeding on Malak, and the shock of it broke her concentration on the spell. The light was extinguished around the scene, but the lightning bolts between the two kept flashing creating a random strobe in the swamps nighttime. Lena made her way to the two of them to see if she could help Malak. She saw the dagger still hanging from his limp grasp and took it. With all of her strength she plunged it into the fiend's back.

An explosion of light and energy blasted through her and knocked her flying backwards into the trunk of the tree. She then fell forward onto the net they had been sleeping on sometime before. As she slipped into unconsciousness, she saw Malak and the thing locked together seemingly frozen within the energy sparking around and between them.

When she fought herself back awake, she was amazed to see the two of them still locked within the embrace. The sparks from before were now huge bolts of energy that cracked in the air like lightning. They both wore expressions of agony and suffering, of horrors beyond belief. Lena didn't notice that she had awakened long before she normally should have after so much magic had coursed through her. She was too enthralled with the vision before her eyes. She didn't know how long they had been like this, but it must have been hours, judging by the size of the energy bolts blasting between them.

Slowly, something changed. The thing holding Malak started to writhe. It was now trying to push him away from itself. The struggle intensified over the next several moments, ending with a blast of black and red energy. They were suddenly blown apart from each other. Malak was thrown from the limb they were on out into space, and fell into the night. The demon was blasted in the opposite direction. It crashed through a branch the size of a mans leg and fell downwards, smashing its way through the foliage.

Instantly, Lena was engulfed in the blackness of the night. She tried to think of what to do, but all that she could concentrate on was getting to Malak. She fought to control her emotions and cast the light spell again. It was there inside her, a little numb, but she thought if she could just calm down, she could recast it and get down the tree to him. Meanwhile, her eyes had adjusted to the darkness, and she noticed that she could make out the faint outline of the branches around her. She realized with a start that it must be almost sunrise.

As quickly as caution allowed she made her way down the tree. She had to avoid the traps that were still set, and keep from slipping on the ever-wet branches. Finally she half slid, half shimmied down the massive trunk to the ground. She had to look carefully around to find him, but finally she did. Malak was lying on his side about twenty feet from the base of the tree.

Lena ran to him and rolled him onto his back. His eyes were closed, and she had to check twice to make sure that he was still breathing. His breaths were shallow and slow, but they were there. Silently she thanked the creator that he was still alive. She tried to make him as comfortable as possible, and think of what to do next. She thought that if she had to, she would carry him as he had carried her the day before. It seemed like a lifetime ago that she had awakened slung over his shoulder. She wondered if she could really carry him like that. Instead she might be able to make some sort of drag that she could put him on, and pull him with.

The possibilities were running through her mind, when Malak suddenly took a large gasp of air, and started breathing more normally. Lena watched him closely, and after a few minutes his eyes fluttered open. He looked around for a few seconds as if trying to get his bearings until he finally saw Lena. A thin smile creased his lips as he looked at her.

"What...what happened?" Was the first hoarse whisper out of his mouth.

---

The llgothi had just managed to stay in this realm. In the last possible seconds, it had broken the connection with the human and doing so had nearly destroyed it. No prey had ever turned the feeding around before. It flew through tree branches and fell until it struck the ground hard. The darkness was a welcome soothing balm to it. It tried to shift to its mist form, but found that it couldn't. The dawn was coming, and the tiny amount of light was already too much for it. Normally this little bit could have been overcome and the entity could have made its escape into the mists. But it was too weak from its wounds and the strange energy transfers to make the shift to its vaporous form.

Hatred again swelled within it. It moved silently through the undergrowth looking for something, anything on which to feed.

If it had too, it could feed from the plants around it, but the energy was so very little that it almost wasn't worth it. It stumbled upon a family of ground squirrels. Normally they would have been safe from the demon, as it preferred larger prey, but at this point it would take anything it could get. Almost immediately they were rooted from their shallow burrow and their life energy absorbed. When the demon finished feeding, there were only a few desiccated bones left. It had sucked the energy completely; even the individual cells had been stripped of life force.

The demon was now more stable in this realm. Not as stable as it should have been with the small amount of energy it had taken on, but it was improving. Only a few minutes had passed since the struggle with the human had ended, and it tried again to become mist so that it could hide from the light that was even now threatening to lock it into its solid form. The task should have been easier than it was. It was as if the energy from the squirrels hadn't all been absorbed. It tried harder, and finally dissolved into a low-lying ground fog. Quickly it seeped underground, safe at last from the light, and able to rest unmolested. It did not understand what had happened this night. These things had never happened before, but if its prey ever did it again, it would kill it immediately and not continue trying to feed. It was sure within its hatred and anger that it would never happen again.

"That's just what I was going to ask you," said Lena. "What happened?"

Malak laid back and tried to think, tried to remember anything of the fight. A moment later he rolled away from Lena and vomited violently. The thought of drinking the sludge sickened him, and he continued to vomit until his chest ached with the effort, and there was nothing left. His body ached all over from the struggle with the monster, and all he wanted to do was relax and lay peacefully for a while. Instead, he continued to dry heave for nearly half an hour.

Lena had to do something to take her mind off of Malak's activities, so she busied herself gathering water from the various leaves in the area around them. With the gathering daylight, she wasn't afraid of the demon-thing, and she could easily hear Malak struggling from quite a distance away. She knew that she couldn't help him, and that if she stayed she might become nauseated herself. That wasn't how she wanted to start the day's hike. She only returned when his gagging stopped and he seemed to be returning to normal.

She gave him the water trying not to look at the ground beside him, and he washed up as best as he could. Then slowly he got to his feet, and staggered back to the base of the tree they had spent the night in. He leaned heavily against it for several minutes trying not to think of the experiences of the night. Every time he did, he felt another wave of nausea overcoming him.

His body ached. He had been sore and wounded before, but this was worse than anything he had ever experienced. It was like being sick, but he felt all right inside. He didn't have any energy, and all of his joints and muscle ached. Even the smallest movement brought a dull agony with it. Try as he might, there was no way he was going to be able to climb the tree. Lena would have to get their belongings by herself. He didn't think he could walk, but he knew that he had to. One more night in the swamps and they would surely be dead. The thought of making one more day's hike in his present condition, made him almost want to give up.

"Lena, do you think you can get our stuff?" he asked in a shaky voice. "I don't think I can make it up the tree."

"I got down the tree on my own, didn't I?" she replied. "I can surely get back up it. Why don't you try to relax for a few minutes while I get it."

Realizing that rest was probably the best thing at the moment, he collapsed where he stood. The jarring impact with the ground caused a new wave of pain to sweep over him. He decided to lie where he had fallen for as long as he could.

"Watch out for the traps," he said to Lena as she started to climb back up the tree.

Although it took Lena nearly an hour to collect their equipment, Malak didn't mind at all. In fact, he didn't move the entire time. From her perch high in the tree she thought a couple of times that he had died. By looking closely though, she could detect his labored breathing. It didn't look like Malak would be able to walk far, let alone carry a pack. But after several minutes of alternately struggling and resting, he was finally standing up with it on. They started off down the trail. Again with Malak in the lead, guiding their course through the endless fog.

Malak felt as if his entire body was made of lead. It took several minutes of walking before his legs seemed to loosen up, and he could walk without feeling like he was going to fall over. Every step was painful and exhausting, but he concentrated on just getting to the next tree, and then the next patch of high ground, and then to the top of that, and then down the other side. His pace was slower than it had ever been. He felt like an old man, and almost laughed out loud with the thought. He almost wept when he thought of the task still ahead of them after they got out of the swamps. There were still miles of open plain and mountains to travel through. And then they would have to find the spot on the map, discover whatever was there, and only then would they know what they really had to do. Whatever it happened to be.

They stopped at lunchtime to rest and gather water. Malak just collapsed in a pile at the base of a tree. Lena found enough for both of them and shared with him. She was worried that they wouldn't get out of the fog and swamp before dark, and that even if they did the creature would follow them. She was also worried about Malak. She didn't understand how he had stayed on his feet all morning. Days ago, there didn't seem to be any end to his reserves, but now it seemed as if each step would be his last, that at any second he would fall over dead. How did he keep going?

They started again after about half an hours rest. Again, Malak took his time getting to his feet, and loosening his muscles up. The water had revived him somewhat and he had thanked Lena for gathering it for him. He didn't understand what had transpired between the demon-thing and him. He didn't know what had kept him alive. Just thinking about the experience made his stomach tighten and he would start to gag. He could still feel the filth and sludge pouring down his throat, and into his guts, coursing through his sinuses and head, no part of his body wasn't filled with the stuff. The taste seemed to be leaving his tongue a little, but it was still in his mind.

About an hour before sunset they suddenly stepped out of the fog. It seemed to just dissipate and fall away from them. Within about fifty feet it was completely gone, and they were on the edge of a vast plain. The sky was clear and bright, and they blinked as their eyes adjusted to it. A wave of relief at having gotten through brought tears to both of their eyes, and after a minute, their faces hurt from smiling. They stepped onto the plain, and looked back at the swamps.

A wall of fog and mist seemed to grow out of the ground behind them. It was unnerving to look at it just sitting there like some kind of border was holding it in. They could see it shifting and moving within itself, but never going beyond its set bounds. The sight reminded them of sailing into it a few days before. It seemed like a lifetime had passed while they were within its borders.

With their mood lightened, they started out into the plains. Malak was still wobbling with most of his steps, but he felt a little better. The sun seemed over bright though, and he had to look down most of the time. When he looked up to check their direction he had to squint to really see where they were going.

Lena felt like she was starving. They hadn't eaten since the night before, and then it hadn't been enough to really call a meal.

They would have to find food soon. There didn't seem to be many options around them so she tried not to say anything to Malak. He was having enough trouble just putting one foot in front of the other. She hoped that he would recover soon.

They made camp that night on the ground for the first time in days. It was comforting to Lena to be able to sleep without the fear of falling to the ground if she should happen to roll over. She was still afraid that the thing in the swamp would follow them, but these fears were put to rest when Malak started a fire with the tufts of dry, dead brush and some dried animal dung that they came across. Lena spent almost an hour after sunset gathering more of the dung that was scattered around the campsite. Not a glamorous activity, but worth doing if it would keep the fire going and the thing from the swamps away.

When she got back to the campsite, she found Malak just starting to cook a rabbit that he had snared. She was delighted with the sight. She had thought he had collapsed again after starting the fire, but he had managed to round up some dinner for them too. The sight of the food starting to cook made her knees go weak.

Malak looked up as Lena came into sight and had to smile in spite of his exhaustion.

"If you haven't lost your appetite carrying that crap around, dinner will be done in a few minutes," he said joking with her.

"Funny," said Lena, "but this way I don't have to worry about keeping you alive tonight," she joked back.

They both laughed. Glad to be out of the pitch-black of the swamp nights, and under the starlit sky and the protective warmth of a fire to cheer them. As soon as they had eaten, Lena volunteered to take the first watch. She could see that Malak was still on the verge of collapse. Normally he would have fought going to sleep first, but instead he silently nodded his head in agreement and rolled onto his side. He knew that he wasn't in any condition to stay awake, let alone stand watch. The food had helped him, but he still felt weaker than he ever had before in his life. If this continued, he didn't know how much longer he could go on.

"Don't let the fire get too big," he warned Lena as he dozed off. It seemed to be very bright to his exhausted eyes.

Lena sat listening to the endless noise of the insects around her. Even they seemed happier out here than in the swamps. She wondered if Malak would be able to go on tomorrow. She wondered about how she had been able to go on herself after the spell she had cast and the little sleep she had had. She even wondered what had happened to Malak in his struggle with the thing in the marshes. What had it done to him? Was he going to be all right, or was he going to be weak for the rest of his life? He hadn't died, and that was another question in her mind. Why not?

---

The llgothi rose from the mud and slime to hunt. It knew instinctively that its prey was beyond the borders of the swamps and the fog. It knew that it had missed the feast. It still couldn't understand what had happened to it during its feeding the night before. Something the human had done had taken something from it.

It began again, hunting for something alive that it could feed from. It came across a long track in the mud and followed it to its source. The giant worm had surfaced to hunt for its favorite ground squirrel, but it wouldn't live to get back underground. The entity leapt upon it as a starving dog does fresh meat. It devoured its life force within moments. There was nothing left but a dried up worm corpse that looked like it had been mummified for a thousand years.

The demon felt itself healing and growing stronger. Its arm grew back and most of the pain it was in disappeared. Such a meal should have healed it fully as well as supplied it with enough food for at least a week. But this time it didn't even fully heal the demon. Something was terribly wrong. The thing knew it, but didn't know what it was or even how to change it.

It hunted again and this time the victim was a wolf that had become separated from the main body of the pack. It died faster than the worm had. The llgothi attacked with a monstrous passion to try and get the full benefits of its feeding. Sucking the energy so fast and hard from the hapless creature that it was merely a skeleton when the fiend finished with it. Finally satisfied, the monster sought out rest from the nights disappointments in the muck where it spent most of its time. It knew that it wouldn't have to feed again for several nights. Now was the time for it to rest and to nurse its pride and hatred towards all things living.

---

Several hours before sunrise, Malak sat bolt upright and looked at Lena.

"I feel a lot better," he said.

Startled, Lena just stared at him for a minute. She had herself been on the verge of dozing off, and his sudden recovery had surprised her.

"What do you mean," she said sounding and acting more animated than she felt. She didn't want to let him see how sleepy she was, but her mind was still semi-numb.

"I just feel better," he said noting the loudness of her voice, but not saying anything. "I feel like I have slept in the most comfortable bed for several weeks."

"Malak," Lena said becoming incredulous, "A few hours ago you looked like you were at deaths door. I don't know how you managed to walk out of that swamp today, and now you say you feel fine. I don't get it."

"I don't really understand it myself, but I actually feel better than fine, I feel really good."

They looked at each other for a moment, and Malak could see how tired Lena really was.

"Why don't you sleep for a couple of hours," he said." "I'll keep watch. The sun will be up in a few minutes, but I'll let you sleep in. Alright?"

"What do you mean, 'the sun will be up in a few minutes'?" Lena asked.

"Look at the sky, Lena," Malak responded. "It's already getting light."

Lena looked even more confused.

"Malak," she said, "It's the middle of the night. The sun won't be up for many hours yet. And furthermore, it is pitch black outside of the firelight. The only things I can see are the stars."

Malak thought about this for a moment. He looked up at the bright sky and located several constellations. Lena was right. It was still several hours until dawn.

"Lena, I can see almost everything around us," he said in a voice that didn't sound so confident anymore. "I could swear it is almost sunrise."

Lena just looked at him with concern. He had always had good night vision, but this was obviously something totally new to him.

"Look, we'll figure it out in the morning," Malak said shaking his head. "Try and get some sleep. I'll keep the watch."

Lena was too tired to argue with him. She laid down where she had been sitting with her blanket wrapped around her and went to sleep. She knew that as tired as she was it would be almost useless to try and figure anything out tonight.

Malak watched her go to sleep and listened to the noises of the night. After the strangeness of the swamp air, it seemed as if he could tell where each sound was coming from, not only the direction to it, but the distance to it as well. It was strange how clear his hearing and vision had become. He decided to scout around the campsite for a while, just to see if there was anything he should know about.

Malak started off moving a short distance outside the circle of firelight. He moved silently from one bit of brush to another. Always changing his direction to circle the campfire. Gradually he widened the radius of the circles, and expanded his search of the surrounding area. He couldn't help noticing all of the small game in the grass and bushes around. He set a few more snares to try his luck and see if he could catch breakfast too. Eventually he returned to stoke the fire and wait for the dawn that was still over an hour away.

As he sat thinking and watching the surrounding area, he heard the snares get tripped one by one. When all three had gone off, he emptied them and started preparing the meat for breakfast. He knew that Lena would probably wake up hungry, and he thought that he could use a bite to eat also. Anything left after breakfast would be stored for lunch. They still had a long way to go to get to the mountains, and they would need their strength.

Lena awoke to the sun just striking the mountains in the west, and the smell of meat cooking over the fire. She felt famished and realized that Malak hadn't been kidding when he had told her he felt better after his brief sleep. He had used the time on watch well. It was almost like getting breakfast in bed. Something her father had done for her on special occasions.

The thought of her father brought the old homesickness back in force again. The dull pain and longing seemed to swell in her head until she thought it would explode. She forced herself to think about the food, and what they had to do before they could return to Shial. Giving her mind something else to do was the only way to keep the thoughts of home and her father from overwhelming her. It was hard to do, but she knew it was the only way she would ever return to him.

"Good morning," said Malak in a bright, cheerful tone. "I thought you might be hungry so I made a little breakfast."

"It smells really good," replied Lena wiping the sleep out of her eyes. "You seem to still be recovered."

"I still feel great," said Malak. "But I can't explain it. Last night when I fell asleep I didn't know if I would wake up at all. I mean I've never felt so incredibly tired and exhausted as well as just plain beat up. And then, in just a few hours, I woke up feeling like a totally new man."

173

"How is that possible?" asked Lena sitting up beside him.

"I don't know," said Malak looking a little concerned. "How did I survive the creature, or whatever it was in the swamps? How did I survive the fall from the tree? There are a lot of things that I don't understand about yesterday."

"Well," said Lena, "I'm glad that you feel better. That's something at least."

"Never look a gift horse in the mouth, eh," said Malak smiling. "Let's eat."

They were hungrier than Malak had thought they would be. When they had eaten their fill, there was no food left over for lunch.

"Don't worry about it," said Malak when Lena pointed it out to him. "There is a lot of small game on these plains. We shouldn't have any problem catching what we need. We'll be across them soon enough. Judging by the amount of dung around, there is a good chance of finding some larger game as well."

"What will we do then," Lena joked, "Walk up and beat it over the head?"

"We'll think about that when the time comes," said Malak playing along with the joke. "Right now we need to find water. There are a lot of streams that come out of the mountains and run into the swamps. All we need to do is find one of them and follow it back into the mountains. The game will come to us. We should probably head in a North-West direction until we find one."

Lena let Malak pack up the breakfast things. She was tired from only getting half a nights sleep, but she was still able to enjoy the morning. The air was filled with the sounds of birds, and she realized after a moment that she hadn't heard birds in a long time. It dawned on her that she hadn't heard any, or at least very many in the fog of the swamps. She gave an involuntary shudder at the thought of the place. She was really glad to be out of there.

When they were finally packed up and ready to hit the trail, Lena noticed that Malak was squinting. In fact it seemed as if he had been squinting all morning.

"What's the matter with your eyes?" she asked.

"What do you mean?" Malak returned.

"You seem to be squinting a lot."

"It just seems like the sun is really bright to me," he said. Then he was thoughtful for several minutes. "The night seemed bright, and now the daylight seem to be almost painfully bright. I thought that it was just from being in the mists and fog for so long, but you aren't squinting, are you."

"I'm glad to finally be in the sunlight," Lena said answering his statement.

"I'm glad to be in it too, I think," Malak said flinching when he tried to look towards the sun. "C'mon, let's go."

They started off heading diagonally toward the mountains. It was a lot easier going than the swamps had been. For one thing the ground underfoot didn't slip and slide out from under their feet like it had for the past several days. For another, there was a lot more to see than just the trees immediately around them. They could see landmarks and stay oriented on their course without even thinking about it. The perpetual dampness of the swamps soon left their clothes as the morning sun burned the dew off the tall grass under their feet. In fact everything began to dry out from their boots to their hair as they made their way away from the fog and mists behind them.

Malak set a fast pace. Lena was pressed to keep up with him, and she asked him once to slow down a little. He seemed surprised by the request, but not at Lena. He was surprised by the speed that he was actually walking at. His pace was faster than he had intended it to be. Although he was carrying the same pack he had for the entire trip, it didn't really feel like he was carrying one at all. That and the sudden realization that he was indeed moving very quickly startled him a little. What had that thing in the swamp done to him? Whatever it was, he was sure that it wasn't what the monster had wanted to do. He had survived, and it had been injured, at least physically if not on some other, deeper level as well. Right now he didn't have the time or the desire to think about it. It still made him physically ill to remember the experience.

Sometime, just after the sun had reached its apex and started down toward the western horizon, they came across a small stream flowing toward the marshes. It bubbled and gurgled invitingly, and after tasting its waters, they both drank deeply. The cool, clear water lifted their spirits even more, and refreshed their heated bodies. They took a break from their hiking, and relaxed for a few minutes. Lena even went so far as to take off her boots and cool her feet in the shimmering waters.

They spoke of pleasantries for a while, and the last of the stresses of the swamps seemed to lift from their minds. Then Malak brought them back to the task at hand. He got the map out and they studied it for a while. It was decided that as long as the stream didn't turn southwards as it went back to the mountains, they would follow it. They would stick with it as long as it led them west, or better yet, northwest. The spot indicated on the map was still several weeks away. They didn't know if anything was really there or not, but they both felt that it was worth checking out. At least if they were lost in the mountains the dark robes couldn't locate them very easily. If there was something there, and if it was dangerous to the rest of the kingdom, they might just be able to do something to thwart the dark-robes plans.

Eventually, they continued their trek, now following the stream back up its course. Malak drew a small throwing knife and held it loosely in his hand as they hiked along. They both kept watch around them for any signs of other humans or larger animals, but there seemed to be no one else on the flat, grassy plains. It felt good to be able to see farther into the distance than just the few yards around them. The nightmares of the marshes were like another life altogether now. Lena thought how funny it was that they could remove themselves so quickly from the experiences of only yesterday.

Malak kept alert for any small game that might flush out of the occasional bushes they passed. Twice a rabbit jumped out and Malak threw the knife. The first time the sudden explosion from the nearby bush and from Malak startled Lena. She let out a little yelp of surprise. Malak's reaction had been so fast that it seemed to have almost been invisible. His arm drew back and shot forward in a blur. He led the target just as he had been taught, and trained to do, but the knife flew so quickly that it struck the ground a full foot in front of the panicked creature. It stumbled through the dust that exploded in front of it, and bolted over a small rise.

Malak stood for a few minutes alternately looking at the knife buried past its hilt in the ground, and his arm as if they were complete strangers to him. He hadn't missed an easy throw like that since he could remember. There wasn't anything between him and his target, and there was no excuse for leading the target that much. Finally in mild frustration, he picked up the knife and looked at Lena. She hadn't said anything, but Malak could see that she was stifling her amusement.

The second time a rabbit flushed, the same thing happened. Although Malak was closer this time, he still led the target by a head. Something was definitely wrong with him. He hadn't missed with a knife for years, and in fact prided himself on his ability and the time he spent practicing with it. To miss twice in one day was inexcusable, and to miss two throws in a row was insulting. What had happened to him?

Since his encounter with the thing in the swamps, his vision had changed considerably. He could see really well at night, in fact almost too well. He could see everything at night. He could see every blade of grass, and all of the leaves on the brush that surrounded them. He could especially see any animal life. He really didn't need to see them though, he knew by some kind of instinct where they were. It seemed as if they glowed within his mind.

During the daytime, it seemed that the sun was entirely too bright. He at first thought that his eyes were having a hard time adjusting to the light after so many days in the fog, but Lena didn't seem to have any trouble with her vision. He really couldn't stand to look toward the light of the sun, and he was squinting and blinking a lot. When he tried to scan the distant horizon and everything in-between he felt like he was looking into a fire on a dark night. He could see everything really clearly, more clearly than he should have been able to. It was almost too painful to look though.

His vision wasn't the only thing to have changed. He didn't feel his muscles getting tired like they used to. Yes, he could hike a long ways before, but now he seemed not to notice the weight of the pack he carried, and his feet moved quicker than normal. When they stopped for a rest, it was for Lena's sake. He could have cared less if they stopped or not. There wasn't any relief to his muscles to be gained with resting. They just didn't feel the strain like they should have. He wondered silently if he would feel the same way when he started into the mountains. They would surely have a tougher time of it then.

Now he found that he couldn't throw right. It seemed like the instant that a rabbit flushed, and his mind locked on the throw, the blade was already almost to the target. His aim was way off, because the speed of his reflexes and the amount of strength used was too fast, and too much. He decided he would concentrate on hitting the animal in the head next time. He wouldn't try to lead it at all, just aim as if it were standing still and see what happened. There must be a way to get used to his new reflexes. The worst thing that could happen was that he would miss again, and give Lena something more to laugh about.

He wasn't too worried about catching food, they could set snares easily enough, but he was more concerned with his skills. If they needed them in an emergency, he had to be able to hit the mark, moving or not. It would mean the difference between life and death in a fight. He had to have it worked out by then. They couldn't afford for him to be sloppy in a fight. He would die, and probably get Lena killed too.

Lena had changed since that night too. Although he hadn't said anything to her about it, she should have slept the entire day away after the light spell she had cast. The intensity of it had been far brighter than anything she had cast before. He didn't know how long she had cast the spell for, but it must have been a while. She hadn't gotten enough sleep to account for the brightness of the light, or for its duration. He had seen magic users before that pushed their abilities beyond their bounds and it did one of two things. It either made them less susceptible to the price, whatever that was for the individual user, or it made them weaker. They couldn't do what they had been able to before. In some, rare, cases it killed them outright. From what Malak knew of her abilities, Lena should have been asleep for at least a day. Instead, she had been the one to keep them going out of the swamps into the relative safety of the open plain.

Another thing Malak didn't understand was the way he had awakened the next night. It seemed as if he could do nothing but fall over and sleep. He had done just that and was in a dreamless state of utter exhaustion when he felt some kind of energy pouring into him. He felt suddenly healed and re-vitalized in a way he never had before. He had come to instantly. He was not only awake, but also ready to go into battle with whoever or whatever happened to be nearby. He felt instantly as good as he ever had in his entire life. Then later on, he had experienced a smaller rush of the same energy. Last night a rush like he had never known in his life hit him. He felt as if he could have leapt to the moon and back in a moment. The feeling didn't go away either. The initial rush waned, but the energy he felt from it seemed to stay with him. He could still feel it coursing through him now. It may be slowly fading, or not, he really couldn't tell. He hadn't told Lena about the experience, because he didn't want her to worry, it didn't seem to harm him, on the contrary, it seemed to strengthen him. He wanted to know more about it before he told Lena anything.

The sun had almost set when they flushed out the third rabbit of the day. It was slightly larger than the other two but a little farther away. Malak threw on instinct, remembering to try and aim at the target rather than lead it. His aim had been at the head, and the knife struck it in the neck, at the base of the skull. The throw was still harder than it needed to be, as the knife passed clear through the neck and embedded itself in the ground behind. When Malak examined the kill, he was surprised to find that the neck was broken, and that only a little strand of flesh was left keeping the head on.

"Well, it's good to see that your aim is improving," said Lena. "I was beginning to wonder if we would have to wait to trap dinner again." She was smiling, but it was obvious that she had noticed something wrong with his throwing.

"Funny," said Malak trying to make light of the situation. "So what are *you* going to eat for dinner?"

"Oh, I'm not stingy, I'll share it with you," she teased back.

"Thanks, that's real nice of you," returned Malak.

Lena just smiled and shrugged in response. It was clear that she had noticed a difference in Malak too. He decided to tell her as much as he could when they made camp. If there was danger in their future, and there probably would be, she needed to know what his new limitations were. It was the only fair thing to do. If something had been wrong with her, he would have wanted to know as soon as possible. He couldn't hold back the truth from her any longer.

They made camp at twilight. They picked a spot several yards from the stream in a low depression so their fire wouldn't be seen. Lena offered to cook the rabbit since Malak had caught it, and he happily turned the duty over to her. While she cooked, he told her about the changes he had noticed in himself.

As they cooked and ate their small meal, Malak described in as much detail as he could about what he was experiencing. Lena sat in mute silence and let him talk. She was glad that he was confiding in her. It made sense that they should know about each other's limitations as they went into potential danger. She had no idea what to do to help Malak, or even if he needed any. All of this could be just a passing result of being locked in that strange embrace with the monster for so long. On the other hand, she had to admit that it might be something that was just starting.

"Have you noticed any other side effects?" she asked when Malak had finished.

"Like what?"

"Like anything else. Are you dizzy? You said that your eyes seemed to be able to see everything, what about your hearing?"

"I haven't notice any changes there," he said. "Well, now that you mention it, are the insects out here on the plains louder at night than they were in the fog?"

"I don't think so," said Lena. I haven't paid that much attention to them. What about your sense of smell?"

"I can't tell any difference there either," said Malak. He took a couple of deep sniffs of the air around them. He could smell the grass around them and the low campfire, and the clearness of the light breeze, but there didn't seem to be anything new or stronger than before. "No, there's nothing new that I can smell either. It seems like some parts if me are more alive than they have ever been, but some parts of me haven't been changed at all. You would think that I would have been dead by now from that thing, but it seems like the exact opposite."

"Well," said Lena, "keep me posted on any other strange things that you start to notice. I don't know many healing spells, but I might be able to help a little if you suddenly take a turn for the worse."

"I'll keep you posted. As long as I feel like I do now, I don't think there will be any need of your healing abilities. I feel really good." He smiled at Lena to reassure her.

They made their beds under the stars that night. Lena offered to take the first watch, and even though Malak was actually not that tired, he agreed to it. In fact he thought it would take him a while to drift off to sleep. Actually his mind went to sleep almost immediately. It seemed as though he just relaxed and told his brain to "go to sleep," and it did. He didn't dream at all. At least not that he could ever remember.

Lena sat up thinking about what Malak had told her. She didn't know enough about magic yet to begin to understand what had happened to him. Something was different though. Not in his attitude towards her, or in his mannerisms, but physically he didn't seem to get tired like he used to. Lena had the feeling that he could have run all day and all night, and still be ready to run some more. The incident with the rabbit hunting also troubled her. He had moved so fast each time that she had not really been able to see it. He had told her about being too fast for his usual aim, and having to adjust a lot to hit the target. It seemed to her that he had somehow been made even more dangerous than he already was.

Malak was in his late twenties. He had outlived most of the king's assassins by a couple of years. Undoubtedly because of his having been allowed to leave the king's service. He was the only one who had ever gotten out, and it was strange to hear her father talk about him as one of the best. Surely if Malak was that good, he wouldn't have been allowed to leave. Unless the king saw some benefit to it at the time. She started to doubt the story of how Malak broke into the dark tower and stole the map and the figurine. She didn't doubt Malak did it, but there was something wrong with the picture. Someone wasn't telling the entire story. That made it all the more important to Lena to get into the mountains and see what was so important up there. Why did the dark-robes put a value on this piece of land, or were they really involved at all.

She didn't think Malak knew anything more than he had told her. He had always been straightforward with her. If there was

182

something going on in the background she was pretty sure he would at least have told her that there was more to the story. As it was, he didn't seem to know any more than she did. She wondered if her father knew anything. He had often told her that he had left the white tower as a kind of resting vacation. He sometimes went back to visit it for one reason or another. He might know something. She had always trusted Shial, and now wasn't the time to change that. He may not have known what was going on when they left, but she was sure that by now he would have learned something. He may even wish he had not sent them away.

Whatever it was that was happening, there was only one way for them to proceed; that was to follow the map into the mountains. They could have just disappeared into the wilds, but then what kind of life would that leave them with. Besides, Malak didn't like the wilderness at all. He could work his craft in it, but he preferred the company of other humans. He was kind of an enigma that way. He liked being with people, but he didn't make any close friends. As far as she knew, Shial and herself were the only friends he had.

Malak slept on beside her. She looked at him for a few minutes and wondered what had happened to him in the swamps. She wondered what was still happening to him. Whatever was going on inside him didn't seem to scare him at all. If it did, he hid it well.

She stood and stretched her tired limbs. She began a walk around the outside of the firelight for a better look at what was out on the grassy plains. She had to climb a short rise to get a better look around. There she got lost in the light of the newly risen, crescent, moon. The prairie seemed truly endless in the pale light, and the millions of stars. To the east they went to the horizon. The mountains to the west seemed to stab weakly up towards them. Out on the open plains, it was hard to remember the pitch-blackness of the swamps, or the darkness of her forest home at night. Under the moonlight the land seemed like a giant gray carpet.

After a while, she went back down the slope and sat next to Malak again. She took a moment to stoke the small fire back to life. There was little to watch for, and the hours passed slowly for her. When Malak finally woke up for his turn, he did so immediately.

It was like a door in his mind had been opened, and light flooded in. Not like the slow sunrise of a new day, but fast. One minute he was sleeping deeply, the next he was wide-awake. It seemed strange to him that he was awake that fast. He had always been quick to fully wake up, but now it seemed to him that there wasn't any transition between sleep and wakefulness at all.

He took over the watch from Lena and she collapsed into her blankets. Within a few short minutes, she was lost to sleep. Malak looked at the surrounding countryside and realized that he could see the small creatures that were all around them in the night. The rabbits and squirrels were busy doing their thing without much of a care in the world. He watched a squirrel get caught by an owl that had swooped low and surprised it. The event was over a mile away, but Malak saw it in full detail. It was almost as if it was ten feet in front of him. He heard the rustle of the wings, and the scream of the rodent as it was grabbed in the bird's talons and lifted into the air.

He was busy thinking about the oddness of being able to hear the sound so far away, when something else caught his attention. Out on the plains behind him there was something coming. At first Malak thought that he was just getting paranoid. Then he knew that it was something a lot bigger than a rabbit. It was coming, and it was hungry. The thought flashed through his mind briefly that it was the thing from the swamps. But just as quickly he knew that it wasn't. He could sense it more clearly now, and he wondered at how he was able to do it. It was a large boar. It had come down from the mountains to get the easier dug roots of the prairie. It had picked up his and Lena's scent, and was following it to investigate.

Malak thought for a moment. If he could get ahead of it, he might be able to distract it and keep it from getting to close to their camp. Who knows, he thought, I might be able to kill it, and then we would have plenty of rations for a while. He headed off across the plain staying downwind of the approaching boar.

Before his encounter with the thing in the swamp, he would have used a lot more caution. Something with the size and temperament of a wild boar was nothing to attack lightly. There were a million things that could go wrong. A wild boar would just as soon eat a person as look at them. Malak realized that he had taken on something that he normally wouldn't have really considered doing. It must be the new energy he felt. He would have to be much more cautious in the future and not run off into the darkness without thinking things through first. He could just imagine what Lena would think of this.

The boar was further away than he thought it was initially. He had time to look for the area that would best favor him in the trap. Quickly he set a loose snare out of the sturdiest rope they had. After considering the trap, he felt sure that it would hold. The biggest question he had now was whether the bush he used to stake the other end of the line would hold. It was the largest bush around, and he hoped that the pig wouldn't uproot it. When all was ready, he hid himself downwind and waited.

It didn't take long for the boar to appear. Malak did a double take when he finally saw it. The thing was enormous. Easily twice the size of any other boar he had ever seen. The rope suddenly looked small, and the scrub brush looked even smaller. He knew that the trap wasn't going to hold.

The boar hit the trap like a herd of stampeding cattle. Its front leg got caught up in the snare, and it stumbled. One good pull of its leg was all that it took to uproot the bush. It tripped itself when its hind leg stepped on the rope, and kept the front leg from moving forward. There was an explosion of dust as the huge animal's face was buried into the ground. It let out a bellow of rage and pain and tore into the rope and bush that were trailing its front leg.

Malak watched the boar tumble and roll on the ground, enraged at the thing on its leg. It only lasted a few moments. The rope was quickly broken, chewed through, and removed from its leg. It took a few more moments to vent its anger on the brush as well. Soon there was nothing recognizable about the rope or the brush. The animal was still furious though, and sniffed the air wildly to find something else to tear into. Malak hiding nearby held perfectly still, not even daring to breath. The boar quickly picked up the scent of the camp again, and charged off in its direction.

Malak had succeeded in pausing the thing for a few moments, which, now that it was in a full charge, didn't really make any difference, in fact it may get to the camp sooner than it would have if left alone. He had also managed to really piss the thing off. Now, anything that happened to cross its path was going to die a very violent and bloody death, to be followed immediately with ingestion into a boar's stomach. And there was nothing between it and Lena.

Malak leaped from his hiding place yelling and screaming to attract the attention of the boar and perhaps even to wake up Lena who was only a couple of hills away. He ran after the thing in a near panic, and ended up slamming into the rear end of the charging animal. The speed with which he had covered the distance shocked him, and he sat down hard in amazement. What had just happened to him? It was almost as if he had been thrown into the back of the charging animal by some incredible force. If he had grown wings and flown, he couldn't have covered the distance faster.

The boar didn't give Malak any time to think about his dizzying run though. It spun around instantly and tried to gore him with its tusks. Malak noticed the swinging head, and tried to roll away from it, knowing it was far too late to escape the blow.

He gritted his teeth and prepared for pain. One tusk lightly grazed his back, and he came to his feet facing the oncoming boar amazed again at the speed at which he was able to move. He reversed his spin and rolled away from the immediate danger. The boar went screaming past him as it too tried to reverse its spin and continue the attack.

As Malak completed his spin, he reflexively threw a sliding sidekick at the beast's hind leg. It was poorly aimed, and he didn't have time to put his full power into it, but there was a loud crack when it connected. Malak felt the huge leg bone snap under his heel. He was thrown forward off balance by the unexpected force of his kick coming back into him, and landed flat on his face in the grass and dirt. He fought to get back to his feet, and came up with his short sword drawn. It was just in time.

The beast was now in a state of insane panic and rage at the pain it was in. It was almost on top of Malak, and it would have been, if not for the hind leg that it held protectively up against its body. The lower half of it was hanging at a grotesque angle. It lunged straight at him, its only intent to kill and destroy its tormentor.

Malak slipped to the opposite side of the way he had spun before. He cut the angle close to the boar, so as to be in range of the animal, but letting it transition the distance. It tried to follow him, but was unable to use its broken leg. Malak lashed out with his sword in a two-handed series of strikes that started low at the front leg, then rolled up and over to strike down at the neck, and finished by flipping the blade in his grasp and stabbing down into the beasts heart. Instantly he yanked the blade free as the boar's momentum carried it past him. The last thing he wanted was to fight with his sword stuck in the boar, and not in his hands.

All three of Malak's blows had connected with their targets, but he had no idea how much damage they had inflicted. Its front leg collapsed, and it rolled towards him. Malak leapt clear at the last moment. He lunged up and backwards. He felt as if he had leapt off the edge of a gully, as it seemed to take a long time before he hit the ground. When he did land, he was off balance, and fell again, this time on his back.

In a flash, he was up again and striking at the beast which was still on the ground struggling to rise. He attacked the head, burying his sword repeatedly into the thick skull, bashing his way to the brain within. The blows finally stopped falling when the brain was fully exposed, and the beast lay twitching on the ground. Malak was panting, but it was more out of reflex. He couldn't believe that he had actually killed the thing, and not been killed himself. He examined the beast for a minute and realized that the first pass with his sword had killed it. Its front leg had been completely severed just below the joint. The neck had been cut almost halfway through. He had just missed the neck bone by a slight angle, and the stab looked like it had at least punctured a lung, if not the heart itself. He surveyed his work, in awe of the results. The boar was still impressive in size. Its shoulder had been at least as high as his, and it must weigh about as much as a bull.

Malak looked at its size, and was still stunned at the fight. He looked up and glanced around the surrounding hills. Towards camp, at the top of the nearest rise, he saw Lena. She was standing silently looking down at him as if she didn't recognize him at all.

# Chapter 11

Lena stood at the top of the hill looking down at Malak. He wondered what she was thinking. She had just witnessed him doing things that no one should be able to do, trained assassin or not. He wondered momentarily what he would do in her shoes. Obviously he had been changed by the encounter with the demon in the swamp. There was no way for her to know how changed he really was, and that was the scary thing. Would he attack her one day? Malak could see the question written in her expression. There was no way for him to know the answer to it. While he had felt a rush of aggression at the boar, it seemed to have come from a desire to protect Lena. Now that he was thinking about it, he wasn't so sure. Had it merely been aggression that was inside him and had found an outlet at the boar? And what about the things he had done? Where had the strength and agility come from? He had always been strong and quick, but this was beyond anything he had ever known.

No, he thought to himself, the aggression was to protect Lena. He decided as long as his instinct was to protect her, she would be safe with him. But then again, if it came to a fight, the instinct to protect her may end up killing them both. He knew that he had to make a decision soon. Should he keep her with him, or make her go back home? He doubted he could make her do anything against her will. He was never able to change her mind before when she had made it up, and he doubted he could change it now. Still, there was uncertainty on her face as she looked down at him.

For now, she should probably stay with him. Shial had sent her with him for a reason. Up until now he had thought it was to help him get through the swamps. Maybe she would be needed even more in the mountains. The changes within him may still be going on, and who knew where they would stop. She was probably in danger if she stayed, but if they didn't stop the dark-robes, there was sure to be more danger for her in the future.

Eventually, they would find out who had stolen from them, and then they would probably find her and Shial too. Right now they must keep working together, and as far as he was concerned, for her safety she should stay with him. Now all he had to do was to get her to feel safe with him again.

He smiled and waved her to come down, "Well, are you going to help me with breakfast or not?" he asked jokingly. She stood for a few moments more, and then started down the hill towards him.

As Lena approached the scene of the battle, her stride became more relaxed. She seemed to come to the same conclusion as Malak regarding their need for each other. Although she was still unsure about the changes in him, they seemed to be only physical; so far. "I thought you could manage it by yourself," she said, her face breaking into a smile.

Malak saw her willingness to lighten the mood, and added to it. "That's gratitude for you," he said. "I go to all that trouble to get us enough food for a real meal, and you want me to clean it and cook it too."

"Well," Lena responded with an air of playful haughtiness, "It really didn't seem to be that much trouble for you. If you really want to impress a girl, you'll have to work much harder for her."

Malak chuckled out loud. "Come on, Lets see how much of this we can dry today. We'll need it when we head into the mountains."

"Do we have time to cure it all?" Lena asked.

"No," Malak said knowing what her concern was, "we'll only be able to carry a portion of it. The rest will have to leave here for the scavengers."

"It just seems like a lot of waste to me,"

"It is a lot of waste, but it can't really be helped. We don't have the time to cure it all, and we couldn't carry it all if we did. Let's take as much as we can and hope it gets us well into the mountains. At least we won't have to stop to hunt for a while."

190

The work went quickly, and soon there was enough meat curing over the fire to last for several days. Malak estimated that they were still at least a day's travel away from the mountains, and then at least several weeks away from the spot marked on the map. He knew they might wander through the mountains all summer and never find the right spot. And if they did find it, he had no idea what they were going to do when they got where they were going. In fact he had to admit to Lena that they might not find anything at all there. One reason for the journey was to keep the dark-robes from finding him. In that regard the journey had been a success, at least so far.

About noon, Malak fell asleep. He sat down to watch the fire for a few minutes, and was suddenly overwhelmed by the activity of the morning, and the sun's warmth. He laid back, and drifted quickly off to sleep. He awoke with a start as Lena came back with her latest load of wood. Again, it seemed to him that there was little, if any change between being asleep and being wide awake. It seemed to Malak that with the wood they had gathered they should have enough to finish curing the meat, and he told her so.

For lunch they ate roasted meat off the bone. "The next time you go kill something," Lena joked, "could you also kill some giant potatoes, and maybe some carrots too. Some salt and spices would be nice. Oh, and perhaps some fresh fruit, and biscuits."

"I'll work on it," said Malak between bites. "The next time a potato charges our camp to eat us, you can rest assured that I'll take care of it."

"I'll count on it," laughed Lena.

They spent the rest of the afternoon napping and tending the fire. Malak would occasionally climb to the top of the nearby rise to scout the surrounding area. He listened to any sounds that he could hear too, and told Lena of his ability to hear bird's wings, and other sounds that he had never been able to hear before. He just had to really concentrate to hear them. They weren't loud, but they were there. As night approached, they gathered wood one final time. By roaming further and further from their camp, they were able to gather armload after armload of dead brush until they figured they had enough to get them through the night and finish curing the meat. The process had cost them a day's travel, and they were both anxious to be on the trail again.

They split the watch the same as the night before. Lena took the first one, spending her time between the cooking fire, and watching the surrounding area. Malak was becoming used to the experience of the instant transition between sleep and consciousness. During his watch, he found his body restless; itching to be moving, almost bounding with energy, aching to be stressed and used. He had to fight to keep from sprinting up the trail. When the sky finally lightened in the east, he was exercising and practicing with his blades. They wove a pattern of death around him that was as beautiful as it was deadly.

When the sun was finally up, Malak went back to camp and found Lena beginning to stir. "How are you this morning?" he asked.

"Good," came the sleepy reply. She stretched and yawned. "I'm ready to get going again if that's what you mean."

"Yeah, that's what I mean."

They quickly packed up their camp and supplies. During the last hours of the night, Malak had let the fire die down to only embers. These were quickly scattered and stomped out. As the sun began its westward climb, the two travelers turned their feet again toward the mountains in the distance. They were refreshed from a day of resting and food. Malak knew that though they were eating; they would soon need to find other things to eat if they were to stay healthy. He was comforted by the fact that they had, in part, replenished their supplies. At least now they could move faster since they didn't have to hunt as they went. They were almost certain to find berries and nuts of one kind or another as they headed into the mountains. These would help them maintain their strength as much as the meat would.

They continued following the stream towards its source. They traveled quickly. Their day's rest served once again to rejuvenate them. The sun was past its zenith when they paused for a short lunch break. Then it was back on the trail again as soon as they were able. Malak was pushing to make up the lost time, and Lena knew it. She kept up with his pace with almost no effort now. The days they had spent traveling together had paid off, and she was getting used to the nomadic life they now found themselves living.

It took them nearly three more days of walking to cross the plains. Later in life, when they thought back to those few days, they were days that seemed like a dream. They talked little, for there was nothing to talk about. The time passed slowly and the walking seemed endless. Time dragged by in its passing, but seemed to not have existed at all at the end of the day looking back. Not even the occasional bird or rodent starting from its hiding place was able to break the spell of the endless effort, and the hypnotizing gurgle of the stream they followed. The mountains that had started out as just a distant blue line on the horizon loomed closer and closer. Every night, it seemed like the next day would bring their arrival, and yet they remained somehow aloof and unattainable.

Inevitably, they succeeded in crossing the plains. About an hour before sunset on the third day, they stood at the bottom of the foothills looking up at the path they must now take. "We're spending the night here," Malak announced. "We'll get a little extra rest, and start the climb in the morning."

"Alright," agreed Lena stoically. She dropped her pack with a heavy thud and sat down next to it.

Malak looked at her thoughtfully. "Some picnic we're having, huh?"

Lena forced a smile to her lips. "Oh, sorry, if I'd known that we were going on a picnic, I would have brought something more than dried meat to eat. Like some fruit preserves and fresh baked bread. You men just don't know how to properly plan a thing like this."

"Well," replied Malak playfully glad to see that her humor was still alive, "the next one of these I'll let you plan all by yourself then. Besides Lena, I've had your fresh baked bread. Don't you think we're better off with what we have?"

"Very funny," Lena said with an exaggerated pout, as she picked up a handful of dirt and threw it in his direction.

They both laughed at the childish banter. Later that evening Malak pulled out the map and they drew close, examining it and planning out their route. Malak thought that they were still southwest of their goal. There were no details on the map showing trails, but there was a specific reference to three peaks and how they should be oriented to find the exact location. Not knowing the road ahead, they would have to proceed on dead reckoning until they were close enough to get the right peaks in line.

"But what if there are more than just these three peaks that align the right way? How will we know we're at the right spot?" she asked.

"I'm guessing that we'll know when we are getting close. There should be something on the ground that will tell us if we are in the right area."

"You mean like some kind of building?"

"Yes, I expect a structure of some kind to be near there, or maybe some kind of defensive traps," Malak answered. "It may be very small and rustic, or it could be something pretty elaborate. I don't know how long they have been working on whatever it is they're planning. There is also the very real chance that we might run into some dark-robes.

Lena stared at Malak trying to decide if he was kidding or not. Finally she decided that he wasn't. "So how many dark-robes do you expect to find?" she asked.

"Not too many, something like this would be too hard to keep secret if more than just a few people were involved. I would think something along the lines of one to three at the most. Any more than that and the odds of a leak go up amazingly."

"What about the other marks on the map? Are there one or two wizards at each of them?"

"It is hard for me to believe," said Malak, "but I think there might be, yes."

"Then there are more than just one or two that know about what is going on," said Lena thinking it through in her mind.

"The question is what do they think they are involved in?" returned Malak. "I mean, the ones at the mark that we are heading for may think they are doing some kind of weather research for Zartho, others may think they are looking for spells to control wild game. There is any number of ruses that could be used if the wizards at one location didn't know about the others. Each group may think that they are the only ones working secretly for Zartho. Dark-robes are notorious for not telling the whole truth, especially to each other. That's one of the reasons so few new wizards follow that path. You have to watch your back constantly. Even your instructors can turn on you if you get on their bad side."

"You mean they kill each other?" asked Lena.

"Well let's just say that more than one novice has died doing a spell that he had no business attempting, or with faulty knowledge about how to safely do it. Sometimes they are just left as hollow shells, alive, but not able to respond to anything. Those with that fate usually starve to death pretty soon."

"I don't think that I can handle taking on a dark-robe, Malak."

"Hopefully you won't have to."

"No," said Lena more forcefully this time, "I don't think we can take on a dark-robe. My father told me about how they train. He told me what they are capable of. Unless they are incompetent, and you are a lot better than you've let on, and I become more powerful than I have ever been, we won't get through this."

195

Malak looked at Lena. There was fear in her eyes, he had seen that before, but there was something else this time. It was almost resolve that they would not survive. If they were to stand a chance at all that look would have to be removed. She would need the resolve to stop the dark-robes at all costs, even if it meant their own deaths. Shial had sent her with him. If he could save her he would, but the more time that passed, the more his guts told him that this mission they were on was important. If he had learned anything, he had learned to trust that feeling. They had to press on.

"Lena," Malak said softly, "I too know what they can do. But they aren't the only ones who have powerful tricks. We can stop them if we are careful, we get to the spot on the map and we hide I'll show you how. We watch what goes on for a while, and make our plans carefully. We don't have to fight them; we just have to stop them from succeeding in whatever they are doing. From the amount of secrecy involved, I think it won't be very hard."

"How do you figure that?" Lena asked.

"Well, first of all if it was hard to stop them, they would just do it. If you're powerful enough to destroy your enemy, you just do it. You tend to publish it too. It makes you look invincible. If you are in a much weaker position, and you are trying to scheme your way through something, secrecy is vital to success. A house of cards will stand, but the slightest puff will knock it down. So it is with strategy. Weak ones can work, but they depend upon the enemy doing exactly what you want them to do. If they find out what is going on, they can easily turn your subtlety against you and destroy you."

"If their position is so weak," asked Lena, "then why are we trying so hard to stop them?"

"Just because their position is weak," replied Malak "doesn't mean that it isn't dangerous. Let's just go see what it is they are up to, and then we'll decide whether we need to stick our noses into it or not."

"From what I know about the dark-robes, we'll need to stick our noses in," said Lena. "This isn't some kind of experiment thing. They don't do anything without a purpose, and it usually involves becoming more powerful."

Malak was silent for a minute. He had been impressed when he had seen Lena's magic use on the ocean. He hadn't known about her training until she had used it to save them. And again in the swamps, she had given them the edge they needed to survive. He still shuddered a little inside when he thought about his too-close encounter with that thing. It surely would have killed them both without the light that Lena had been able to make. Now she was trying to tell him about how dark-robes thought. As he looked at her in the fading light, he knew that she was more than the little girl he had played with. Shial had taught her and raised her well. There was no use in trying to soften the situation in her mind. He knew all too well that a dark-robe was not only dangerous, but they wrote the laws that they lived by according to the current power structure they found themselves in. If they felt they had an advantage they would do anything to exploit it, and they would never stop trying. Tenacity was their only religion.

"You're right," he finally said. "We will probably have to stick our noses into whatever is going on. And there's a good chance we might loose our noses in the process."

"You mean we might die," said Lena flatly.

"That is exactly what I mean," Malak answered. "And worse. One of us may have to watch the other one die. If it comes down to stopping them or saving me, will you be able to let me die and keep going?"

Lena was shocked at the thought. All along she had been worried that they would die, or that she would be killed. She had never considered the possibility that she would have to watch Malak die and do nothing about it in order to stop the dark-robes. The question wasn't one that he would normally have asked her. It was blunt and to the point. Almost inhumanly cold, but a

197

question whose answer one warrior would expect fixed in another warriors mind and heart. "I don't know," she answered after a moment.

"You must know," said Malak looking her in the eyes. "If I can't trust you to let me die to accomplish our goal, then we can't go any further together. It isn't a question of whether you would try to save me if possible, that I know you would. But this goes beyond just us; it involves the rights and lives of everyone in the kingdom. That is worth more than my life, and your life, and both of them together. I don't question your abilities, or your courage with your own life. But you must be willing to let me die if that is necessary. So I'm asking again, can you let me die to see this through?"

Lena thought hard for several minutes before she could answer. She had known Malak since she was very young. Many of the hours they had spent together came back to her now. She tried to imagine her life without ever seeing him again, and it just didn't make any sense. Finally, she answered, "I don't know."

Malak looked at her hard for a moment, then his expression softened a little. "That's as honest an answer as I've ever had," he said. "Hopefully we won't come to that situation."

They were quiet for a while after that. Each trying inside to face the others death in case it happened. It would help to be a little prepared for the emotional blow. But at the same time they tried to not think about the possibility of the others death. The sun had set, and the last glow of twilight was leaving the sky when Lena finally broke the silence. "I've got first watch, right?"

Malak looked up at her and nodded his head. "Yeah."

"You know," Lena said smiling, "there have been times when I wanted to kill you myself. If anything does happen to you, I might actually consider it a favor from the dark-robes."

"Oh, very nice," replied Malak making a face and playing along to lighten the mood. "I love you too."

Lena laughed and watched him roll away from her and go to sleep. She thought for a minute about what he had said. When he had said he loved her, even though it was in a joking manner, she had felt something nice inside. She wasn't sure what, but there was definitely something nice about it. She knew that he cared for her just as he cared for Shial, her father, but the thought that there might one day be more to their relationship than just friendship had never really occurred to her. She wondered for a moment what her father would say if something ever did evolve between them. It was impossible to say. Shial cared a great deal for Malak, which had been obvious for years. But he had always tempered the relationship, never letting it get too close. Maybe he knew things about the young man that Lena didn't. Maybe it was because of Malak's training to kill. She didn't know for sure why there was a distance kept, but she was sure that it was there.

Her own feelings for Malak were more complex. They had started the trip as friends, almost siblings. They had been through so much together now that they had somehow become more. It hadn't ever come out in words, but there was a difference in the way they looked at each other. They had learned to work together, using each other's strengths, and complementing each other's weaknesses. Hadn't they survived the swamps together?

The question brought a cloud to Lena's mind. They had indeed walked out of the marshes alive into the sunlight of the open plains that was true. But Malak had been changed by the encounter with the demon in those marshes. He had changed in ways that seemed only evident in battle. She wondered if there were other changes that were only to be seen in other ways. Perhaps he was still changing.

She swept all these thoughts out of her mind. It was all pretty irrelevant at this point. They still had miles to travel through some very rough country to get to their goal, and then what? They would very likely die trying to stop some dark wizards from taking over the kingdom, or worse. Although she didn't want to know what would be worse than them taking over the kingdom.

There were too many 'ifs' right now to think about relationships. She mentally switched her thoughts to the task at hand and scanned the countryside. She spent some time studying the mountains carefully. They seemed the more likely source of any danger that may approach. They had come from the other way, and the plains were open and easy to watch. The foothills and mountains beyond that now faced them seemed much more dangerous. They were the unknowns. They had places to hide and ambush from. They had shadows.

A long time later, when the stars seemed right, Lena woke Malak for his turn at watch. He woke up immediately. There just seemed to be no real transition between waking and sleeping for him now. He noticed it again. There wasn't any use in denying it. He wondered what other changes were going on in his psyche. He couldn't remember dreaming at all. The last dream he could remember having had been before the thing in the swamps attacked him. Since then, sleep seemed empty. Although he did feel rested when he awoke, there just wasn't any sense of having slept. Rather just the quick passing of time.

As Lena turned in, he made his first scan of the horizon, and everything in between. Then he listened intently to everything he could hear. Lena's breathing seemed loud against the backdrop of other noises. The light breeze that had been blowing up the mountain all day had reversed and was now blowing down, away from the hills. Malak sniffed it wondering at the smells it carried. When he really tried, he could pick up the scent of evergreen pines, and the sweet of meadow flowers. There also came smells that he didn't know. Some he recognized as grasses, but some he thought were totally new to him, a whiff now and then of heavier, muskier smells that he couldn't identify.

He realized suddenly that he had been focusing on these smells for quite a while, lost in their secrets, and quickly resumed scanning the horizon. The night seemed unusually bright out here on the plains. He was sure that it would be a lot different in the forest of the mountains. Tomorrow night it would be much harder to see the things around them. On the other hand, tomorrow night they would also have some cover to protect them. What advantage they lost in the forest from not being able to see would be replaced with places to hide. There always seemed to be a balance to the world Malak thought, you just had to know what the options were and how best to use them.

The next several hours were spent repeating the endless cycle of observing their surroundings with the minutest detail. The sun finally began to make its appearance with the first few rays of the new day.

Malak woke Lena well before the sun rose above the distant horizon behind them. They ate and packed up their camp quickly. Immediately they started up the trail. Malak was feeling restless, bounding with energy for the challenges ahead. The last hour of his watch, he could hardly hold still. Lena, on the other hand felt the change in the terrain immediately. The going was rougher than she had been used to for the last several days, hiking through the relatively flat swamps and prairie. Now they climbed higher and higher up the foothills towards the mouth of the canyon that the stream flowed from. Malak noticed the change on Lena, and slowed the pace slightly to let her adjust to the new demands. He knew that what they were now doing was a lot different on the body than what they had been doing. Muscles were now working differently since the walking had become climbing.

Still, Malak had to admire Lena's determination to press on. She had been willing to face the dangers and terrors that they had encountered without complaining or showing weakness. She was even willing to continue with a person who had been changed by some kind of demon. Neither of them knew what the end of those changes might be. Malak was a little worried that he might die from it yet. He was greatly worried that he would change on the inside, and become a danger to Lena, or others. That was the worry he had tried to keep out of his mind, while still monitoring his thoughts and motivations.

They had been climbing for a couple of hours when it dawned on Malak that he didn't feel any different than he had walking in the open grasslands. They had made it past the foothills of the mountains, and were now climbing through a long canyon. Trees had slowly surrounded them as they had worked their way up, and now they were in the forest proper. Lena had shown signs of the strain of the climb within a few minutes of starting up the trail. But her body had adjusted, and within an hour, though slower, she was moving along well.

They were just about to the top of a hill when the game trail they had been on forked. The trail to the right took them across the stream, and to the north; the left looked like it went to the south. They consulted the map together. It seemed like they had come to the mountains south of the mark on the map, and that they should take the trail to the right and head in a northerly direction. They ate a brief meal of dried meat and water, and started out again. This time Lena took the lead, and Malak followed a ways behind. They still had a few weeks left of traveling before they would need to be careful of their movements. Letting Lena set the pace would save her strength.

The trail wandered northwards. After several more hours, it turned back to the east, towards the plains. It was now following another small stream that flowed out of the hills, and onto the flatlands. Malak called a halt to their march.

"I think we need to go back to the other trail," he said to a tired looking Lena.

Lena stared at him like she wanted to punch him. "Do we really have to go all the way back? Maybe this trail meets another one."

"It won't," said Malak. "This trail has almost taken us back into the foothills, and it is heading straight out onto the prairies again. The game that uses it has only one purpose for going this close to the lowlands. They want to graze, and then hide in the mountains again as soon as possible."

"But the other trail went to the south, remember?"

"Yes, but it may also lead into the mountains and then curve back to the north. Or it may lead to other trails. This one is definitely not going our way."

"How many trails are we going to have to backtrack?" asked Lena resigned to the fact that they had wasted nearly half a days labor, and they would waste that much again before they made it back to the fork.

"I don't know," answered Malak honestly. "It may take us a lot longer than I thought it would, but we'll make it." He could see that she was looking exasperated and tired.

Lena had spent her youth hiking in the woods around her farm. These hikes were never very long, and were over usually before sundown. Those day hikes were also in relatively flat lands. The last several hours, had been spent hiking downhill, but Malak knew from experience that downhill could be harder than uphill after a long time as the leg joints got pounded with every step. They would begin to ache after a while.

"Lets make camp here tonight," said Malak. "We'll head back in the morning and try again. Oh, another thing, I want to start training you more with weapons in the morning. We should spend about an hour each day practicing together."

Lena sighed and let her pack fall to the ground with a thump. She didn't like the thought of having to backtrack back up the trail they had just been coming down, or the thoughts of the bruises that she was likely to gain from practicing with Malak. She felt like they were wasting time and energy that they didn't have. But she knew that the search might be a long one, so they should be careful and try to prepare as best they could for whatever was ahead of them. They made camp just off the side of the trail in the flattest place that they could find. It wasn't long before they had eaten and set up their watches for the night. There wasn't much to do, so they turned in early.

Lena watched the dark woods quietly. She listened for any sound of animals that would come down the trail towards the plains. There didn't seem to be anything going on. Even the insects were quieter than normal. Lena thought about how far they had come as she listened to the forest around her. The light breeze blowing through the trees calmed her, and after a while, she resolved herself to the rest of the journey. It may take longer than she thought, but it would be done all the same.

Malak woke an hour early for his turn on watch. Lena didn't mind, and it was obvious to him that she had somehow changed her attitude during her time on watch. Malak watched her quietly as she drifted off to sleep. He was amazed at her powers of recuperation.

In the few hours she had been on watch she had renewed her morale and rejuvenated her energy and outlook. He could remember men he had known trained in the military arts with much less self-discipline and internal strength. They would complain about everything and the least little setback would destroy their will to win. It had made him sick inside many times that those men, older than himself, would give up so easily and lay down. He hated them for the insult they were to anyone who worked for something worth having. He had met the same type of people in all walks of life. There were those who quit at the smallest resistance to them. Malak had to admit that she had earned his respect. He was learning about her abilities, and to trust them.

The sun rose the next day hidden behind an overcast sky. It was going to be cooler today than it had been for several days. Chances were that they would be wet before the afternoon. As they started back up the trail the sky seemed to grow darker. By noon they were back at the fork. They ate a quick lunch and took the left fork, seemingly heading in the wrong direction.

"Do you think this will take us the right way?" asked Lena still a little doubtful.

"Well, it should," said Malak. "As long as it doesn't take us back onto the plains. Any trail heading to the west will do for now."

As he finished speaking, the sky started to sprinkle. It soon settled into a steady drizzle that had them soaked through in less than a half hour. Within a couple of miles, the trail wound back to the north. It wound its way around mountain peaks and over smaller passes. The trail became muddy and slippery as the rain continued. They walked on through the wet gray daylight hours. There wasn't any end to the drizzle in sight as they ate their cold dinner and tried to find a dry place to sleep in the gathering darkness. Malak built a crude shelter against a tree that kept most of the rain out. The night would still be a miserable one. The next day promised only more walking and perhaps even more rain.

# Chapter 12

The army had been marching for a couple of months. Since King Nolan had sent them to discover what had happened to the previous scouting parties there had been no contact with either the king or any of the people that should have inhabited the mountainous areas they were traveling through. It wasn't uncommon for the peoples of the mountains to hide from the king's forces though. Many of them were avoiding the tax collectors. Many of them were easily frightened by shows of force, and the army that was now moving through the area was nothing if not that. Some of the people who inhabited this rough country were even outlaws seeking to escape capture and justice.

Even though most of the people in the area had reason to hide from the approaching army, there surely should be some sign of them. A cold campsite or fire ring would have been evidence that someone had been there. Only the empty mountains greeted them. There was only the sound of the wind, and the toil of the mountain road.

They had headed southwest out of Thosh a couple of months ago. They were going to the isolated white tower on the west coast of the kingdom. It was nestled within the mountains, and overlooked the Sword Sea. This body of water was named for the violence that accompanied the invading forces from the mainland to the West. There was a narrow bridge of land further to the south that forces could have crossed instead of the sea, but that route involved several hundred miles of desert. It was much easier to cross the sea, and attack from the water. The tower was put there to serve both as a watchtower for the king, and to house wizards working on more delicate magic. They required more time, study and attention than were easily available in the tower in Thosh. Slower students were also assigned to the tower as a last resort.

The tower could report by magical means to the king if there was any attack coming, but they were usually in contact with the white tower in Thosh only once or twice a year. Usually only about ten men were assigned this duty as it lasted for almost a full year. Another small contingent of guards had been sent, to replace what seemed to be a desertion, and they too had disappeared. The king, now a little concerned, sent a larger force to man the garrison, but they never arrived. All thirty of this larger force were seemingly wiped off the face of the earth, and never heard from again.

King Nolan decided that fifty men were too many to loose, and sent the bulk of his army into the mountains to solve the problem. They were to secure the tower, and then scout the country around to find out what happened to the missing troops. The generals in charge of the force had hoped to encounter people who could, perhaps, give some clues as to what was going on. So far, they hadn't seen anyone at all. It was as if they had entered another world when they marched into the mountains. On the other hand, the plants and forest animals seemed to be fine. They were growing and acting normal, but there were no people. It seemed that whatever had happened to the troops, had also happened to everyone else in the region.

The absence of humans had a depressing effect on the troops. They started out the trip in their usual spirits, aggressively joking in the ranks and looking forward to destroying a presumed band of highwaymen. A battle was almost hoped for, as it had been years since there was any real use for the king's army. As the days passed without any signs of other people, the troops had become silent and watchful. They were jumping at every sound, and had even started marching with swords drawn and arrows notched. If anyone were to jump out at them unexpectedly, there was a good chance that they would be killed before they could say "hello."

The men who were sent out to scout the path ahead were pale with fear going out, and visibly relieved when they returned to the main body of the force. Soon only the hardiest of the men were assigned to this duty, those who had been in battles before, and who were experienced in the ways of subterfuge and ambush. Still, there was no sign that anyone had inhabited the areas they traveled through for several months. Where had all of the people gone? What had happened to them?

If the people's departure from the area had been voluntary, then what was the reason? There was obviously food and game in the area. The streams were clear and their waters pure and sweet. There was plenty of dead wood for fires. All the necessities of life were present, and relatively easy to obtain. If the people had been forced to leave, then where had they gone? Why hadn't there been any reports, or appeals to the king for protection? People always went straight to the authorities if they thought they had been wronged in some way. There was tactically no way to capture all of the people without at least a few getting away. Unless everyone had been killed, again tactically almost impossible to achieve, so they must have wanted to leave.

There was another possibility; that of disease and epidemic. It would have had to make everyone sick at the same time, or there would have been some kind of alert to the rest of the kingdom. Again a scenario that seemed impossible. There was no evidence of it either. There would have been campsites somewhere full of bodies, as no one would have been left to bury the dead. There were no such campsites. Even if wolves or other predators had been at the bodies, there would have been bones scattered about. There was no trace of humans anywhere. It was as if some giant hand had reached out and swept them all up so fast that no alarm could be given, and so completely that there was no escape. It was impossible to come to any conclusions. Every logical explanation only led to more questions.

There wasn't anything to do but press on. The answers would hopefully come when they took over the garrison at the white tower. Perhaps they could work with the wizards there to find the answers to the de-population of the area as well as the disappearance of the guards. Perhaps they had seen something, or could find a way to see what had happened to the people.

In the absence of any rational explanations, the men began to make up irrational ones. The rumor mill went into full production, with every new rumor worse than the last. Everything from demons left over from the Wizard's War, to new attacks from the West, to ghosts of highwaymen that had been captured and put to death were extrapolated to the ends of the men's minds. There was less and less logic used as the days went on. Finally the commanding officers had to step in and snap the men out of their fear and foolishness. They had watched an eager, strong fighting force become fearful, and loose its will to fight in a matter of weeks. There was no excuse for it, but the relative silence of the surrounding forest had had its effect on the men.

The day after the commanders had inspired the men, and shamed them into logic again, the army came across what must have been a small village. There were several fire pits on the ground. There had, evidently, been several buildings as well, as the outlines of the foundations were evident. The wood of these buildings had been scattered and charred, and lay in total disarray about the site. There were a few personal items lying around as well. They shed no light on what had happened though. And only re-fuelled the gossip among the men.

They spent the night there to look around, and search for any kind of clue as to what had happened. All around was the appearance of abandonment. They first thought that a whirlwind of fantastic proportions was responsible for the village's destruction. But the timbers of the buildings were charred and blackened as if by fire. The men spread out to search for more clues in the surrounding woods, but after several hours the search revealed nothing. It was as if the people had been chased off. They had just picked up and left many of their possessions lying about. Abandoning them to the elements with no thought of returning to claim them.

The men's commanders were confident they could keep the men's spirits up in spite of the abandoned village. It appeared that several weeks if not months had gone by since it was inhabited. As the men were returning to camp for the night, there was a cry of astonishment from one of them. He dove under some brush, and came up holding a skull. It was small, clearly from a child. There were scorch marks on it as if a fire had burned all the flesh off it. Something had clearly happened to the people of the region. They hadn't just abandoned their lands. They had been cut down and disposed of by someone or something. That night the guards were more alert than they had ever been. Many positions were re-enforced by men who chose not to sleep, and many more by those who couldn't sleep.

There wasn't any use in denying the danger anymore. The next day as the army continued its way to the white tower, the men were silent. The only sounds that marked their passing was the jingle of swords in sheaths and the soft sound of booted feet and horses hooves on the ground. Every eye was on the surrounding forests and hills. Every turn in the road held the terror of the unknown. The scouts kept in sight of each other as they crossed and re-crossed the path of the trailing units. No one wanted to be left alone, or leave another alone. Whatever happened to the village, they weren't about to let it happen to them, at least not without a fight.

There were also rumors about what had happened to the men on guard duty up at the garrison. Had they met the same fate as the village? There wasn't any other evidence around the village site to reveal what had happened. Just the one skull was found. Too many opinions were given to count; most of them were slightly possible, while some were outrageous. All were terrifying.

General Leland, the commander of the entire force had the men gather around the next night after the evening meal to calm them.

"I don't know what has happened to the people around these mountains, but we will surely find out soon. We will be at the garrison within two days, and we will be able to protect ourselves better there than out here in the open. If there is anyone with a reasonable idea as to the whereabouts of the people, I'd like to hear it."

There was only silence in the air. The ridiculous stories seemed like just that in the silence after the general had spoken. No one was going to talk about dragons, or demons. The general had the reputation of being a patient man, but not one given to follies of any kind. Most of the rumors were clearly that, just stories to frighten each other.

"Very well then," continued the general, "until we arrive at the garrison and can find out some answers there will be a double guard posted each night. Your unit commanders will let you know how things are to be arranged. Until we know more, no soldier will be allowed to be alone. You will always have a buddy with you. I'm not kidding about this people. Whatever happened to the folks that lived in these mountains will not happen to us. We will get the answers that we need, and report back to the king. If there is foul play anywhere, it will be dealt with severely. Until we find out something, there is no need for you to work yourselves into hysterics like a bunch of women. Stay alert, and do your duty. That is all."

With that the men broke up. Many of them were not able to hear the general's words, but their chain of command repeated them so that all understood. The guards were posted. Soon the night settled down to its usual routine. Cooking fires were blazing; the air was charged with alertness. The men ate in shifts, so that the sentries on duty wouldn't have to watch and eat at the same time. Nothing was left to chance. There wouldn't be any surprise attacks tonight. Not as long as they could help it. The penalty of falling asleep on guard duty was so severe that nobody even came close to it that night.

The following day was like the others had been. There were seemingly endless miles to travel, and nothing but wild creatures to note their passing. The men were under orders not to hunt, as it would waste valuable arrows and time. They had to subsist on their rations. This had been a sore spot for some of the men earlier on in the mountains. As their trek through the rugged country had continued, they had looked at the fleeing venison with less and less appetite. For all they knew, there could be something wrong with the meat. There wasn't any way to tell for sure, and by now there wasn't any man among the whole army that wanted to try some and find out. It wasn't that they were afraid. They just didn't want to be the first to learn the hard way. There wasn't any shortage of drinking water from the many streams that crossed their path. They drank freely, and no one had suffered any ill effects yet.

The next night passed as uneventfully as the rest of the nights had. Double guard duty started to seem like overkill as the men started getting used to the strange absence of people. Had there really been that many folks in the mountains any way? Only a few of the soldiers had been through the mountains before, and so few of them knew of the people who were missing. There weren't many in the mountains, but you would normally see several every day. Most were curious about soldiers passing through. There were many that you didn't see too. Now though, there was no one to try and sell them trinkets or jerked deer meat or any of the hundreds of things that the mountain people could make to sell at a small price.

Finally the expedition reached the end of their march. Away over a mountain pass, they first caught sight of the white tower. Its silhouette showed against the low, afternoon sun like a black finger standing straight into the air. Just the sight of it lifted the men's spirits. At last there was evidence that something of civilization still existed. Many of the men had wondered if it would still be there.

As the sun sank behind the ocean horizon to the west, they arrived at the garrison. It was built on an outcropping of rock about half a mile east of the tower. The outer walls were high and smooth to help keep out any invading forces. It was stocked with enough supplies to last for a couple of months if need be. The inner buildings were storehouses and supply rooms where hundreds of arrows, swords, armor, and every other tool imaginable for the waging of war and the defense of the keep were stored. The troop's sleeping quarters, mess hall, kitchens, and other quarters were dug into the rock itself. Located underground, they were always cool in the summer, and provided warmth in the winter. The temperature rarely varied from the comfortable but cool. Other than boredom, there was little to worry about.

Usually the soldiers kept to themselves, preferring to leave the studious wizards to their own devices. They would make annual contact with them as a means of reporting to the king. But most of their time was spent practicing their swordsmanship or archery or any number of combat methods. They would drill for endless hours day after day. They cared little for the wizards. As for the wizards, they neither knew nor cared when the garrison was re-supplied or when the men posted there were relieved and new troops began their tour of duty.

Now, the commanders made it clear that beginning on the morrow, they would be in close contact with the wizards and with the king. It may be that the disappearances could have been avoided if the two groups would have had a closer watch on each other. There was strength in numbers. The warriors and the wizards would be much stronger together than they would be alone.

As the troops set up residence in the abandoned garrison, General Leland called the officers to his quarters. When they had all arrived and were settled, the General addressed them.

"Tonight we will keep up the double watches. Until I know what has been happening to our men, and the people who should be living in these mountains, double watches will be the standing order," he said.

There was no noise in the room. Each officer knew his duty, and would follow Leland's orders. They would accept nothing less from their men. "Tomorrow morning," continued the general, "we will contact the wizards in the tower. They are probably already aware of our arrival, but the night is too late to begin working with them. Besides, we have plenty of our own work to do tonight just making sure that the garrison is secure both within and without."

One of the lower grade officers raised his hand and waited to be recognized by the general.

"Yes?" He asked.

"General Leland," began the young officer, "you seem to be worried about something happening tonight. Is there something specific we should be alert for?"

"I don't know of any particular danger," said the general. "But something is happening. I'm sure of that. It would be foolish to think we are safe just because we are a larger force than has been here before. Make sure the men are aware of this. I don't want to loose even one man on this deployment if I can help it."

There was silence in the room for a few moments before General Leland continued.

"Tomorrow, several of you will accompany me to the white tower. There we will see what we can learn from the wizards. If they can tell us anything at all, it might be helpful. I will make the assignments in the morning. Are there any questions?"

Again the room was silent. In classic military discipline, not even the scuffing of boots was heard.

"Then you are all dismissed. Make sure your men realize that just because we are here we aren't safe yet. They must stay alert until we are. That is all."

The general's quarters emptied quickly and he was soon alone. Lost in his thoughts about the night ahead of them. He didn't think that anything would happen tonight. Nevertheless, it was better to be safe than sorry, and he wanted the men to be especially aware of their surroundings tonight. Just in case. He hated to have to send word to families that a loved one had been killed. He knew that men died in battle, and he had seen it many times. There was no help for it. Many times men died in training. That was even harder for him to tell a family. If he could help it, there would be as few deaths among his men as possible.

The guards were quickly posted around the fort. They were relieved to take their meals just as they had been on the trail, with others standing in for them while they ate. The officers made doubly sure of the security of the garrison before they turned in for the night. Many of the officers elected to stand watch themselves. General LeLand trained them that their positions over the men were more than just a difference in rank. Being an officer to him meant action. Officers weren't to order the men to do anything that they weren't willing to do themselves. The men should know that they were willing to do it, because they should have already seen them doing it. Thus it was that the officers who opted out of guard duty had already been on duty the preceding nights on the trail. Having several officers around also helped to steel the men's nerves in the darkest hours of the night.

The darkness of the night within the garrison was broken here and there by the watch fires of the guards on duty. The night was quiet as the rest of the troops bedded down. They had taken up residences underground in the barracks areas of the keep to stay out of the weather. The night progressed quietly. All seemed to be in proper order. The men on duty stayed alert, and helped make sure that those around them stayed awake as well.

The guard was changed in the middle of the night. All had been quiet up until then. There had been nothing out of the ordinary. The only difference between this night and those of the previous weeks was that tonight, for the first time in a while, the men had roofs over their heads. Most of them actually felt comfortable when it started raining. The only ones who would be soaked in it were the newly posted sentries, and even they felt comforted by the cold, stone, walls surrounding them.

The clouds had moved in silently from the west. They had started as mere wisps, blocking out a thin line of stars every so often, and obscuring parts of the thin crescent of the moon. Gradually they had increased until they blocked out all the lights in the night sky. The forest outside the keep was dark. It was useless for the men inside to look out into the night. But the guard watched still. The forest was alive with the sounds of the occasional nocturnal animal and insects of the night. The rain started as a light sprinkle. It soon increased into a steady drizzle that soaked everything that wasn't under cover. The men on duty complained to each other as they passed. Some on stationary posts, others on roving patrols, they kept the camp safe from attack or invasion. The morning dawned slowly. Going from pitch black to dark gray and lighter. Still the thick clouds slowly wept.

The cooks had had the foresight to put some wood under cover the night before, so the cooking fires started easily. The rest of the camp woke up to the steady drizzle. Reveille caught most of the men already awake and at least half dressed. Early morning exercises and roll call went without a hitch, and the men breakfasted in the usual rotation of shifts.

General Leland assembled a small group of his officers and men to go and meet with the wizards in the tower. They left about an hour after the last breakfast had been served, and the rest of the men had been given their duties for the day. The trail to the tower was overgrown with grass and weeds. It clearly hadn't been used in a long time. As the small force approached, the general began to get a sick feeling inside his guts.

There wasn't any sign of life in the tower. There was no sign of smoke from the cooking fires that should have been burning by now. As the force got closer to the tower, it looked as if it had been deserted for a long time too. The front door had been hit by something big, and was hanging at a strange angle by a single hinge. It almost looked as if the force of the blow had come from inside.

The general first separated his men into two groups, sending one in each direction around the outer perimeter of the tower. They were to look for signs of life or anything out of the ordinary. Both groups soon returned to the front door with nothing to report. They cautiously entered the tower, weapons drawn and at the ready.

Inside, they could see that there hadn't been anyone living there for some time. Everything in the entryway had a thick covering of dust. Thick cobwebs covered the few pieces of furniture that had been knocked around the room as if by some powerful wind. Here and there along the walls were traces of burn marks, as if some careless person had placed a torch there for a few minutes.

Again, the general separated his men, sending one group upstairs to search out the upper levels of the tower, and the other group to search out the lower levels that were underground. The second group found that the candles along the walls of the lower stairways and corridors were still in their sconces, and quickly began lighting them as they went.

Soon the men from the upper levels were back with their report. The upper levels had the living quarters and the library in them. Everything had the same covering of dust as the downstairs, but there was one strange thing. The men reported that almost every bed looked as if someone had been sleeping in it, and had gotten up in a hurry. The bedclothes were in disarray, as if they had been thrown off their sleepers quickly and never remade. There was another strange thing; all of the rooms that had beds in this condition also had personal affects in them. The wardrobes were full of clothes; their toiletries were laid out as if in readiness for the morning to come. It looked as if something had awakened them and they had left their rooms fully expecting to return, but they never had.

The report didn't set the general's mind at ease. What could make nearly a half-dozen wizards disappear so quickly that they didn't have time to pack? Where had they gone? How long had they been gone? To the best of General Leland's knowledge, they had been fine the last time they had checked in, about six months ago. Since they rarely, if ever, had anything to do with the soldiers, so they may not have realized they were gone. There were clearly several months worth of dust covering everything. Whatever happened must have happened a long time ago.

General Leland ordered the men returning from upper rooms to wait in the main entrance, while he personally inspected the lower levels. He quickly caught up with the troops he had sent to inspect the catacombs. They reported to him all that they had found, which consisted of a description of the tunnels and rooms that had been searched so far.

These were mostly deserted classrooms and a few small laboratories. They had also found a few store rooms packed with old food and supplies. As they continued down through the levels, they continued to find these same things. They also began to notice a smell.

It started as just a faint, unpleasant whiff now and then. Soon everyone noticed it, and as they descended it became an intolerable stench. The men started to gag. They began covering their faces with whatever they could find. But as they continued, the smell got worse and worse. Several of the men began to vomit. The general sent them back up the passageway to clearer air. They were to wait as close as they could stand it, in case there was some kind of emergency. The general himself began to feel like vomiting in the horrendous stench. There was no doubt in his mind that somewhere ahead something big had died and was rotting.

The stench continued to get worse and overpower men as they continued down the passageway. By the time they came to the last door in the bottom of the tunnels, there were only two captains remaining with the general.  They had pressed on until this point through sheer willpower.  Refusing to let the general see their weakened condition.  They threw open the last door and were overpowered by the wave of stench that seemed to explode from the room.  The general grabbed a torch, and thrust it into the room to see what was inside.  All three men stopped breathing at once.

The room opened up into a round dome.  It was by far the largest room in the keep, and had probably been some kind of huge amphitheatre.  The bottom dropped down, and the ceiling rose to a height of nearly forty feet above the level of the door.  The room was now a charnel house.

Bodies were strewn everywhere.  They seemed to have been thrown in without care.  There was no way to know how deep the floor descended, as the bodies filled it completely, and were stacked up over the men's heads.  There must have been over a thousand corpses in the room.  The general and captains stood looking in horror as rats climbed here and there among the bodies.  Their eyes began to identify the remains of men, women and even children in the room.  Suddenly the general slammed the door shut and motioned the officers back up the way they had come.

They ascended without saying a word until they reached the other men above.  Together they made their way up to the main entryway, where the rest of the men were waiting.

"I think," said General Leland between gasps for breath, " that we have found not only the wizards, but also the missing inhabitants of these mountains."

Without saying another word, he motioned the men forward, and they left the tower and headed back to the keep.  No one looked back at the silent, empty structure as they left.  There was no reason to.  The empty windows stared at their backs, silently watching the soldiers leave.

Later that afternoon, the general assembled all of his commanders.  He told them what they had found in the wizard's tower. They already knew. The story had run its course through the rumor mill three times already, becoming more gruesome with each telling. General Leland knew this would happen, and that it would just get worse if there wasn't some announcement to the men to clear up the details. By nightfall the guards would be jumping out of their skin. He had to quell any overtones of the supernatural before things got out of hand. A man could stand the face of many dangers, and still run willing into battle, but get him afraid of the dark, and he was likely to kill another guard before recognizing him as an old friend.

The general opened the meeting without fanfare. "We are going to send a small force back to report to the king," he began. "He needs to be aware of the situation. The tower has obviously been deserted for several months. We just don't know enough about anything yet to make any conclusions."

"We'll send a force of twenty men back to the king to inform him of what we have found," the general continued. "While we are waiting, we will search the surrounding area for clues or anything that might point out the answer to what has happened here. Someone or something killed a lot of people and hid their bodies in the deepest part of the keep."

An officer on the first row signaled the general to be recognized.

"Yes?" he asked the young captain.

"To do something like this would have required a fairly large force, wouldn't it?" he asked.

"I tend to think so," replied the general. "But then again, there are reports from time to time of demons left over from the Wizard War. Granted those reports have nearly stopped in the last fifty years, but I'm not in a position to ignore any possibilities yet."

"General Leland," said another officer, "do you think an army from the west has done this?"

"I don't think so. An army would have taken time to assemble. Even if they had been able to surprise the tower and the keep, the local populations would have been too hard to entirely round up. News of an invasion would have leaked out of the area. Besides, there is plenty of game in the region. An army large enough to kill everyone for miles around without the alarm being given would have killed nearly everything in the area to survive. No I don't think this was done by a large force of men."

"Until we know for sure," the general continued, "we will have to send out patrols. I want the men divided up into forces of no less than ten. They will take turns going into different areas to search, but they are to return by nightfall. I don't want patrols out in the middle of the night. We should stay together here in the keep during the dark hours at least for the first few days.

"Major Sisax, you will be in charge of the patrol returning to report to the king. Take the twenty men you want. Feel free to pull them from any unit, but make sure they are good ones. Report to the king on our findings, and await his orders. The rest of us will hold the post, and see if we can figure out this mystery."

The general paused before adding, " I don't need to tell you to be careful." Then addressing the general assembly, "I want the first patrols to be into the woods within the hour. This meeting is adjourned."

The officers quickly emptied the room, and began to assemble the various groups of men. Those chosen for the return trip to Thosh were excused from other duties, and given two hours to prepare for the return to the city. As the first patrols entered the woods in different directions, the sunlight that had peaked through the clouds began to disappear again as more dark rain clouds rolled in from the southwest.

# Chapter 13

Shial Fonth sat in front of the table trying to think of the work ahead of him that day. For the past several mornings he had cast the mental signal out in hopes of contacting their man inside the black tower. As yet there had been no reply to his mental summons. He had known that it would take some time to work, but at this point, he didn't even know if the man was alive or not. It wasn't in his nature to give up easily, or to admit defeat until there was no other option. The man could be dead, yes, or he could just not have recognized the signal, or he may not be able to answer yet. Shial just didn't know.

After signaling each morning, he had tried to remain alert for the return signal the rest of the day. He wondered if he had missed it. Had he been too engrossed in some task about the farm that he had missed the delicate mental push? He thought about this possibility, but it didn't seem very likely. He would just have to wait and try again tomorrow if there was nothing today. He knew Dalryms would want to hear something soon, but there just wasn't anything to tell yet.

Shial got up and cleared the breakfast dishes away from the table. Since Lena had gone, his meals had been simpler and less frequent. A simple pot of cooked oats or corn mush for breakfast, a crust of bread for lunch, and something small from the garden for dinner was the sum of his daily fare. He knew that Lena would have scolded him gently for eating like this, but without her near him there just wasn't the desire to cook a proper meal.

The daily chores started as normal. Tending to the animals took a couple of hours, and then it was into the garden, field, and orchard. The spring planting was done, but there was never an end to the work. Something else would come to take the place of the last job, and something else after that. It was a never-ending cycle. Life kept coming.

The day passed uneventfully for Shial. Again, there had been nothing from the spy that he could detect. He lay in his bed with the same stoic determination that he had felt in the morning. He would get up early again, and try again. He would do this until he got a response, or until Dalryms told him to stop. There wasn't any other option he knew of. He drifted off to sleep listening to the sounds of the night.

Just on the verge of deep sleep, Shial suddenly felt that there was something he had to do before he could sleep. He tried to remember what it was, but he couldn't. The thought nagged at him for several minutes but he couldn't remember, and he couldn't get it out of his mind. Suddenly, it dawned on him that he had just had the signal he was waiting for. He knew it would come in a very gentle way, but this was almost too soft to hear and recognize.

Shial took the ball and its stand out of the trunk in a hurry and was soon sitting in front of them at the table, beginning the spell that would connect him to the spy in the dark tower. He had to make a conscious effort to calm down. Again, he had to use caution in the spell, or it would surely be noticed. Smokey vapors finally began to rise from the ball and started to form above it. This time though the image never really became solid. It seemed like smoke trying to withstand a breeze. Now and then it would almost form the image of a black, heavily cowled figure. No features were distinguishable on the figure at all. Just a vague shape and then it would dissolve again into wisps of smoke.

"It is dangerous to talk now," a whispered voice came out of the smoke.

"We have lost the statue," Shial whispered back to the smoke. "It was taken back by force."

"I know this already," replied the smoke. "I was there when it was taken back. I had to help recover it."

"You what?" asked Shial incredulously.

"Zartho found it much faster than I anticipated," answered the wraithlike form of smoke. "I had no choice but to help him

223

recover it. If I hadn't helped I would have been discovered. That would have been disastrous for us."

"I'm glad you could help," said Shial. There was a hint of sarcasm in his whispered voice but inside he knew the spy had acted wisely under the circumstances. "Have you learned any more of its purpose?"

"Nothing new," the cloaked figure responded, "Zartho gaurds its secrets too closely. He thinks he has control of us, and yet he still doesn't trust us completely. All I know is that soon he will use it. He may not wait until the solstice. He is growing impatient. I think he also fears another attempt to take it from him. He knows there is a spy."

"Do you think he suspects you?" asked Shial.

"If he did, I'd be dead already," was the reply. "Whatever it is, it's big. Zartho has sent others faithful to him away. I don't know where but I know of at least four wizards that have left the tower on some assignment from him."

"Do you think they know what is going on?" asked Shial.

"No more than anyone else," whispered the billowing smoke. "I'm sure that only Zartho knows what is really going on. He has said different things about the statue from time to time, but I'm sure that's meant to mislead us."

"Is there anything else you can tell us?"

"Stay alert for my signals," said the smoke dissolving. "I'll try to have something more for you in a day or two." The voice said as the image faded away so quickly that Shial had to strain to hear the last couple of words.

Shial sat staring at the now silent ball in front of him. There was nothing new in the spy's report, except to confirm their worst fears that they may need to act sooner than they thought. They also knew that the spy was still alive and that he hadn't been caught or killed yet. That at least was something to report to Dalryms. The white robed wizard wouldn't be happy with the details of the report, but at least he would know that the spy was still alive and seemingly working for them.

The report to Dalryms was quick. Shial thought he seemed tired, which was certainly understandable considering the lateness of the hour. He took the information stoically and quickly cut off the communication spell. It didn't help Shial to sleep well that night. Knowing that something really was wrong, and that they didn't even know what it was. All they could do was to wait for the spy to report again, if he didn't get caught snooping, or in the act of reporting back to them. If that happened they would never know about it until it was too late.

A frightening thought occurred to Shial then. What if the spy had already been caught? What if the report he had just gotten was from Zartho himself? The person in the smoke had only been a blurry figure at best. He had only spoken in a quiet whisper. What if they never heard from the spy again? How long should they wait before they acted for themselves? No, the voice warned them that it was coming sooner than they probably thought. Zartho would have put them on a longer time scale so he could catch them unprepared. At least that is what Shial was hoping. He didn't know for sure who the spy was. Thinking back, there were only a couple of people that it could be, but he wasn't sure. Anyway, he didn't really want to know. If he was caught, he might be made to talk, and what he didn't know, he couldn't tell.

There wasn't anything more that Shial could do tonight, and he knew it. He decided to go to bed and get what rest he could. He thought about the days ahead, knowing that he would need to be well rested for them. There may be some days that he didn't get any rest at all. Sleeping, while he could, would help prepare for them.

But as he lay in his bed his mind kept running over the dangers ahead. His mind jumping from one idea to another only to discover another dreadful scenario that he hadn't thought of before. Overlying all of these thoughts were the poignant concerns and feelings for his daughter and Malak. Where were they now? Were they in the marshes still fighting through the mud and mist? Had the evil that had wiped out an entire expedition found them and killed them too? Had they even reached the marshes, or had they fallen prey to the pirates? Or had the evil of the dark robes located and destroyed them? All of these fears brought angry tears to Shial's eyes. He was sure that he had done the right thing by sending them away from the dark robes, but the dangers they faced were just as real, and just as deadly as Zartho and his quest for power. The only advantage they had by going was that the dangers they might encounter on the journey weren't actively looking for them.

Shial finally dozed off. He had to put everything out of his mind and force himself to relax. Thinking about the mundane tasks of the farm helped. There was still the daily routine to keep up with if he were not to fall under any more suspicion. He figured that he was already under some, but as long as he didn't do anything out of the ordinary that Zartho would think twice about, he stood a chance of keeping in contact with the man inside the tower. It was difficult, but years of mental discipline helped him to succeed in finally dozing off.

---

Dalryms sat thinking long into the night about the message from Shial. There were still too many questions that needed to be answered before anything decisive could be done. He still hadn't heard from the force that went into the mountains to check on the outposts of the king. He instinctively felt that there was somehow a connection between the disappearance of the outpost guards, and the activities of the dark robes in Chistock. He decided that he would go and personally talk to the guards that were on duty tonight.

He walked the halls and stairways alone in the dark. Every guard post had been doubled since he had returned from Chistock, and he had most of the wizards in the tower perfecting their combat spells and honing their skills. Each knew that there was some kind of impending struggle in the not-too-distant future, and they were serious in their preparations. They all knew well the history of the last wizards war, and knew the importance of the work ahead of them.

As Dalryms inspected the guards, he found them all alert and at their posts. He again reminded them of the importance of their duties, and commented on their vigilance. He knew from experience that a man worked harder, and with his whole heart in something when he knew his efforts were recognized and appreciated. It was a lot more effective than threats or intimidation. A truly willing heart was worth five hired mercenaries.

Dalryms continued his inspection into the wizard's quarters where he had several wizards keeping watch magically. They were not only looking for intruders into the tower, but were trying to detect any and all magical activity in the local tower and anywhere else magic may be being used. So far there had been nothing of consequence to report. And it was the same tonight.

By the time Dalryms turned his footsteps back toward his quarters, it was deep into the middle of the night. He was troubled still by all of the things he didn't know about what was coming, but he knew that he was doing everything that he could with what little information he now possessed. Tomorrow would bring a new day, and new tasks to perform as well as new worries to ponder. Among all of his worries the topmost were for Shial and Lena. He doubted that Lena even knew of her fathers spying on the dark tower all of these years. The danger it put her in was real and also greater than she could understand. He hoped that she would be safe through all of this, for Shial's sake as well as for her own.

# Chapter 14

Zartho awoke to the new day.  Normally he was moody and angry in the morning hours.  Today was different.  Today was the day he would put the final stages of his plans into action.  He dressed quicker than normal and made his way to breakfast with a lightness in his step that strangely, no one detected.  In the dark towers, the only time anyone paid attention to anyone else was when paranoia was involved, and that meant frequently.

As Zartho ate his breakfast, he silently gloated to himself.  After today, there would be nothing to stop his plans.  A couple of months had passed since the theft of the figurine, and since that night and its recovery, there hadn't been any other delays.  Soon he would rule all of the magical towers as well as the kingdom.  There were future plans, of course, but in one stroke he would set himself up as the ruler of all, and there would be none to oppose him.  Soon no one would dare challenge his authority.  If they tried, they would meet a horrific end as well as their family, friends, and anyone else sympathetic to them.

The only thing that bothered him was the elusive spy.  He should die first.  All of Zartho's attempts to discover his identity had failed.  He couldn't imagine that one of his three assistants had revealed the symbiot to the white robes.  His enchantment should have picked the treasonous thoughts up and alerted him.  Unless the spy was already enchanted!

The thought struck Zartho like a blow in his guts!  That had to be it.  One of the three was the spy, and had been a spy for a very long time.  All of them had been in the tower for years.  Whoever it was would have been spying on the dark robes for a very long time.  Not only learning their secrets, but also giving them to the white-robes freely!  The very thought of it enraged him.

As Zartho sat motionless looking at the other wizards in the dining hall, he swore silently to himself that the spy would die horribly.  He knew it was probably one of the three assistants he had chosen. It had to be. There was no one else whom it could have been. He was sure of this now.

His appetite suddenly gone, Zartho stormed out of the dinning hall. He had to make sure the ship sailed today! The captain had taken quite a bit of coaxing to agree to sail to the Bay of Blood. In fact, just as Zartho had planned, he had to promise that a wizard would sail with them for protection. Neither the captain, nor the wizard in training had any idea about the true nature of the trip. The young wizard only knew that at a certain point on the map he was supposed to place a crystal on the top of the mast, and magically lift and hold the ship in place. Zartho had told him that it was an experiment in weather, and the young wizard, anxious for a chance to impress the head of the tower, had readily agreed to help. Now it was finally time to send them on their way.

After Zartho sent the young wizard off, he stopped at the rooms of his three trusted assistants. He told them to come to his quarters after lights out for a special meeting. They all readily agreed, and said they would be there, taking the usual precautions for secrecy. Zartho then went to several other wizards' quarters on pretense of some minor item of tower business or other.

By lunchtime Zartho's appetite had returned. He knew that the ship had set sail on time with the morning tide. He had watched it from the tower's top. He enjoyed a swelling feeling of anticipation as it turned southeast and headed out to sea on the late-morning breeze.

He ate his lunch almost without tasting it. The plans for later tonight were running through his head. The main problem he faced was how to go about capturing the spy, and what to do with him once he was identified and subdued. He would torture him until he died, that was for sure. Before he allowed death to take him though, he would find out who his contacts were, and who the actual thief was. He wanted to get his hands on everyone involved.

Zartho finished eating and went to his quarters. Tonight would require a lot of energy. He knew that he would probably be up for most, if not all, of the night. He would also have to be at his best for the fight that would surely come. His plan was simple. He would reveal some of his true plans to all three of his assistants, nothing too specific though, just enough to panic the spy and make him contact his people outside. This time he would be watching. This time he would be ready.

Zartho got undressed and went back to bed to sleep the afternoon away. He wanted to be especially rested for what was sure to be an eventful night. There was no way to know if there was more than one spy or not within the walls of the tower. By sleeping during the afternoon, he felt confident that he would be up to any task ahead. It took a while longer than normal for him to drift off to sleep. But it always did when he chose to sleep during the day in preparation for a long night. When he finally dozed off, he dreamt of what he would do to the spy. His face wore an uncharacteristic smile as he slept.

Zartho awoke just before the evening meal was to be served. He dressed quickly, and at the appropriate time made his appearance in the dinning hall. As he ate he had to concentrate on not watching his three coconspirators any more than normal. He didn't want to tip them off that anything was wrong. After all, two of them were probably innocent, and would still be helpful in his plans. In fact, he would probably need their help at some point that he was now unaware of. There was always the unexpected that could mess up plans. The meal progressed, and he finished without watching anyone too intently. He managed to avoid doing anything that would draw attention to him as well.

Back in his quarters, Zartho carefully prepared for the upcoming meeting. He made mental notes of what to tell the three and how to carefully mark them so that he could watch them. The mental spells already in place could be blocked by the spy's protections. He would also have to passively watch what was going on in the tower until the spy made his move. Only then would he be sure to catch the traitor. The marking would help him track their activities, but could be fooled. If the spy was very clever, he may already have a fake locations spell in place. The possibilities in this game were as varied as they were endless. Yes, watching until the spy made his move was the only way to be certain of catching him.

When the appointed hour finally arrived there was a knock at the door, followed by Lorban silently entering. He and Zartho waited quietly for the others to arrive. They didn't have long to wait. Golan and Harnthiston each made their respective arrivals before a quarter of an hour had passed. Each of the three assistants figured that something was going to be different about tonight. Zartho rarely called a surprise meeting, but when he did there was a purpose behind it.

Zartho quickly took charge, and showed them into the inner chamber where they were less likely to be disturbed, or overheard. When they were all seated within, he looked each of them in the eye feigning a smile of triumph.

"My friends," he began, "very soon we will be successful in our efforts."

The three assistants looked from one to the other questioningly. Though they had been working on spells like the ship-holder for many months under Zartho's direction, they had never understood exactly why. All control had been Zartho's and there was never any explanations or adjustments to what he wanted. They had to create spells that met his exacting requirements and standards without knowing why. Now, it seemed they were about to be let in on the reason for all of their efforts. None of them made a sound, they just waited for Zartho to continue.

"You may have wondered," Zartho said, "about the strange little statue that was stolen and which we had to recover. I have told you different things about it in the past for the secrecy of our business. Believe me now when I tell you it is a symbiot, a very special symbiot. The plane it is connected to is full of the

231

creatures that it represents. There are, as I understand it, hundreds of the little things. That is our goal, to bring hundreds of them here under my control." Though he said hundreds, he knew deep inside that he really meant to bring millions of them into the world.

"But," interjected Harnthiston, "a symbiot will only connect with a single entity. Only one of them will come to our world."

"In the case of any usual symbiot," continued Zartho, "that is certainly true. But this one is different. This one is linked to an entire species or race. This one is truly powerful. And with that kind of power we, the four of us, will be able to rule the entire kingdom, and perhaps even the world. Think of it, an army of small demons who can't be killed because they aren't from this dimension. They can only be sent back to their own dimension, and when they've healed, they can be brought back again, and again."

The effect of Zartho's words was exciting to the others. Partly due to the promise of greater power than they had ever dared hope for, and partly due to the mental spell each of them was under. He didn't tell them that they would all come through at once, or that all other wizards would be destroyed with the king and his army. But each of them knew enough to see problems with the plan. Lorban spoke first.

"But even if that's true, and it is the key that controls an entire species, there's no way to bring more than one at a time into our world. The doorways are just too small."

"How do you know these things about the statue?" asked Golan. "Where did it come from? Did you create it?"

Zartho smiled and held up his hands to quiet the questions that were just beginning to come.

"I'll answer what questions I can at this time. So many wills will be difficult to control, so I need you three to back up my will with your own. Otherwise... well, I don't have to tell you what could happen if we lost control of so many demons. It would be catastrophic to ourselves as well as our enemies."

"As for where it came from, and how I know about what it does, that is an interesting story," began Zartho. "No, I didn't create it. I have no idea who did. I found it several years ago when I was visiting ruins from before the Wizard War. I was on a good-will pilgrimage with several white robes. The statue was carefully concealed inside a stone wall. I happened on it when I stumbled and fell against that wall. While catching my balance and my breath, I noticed one stone was looser than the others. After a few minutes of working out the mortar and wiggling the stone it came free. Behind it was a small hollow space, which contained the figurine and a piece of parchment. I had no idea what it might be at first; the writing on the parchment was unknown to me. I had never seen anything like it before. I decided, of course, to keep both items for myself.

"I spent the next several years trying to decipher the writing on the parchment. I wondered why anyone would hide a statue in a wall, and just exactly what it was for. If it turned out to be nothing, I could always return it to its resting place. No one would ever be the wiser.

"I still don't know the full translation of the parchment. It appears to be some kind of warning about the power of the thing. But I have only been able to find about half of the characters in the most ancient of records in the libraries of the kingdom. Of the characters I have found, there are still a few I haven't been able to translate. It appears that most of the parts that I can't translate are an account of who made it and how it was made. What I have translated though gives me enough information to know how to use it."

"It's pretty risky, don't you think?" asked Lorban. "I mean there are so many things that could go wrong with a magic that isn't fully understood."

"Rest assured, Lorban," said Zartho, "I know what I'm doing. Individually, the little dragons, or whatever they are, are easily controlled and used. The only question I have is how many will be able to be controlled. If it gets to dangerous, we can always close the portal and stop any more from coming."

"Zartho, we are ready to help in any way we can, of course," interrupted Lorban again. "The portal is going to have to be huge to deal with the number of creatures you're talking about. Where are you going to be able to open one that big?"

"That is a good question, Lorban. I have come up with a good answer for it too," said Zartho pleased with himself and with the support the others were giving. He knew that there were terrible risks involved, but the payoffs would be phenomenal when it worked. (He had never given consideration to the possibility that it wouldn't work.) "The portal actually doesn't need to be that large," he lied. "It could be opened on the top of our tower. With all of us working together, we will be able to control them as they trickle through. I won't tell you where we will open it yet, but once enough are through we will launch our attack on the king. People will suddenly be aware that the kingdom has changed dramatically. They will also understand very quickly that they have no chance of resisting, and we will be in charge."

"But when will this happen," broke in Golan. "When will we open the portal?"

"Relax," said Zartho. "We will open it soon. As soon as the people are in place with the crystals Harnthiston has been working on for so long."

"So what are the crystals for?" asked Harnthiston.

"To help in long range control of the demons," Zartho lied. "The crystals are on their way now, and will be in place on a certain day and time in the near future. All of you need to be ready at a moments notice for me to call you. We won't meet again until that time."

"But," Golan began only to be cut off by Zartho.

"There is nothing more to tell you tonight. I don't need to emphasize the importance of keeping all of this in the strictest of confidence. We have come too far now to stop or to be stopped by anyone. Remember, when the dust settles, we will rule the entire kingdom, and there won't be any white-robes or king to keep us from taking anything we want."

The room was silent when Zartho finished talking. Each of the three others was thinking of the power and glory to be gained. The risks were great, true, but the payoffs were worth it. Black robes were notorious for their lust for power and control. They craved it like a drug. The proposed plan was not only dangerous from a magical point of view, but also treasonous. If any part of the spells failed, there was no telling what would happen. If their control of the creatures failed, they would die, as the creatures would know exactly where their failed masters were. There wouldn't be anyplace they could hide. Their slaves would find them first, and the four of them would meet a horrific end. The rest of the world would then face a terrible struggle for survival.

On the other hand, not taking advantage of the opportunity would be inexcusable and cowardly by their way of thinking. This was the stuff dreams were made of to almost every dark robed wizard from their earliest venturing into magic. Most dark-robes had started in white towers, and later gravitated to a dark tower when their true natures began to come out. Many of them still harbored deep grudges against specific white-robes, and all of them hated white-robes in general because of their perceived wrongs. In truth, if any wrongs had been committed, the dark-robes were usually the perpetrators.

Zartho could feel the emotions of each of his assistants. Of course he never had any intention of sharing any power with them, but they didn't need to know that until it was time to get rid of them. Until then, they may be useful if he couldn't control the hordes of monsters he was going to unleash on the world. With three minds united under his direction, he would be sure to maintain control. Only two minds under his direction, he corrected himself. One of the assistants would soon die.

"Go now, and be ready." Zartho said waving his hand in dismissal.

The others all filed out silently. They all felt excited and emotionally high as they left and went to their separate quarters. At the moment, Zartho couldn't tell if there was anything suspicious about any of them. He knew one of them was hiding. One of them would have to try and contact the outside world, or someone who could make contact for him. Either way, Zartho would be watching them all closely. He sat down in his chair and closed his eyes. The spell was working. He knew where each of them was, and what they were doing and thinking. He watched them get ready for bed and go to sleep. He kept a silent watch all night and noted with some displeasure that they all seemed to be excited and happy about the plan. If he didn't know better, he would have looked elsewhere for the spy again. He could wait. The spy would be revealed, of that he was certain.

The remainder of the night passed quietly. None of the assistants woke, although due to the excitement, they did take a while longer to fall asleep. Zartho detected no communication into or out of the tower. He was feeling tired as the windows of his quarters began to show the morning's light through them. He had to stretch himself several times to keep from falling asleep. He couldn't let himself doze off and become distracted from the vigil. If he failed to discover the spy this time, there wouldn't be another chance. He would have to go on without the help of the others. He would have to kill them all before the portal opened.

Breakfast in the dinning hall came and went while Zartho sat in his quarters watching and waiting. The morning hours and noon meal passed, as did the afternoon hours. For Zartho, the waiting was beginning to take its toll. He had almost slipped into semi-consciousness a couple of times. Each time he jerked awake, stood up and paced the room several times to revive. When dinnertime came Zartho descended from his quarters long enough to get a small plate of food and return to his vigil.

He ate the food slowly, making sure that his mind was still focused on the tower and the magic of the surrounding area. At the same time he had to keep track mentally of his three helpers.

The food helped to re-energize him and bring him back to full alertness. But he avoided eating so much that he would become sleepy. There was no telling how long he would have to stay awake before the spy made his move. He began to wonder how long he could wait before sleep closed his eyes whether he wanted them closed or not. He had his limits, and although he could have gone many days taking only short 'cat naps', he couldn't go much longer without any sleep at all. The human body and mind wouldn't last long without it. Sleep had always been a limitation that he had hated.

As the sun slowly set into the western sea, the gathering darkness began to have an almost narcotic affect on Zartho. As the light through his window dimmed he had to fight harder to keep his mind centered on the seemingly endless task at hand. More and more frequently he had to stand up and exercise himself to keep alert. The hours passed slowly.

---

Shial went to bed at his usual time. He was tired from the activities of the day and from worrying about what might or might not happen in the near future. The summer solstice was nearly here, and nothing further had been heard from within the dark tower. He was also worried about Lena. He had a strange feeling that she was in trouble. There was no safe way of trying to see her or help her. He had to depend on Malak. In any other place on earth, he would have felt confident with the situation. He didn't have any idea where they were now, but he hoped they had gotten through the swamp. If anyone could get through the swamp, he thought Malak had a pretty good chance. He knew that the ex-assassin thought quickly in high-stress situations, and never let his emotions control his actions. Not to mention the fact that he was skilled at survival, and deadly. As long as they avoided the entity that he was sure still existed in the area. But by now they could be anywhere. He relaxed and tried to clear the cares from his mind. He went to sleep with his mind open to any prompting from the spy.

The spy had been silent for a couple of months. Shial had no way of knowing when he would try to make contact again, so he tried to be ready at all times. As his mind drifted off to sleep, he thought again of Lena and the hopes of seeing her again. Sometime long after midnight, he awoke to a sound that he thought he heard. After several minutes of quiet, he was on the verge of sleep again, when he felt an invisible hand reach inside his head and gently stroke his mind.

He sat bolt upright. At last, the signal from the spy in the tower! Without losing a moment, he ran to the front of the cabin and threw open the chest. He quickly set up the crystal on its stand and concentrated on the communication spell. It was hard to keep the power of the spell low, so as not to draw attention to it. Deciding to err on the side of caution, he fought back his eagerness and excitement even more, and bled off more power from the spell before releasing its answering pulse.

Almost immediately the crystal before him began to give off smoke, which soon coalesced into the robed and cloaked figure that had reported to him before. Although the figure was the same, the spell seemed even weaker than before.

"Soon a portal will open," began the figure immediately, "I don't know where for sure, Zartho hinted at the top of the tower, but it could be anywhere. At that time hundreds of small demons are going to come through and be under Zartho's control. He plans to take over the kingdom at least, probably more."

"What?" Shial asked.

"Don't interrupt," hissed the cloaked figure. "I'm probably being watched right now, and will be dead soon. I don't know for sure how long you have, but if Zartho's not lying it can't be more than a couple of days. You must destroy the crystals; he said they help control the demons somehow. If they are destroyed, I believe the demons will kill Zartho first as soon as they come through the portal, hopefully before there are very many to deal with. It will be soon, I don't know exactly when."

The figure in the smoke disappeared and the room went silent. Shial stared at the dissipating smoke with his mouth hanging open. So that was the power behind the statue, control of not a single entity from another dimension, but many of them. He knew what that could mean to the peace of the kingdom. He also knew that a portal held open as long as would be needed might allow other things in as well. That's if it wasn't done just right. But even if only the one species came through, hundreds of them could spell the end of the world. Zartho was surely mad to even consider trying it. He prayed silently that if Zartho did open the portal, whatever came through would kill him immediately.

He doubted for a moment that the spy had heard correctly. He had heard of symbiots and even seen them used to bring and control demons into the world, but he had never heard of one that defined more than one specific creature. Still, the spy had been specific, that "hundreds" were involved. The spy had also been specific about his impending death. If they caught the spy, they would probably soon catch him too. He had to contact Dalryms immediately.

Without attempting to hide the signal, Shial sent a single powerful mental jolt to Dalryms, one that would wake even the deepest of sleepers. There would be no doubt about where it had come from. Within a few minutes the crystal again began issuing forth its smoke and the figure of Dalryms took shape.

"What are you trying to do?" he demanded, "break my mind?"

"The spy just made contact. I don't know if I have much time," replied Shial calmly. Then he went on to tell Dalryms everything that he had heard and that the spy's continued existence was not very likely. They discussed the possibility of Zartho lying to his own men, exactly what the crystals might be, where they might be located, and how to go about destroying them and protecting the kingdom. Their brief conversation ended with Dalryms telling Shial to get out of his cabin, and hide.

Zartho snapped awake suddenly. He realized after a moment that he had lost the three he was watching. He quickly recast the spell and connected to them. All three seemed to sleeping in their quarters. He then sent out the probe of the tower. There was a very small trace of energy, fading quickly, extending from the tower.

Zartho knew immediately that a message had been sent. One of the three was not truly asleep and it enraged him. Blind with rage he stormed out of his room to kill them all. His discipline caught up with him, though, as he was raging down the first flight of steps.

Now wasn't the time to act. If he attacked them now, the entire keep would be awakened. He would only be able to kill one of them before the rest of the wizards in the keep stopped him. He was powerful, but not powerful enough to take on the entire tower. The spy had a 2/3 chance of escaping, and the entire plan would fail. Besides, he was already weak from keeping his long vigil. No, now was not the time or place to kill them. He would arrange another meeting. This one would be the last. The spy wouldn't have time to report this one.

# Chapter 15

The soldiers were happy for the first couple of days on the return trip to Thosh. They were lucky enough to have been picked for the homeward journey. Soon they would be back with their wives and girlfriends. Back to the comforts of their homes and barracks; loved ones and friends.

Some of them were young with a lot of promise in their soldiering careers ahead of them. Some were older and more experienced. All were glad to be getting out of these strange, silent mountains. With the discovery in the bottom of the tower, the beauty of the land had disappeared, and been replaced by suspicion. Suspicion and fear that ran through the entire force. The men feared the unexpected sounds around them, sounds that occur frequently as a small group marches through the mountains. Every squirrel that ran up a tree; every bird that suddenly took flight seemed to startle the men and put them even more on edge.

The officers in charge of the force were concerned. They knew of cases where men became so jumpy that they had actually turned on each other. The dark nights ahead would be dangerous enough without the men panicking and tearing themselves apart. They could order all weapons picketed together as the men slept, but then they were basically unarmed, and unprepared if a surprise attack should come. There were no easy answers. The officers consulted with each other, and decided that the best course of action would be to pair the men up on watch so they weren't alone, and then try to get the other men to relax a bit.

The first night away from the fort was uninterrupted. The men slept well, and the watches went without any problem or anything out of the ordinary to report.

The second day's march took them even further from the main body of the army. The men were more relaxed than on the previous day. The weather clouded up in the afternoon, and a few thunderstorms passed overhead, but only dropped a few sprinkles on the men. The air became muggy with humidity. Still they pressed on. Most of the force were experienced enough to have marched through days of rain before, slipping and sliding both up and down hills. These brief storms were nothing by comparison. They cooled the air for a few minutes before the sun came out again and evaporated what little water had made it to the ground so that the air was now hot and humid. It seemed worse than if there had been no rain at all.

By nightfall the men were tired and welcomed the rest that was to come. As the men were assigned their various shifts for watch, they cooked and ate their rations. Most were thinking about getting back to Thosh and the routine of life there. The first watch was set for sunset with watch changes every two hours. At the midnight watch change an alarm was sounded.

The entire camp roused from their beds. There were two missing guards. The post was one of the furthest ones from camp, and the relief sentries had come on duty to find no one there to relieve. The men were quickly in formation, and counted. The two sentries had just disappeared. As soon as it was clear that men were missing, a search was organized. The camp was searched first. New fires were lighted to give additional light so they wouldn't miss anything. The search of the camp revealed nothing except what was already known, two men were missing. Two patrols of four men each were organized and sent into the woods.

The patrols were to look for the men or their bodies if that was all that was left of them. After two hours, they were called back into camp. It was then that fear began to take shape in the hearts of the men. Only one patrol returned. There was no sign of the other.

Again and again, the call to return to camp was sounded. Finally it was evident that the sound of the horn was falling on either deaf ears, or more likely, dead ears. It was decided to pull the sentries closer to the firelight, and to wait out the night with all of the men awake. The men whispered their fears during the remaining hours. What could take six men so quickly that no alarm could be raised? What had happened to them? Were they dead? If so, where were their bodies? No one had any answers to these questions.

Wild stories started to abound around the fires. Some men thought that whatever had happened to the missing troops was intelligently controlled. It had waited to attack until they were too far from the outpost to make it back in one day's march. They obviously couldn't go further, and they couldn't make it back to the relative safety of the army while daylight was shining. Above all, they knew they couldn't stay where they were.

At dawn, it was decided to head back to the main force at the tower outpost. The two fastest men were chosen to run ahead and let General Leland know what had happened, and that they were coming back. They were each given a small amount of water, and others carried their packs. They also were each allowed to carry their weapon of choice. They left while the others were breaking camp.

General Leland had been in a fowl mood all day long. There was something wrong with the area that his troops now lived in. It had been only two days since the small force had left to take word back to King Nolan about what had happened to their outpost. The first night had gone smoothly, and there had been nothing out of the ordinary to report from any of the sentries on duty.

The next day, they had again sent out scouting parties into the surrounding countryside. Again there had been nothing out of the ordinary to report. One of the groups had even managed to kill a deer, for some fresh meat for the camp. Yet still, there was no explanation for the bodies under the tower. Murder had been done on a larger scale than he had ever thought possible, and there was no evidence as to who or what had done it. He thought about magic being at play, but then wouldn't the wizards in the tower have noticed what was going on? Surely they would have said something about it in their reports to the king, unless they were the first ones dead.

The more he chased the facts at hand around in his head, the more he knew that he needed more facts. There just wasn't enough to go on. The worst part of not knowing was that his men were depending on him to keep them safe. At the present time, he didn't know if any of them were. He didn't even know where to look to find out. All he could do was to continue the patrols, and hope that word from the king would come soon. He knew it would take several weeks, perhaps even months before any word arrived. He wondered if there was anything the king could do about the present situation. He hoped some wizards would be sent to take over the tower again. Maybe they could help figure out what had happened.

Until they arrived, all the general could do was sit and wait. It was a game he hated most of all. Until he learned more, he felt that he, and everyone under his command were at risk. Yet, there didn't seem any way for him to learn more. The thought of going back inside the tower to the lowest chamber filled him with dread. However, if that was where the answers lay, that was where he was going. He would start tomorrow morning. It was almost sunset now, there would be only more danger going after dark. For some reason he was apprehensive about the darkness. When he thought about the night in the forest or in the tower the hair on the back of his neck stood on end. He'd had the feeling before; it was his intuitive reaction to unseen danger. There wasn't any specific cause he could think of, but he knew he shouldn't ignore this feeling. Neither should he let it rule his actions. Yes, the morning would be soon enough for visiting the charnel house.

An alarm sounded outside from the fort's gate. General Leland rushed outside to see what was going on. When he got there, the guards were holding a man to keep him from collapsing onto the ground. He recognized the man as one of those sent to Thosh with the return party.

"Bring him to my quarters," he ordered the guards. Obviously there was trouble, and he wanted some control about what leaked out. The men were edgy enough already, but this could send their morale spiraling out of control.

On his way back to his quarters, he ordered a man to find his second in command and have him also report. Once everyone was settled, he dismissed the guards and sent them back to their posts.

"What's your name soldier?" he began.

"Corporal Binder, sir,"

"Now Corporal, tell me what is going on."

The corporal told his story between gasps, as he was still trying to catch his breath. It was obvious that he had exhausted himself in his efforts to reach the camp. The other man, a Private Jentz had fallen behind in the early afternoon, and he had pressed on alone. As to the rest of the force, it should arrive tomorrow afternoon at the earliest.

"How far behind you was Private Jentz?" asked the general.

"He should be here within the hour. Two at the outside."

"And there was no sign of what happened to the missing men?"

"None at all sir. We tried to follow the footprints as best we could, but they just disappeared."

"Well then, return to your barracks Corporal. Don't talk to anyone about this. You will be excused from guard duties tonight. The last thing I need is someone falling asleep on watch."

With that dismissal, Corporal Binder left the room, and the two officers were left alone with their thoughts. It was a few moments before the general spoke. He wondered how long it would take for the stories to start running around the camp. Once the main body returned tomorrow they would surely make their experiences known.

"What do you think," the general asked.

"I don't know what to make of it. We put competent men in charge of the return force."

"I'm not blaming the men in charge. From what Corporal Binder said, they followed standard protocol. I would have done no different."

"Surely, he must have been exaggerating a little. To take a four-man search party without a sound, that's hard to believe, in fact I think it's just about impossible."

"I agree," said the general. "But his story may be correct. We'll just have to see what the other men have to say when they return. Someone must have seen or heard more than what we have been told. We'll have to interview every man individually so they don't get their versions mixed up. You know how they tend to build on a good story."

"What do you want me to do until tomorrow?"

"Tell the guard to be on the lookout for them tonight in case they force-march all night. Also watch for the other runner. Bring him to me as soon as he comes in. I want to get to the bottom of whatever is going on around here."

"I'll keep watch for the other man myself."

Then the second in command left the general with his thoughts. He didn't like what was going on. They were now completely cut off from the kingdom. He considered retreating and moving the entire force back to Thosh, but decided that would be a last resort. That would mean leaving the entire fort and tower abandoned, and the west coast open to attack. Then again, hadn't there already been some kind of attack, and those who had been here originally had lost.

He wondered if there was some kind of explanation for the disappearances. Maybe some kind of mass desertion was afoot. There was no evidence of that though. They would have to know that the safest place for them would be together in the largest group possible. To want to risk the mountains alone or even in groups of four would be crazy. Something had seemingly captured and killed entire villages and dumped the bodies under the tower, and they knew it. To try the mountains alone would be madness. Especially when no one knew what had happened.

A soldier would show the greatest of courage and fight to the death against incredible odds if they were fighting something they knew. Give them an unknown or worse something that smacked of ghosts or phantoms and they would cower away their lives. No, there was no way that the general could see that the men would desert. They needed each other too badly.

He sat thinking until nearly midnight. His thoughts going around in circles until he decided to give up and go to sleep. As he was preparing for bed, he remembered the other runner. Quickly he dressed and went out to inspect the troops. He found them all alert and dutifully standing their watches. Some of them seemed a bit pale undoubtedly they knew that something had happened to the returning force. When he got to the main gate, he found the second in command still at the post pacing nervously.

"No sign of the other runner?" he asked.

"No sir. There hasn't been so much as a squirrel come up that trail. Do you suppose that he decided to sleep through the night and come in in the morning?"

"I doubt that very much. I think that he would have kept moving as if the hounds of hell were on his heels. Keep a watch though. It is possible that he hurt himself. That last man practically fell through the gate. Maybe he's out there hurt, a broken leg or something, we'll send a patrol out in the morning to see if they can find him. They can also meet up with the returning force and help them along.

"Go and get some rest. I have the feeling that he won't be coming in tonight. Tomorrow promises to be a very long day."

With that the general returned to his quarters. He felt that tomorrow would indeed be a long day. The second stayed to give the guards some final orders, and then, as ordered, he too retired for the night.

The morning dawned cloudy and cooler. There was still no sign of the other runner, and a patrol was soon dispatched to find out where he was as well as the rest of the returning group. Meanwhile, General Leland decided to take some of the more battle-hardened men and return to the tower. He was sure that somewhere there had to be some evidence that he had overlooked before. Something that would make sense out of what was going on.

They started just after the last breakfast shift had eaten. Several groups of men were sent into the woods to hunt for meat and scout around again. If they had to stay here a while, the general wanted to make sure his supplies would last. Besides, fresh meat would lift the men's spirits.

After the short walk down to the tower, they divided the men up into teams to search the tower top to bottom again. There was to be nothing left unturned. No book was to be unopened and unshaken. Several of the bravest accompanied the general into the tunnels where they also searched. They started with the rooms closest to the main floor. These were studies and some small laboratories. They found nothing of interest in the first few and so they continued downwards. Room after room was searched with nothing found. They were well into the lower levels by lunchtime. None of the men wanted to go back to camp to eat though. They knew what was ahead of them. The smell of the rotting corpses was beginning to become evident. None of them wanted to face that room on a full stomach. Most of them doubted that they would be eating dinner that night either.

Toward sunset, they still had a few rooms left before they entered the horrors of what had become a crypt ahead of them. General Leland thought it better to come back in the morning and finish. Something told him that he would be better off doing this in the daytime. They retraced their steps and met up with the men searching the upper levels. They too had been looking all day with nothing to show for the effort.

Tired, the men formed up and marched back to the outpost. They knew that there was probably nothing to find that would shed any light on the mystery they faced. They also knew that they would have to return to the worst of the underground the next day. They had not completed their mission, and so it would fall upon them again tomorrow. The ones who had worked in the lower levels had it the worst. All day they had endured the stress of what was to come, and now they would have it all night as well. It wouldn't go away until it had been faced and they knew it. They had only prolonged the stress. Many thought to themselves it would have been better to face it now and get it over with regardless of the time of day or night. Down there, they reasoned, it didn't matter how bright the sun was shining.

When they got back, General Leland was surprised that nothing had been heard from the scouting party that was supposed to escort the returning troops. The evening meal was spent worrying about what was going on. At least there was fresh venison to eat, as one of the other patrols had killed another deer. The meal was better than the usual military fare, and he made a mental note to compliment the cook on it. Just as he was finishing his meal, there was an alert from the gate sentries.

General Leland ran to the gate to see what was going on. Off in the distance, just coming into view was a small group of men. They seemed tired and footsore, but they were moving towards the fort at quick-step march. They were quickly recognized as the men who were sent out to escort the returning force and the missing runner back to the fort. The general looked at them for a moment. They were not only tired, but they were exhausted. It didn't look as if they could have gone another mile.

"What is your report?" he asked the officer in charge.

"Sir," the man gasped between heavily drawn breaths. "We began this morning at a quick-time. We wanted to be sure we made it back by dark with the other troops. By noon, we hadn't caught up with them yet, and we still hadn't seen any sign of the other runner either. We decided to go on for another hour at a run. After that, we still hadn't seen any sign of them; we decided to go a half-hour more. That's when we found their campsite. The tents were all there, set up just like they should be, all neat and regulation style. But there were no men to be found.

"We spent another half-hour yelling our heads off, but we never found anyone either. We looked for tracks around the camp, to see if they went anywhere, but we couldn't find any. At least not any leaving the campsite."

"What do you mean?" interrupted General Leland.

"I mean, sir, that we could see the tracks of the group coming into the campsite, and tracks in the camp itself, but there were none leaving it. It was like they had been marching back here, and made camp for the night, and then they just disappeared."

"Then what did you do?""

"Well, sir, we figured that we should start back. There wasn't any sense waiting for people who weren't there anymore, and who we couldn't track, so we double-timed it nearly all the way back to camp. We were trying to get back here before it got dark, but we didn't quite make it."

The general was silent for a moment.

"Why did you want to make it back before dark?"

"Well sir, I can't explain it any better than a feeling. The campsite didn't feel right. It seemed that something was waiting to happen. There wasn't any way we could help the others. There wasn't anyone left there to help. We figured the best thing to do would be to get back and report. That was about three o'clock this afternoon. We pretty much ran all the way back here. When the sun went down, we were forced to walk or risk injury in the dark.

"Thank you, I'm glad you made it back safely. Go get some food. You've all had a hard day."

When they had left, the general told the captain of the guard to keep those men off watch tonight. They were practically done in, and he knew they needed rest.

250

Back in his quarters, he hoped that there would be some answers soon. The men who had returned had begun to show their fear openly. The fact that they had maintained ranks all the way back to the fort attested to their bravery. It would have been very easy to slip into a panicked route at the setting of the sun. Instead, they had stayed together in reasonable formation and made it back together. He would have to remember the name of the officer in command. He spent the rest of the evening seeing that the mundane aspects of running an army were all addressed.

In the morning, he again went back to the tower to finish looking in the lower levels. There didn't seem to be any reason for doing it other than he couldn't figure any better direction to take in his search for answers. This time he left only a couple of greatly relieved guards in the upper levels. The rest of the men followed him into the darkness. They moved quickly, looking for anything that might be in the last couple of rooms. There wasn't anything of interest, and they were soon in the overwhelming stench that surrounded the entrance to the great amphitheatre. Leland took two men inside with him; the rest would stay outside and try not to get sick.

The room was as it had been before. The stench made a physical horror of every breath. They tried breathing only shallowly, but it was a useless effort. There didn't seem to be any change to the bodies, and there wasn't any other way out of the chamber that could be detected. Finally, the general relented. Short of going through the bodies one at a time there just wasn't anything to find. It would be a long time before he was reduced to digging through the dead for clues. Just as he was turning to go back, the flickering torchlight caught something.

He hailed the other two men to come with him as he checked it out. There was something different about one of the corpses toward the back of the pile. They skirted the edge of the pile of decaying bodies until they could see the back of it. To their horror they began to recognize the uniforms and then the bodies of the men who had disappeared on their way back to Thosh. They looked like they had been torn apart.

The men had died horribly. Like the other bodies in the room, they were mutilated. Deep slashes marked the torsos, and their limbs were at grotesque angles that marked them as broken or dislocated, sometimes both. Their silent screams were cast forever on their pale, stiff faces. Eyes bulged from sockets as if disbelieving what was being seen at the last moment of life.

One of the men with the general started to vomit, and the sound forced him and the other soldier to follow suite. They ran for the exit vomiting as they went. As they burst through the entrance, they were met by the questioning stares of the other troops.

"Out," yelled the general through clenched teeth. "Get going." In an act of sheer willpower, he forced himself to be the last one in the climb to the upper levels. All the way along, he thought he could feel some unknown presence following him back up the tunnels. Mercifully, his stomach had started to settle by the time they reached the surface. Here there were more questioning stares at him and the other two who were with him.

"We found where the missing soldiers went," was all he said for several minutes. He and the other two stood around trying to breath and forget what they never could. "Let's get back to the fort, there isn't anything we can do here."

When they arrived back at the fort, General Leland quickly gave orders to double the guard again, although he doubted that even this would help. Hadn't the entire returning force been killed and somehow transported back to the tower to be buried with the other people who used to live in these mountains? How had it been done? One thing was certain now in his mind. There was magic of some kind at work here.

It had to be the work of dark-robes. He had never heard of them killing on this scale before, but they must be behind it. There was no other way. Oh, they may be employing demons of one kind or another, but they would have had to bring them into the world, and be helping them to escape detection. There wasn't any way around it. There was no way, short of a full retreat back to Thosh, to get word to the King. Even then, a retreat would mean that most of them would die on the way. They would be a couple of months in the mountains without any cover for the sentries. The only man to survive the last attempt to get back had said that sentries were exposed, even in numbers.

Besides, retreating back into the mountains would leave the western shore of the kingdom exposed to attack. He was sure that the dark-robes were up to something, and they didn't want anyone to interfere with it. If he pulled back, that would leave them to their devices unopposed. That wasn't acceptable either. The only option for the time being seemed to be to sit in the fort and cower with fear. That didn't suit the general at all. In fact it angered him beyond anything he had experienced in a long time, even more than the sight of his mutilated troops.

He felt like a frightened schoolgirl about to wet her pants in fear of the local bully. They would not give in to the fear! He was determined about that. They would do their duty, by thunder, if it got them all killed, then so be it. That's what they were paid for. He was going to find out exactly what was going on, and he was going to be careful about how he did it. There wasn't any sense to killing men uselessly. Too many had already died for nothing. But it wouldn't stay for nothing if he had his way.

In a fit of decisiveness, he called for the officers of the camp, and addressed them.

"Gentlemen, I've called this meeting to make sure that everyone is aware of what is happening. The force that we sent back to Thosh has been completely wiped out. I found their bodies inside that pit of death this morning. I think we are dealing with some dark-robes that are using demons. I don't know how many there are, but we need to gather more information than we now have. Suggestions?"

The room was quiet for several moments. Slowly, a hand went up here and there. Ideas were soon flowing from the officers. Some good, some would need work before they could be implemented. But they were all engaged now that they had a direction to focus their energy in. If the general was right, they faced formidable foes. At least they had an idea of what they were up against now, and that alone bolstered their courage.

At the end of the meeting, there were several good ideas that would be immediately put into effect. The men would be told to be on the lookout for each other, as well as what the general thought they were dealing with. The best defense, it was decided was to have the guards placed around the entire perimeter of the camp. They were to space themselves out about every twenty feet so they weren't bunched up, but so that they could always see the sentries to either side of them. They were to watch both the area inside and outside the camp as well as the other guards. The consensus was that if anyone disappeared, it would be immediately known, and only one man would be at risk at any given time. Under no circumstances were they to bunch up.

Other plans were also put into work. The men, who had earlier been showing signs of fear and indecision, were now resolved and purposeful. They had a plan, and would see it through until something better came along. As the sun went down on the camp, they had one final head count, and set up both the guards and the roving patrols that would walk around inside the fort to be doubly safe. If anything at all happened, the alarm would be quickly given. So far there had been no problems in the fort. The officers reassured their men that nothing was likely to happen, but they also knew that their safety wasn't assured by any means.

The entire camp was on watch at one time or another during the night. Officers included. They worked in two-hour shifts, and reported every change. The night went without incident, and soon the men were relaxing in the pre-dawn glow that backlit the mountains to the east.

General Leland had served his shift just as everyone else. He had taken one in the middle of the night, so there would be no lapses in the concentration of the men. Then he had turned in to get what sleep he could before the new day. The morning roll call was just beginning when he stepped out of his quarters to breakfast and start the day. It was a routine that had been going on for his entire adult life. The cooks had been busy since before dawn, and now the meal was ready to serve. The troops would eat in two shifts, and the day's work would begin. More patrols were scheduled for the surrounding mountains today. There must be something to find out there. Something that would make some sense about the killings. If they didn't find something soon, he would have to send out another return party. And this time, he knew, there would be a lot less enthusiasm towards going.

The general's thoughts were interrupted as his attention was drawn to one of the platoons. There seemed to be something wrong with the count. The officer in charge had started the count again. Usually the men held their swords above their heads, and as each man counted off his number, he lowered the weapon. This way no one was missed, and no numbers were left out. On occasion the soldiers were in a hurry and would count out of turn. Thus forcing them to start the count again from the beginning. When finished, the count would be accurate, and if there were any missing men they would be evident.

The platoon had already counted off once, and the officer was making them do it again. The general watched to see that it went correctly. He could hear the sound of each man's yell, and see their sword lower to their chest as they called out.

"One, sir."

"Two, sir."

"Three, sir."

And so it went down the four rows of troops. As the count was nearing its end the general's mind again began to wander to the problem at hand. A moment later, he was drawn back to the platoon as they started the count for the third time. A knot seemed to twist in his guts. The officer seemed a bit paler than he had been before.

General Leland approached the officer as he was watching the count most carefully this time. When it ended, the man let out a quiet groan.

"Is there a problem?" asked Leland.

"Sir," the officer spun around startled. "The count is off sir. Three men are unaccounted for."

The general's blood ran cold in his veins.

"Which three men?" the general asked.

The three missing men were soon identified, much to their comrade's despair.

"Is it likely they are at the latrine?" asked General Leland.

"I'll send two men to check sir, but I personally checked the latrine as the men were assembling for roll call, and there were no men there."

"Send the men now," said the general, the knot twisting tighter in his guts.

Soon word was back that they were not in the latrine, and a general search was begun of the camp. They were never located. They had simply disappeared. Tracking their movements, they had stood one of the final watches, and retired to their racks as soon as they had gone off-duty. No one had seen or heard of them since then.

General Leland fumed inside, how could three men disappear without any trace from within the camp? The fact that it had happened was clear. But the question as to how remained. No guards had fallen asleep during the night, he was sure of that. There had been no sightings of anything coming into or going out of the camp. They had vanished completely, leaving all of their personal belongings, and their weapons behind at their bedsides. How had it been done?

Another problem was now developing. What was the use of watches when something like this could happen? The men knew about it, and they had to assume that they were next if they stayed here much longer. General Leland had to admit that it looked like they were correct in their fears. They were not safe anymore inside the fort. The only time that it seemed they were safe, was while the sun was shining. But even that wasn't a certainty.

There was one thing that he had to do today, and the general loathed the idea of it. He had to go back down into the pit of corpses and look for the missing men's bodies. If they were there, and he knew that they would be, there was one thing he thought would smoke out their unseen enemies.

Meanwhile, the troops went about their usual morning routine quietly. They moved silently and quickly formed into patrols. When these had gone out on their assigned rounds, the general took two of the remaining troops and went again to the tower. He was not gone long. When he returned to the fort he met with the officers who hadn't gone on patrol. They soon came up with a plan to defend themselves. It would take a lot of courage, and they knew at least one more man would die. But if it worked, they might save the rest of the men.

Later that day as the sun was going down, the general and three of the most experienced men left for the tower. General Leland had always believed in leading from the front, and thus it was tonight. He couldn't assign this duty to anyone else. It would be horrific, and the thought of it made him sick to his stomach. He was glad for the company of the other men. They had no idea what was being planned. He had chosen them from among the ranks of the enlisted because of their bravery, and their ability with both the bow and the blade. They may need both by the end of the night.

The patrols had all returned without incident, proving at least for the time being that their enemies preferred the cover of darkness to do their dirty work. How long that would last, no one knew. The troops had been fed, and assigned to the same guard routines as the night before with the exception that now there were guards in the men's sleeping quarters as well. They were taking no chances tonight. In spite of all these precautions, the general was pretty sure they would loose another man or perhaps more. There just wasn't anyway to watch all of the men all of the time.

With the additional security, and the other plan, he thought they might just stand a pretty good chance of surviving to make it back to Thosh. But first he had to make sure they killed the thing, or things that were killing them. If they could pull it off, there would be some small retribution for the murders that had been going on for these past months.

The windows of the tower looked like black eyes staring down at the approaching men in the dimming light. As they arrived in the outer courtyard, a chill breeze sprang up as if to warn them of the approaching danger. It was too late to turn back now. The general was sure that if they tried to return to the fort at night, they would either disappear like the others, or their own panicky guard would kill them. Only a few of the men in the fort knew they were gone, and none but officers knew what the plan was.

As they entered the main hall of the tower, the general signaled them to gather around him.

"Tonight," he began in a faint whisper, "we will see if there is a chance to make it back to Thosh. You, no doubt, have heard about the amphitheater at the lowest level of the tunnels. It is filled with the bodies of those who have gone missing. There are hundreds stacked there. I warn you, it isn't a pretty sight or smell. I warn you of this because that is where we are going to spend the night."

There was a hiss of air from the men as they realized what the general was saying. "We will go down together. We will all carry the torches with us, but only one will light our way down. I want you to understand exactly what we are going to do before we go down so that we won't need to talk while down there." The men stood silently waiting for the general to continue. There was no sign of doubt or question on their faces. They would follow Leland where his orders took them, and they would do so without a word of complaint.

"When we arrive in the amphitheater, we will spread out. Each taking a portion of the room to cover, but make sure that you have a clear shot of the ceiling. You're probably wondering why you each have a crossbow as well as your long bows. I'll explain that now.

"We will be looking for something to happen down there. I don't know what it will be or even if it will be visible. I believe it will be though. Look and listen for anything to happen. When it does, fire the crossbow immediately into it. You won't have time to reload them, so use your longbows after the first volley. If it comes to a close battle with blades, you know what to do. In order for this to work, we must be able to surprise them completely." The general paused for a moment. This part was going to make them unhappy. "When we get into our positions, I want you to camouflage yourselves. In this place, that means use the bodies. Bury yourselves under them, other than your crossbows, so they can be fired on a moments notice. Also, make sure you can get out from under the bodies quickly so you can fight whatever comes after the first volley."

The faces of the men were unreadable. They knew now what their commander asked of them, but there was no trace of emotion on their faces. It was just as well he couldn't see the revulsion that must be going on behind their eyes. "When we get situated, I'm going to douse the torch," Leland continued. "We will be totally enclosed in darkness and stench and cold. Are there any questions?"

"General," whispered the man to Leland's left, "if we do fire at something, in the blackness how will we be able to fight, or see to aim a long bow?"

"Good question, if we are in blackness, and I hear or shoot at something myself, I'll light a torch to see by. There won't be any surprise left after the initial attack. I'm hoping that we can wound or even kill whatever it is in the first volley. I'm hoping for time. We'll need it to get out from under the bodies, and ready to fight. I'll use it also to light the torch."

With another glance at their faces to make sure that there were no more questions, Leland lit a torch, and led the way into the tunnels. They were all steeling themselves for the horrors of the night to come. As they made their way downwards into the blackness, each wondered if they would see the light of day again.

When they finally reached the pit, the stench was nearly overpowering. General Leland took a last breath and entered the charnel house. The other three quickly followed. They could see just enough by the one torchlight to get into their positions. Leland pointed to each man in turn, and then to the general area where he wanted him to hide. Then he quickly placed himself. He set up the torches and striker where he could find them with his hands in total darkness. Then he watched as the others camouflaged themselves. He could tell by the iron set to their jaws, they would do what was required of them, but they would rather be anywhere else.

After making sure of his men's positions, he got into one himself. He nearly gagged when he pulled the stiff rotting corpse of an old, toothless woman on top of himself. He calmed his nerves with the fierce determination of having faced death many times before. He made sure of the position of the torches, and the set of the crossbow in one hand, then smothered the torch.

Cold blackness engulfed them. The urge to wretch came again, more powerful than ever before with the weight of the corpse on top of him, but he fought it back again. How long they would wait, he didn't know. He thought they might have to wait until someone came from the fort the next day to see if they were alive or not. He doubted that anyone would come looking for them. If they didn't return to the fort, they would be dead. He was going to wait until that happened or until they had some success.

Hours passed without anything at all happening. Sometimes Leland almost thought he could hear breathing from one of the other men, but there wasn't anything really there. They were all being absolutely silent. At other times the sound of his own heartbeat hammered so loudly in his ears, that he thought the walls would come down from the noise. Still there wasn't any sound at all that was made by him or any of the others.

His muscles began to ache. They cried out for movement. The corpse on top of him, and the stone underneath began to dig into his flesh. When he started his vigil, places where his bones lay on the floor, and where the bones of the corpse on top of him rested had merely been slightly uncomfortable. As the hours drug by, these points began to ache, and then to scream in agony to be relieved from the constant pressure. Yet he dared not move. The other men were feeling the same thing and they had been true. He wouldn't fail them.

The cold was a living thing altogether. It seeped into his bones like a thick fog. He fought the urge to shiver for what seemed like an eternity. The longer he lay there, the colder he got until it caused him to ache inside. Still he didn't move. He forced himself to listen more carefully for any sound however slight.

He strained to see anything in the infinite blackness that surrounded him. If there were anything, anything at all, he would see it. But there was nothing to see. At times he fought the urge to sleep. It didn't last long because of the discomfort, but it did come from time to time. He wouldn't yield to it any more than he would yield to any of his other discomforts. He would only get one shot at this, and he was not going to blow it.

It never occurred to the general to wonder where the rats were. There should have been thousands of the vermin, but there weren't any. Not here. Not in the charnel house this night.

After an indeterminate length of time, a light burst into the chamber. It was so bright that the men had to blink several times until they could focus on it. The general brought his weapon to bear slowly so as to not alert it to his presence, he wanted to see what they were facing a little more clearly. He hoped that the other men in the room would wait just a second to identify their target, but he knew he had to be ready to fire immediately if someone else did. They had to wait just a moment. They were seeing no more than a candle's illumination, but after the endless night, it was almost more than they could bear to look at. Then, just as their eyes were adjusting, they heard the voices.

"No rats tonight for the demon. I think he cleaned them all out."

It looked to General Leland as if a window had opened in the air above the center of the room. It floated in mid-air, and he finally could see a pair of dark robed wizards within it. Something else was in it as well. It looked vaguely human in shape, but it was heavily muscled, and greenish in color. It stood hunched over, but was still larger than the two dark-robes.

"Sorry Igelnisxus," a voice from the window said, "No rats tonight. I think they can smell you, they won't come around after you've been eating them." There was a low, guttural sound from the green behemoth. "Throw the body in, and we'll go back to the camp for another. You *would* like another to rip up tonight, wouldn't you?" A hiss of excitement escaped from between the things lips.

Leland watched as the demon picked up what was left of one of his troops, and lumbered to the portal's opening. As it lifted the body to hurl it through and onto the pile, all four crossbows fired at once. It screamed in agony as bolts pierced its eyes, neck and mouth. The thing thrashed around blindly, tripped, and fell through the window onto the pile of corpses, still holding the dead soldier.

"Close it," screamed one of the dark-robes as an arrow fired from a longbow flew through the opening in space and struck him in the chest. Immediately the pit was bathed in utter blackness. The window and light were both gone. The room was filled with the bellowing of the demon that was now trapped in the charnel house with them, and really pissed-off.

Leland fought to light the torch. The first two strikes of the flint merely flashed uselessly, but the third caught in the oil-soaked tinder around its head and began to flame brightly. The men were already surrounding the thing. It had fallen nearly on top of the pile, and rolled down to ward one of the men. It was swinging blindly about and screaming in panic. The man was already on his feet, and drawing his sword. The others had their bows notched and were maneuvering for a clear shot.

As the beast swung close to the swordsman, he swung his great, two-handed blade in a lightning arc that cleaved the demon's arm in two just below the elbow. The thing reared and screamed, only to have arrows thunder into it from several angles. It dove off the rotting pile of corpses, head down toward the man who had cut off its arm, not knowing for sure where he was, but knowing he was there somewhere.

Instead of ducking out of the way, the soldier stood his ground and pointed the tip of his sword straight at the things diving face. It was struck between the eyes. The sword tip drove downward through the head, missing the things brain, but lodging somewhere at the top of the throat. The demon had never known such pain. It thrashed uncontrollably throwing the soldier across the chamber, slamming him into the wall where he collapsed in a heap. More arrows found the thrashing monstrosity. It was defeated, and it knew it. It would soon be back in it's own dimension where it was just another of the minor beings. It hated the ones causing it so much agony, and wanted nothing more than to rend them with its bare hands as it had so many others. But it couldn't find them.

Slowly the thing began to loose its fight. It lumbered around chasing the pain of the latest arrow to strike it. They came from all directions now; it would attack one way only to feel the sting of an arrow from another. The dance went on for several minutes. The soldiers were breathing heavily now as they fired volley after volley into their foe. They were nearly out of arrows when the screaming pincushion with the sword still sticking out of its face faltered and collapsed onto the other bodies in the room. It lay there gasping for air, and struggling to remove the sword from its face. Finally it lay still.

The soldiers watched it as it slowly disintegrated into the smoke which hade made its form in this dimension. The sword and arrows dropped through it and soon there was nothing but a pile of weapons that had been imbedded in the thing. All other traces of it were gone.

The perfect murderer thought Leland. But they had all witnessed it. There were going to be heads rolling when word got back to Thosh. He remembered the man flung against the wall and rushed to him. He was still alive, only semi-conscious though. They lit up all of the remaining torches, and helped him get to his feet. With one soldier under each of the wounded man's arms and Leland bringing up the rear they made their way out of the mass grave into the tunnels above.

The air was immediately easier to breathe. Leland realized that he had forgotten about the stench in the heat of the battle, and now the air outside of the crypt smelled incredibly good. They were still in the tunnels, and there was still the trace of decomposing flesh in the musty air, but the difference was amazing. Even the wounded man started to breathe easier and come out of his daze. Before long he was taking steps by himself, and though the others never let go of him, by the time they reached the tower's entrance, he was able to carry most of his weight himself.

Leland was considering putting him in for a commendation. It had taken unbelievable courage not to duck the beast, but to stand there and drive home what had undoubtedly been the killing stroke. It had taken more than bravery. That kind of self-sacrifice was meant for companions. The fact that it hadn't killed him was merely a chance of luck. There would be recognition of some kind in the works, and soon.

It was still dark outside the tower. The general decided to remain there and wait for dawn so they wouldn't get shot approaching the fort in the night. There was one man already dead tonight. Those in the fort might not know about it yet, but then again they might. Anything could set off the guards, especially if they thought they were next. They were all safe enough for now, and even the wounded man was coming around. He would be sore the next couple of days, but he assured them that nothing was broken, only heavily bruised. They all agreed that it would be a lot safer to return to the fort after sunrise.

---

Zartho was furious. How had the commander figured out what was going on in the west. He had counted on the three wizards to get everyone out of the western area of the kingdom so they couldn't interfere on the night of the solstice. He had even built a copy of the traveler for them to use to move about undetected. There was no time to find and recruit another homicidal wizard and summon another demon. When the wizard had told him about the accident and the loss of the demon, he had thought that everything was going to come apart in the west. Then he realized that he could make this work for him.

He didn't need to get rid of everybody, no one would be able to stop the flow of demons once they had started, at least he didn't think so. He only needed the wizards to place the stone in the tower and he still had two there. All he had to do was make sure that they weren't found, and that they would do what was needed at the right time. Zartho knew that if he acted like all was forgiven, they were sure to give extra attention to the orders they received from now on. This could still work. The loss of one of the wizards didn't concern him at all. In fact, they were all going to be killed as soon as possible after the kingdom was his.

It was time to get ready now for the greatest summoning of all time. Whoever had made the symbiot, had truly been unwise never to use it. In fact he had decided that with it in his possession he would surely be able to control the demons he would bring over. It would be necessary to kill his three helpers before the casting of the pentagon. There was a spy among them, he was sure of it now. Everything pointed to it. He would let them think they were going through with the ceremony as planned, but he would kill them. Then he would complete his plans alone, and there wouldn't be anyone to stop him or try to steal the symbiot again.

# Chapter 16

Over a week had passed since the spy's last contact. Shial had expected some kind of report from him that would shed some more light on what was happening. The silence was driving him mad. If he were to judge by the last day or two, it seemed like there wasn't anything at all going on, at least not soon enough for Shial to have to worry about right now. The spy's last message had seemed too urgent, that things were going to begin immediately and they hadn't yet. There was a saying in the town among the fishermen's wives that, "no storm reports were good storm reports." The thought that something was going on would not leave him though. He knew that there might be a lot of things happening that he should know about. The spy might have been caught and killed before he could send a warning. Or he may not be able to send one for any number of reasons.

Shial felt secure in assuming that the spy was either dead or safe. If he had been captured, he would have been tortured. There were other ways of breaking someone's will and making them more talkative, magical means were quicker, and more effective than torture. But the dark-robes tended to use these more humane methods after the torture had given them everything they wanted. Then they would use magic to make sure they hadn't missed anything or been lied to. Usually the spells they chose were the most damaging ones too. There had never been evidence that they had done it, but the dark-robes were known for suspiciously not being around when the leftovers were found.

There was no doubt that something was brewing in the tower, but whether it was boiling now, or merely heating up, Shial didn't have a clue. He wished that the spy would make some kind of contact. Even a warning to get out fast would be better than the uncertainty of not knowing anything. He had spent whole weeks working the farm with only half of his mind on it.

The other half was tuned for even the slightest signal from the spy. Still nothing had come to him.

Even the unknown spy's fate was better to contemplate than to allow his mind to wander to the fate of his daughter. When he had sent her with Malak, he knew that she was going into danger. But there was no way he wanted her here to get caught by the dark-robes. If she fell into their hands, there would be no such thing as a quick death. Shial wouldn't allow himself to think about what the dark-robes would do to her if they got hold of her. No one would ever see her again, that was for sure. There would be no leftovers.

At least with Malak, he was sure that she had a chance of hiding. He had felt that night that things were going to go bad eventually, and now it was more likely than ever. The last report from the spy had worried him. The information about the demons had him worried about a second Wizard War. Dalryms had not liked it at all. The fact that the symbiot was now back in the hands of Zartho was cause for worry in itself. If Zartho wanted it back so bad he was willing to kill out in the open for it, then the danger was very real. It was surely too dangerous in Zartho's hands to wait for him to act. But there wasn't anything he could do until he knew what was coming, or at least until he had a vague idea of what was coming. The waiting game was turning his hair gray. He could almost feel it happening.

He would continue though, for as long as it took. There wasn't anything else to do. He could make a run for safety, but that would leave the spy alone, with no one he could report to, and no help if he needed it. No, Shial would not abandon his post. It had granted him the bliss of life outside of the world of magic while his daughter grew up.

Often times during the past years, he had wondered about the many people who lived near him. To them he was a simple farmer. To him, they lived an ideal life. They didn't know the horrors of magic, and the power games that went on, even in the white towers. They lived peacefully, tending to their affairs with no thought of power or manipulations. Theirs was a life of struggle yes, he had learned that first hand. But it was also a life of calm, and bliss.

He had, in his earlier life, had dreams of power himself. They had faded away slowly over the years. First, when he had married. Few wizards ever took the commitment of marriage on. But then again, no other woman had been like Terina. She had filled his world with light, when she died giving birth to Lena, he had thought his world was over.

Lena had filled him with new purpose though. One look at her, and he had found a far higher calling than that of magic. She had filled him with a joy that power never could. Just thinking of the years that had gone by made him choke up, filled his eyes with tears, and his head with an intense, dull pain that he had to make a conscious effort to release. Otherwise he would breakdown and weep. Now was not the time for that, later perhaps, but not now. Besides, she was with Malak.

The young man didn't know his own skill. He was the only one of the many assassins trained by the king to complete the final test. There wasn't supposed to be any way to complete the test. It was too hard. It had been designed that way to make sure that the assassin being tested knew that he was still mortal. Yes, they were dangerous men, but they were still just that, men. Except Malak had finished the test. It had almost killed him, but not knowing that he was supposed to fail, he had succeeded where no other ever had.

Lena was as safe as he could make her. Soon his life of exile from the towers would be over. He would soon have to go back to them, or he would be dead. Either way he was sad to leave behind the simple farming life that had helped him raise his daughter to the beautiful young woman that she was now. As he thought about his choice for her protector, he knew that he couldn't have hoped for one as good as Malak. If anyone could see her through this, he could. He wondered briefly where they were, and the tears started to creep back into his eyes.

Day after day he waited with his thoughts growing sometimes dark, and sometimes cheerful. He was always alert for the signal from the spy. And every night he tried to sleep as lightly as possible so that if it came, he would wake up. One of his greatest fears now was that the signal would come, and he would miss it. That could be disastrous. A wry chuckle escaped his lips as he thought of all the years spent watching the dark tower and waiting, only to miss the signal that could have saved the kingdom, and possibly the world.

Then one day, while he was milking the cows the signal came. It seemed to gently push into his mind from somewhere behind his eyes. He immediately went into the cabin, and bolted the door. The windows were shuttered just as quickly, and he went immediately to the chest in the corner. When the crystal was on its stand, and everything was ready, he answered the call.

Smoke curled lazily at first from the crystal. Then with increasing urgency and power until it coalesced into the hooded shape that Shial knew so well. He waited patiently while the form took its shape. Then it began to speak in its familiar whisper.

"Something is about to happen," it began. "I don't know what just yet, but Zartho has called another meeting. It has been a while since the last one. He has been strangely quiet. I know that he's up to something that we don't expect. The meeting will take place tonight. I don't have to remind you that tomorrow night is the summer solstice. I think that he means to act then. He has put a lot of effort into this. Be ready. I will contact you again after the meeting tonight if I learn anything more."

The image in the smoke broke up immediately after the last word, and Shial was left wondering what it all meant. Clearly tomorrow night would bring some kind of danger. Maybe the spy would learn what form that danger was going to take tonight. If they were lucky, it would be in time for them to take action. If not then all of this would have been for nothing. The spy had been in place for years, rising slowly in the ranks of the tower until he was finally in a place where he could be useful. It would be ironic if they finally found out where the danger was going to come from, only to have the information arrive too late to do anything about it.

He sent a quick signal to Dalryms and waited for his reply. He would pass the information of the meeting tonight to him, and wait for the spy to call again. What else was there to do now? He was still playing the waiting game. At least now he had a little more knowledge to aid his patience. With the contact from the spy, he didn't feel so alone anymore.

A few minutes after sending the signal to Dalryms, he felt the answering tug in his mind. He concentrated on the crystal, and the smoke again issued from within it. Slowly Dalryms familiar features appeared within the smoky coils.

"The man inside has finally made contact," he began his report. "There is a meeting tonight. He thinks it will be in preparation for something to occur on the solstice."

"That is tomorrow night!"

"Yes, Dalryms. "

"It doesn't give us much time to prepare. Did he give any indication at all as to what we can expect?"

"He doesn't know anything yet, but he will contact me again tonight, and hopefully he will know something then."

"This couldn't have come at a worst time," said Dalryms half to himself.

"What do you mean?"

"The army still hasn't returned from the west. In fact we haven't heard anything from them at all yet."

"Is general Leland still in charge of it?"

"Yes, and more importantly, he is still the soldier that he has always been. We can count on him to do his duty. But if there is an attack here on the king and the capital, what good can he do from so many leagues away."

Shial was silent for a minute. "Do not despair, old friend. Perhaps tonight will bring us some good news. I'll contact you the minute I know more."

The smoky image shifted and fell apart as it floated lazily up to the ceiling. Shial watched it move upwards wondering what the next few days would bring. Tonight he hoped he would finally find something out. He cleared the table, and re-locked the trunk. There was still a lot of daylight left, and there were a few mundane things left to do on the farm. If he were being watched, although he didn't think he was, it would be best to go about his normal routine as if nothing was happening. The thought occurred to him that in two days time the entire farm might not exist anymore. War could come quickly. When wizards were involved, they tended to come very quickly.

The daylight hours seemed to drag on and on. It seemed like the day was as long as, or longer than the month before. The chores were done long before sunset, and Shial took the time to do some maintenance around the old place. It was almost as if he were saying goodbye to the farm. It had been there to help raise his daughter, and had taken good care of them over the years. Perhaps nothing would happen to it. But, then again, anything might. He may even be recalled to the tower before all of this was over. It frustrated him that he still didn't really know anything at all.

---

Malak and Lena had been wandering in the mountains forever. At least that's how it seemed to Lena. They had been hiking up one mountain and down another for weeks on end with no sight of their goal. Malak wondered how much longer they would have to last. He had begun to wonder if there was anything at the end of the trail after all. To the best of his ability he had led them as close to the spot on the map as he could. It was now a matter of luck to see if they could find anything there.

They had been wandering from one peak to another in a circle for two days now. They were only hoping to get lucky and see something out of the ordinary. They had run out of food several times, and Malak had been forced to stop and fish in one of the streams that ran through the high country, or hunt bigger game. It had been tricky catching the fish by hand, but he had finally managed to get the hang of it. He had also had some luck with a couple snares overnight. They had enough food for their needs. Although the forest was in the heat of summer, the higher elevations were still cold, especially at night.

Malak and Lena had taken to sleeping close to each other to keep warm. One would sleep while the other watched. It had worked out pretty well. The only problem was that Lena would wake up if Malak moved away from her. Several nights he had wanted to scout around in the dark and see if there was something he was missing during the day. He had to admit to himself that he had an urge to run at night that he couldn't explain. It was almost like something was driving him during the dark hours. He didn't seem to need or even want sleep, but he took it anyway.

The schedule they had been forced to keep was taking its toll on Lena. She had held up well for a long time now with only half as much sleep as she should be getting. Malak knew that she would soon get sick if they didn't start taking it a little easier. If they could just find whatever it was they were looking for, they might be able to relax a bit. If the coming solstice passed uneventfully, they could continue the search for a couple more months, even longer if need be before they would have to leave the higher mountains or risk getting caught in the first snows of winter.

If they got snowed in, they would probably freeze or starve before they could get to safer country. During his training years he had studied how to survive in the winter outside the safety of civilization. There were a couple of rules that had to be followed though, and he doubted that they would survive without a lot more preparation.

This day had gone like the one before, up and down without any sight of anything that shouldn't be in the mountains. Or, for that matter, any sight of something that should be in the mountains but not as it should be. If there was something up here, it was well hidden.

During dinner that night Malak had an idea.

"Lena," he said as she was picking the last of the meat off a rabbit. "I want to spend the night on top of the peak behind us." They had climbed to the top earlier in the day to see the country around them. When the sun had begun to set, they had hiked back down a ways to find shelter from the wind and bitterest cold.

Lena looked at him for a moment. She was tired from the day's hiking, and all she wanted to do was curl up in a ball and sleep before her turn at watch.

"How cold will it be up there?" she asked, knowing that she wouldn't like the answer.

"Colder than it will be down here in the cover of the trees. But we might be able to see something."

"Like what?" she asked before she could stop herself.

He didn't know, and he merely shrugged.

"Like something we won't be able to see hiding down in the trees. You don't have to come. You can stay by the fire. Just keep it small."

Lena thought about it for a minute. She knew there was no way Malak would allow a fire up on top of the peak. She also knew that the wind would be terrible up there. She didn't think she would be able to sleep down in the trees alone though.

"I'll go up there with you, but I get a shorter watch."

"I'll do you one better, I'll give you my cloak, and I'll take both watches tonight." He hadn't wanted her down in the forest alone. The last thing they needed was to become separated somehow. He could track her, that was true, but why go through the effort if they could just stay together.

"But you'll be useless tomorrow," said Lena decisively. "No way, you'll get sick."

"Then how about this, I'll keep my cloak, but take both watches. If we don't see anything we'll spend tomorrow here in camp resting, and then we'll figure out what to do."

"Alright," agreed Lena. She couldn't believe he was offering a days rest. Malak had always had great stamina, but the past several weeks he had seemed to never tire much at all. He would breathe harder when he was exerting himself, but he didn't seem to notice the strain. There were times when she doubted that she would be able to keep up with him. At those times, he had slowed down, but it wasn't from fatigue or exhaustion in himself, it was for her.

Quickly they packed their meager belongings and doused the small fire. Lena regretted her decision as soon as they started back up the steep climb to the top. It took nearly an hour to get where Malak wanted to be. By the time he did, the wind was whipping over the exposed peak. Lena bundled up tighter in her thin coverings, and tried to get comfortable on the ground. It was hard and cold, just like all the other ground she had slept on since stowing away in Malak's small boat. Had that night ever really happened? It seemed like a lifetime ago to her.

Malak knew that Lena would sleep. He couldn't leave her to scout around, but he could see for miles in every direction. It wouldn't be long, he thought, if something was going to happen, he thought it would happen earlier in the night rather than later. In the end, he had to confess to himself that he was wrong about that.

After several hours, Malak had to admit that they might just be wasting their time and effort. Like chasing a headless chicken. It was dangerous and unpredictable work that, in the end, would prove just about useless. Dangerous because of where the thing might lead you. Dangerous because you had to focus too closely on the thing and you couldn't see what was happening around you. Unpredictable, because you never knew where it would lead you next, and what it would do on the spur of the moment. One of the exercises they had to do as trainees was

275

to catch a chicken. The masters said it would quicken their legs. After they had mastered the chicken, they had to catch one without its head, in a room piled high with junk that was laid and piled up to form thousands of traps just waiting to maim or kill. More than one trainee's career had ended in that room.

He stood in the cold wind looking in every direction and listening. The wind howled around him so that all he could hear was its mournful howl. He thought about nothing for a long while, only the wind kept company with him this night.

Then a tiny spark of light flared in the corner of his vision. Malak jerked his head around to look at the top of another peak. It wasn't far off, about two peaks away. It was one of exceptional height. In fact, it was probably the highest in the area. As he stared at the top of the peak, another flash shot out into the night. This flash was stronger, and lasted for nearly two heartbeats. Again the light went out, but this time he was sure he had seen it.

Malak squatted reflexively to hide himself. He suddenly felt exposed and vulnerable on the top of the peak. Once more the light flared, then seemed to stabilize for a second. A single intense beam shot out of the peak towards the northeast. It ran straight and true into the distant horizon. Then, to his astonishment, another beam of light appeared from the tip of the mountain. This new line ran more northward than the original, almost, but not quite, due north. In fact the two lines formed a very narrow angle with the peak as a point of origin. That was what they had been searching for, he was sure of it.

Without thinking of her comfort, Malak reached down and shook Lena awake. She opened her eyes slowly and started to mumble something when she saw the lines in the sky and sat bolt upright. They lasted for only a few more seconds, but it was long enough for Lena to believe that she hadn't just imagined part of a dream. Then they both disappeared as if a curtain had been drawn across a stage.

"That peak," said Malak in a hoarse whisper, "is where we are going tomorrow.

"I knew you were going to say that," said Lena still wondering what exactly it was they had seen.

Malak motioned for Lena to follow him, and they moved off the peak a few yards to shield themselves from most of the wind. Lena thought it was strange that Malak was going to sleep.

"Don't you have the rest of the watch tonight?" she asked.

"We don't need a watch tonight. We know where they are, and they don't know that we're here."

"How do you figure that?"

"Well, whoever just lit up the night wouldn't have done it if they knew we were here to see it, and they are doubtless planning something besides just lighting the sky. They are up to something, and they are going to be busy getting ready to do it."

"You don't think all of this is to make the sky pretty?"

"No, I don't," said Malak refusing to compliment her sarcastic tone.

"Dark robes have gone to a lot of trouble to set this up, and they aren't known for their sense of ambiance. I feel like there is something bad happening here, and I want to stop it if I can. What happened tonight looked like they were testing themselves. They're getting ready to do a lot more than put some red lines in the sky, but that is definitely part of it. We'll both need as much sleep as we can get tonight." He looked at Lena almost apologetically. "Tomorrow is going to be a long day."

Lena watched him roll over and go to sleep. *It may be our last day too,* she thought. *You didn't say it, but you thought it.* And she too rolled into her blanket and went to sleep. The ghosts of those bright lines were still etched across her retinas.

Zartho stood before the trio. He had told them to be in his quarters an hour after lights-out. They had all been there as ordered. He had excused himself for several hours, and left them to wonder about his activities. Surely the spy would be sweating it out by now. He wouldn't tell them everything yet. The test had gone perfectly. The ship was on station exactly where it should be. The spells to lift it had worked and the pentagon inside the pentagram had formed exactly as planned. He had made sure that his three confederates had been in his quarters when the beams had appeared in the sky so they wouldn't suspect anything about what was really going to happen. Tomorrow night at this time, there would be a lot of trouble for the king, and the white-robes. The next night should see him as the supreme ruler in the kingdom. There wasn't anything to stop him now.

The trio knew instinctively that Zartho was happy about something. He could tell that they knew, and he decided that keeping them entirely in the dark for his pleasure would serve no real purpose. No there would be no point in telling them anything really useful. He had decided, after all that they wouldn't be around to share his power. But there was still the spy. He wanted to find out who it was. There was a special death waiting for him! Now, if he could just get the spy to reveal himself. Then he could finish planning his end.

"The time is finally here," he announced to the three. "I have just finished the testing of the final spells. Our destiny is upon us at last." He paused a moment for effect.

"What are we to do?" asked Lorban.

"The night after tomorrow will see us in charge of the kingdom. No one will dare oppose us."

"Be careful," warned Golan, "If any one hears this we will be executed for treason."

"I don't care if the king himself is listening now," growled Zartho. "There isn't anything they can do before tomorrow night. I have all but won the crown now. And you three, of course have just about won the prize I promised."

The three remained motionless. They knew that they were to receive command of part of the kingdom for their direct control. Each knew which they wanted, and unfortunately it was all the same part. They had all been trying to win the best part of the kingdom for themselves since Zartho had confided to them what the statue did. Of course, Zartho would be over them in command, but they would be directly in control.

"We must keep this all a secret from those within this tower though. They are the only ones who can stop us now."

They were still in the dark regarding most of what had been set up by Zartho over the past year. He hadn't told them until recently anything about what the statue did, only that it was the key to some great power. They had helped him create the crystals and the spells to cast the light beams that would create the huge pentagon within a pentagram, not knowing what the beam of light was truly for. They had invented and experimented until they could raise a ship and hold it in a specific position in the air on Zartho's demand because he said they would need it for their navy when they were in power. The other spells to open portals had been done in pieces without any seeming continuity. Despite all of their help, there was no way they could have conceived the true magnitude of the portal that he was creating. Others he had working throughout the kingdom at the different locations would also help create the portal. They had also believed his lies and half-truths about their role and purpose. All of the pieces were coming together now. And the thing that made Zartho want to laugh the most was that none of the pieces knew anything about any of the others.

" Tomorrow night we will finally be done with it. Get what rest you can with the rest of this night, tomorrow night we will meet here an hour after lights-out. There will probably be some resistance from a few of the wizards in this tower, but we will deal with that quickly. They won't be any challenge for the four of us. After we start the final spell casting, most of the kingdom will know that something is going on. That is when we will find out who will try to oppose us, and must be destroyed. That is when you three will need to be at your best, and toughest. When it comes time to fight, there must be no hesitation. Those who will challenge us must be dealt with instantly, and permanently. Can you do this?"

"Yes, Zartho," spoke Golan. All three of them were nodding their heads.

"We look forward to completing our goals with you," said Harnthiston. "There isn't anyone that will be allowed to stand in our way."

"We will be ready," said Lorban, "there won't be anything we can't handle."

"Excellent," said Zartho smiling. "That is what I needed to hear. Now I know that I have the right three to rule with me when all of this is done." He appeared thoughtful for a moment. "Go now, the hour is late and you all need to sleep before the final battle tomorrow night."

They left quickly. If anyone had observed them leaving, they would have shuddered at the tyrannical smirks that each wore. The only one not smiling was Zartho. He waited until they had all left and the door to his chambers was locked before the grin was allowed to cross his face, and then it was a maniacal leer. All three of them would be dead before he cast the final spell tomorrow night. And it wouldn't take much effort on his part. In fact, the more he thought about it, the more he realized that he wouldn't need to do much more than put the proper words in the proper ears. They had duties and responsibilities that would hound them most of the day. That would keep them from any rest. He, on the other hand, would sleep most of the day away.

As he retired to his bed, he paused long enough to take a bottle from his laboratory and set it on his desk. By adding a drop to their meal tomorrow evening, they would be especially weakened. Then the others who would do his dirty work for him would have quick work of it. He suddenly wasn't worried about the spy any more. Better to have him done away with entirely than risk something going wrong for the sake of revenge. He lay down on his bed knowing that the next time he laid down he would be ruler of the entire kingdom. That thought brought another smile to his lips, the second one today. In fact, it very well may have been the second one this month.

---

The spy returned to his quarters before he let the leer; mimicking his fellow conspirators, slip from his features. They were about to do something horrific, and he knew it. Hadn't he already helped them to do murderous things? They had committed acts of piracy, torture and murder in addition to developing spells that didn't make sense. Why would you want to float a ship in the air? Why would you want to make a beam of light, when it could be interrupted so easily? Did it somehow work with the crystals to control the demons? Where was the doorway going to open? Why would there be a reason to copy the Traveller, if these demons could fly? Why the other spells that he had helped to create? And why were there so many secrecy spells around various parts of the tower? He was pretty sure that he and the other two weren't the only group of Zartho's helpers. That, thought alone was enough to make him afraid of what the next day would bring.

Stealing the statue had been incredibly dangerous. He had no way of knowing how many other wizards knew about it. He had hoped that he could hide inside the group of three and not be caught. It had worked so far, but tomorrow all of that would change. If Zartho had other people working for him too, then what reward had he promised them? Would any of them actually live to collect a reward? It seemed suddenly that Zartho would enjoy ruling the kingdom a lot more if there were fewer wizards to threaten his power. It also seemed that they really hadn't been told any specifics of what was about to happen. He only knew the time it would happen, if Zartho hadn't lied about that too.

It was time to contact Shial and let him know that whatever was going to happen, it was coming soon.

---

By the time Shial had finished his brief exchange with the spy, it was clear that tomorrow night was going to be a bad one. He had immediately signaled Dalryms, and let him know of the situation. A while later, he had been awakened by a mental push from Dalryms. It took a couple of minutes to set up the crystal and make contact. Daylight was only about an hour away now.

"Our best defense against the dark robes is that they don't trust each other, and so they fight amongst themselves. Is there anything the spy can do to help them?" asked Dalryms.

"We could have him try and leak the information out that something was going on, but we don't know if anyone would be interested until things actually start happening. By then it may be too late to stop Zartho. I'm sure he is going to try and sabotage the nights activities, but since he isn't sure exactly what is going to happen, he might not be too successful."

The shade of Dalryms was silent for a moment, "I will appeal to the king once more to try and find out what is going on. I still think that someone in the dark tower here knows something about this. Or at least they are helping Zartho without knowing what they are really doing. A couple of hours ago, one of our lookouts reported that something happened at the dark tower. He said that a couple of small beams of light shot out of the tower."

"Was one of them pointing to the tower here?"

"Not according to the man who saw them. He said one of them went southwest, and the other nearly due south."

"Did he see anything else?"

"He did mention one other thing, he said he thought he saw another beam of light, very dim, running east to west. It was far off in the southern sky between the other two."

"I have been inside all night, so I didn't notice anything. How long were they in the sky?"

"Only for a moment. The guard said he sounded the alert, but before anyone could come and verify what he was seeing, they all disappeared."

"What do you think it was?" asked Shial.

"I don't know. There really isn't anything to fear from a light in the sky."

"I don't think we've seen the last of that light."

"What do you mean?" asked the smoky head hovering above the stone.

"Well, I think that what was seen tonight was a test of some kind, or a precursor to something bigger. If the real danger is going to come tomorrow night, then tonight must have been some kind of dress-rehearsal for it."

"I think you're right, Shial. I don't know what is happening, but I'll talk to the king again in the morning, and see if there isn't anything we can do to stop them."

"I'll keep an eye on the tower here, and also try to help our man on the inside if there's any way I can."

"Listen for a signal from me," instructed Dalryms' shade. "I will let you know if there is any success with the king." The form began to dissolve before the last of the words were spoken.

Shial quickly put the stone and its stand away, and headed for bed. If there was going to be a time to sleep, it was now. There would be no napping tomorrow, for surely Dalryms would contact the king as early in the morning as he could. Sometime later in the day the signal to contact Dalryms would come again, but he didn't know when. He also had to listen for any signal from the spy. There wouldn't be any chance at all for sleep tomorrow night.

He lay in bed for many long minutes before he finally managed to drift off. Once asleep his dreams were filled with frightening images that never fully took shape. He ran in fear through darkened dreamscapes never fully knowing what was chasing him, and never able to turn and face them.

# Chapter 17

Malak awoke just before the sun crested the mountains to the east. Lena was still sleeping, and he woke her with a gentle shake. She opened one bleary, tired eye and aimed it at Malak for a moment before closing it again, and rolling over.

"C'mon sleepy," Malak said teasing her. He was in a good mood. Today they had a specific goal to achieve, not just wandering aimlessly about the mountains. They could actually make something happen today. "Pack up your bed. We'll have some breakfast and leave in about an hour. I want to get to that peak as quickly as we can, so that we can scout it a little before darkness."

"Why don't we pretend that we did," replied Lena without opening her eyes, or lifting her head. "We could pretend that we hiked all day towards our doom, and instead we could just stay right here."

"Up!" said Malak rolling her shoulder back and forth to disturb her relaxation. "You know it won't be any fun having dark-robes trying to kill me without you there."

"Yeah," moaned Lena sitting up. "I need to be there to cheer them on."

"Funny."

"It will be to them."

"Well we shouldn't keep them waiting then, should we?"

"It would be terribly rude of us," Lena laughed shaking the last wisps of sleep from her head.

"Just think," Malak said trying to sound encouraging, "if all goes well today, we might be heading home at this time tomorrow."

"Now *that*, I'd enjoy waking up to."

They packed their things quickly and began their march. They took one last bearing on their target peak, and headed down the mountain. Once they were back under the cover of the forest trees, they stopped and ate their meager breakfast. They would be out of food by noon today. Again, they would have to hunt and gather things to eat. Malak thought it wasn't going to be a problem until tomorrow. They didn't have time today, and if they died tonight, they wouldn't have to worry about it at all. Besides, if they survived the night, they might be able to steal something to eat from the dark-robes.

After they had finished their small meal, they again headed for the not so distant peak. Malak lead them through the forest along the less used trails. The last thing he wanted right now was to stumble into a trap of some kind. He didn't know for sure that there were dark robes ahead, but he figured it would be safe to assume that there were probably several.

"It seems like we're taking the scenic route today," commented Lena when she noticed them taking about the third side trail. "I thought you wanted to get there early to scout around a bit."

"I do want to get there early, but if there are any traps around the peak, we don't want to set them off."

"You think they would set traps? Here in the woods?"

"If it was me, I would want to know about intruders as soon as I could. Yes, I think there could be traps around us."

At this remark Lena stopped. She looked around carefully, and then asked, "What do they look like?"

Malak just caught the sarcasm in her voice. He decided that he had to explain a little more to her than he had. If she could use her eyes too, they would stand a better chance of getting to the peak alive.

"Lena, please be more serious. We can't risk just walking up the main trails onto the peak. The dark-robes must be watching them like a hawk. We have to try and find a back way in. Remember when we used to play in the snow?"

"Yes," said Lena. She remembered the last couple of winters when Malak had come to visit for a few of days. They had made forts in the snow with Shial, and then tried to attack each other with snowballs. The object of the game had been to try and take over the other person's fort. Malak had often caught her from where she least expected it. On the other hand, when she had tried to attack him, he always seemed to be ready for her.

"It's the same game here. We want to get to them without them knowing that we're coming. The best way to do that is to come from somewhere that they don't expect anyone to come from."

"Oh, of course," said Lena still thinking that the game analogy was a bit trite for what they were actually facing. "Why don't we skip the trail altogether?"

"That would be really slow," said Malak. "We would be too late, and even if we could move quietly through the underbrush, we would flush every animal around. They can't help knowing we're coming if the deer start running from us."

"But what if they have traps on all of the trails?"

"Good point. When we get close we will have to get off the trails. Until then keep a sharp eye for anything out of the ordinary."

"But won't we flush animals near them?"

"I'm hoping that the animals like dark-robes as much as we do. If so, the area around the peak should be clear of most of the wildlife." Malak knew he could be wrong. If the dark-robes had been there a long enough time without disturbing the surrounding forest, the animals would have learned to ignore them for the most part. But if they were new to the forest, or if they were actively hunting the animals, then the area wouldn't have anything more than the occasional squirrel.

"Now," continued Malak, "If we can be really quiet, we might be able to pass unnoticed through this area."

Lena took the hint well. She stuck her tongue out at the back of Malak's head.

For the next couple of hours, they moved silently through the woods. After traversing their way around the base of peaks that they weren't interested in, they finally arrived at their goal. They ate the last of their dried meat, and rested before beginning the climb up and out of the forest.

They hadn't gone far when Malak held his hand up signaling Lena to stop where she was. She had been watching the forest around her trying to see anything out of the ordinary, and just happened to see him signal. Otherwise she would have walked straight into the back of him. He pointed at the ground in front of them. At first, there wasn't anything to see. But then she noticed that there was a thread stretched across the trail in front of them.

It wouldn't have taken much to miss the thread. Malak had just happened to notice it in time. He carefully stepped over it and traced it to the side of the trail. There, hidden under some leaves, was a thin stick with
several sharpened barbs attached to it. They were covered in some kind of sticky black stuff that Lena had never seen before.

Malak motioned her forward. She gingerly stepped over the thread too.

"Poison," was all Malak said pointing to the black substance on the barbs.

They continued their trek up the mountainside. Every now and then Malak would stop and look around very carefully. He would listen for even the slightest sounds in the forest around them. He was in his element here. Tracking his target with the stealth of a hunter, he moved along the forest paths. Working his way higher and higher, he moved like some kind of feral animal. Even sniffing the air for any scent that would betray an enemy. He was aware of Lena behind him, and kept his speed slower than normal to let her move silently with him. Normally, he would have moved about as fast as they were now, but lately he had been able—almost driven—to move faster. He knew that it might have something to do with the thing in the swamps, and what had passed between them. He just knew that he could have moved along the paths faster than he was now. The biggest problem was the crisp dead leaves that seemed to be everywhere. Most of the trees were evergreens, but there was scrub brush all along their path that had shed its leaves and they had to move like they were walking on needles sometimes. Oftentimes the slightest misstep could have given them away. Something was nagging at the back of Malak's mind, but he couldn't put his finger on it. There was something that he should know or realize, but he couldn't force it from his brain. The more he tried to pin it down, the more it eluded him. These things usually either went away, or became blatantly obvious at the worst possible times, and then you were in real trouble.

Suddenly Malak held up his hand to stop. Lena froze in her tracks. His body was rigid, and his eyes scanned carefully ahead without his head moving. The muscles along the back of his neck flexed a little as he tried vainly to extend his ears to hear more. Lena stood motionless holding her breath so that there would be absolutely no noise. Finally, after several minutes, Malak waved Lena forward to him.

"Look ahead," he whispered in her ear. He waited for almost a minute for her to take in the sight before her. Then he asked, "What do you see?"

Lena looked at the trail before them. It looked just like the rest of the trails that they had been following since starting up the mountain. There were a couple of spider webs across it, but other than that she could see nothing out of the ordinary. The ground in front of them was covered in the dead leaves of autumns past, and they would probably make noise going through it. Was that what Malak wanted her to see? If so, she thought they could get through it without making too much noise. They hadn't seen any evidence of people other than the traps that they had dodged.

"All I see are those leaves that we have to cross over," she finally answered.

"See the little stick poking out from under the closest leaves?"

"Yes," she had seen it, but thought nothing of it.

"That tells me there isn't any ground under those leaves. It also tells me that there is probably some sharp pointy sticks at the

289

bottom of the hole under those leaves. See those branches that sweep back away from the trail?"

Lena looked closer at the trunks of the trees that stood to either side of the trail. There were a several branches that sprouted from the trunk toward the trail, then bent sharply back behind the tree. "Yes," she whispered finally.

"There are several more going up the trail, and off into the forest to either side of us. We must be getting close to something. I haven't seen this many traps all in the same place before. I think they are watching this area really closely."

"Why do you think that? Maybe they just set a lot of traps and forgot about them?"

"Lena, I haven't seen anything larger than a squirrel on this peak. I haven't even seen any tracks or other signs of anything bigger than a mouse. They are checking these trails daily, and wiping their tracks as they go."

"Malak, if they were checking these trails daily, we would have seen them by now, wouldn't we?"

"Not if they check them at night. Now aren't you glad we waited until daylight to try this?"

Lena rolled her eyes at the thought of trying to move through the traps in the dark. Malak had pretty good eyes in the nighttime, but she didn't think they were that good.

Malak continued, all the while watching the forest, "I think we should backtrack and try another way. We may have to leave the trails altogether now, but we'll make a lot of noise through the dead leaves and underbrush. There should have been a lot more leaves on these trails, now that I think about it." His subconscious mind finally gave up its secret. The missing leaves seemed to scream at him. The trails were void of them in many places. They were, with a few spot exceptions, almost swept clean. For the trails to be as clean as they were, there should have been hundreds of animals using them, but there weren't any.

They needed to get off the trails as soon as they could. He knew they may have already been detected.

"Lena, do you know any spell that can detect magical traps?" he asked in a hoarse whisper.

"Only one. But I also know one that detects magic generally."

"I know one for traps too. Let's back out of here, and see if we can find a safer way in. We'll have to get off the trails soon. First, check and see if there are any magical traps we need to be aware of."

Lena closed her eyes, and muttered the words of the spell under her breath. When she opened her eyes again, the forest around and behind her looked normal, but there were several areas ahead of her that seemed to glow with various colors.

"There aren't any that I can see behind us, or to the sides of us, but there are a lot ahead of us," she told Malak in a whisper. "There are different kinds, too. I don't know all of what I'm seeing, but the trail is really scary."

"Alright, let's go back a ways and then get off the trails."

They headed back the way they had come. At the previous fork in the trail, Malak told Lena to stay there for a minute while he scouted ahead. When he got back, the scowl on his face told her enough of what he had found.

"There isn't a way through here either," he began. "I think that they might have traps on all the trails from here up to the top. We'll have to get up by our own way." With that, he stepped cautiously off the trail. As he stepped tenderly through the leaves trying to make as little noise as possible he began his own spell to detect traps. Lena followed behind him softly rustling the ground as she went.

They climbed for a couple more hours. Several times they had to turn back because of the magical traps as well as the occasional mundane ones. They worked their way around the peak slowly. Trying to blend into the forest around them. They just couldn't get to the timberline. Hours passed without seeming to make any real progress up the mountain. Finally, Malak held up his hand to signal a stop.

He again was alert. Lena thought he had come to another batch of traps. The entire time he had been using his own spell to detect magical traps, and avoid them. Now he couldn't tell anything anymore. The spell had failed him. Like a muscle that was worked to failure, the spell had taken more and more effort to maintain. It had been less and less effective too. The colored areas in his vision had grown fainter and fainter, less and less clear, until they had disappeared entirely. He hadn't seen any in the past few minutes, and he realized the spell had left him completely. It would be a couple of days before he could cast it again, and then it wouldn't be very strong, at least it didn't hurt like every other time he had cast it. What he needed now was time. It would be a month before he could cast it again with the same power.

"Lena," he whispered. It was the first communication between them in several hours. "I can't see the traps anymore. The spell's gone. I'm burned out."

"I can look for a while," Lena volunteered. She realized suddenly that Malak had just told her at least part of his price for using magic. He was a burner. While Lena had to sleep to recharge herself, Malak wouldn't be able to use magic again for a long time indeed, at least not that particular spell. When he said he was "burned out," he was saying it would be weeks or months before he could cast this, and perhaps any other spell again. No wonder he had never been taught much.

"That's not the only problem," Malak continued. "I'm beginning to wonder if there is a way to the top at all."

"What do you mean?"

"Every time we start to get close to the timberline there is a veritable wall of traps. They are layered up the mountain for a hundred yards or more. Even if we could get past the timberline, we would be in open country. Anyone watching from the top of the mountain would see us in an instant. Even if there aren't any traps on the face of the peak, we would be easy targets."

"We aren't giving up are we?" asked Lena.

"Let's think a minute or two. You said you knew a spell that would detect magic in general, right?"

"Yes, that's true."

"I think I've been looking for the wrong thing."

"What do you mean?"

"Well, the dark-robes have to get down to maintain the trails somehow. I can't see them nightly destroying the magical traps and resetting them. They have to have a different way down here, unless they can fly."

"I've never heard of a wizard that could fly."

"Neither have I," said Malak nodding agreement. "So there must be a hidden way in. I've been looking for things that block our path. Can you look for paths that we can't see?"

"Malak, I can do that, but how long will I have to do it for? I mean, I get tired and go to sleep when I cast a spell too long, but it doesn't burn out of me like you."

"I know that," whispered Malak. He didn't admit that there were other problems with his spell casting too. That was a discussion he hoped he would never have with her. "But I can't see any other way to get up to the top. We're loosing the daylight."

"I'll try it. What am I looking for?"

"Anything magical that doesn't look like a trap."

She knew that it would be days or even weeks before the spell could be cast again. Her own price was more profound in the short term, but as soon as she woke up she could cast it again. In the end, she thought Malak paid the higher price for the use of the magic. She had no idea how right she was about that.

Lena took the lead, with Malak close behind. He kept a close watch on the area ahead looking for mundane traps that were just as deadly as the magical ones. He hadn't seen any except for on the trails. But he knew it would only take one to kill them. If Lena was watching the magic in the area, she was more likely to miss a pitfall than ever before. He, on the other hand had set hundreds of similar traps, and knew what to look for. While there were as many ways to set snares and pitfalls as there were people setting them, there was a pattern to them, and you could see them if you knew what to look for.

Lena muttered her spell, wondering how long she could keep it up. After about ten minutes of walking and seeing nothing but traps, she noticed a bush about fifty feet down the mountain from them that seemed to glow in a pleasant, soothing color. It didn't seem to her as if the spell was cast on the bush, but that it was the bush itself. She pointed it out to Malak, and they made their way down to it.

"Is this what you were looking for?"

"I don't know," admitted Malak looking at the bush. It seemed like every other one on the mountain. "What does it look like to you?"

"It looks like it's made of magic. Not like there is magic all over it, but like it is pure magical energy."

"What do you think we should do?"

"I think we will have to touch it."

"Are you out of your mind?" asked Malak whispering angrily. "There are thousands of nasty traps on this mountain, any or all of which would kill us, and you want me to touch something that is definitely magical?"

"No," said Lena patiently. "I'm going to touch it."

"The hell you are," said Malak without thinking. "What would Shial do to you if he knew you were trying a stunt like this? Not to mention what he will do to me when he finds out I let you try it."

"Listen Malak, if I'm right, and nothing happens, then we may have found a way to the top. If I'm wrong, and I get torn to pieces, then you can still get out of here. On the other hand, I wouldn't stand a chance of getting past all of the traps on the mountainside. I've watched you find them all day and I still didn't see most of them as I walked past them."

Malak knew that she was right. There wasn't anything he could do. If either of them was going to have a chance of getting out alive, let alone stopping the dark-robes, then she would have to take the first step. It galled him to think he might have to explain this to Shial. He felt something different when he thought about what might happen to Lena, but he didn't have a label for the feeling. Only part of this feeling was worry. The rest of it was painful. He didn't like it at all.

"Alright, you go first," he finally said. "Do me a favor though, try a stick first, just in case."

"Good idea," said Lena. She looked around for a suitable stick, and picked it up. Very gingerly she pushed at one of the branches of the bush. It moved as any normal bush would, and Malak wondered if Lena was really seeing what she said she was. He had to trust her. She swung at the bush harder. The stick slapped through the leaves looking and sounding like any other bush would. She shrugged her shoulders and looked at Malak.

"Oh, all right," he said exasperated. "Go ahead and touch it."

Lena dropped the stick and tentatively reached out her hand. It passed through the branches of the bush as if there wasn't anything there at all. Malak and Lena stared at each other for a moment in surprise. Malak spoke first.

"Do that again."

Lena reach out a second time and again her hand passed through the bush as if passing through air. Not a single leaf moved; there wasn't a sound.

"What now?" she asked Malak.

"Hold onto my hand, and step into the bush."

Lena took his hand, closed her eyes and stepped forward purposefully, into empty space.

Malak gasped out a breath as Lena disappeared, and his arm was yanked to the ground.

"Aaiiight!" she cried out in surprise. "Don't let go!"

Malak could hear her rapid breathing, and felt her entire weight swinging from his arm. His hand had slipped a little when she had unexpectedly fallen out of sight. He tightened his grip and heard a gasp of pain.

"Not so tight!" Lena gasped. "You're crushing my hand."

Malak didn't squeeze any harder, but he also didn't relax a bit. Lena could see that she was in a cave. It was a sheer drop straight down into the darkness. When she looked up, she could see Malak holding onto her. He was kneeling on the edge of the pit she had fallen into. He started to raise her up when she noticed the metal rungs driven into the side of the shaft.

"Wait," she said. "There's a ladder here."

Malak couldn't see Lena or anything of his own arm from just below his shoulder. It looked as if it had been cut off at ground level. He felt her moving around a little, and then her weight eased off of his arm.

"It looks safe enough," said a voice from under the base of the bush. "Put your foot over here." Lena's hand appeared out of the ground, like some nightmarish corpse rising from the grave.

Malak turned around and put his ankle into Lena's hand. He watched amazed as first his foot and then his leg disappeared into the ground. He swung his other leg into the hole that he couldn't see, and felt around with his feet until they were both on a thin support. Then, feeling his way down, he moved to the next rung on the ladder. Carefully he worked himself over the edge and down into the invisible hole within the bush. When his eyes dropped below the ground, he could finally see the rim of the hole, and the ladder that he was now standing on. The hole descended into darkness that concealed its true depth. Lena was a little ways below him, working her way down the ladder.

"Be careful," Malak said. "Some of these rungs could be loose, or magically rigged somehow."

Lena looked up at him with a worried look. "Now I wish you were going first." She hesitated looking down, and then began her descent again. Malak followed carefully checking each rung before he put his weight on it. The going was slow, and the darkness became nearly absolute around them. He could only see a very dim point of light over their heads when he heard Lena say she was at the bottom.

"Stay next to the Ladder until we can make a light of some kind," he said to her speeding up a little. "There could be more holes to fall into."

Malak struck a small piece of tinder and blew on it until it flamed briefly. In the small light, they could see torches set on the wall near them. Malak took one, and with the remaining bit of fire from the tinder, he managed to get it to light.

There wasn't much to see, there was only one tunnel leading into the mountain and gradually sloping upwards. It seemed to Malak that they would be in a lot of trouble if they were caught in its narrow confines. There was nowhere for them to hide now. They would surely be seen by anyone looking, and that meant they would probably die. The dark-robes that were surely down here, had been good at laying traps.

"Are there any traps?" he asked Lena.

"Not that I can see," she replied a little sleepily.

"Let go of the spell," said Malak not wanting her to fall into a comatose sleep. This wasn't the time or place for resting.

"I'm alright, I think we should hurry though."

"I think you're right. But let's try to be as quiet as we can."

They started off walking side by side. Every so often Lena would check to see if there were any traps ahead. There never were, but she felt safer trying. There was always the chance that there was something hidden beyond her abilities to detect. But there wasn't anything she could do about that. They continued up the tunnel at a fast pace. Finally they stepped into larger chamber. It served as an intersection for several tunnels. Five dark openings stared silently back at them. Malak immediately scraped a mark on the left of the tunnel that they had just exited. It was a small mark, and hard to see if you weren't looking for it.

"Well, which way do we go now?" asked Lena slightly out of breath from their run up the tunnel.

"Look at each opening, and see if there is one that looks more used than the others."

"Like what?"

"Like one with more soot on the ceiling than the others. Or, maybe more wear on the floor than the others."

The two of them looked closely at each of the tunnels, but could find nothing different to speak of. They all appeared old. The tops of the tunnels were thickly coated with soot as if from years of torches passing underneath. Malak wondered how long the tunnels had been used. How long had this mountain housed the dark-robes? How many dark-robes knew it existed? There were no answers to these questions, only the black openings waiting for them to choose.

"Pick one," said Malak. "We need to get going."

"That one," Lena said pointing to one of the four other tunnels.

They started into it moving slower and quieter than they had come up the last tunnel. Soon they were heading downwards again, and Malak stopped them.

"We're not going to get to the top of the mountain going downwards. Let's go back and try another one," said Malak.

When they were back in the junction chamber, Malak scraped a mark by the tunnel, and they started into another. Just then they heard something up ahead. They listened intently for a minute. The sounds were getting closer. Malak motioned for Lena to go back. They moved silently into the room they had just left, and Malak quickly picked another tunnel to explore. They headed into it fast, moving as if their lives were on the line, they maneuvered around several bends, and up a couple of staircases, there they stopped and listened for several minutes.

"Why didn't we stay and see where they were going?" asked Lena.

"Because we can't hide the torch. If I put it out, they would smell the smoke, and know that something was wrong. Unless we doused the torch, and killed them as soon as they came out of the tunnel, we would have a real fight on our hands. They could end up wounding both of us, maybe even killing us.

"But what if they come up this tunnel?"

"Then we move up it as quickly as we can, and hope that there isn't anyone up ahead. If we get lucky, we won't step into a room full of dark-robes. Besides, they might be on trap duty tonight. That means they are going down the tunnel we came in through. If they come up this one and it's a dead end, we'll have to fight them."

"How many were there?"

"I don't know for sure, but there was definitely at least one of them."

They slowed their ascent, and moved more quietly so that they could hear anything in the tunnel both behind them, or ahead. After an undetermined amount of time, they entered a large room full of casks and crates. There seemed to be enough food for several people to survive on for a long time. Maybe a year or even longer depending on how many people were there.

As they looked closely at the supplies that were laid in store, they found dried fruits, casks of flour and ale, cases of dried meats and cured sausages. Huge cheeses encased in wax. There were also dried goods, and supplies of every kind and assortment.

"Can we load up?" asked Lena.

"Grab some dried fruit quickly. If we get the chance to come back later, we will. But don't count on it. There isn't any guarantee from here on out."

"Did I ever have a guarantee?"

"Yes, I guaranteed you that you might be killed on this little trip of ours. Remember the first night in the swamps? Let's get out of here and back down to the intersection. We still have a lot to do before we are through tonight."

They quickly put some of the supplies in their packs. A little of everything went here and there, and then they were out of the room, moving back down the tunnel. Moving cautiously they made their way back through the tunnel that they had run out of just a little while ago. They moved slower than they had in a long time, often Lena wondered if they would ever get wherever it was they were going. Malak was listening to the tunnel ahead more than he was watching with his eyes. The circle of light from their torch only penetrated the darkness of the tunnel a short distance ahead. It was never bright, but now it was beginning to burn down. He couldn't tell for sure, but there seemed to be only silence ahead.

"How long do you think those wizards will be gone?" Lena whispered in the darkening tunnel.

"I don't know," answered Malak. "It depends on how long it takes them to check their traps on the trails. It also depends on whether they realize this torch is missing or not."

"So they could be on their way back right now."

"That's what I'm saying."

"Why are we going so slowly?"

"We don't know what is up ahead. Right now the only thing we know for sure is that some men came down this tunnel. I assume that they were wizards, because of the map, and the lines of light we saw last night. I don't know it for sure, but we could be walking into an empty mountain, or into a hornets nest of angry wizards."

"Malak, don't play games with me," Lena said. "Your talking as if you don't have a clue about what is going on here. You usually have some idea about what is ahead. It would be nice if you'd tell me what we might be up against."

"I just did. If you were asking which of the two extremes I think we now face, I would have to say both. I don't think that there are a lot of wizards in this mountain. But I also don't think they all went to check the traps. I don't even know for sure that they went to check the traps. We didn't see which tunnel they went down. We just assumed they went down the tunnel we came out of. They could be anywhere. Maybe they even went back up this tunnel."

"I don't think I liked that answer," said Lena more to herself than to Malak.

"I didn't think that you would," replied Malak.

"Well, it didn't give me any comfort to hear a longer version of the same thing."

Malak let the conversation die. They continued making their way up the tunnel. It seemed to go on indefinitely. Finally they came to a stop as the torch burned out. The darkness was absolute around them. They couldn't see their hands held in front of their faces. Taking Lena by the hand, Malak started moving forward again. They both knew that they couldn't stay where they were, and they couldn't go back without risking running into the wizards who might be returning. So onward they went.

Malak thought he could see the outlines of the tunnel ahead of them. He knew instinctively that there was no way he could be seeing the sides of the tunnel. No way he could see the uneven surface of the tunnel's wall, or the slight irregularities on the floor. Yet when he reached out his hand to touch a particularly large lump on the side of the tunnel, he found that he was indeed seeing. There must have been light from someplace, but Malak couldn't seem to locate it. Everything was in shades of blackness, and part of his mind couldn't believe he was doing it, but he was able to see.

"Do you want me to use the light spell?" Lena asked.

"Lena, can you see anything?" he asked quietly.

"You're kidding, right?"

"No, really, can you see anything?"

"No, Malak, I can't see anything at all. Why?"

"Look closely at the side of the tunnel, and tell me if you can see anything at all."

"No, Malak, I don't see anything at all, just a lot of black. Why?"

"Because somehow I am seeing the tunnel wall."

"What?"

"Not very well of course, but I am able to see a little."

Lena's grip tightened on his hand and Malak looked back at her. He gasped and yanked his hand away from her.

"What?" Lena asked a little scared.

Malak just stood looking at the thing before him. Lena's face was lit up in an array of glowing colors and intensities. Even her clothes seemed to glow although a lot dimmer than her face and head. He looked down at her hands, and was amazed that they were glowing too.

"Malak what's going on?" Lena repeated fear starting to sound in her voice.

"Hold still," Malak answered softly trying to sooth her. "I'm not sure what's happening. How do you feel?"

"I feel fine."

Malak reached out to touch her hand, and gasped again when he saw his own hand glowing brighter than hers.

"What is it? What's wrong?" she asked again.

Malak held his hand up in front of her. "This."

"What?" this time her voice was louder.

"Sshhh!" he whispered. "Can't you see my hand?"

"Malak I can't see anything," she whispered back.

It dawned on Malak then that he was seeing in someway that he had never done before. He wasn't sure exactly what he was seeing, but it wasn't light.

"We are glowing," he tried to explain. "We are both lit up like candles."

"You can see light on us?"

"No, I can see light *from* us."

"What are you talking about? Like our auras?"

"No," said Malak. "I think it is something different. I've never heard of an aura being so bright. And they are only one color. We look like rainbow people."

"Malak, I don't know what you think you see, but there is nothing but darkness here."

Malak reached out and took her by the hand. It felt cool to his touch, and he wondered silently if that had something to do with the difference in brightness. "Lena, if there isn't anything to see, how can I do this?" He let go of her hand and reached toward her face. "This is your nose." He rested his finger lightly on the tip of her nose.

"You know how tall I am, and you just had my hand," she replied slightly annoyed now. "I would think that with your skill, you would be able to stick a knife in my eye in this blackness if you were holding my hand." On the spur of the moment she came on a way to test Malak; closing her eyes, she stuck out her tongue.

"That's true," said Malak. "Very astute of you. But you don't need to stick your tongue out at me. And closing your eyes won't make it go away."

Lena was taken aback. There was nothing for them to see. It was total blackness around them. And yet Malak had seen. It should have made her feel better, knowing that one of them could see, just in case there were traps in the tunnel. But it made her feel uneasy instead. Malak wasn't supposed to be able to do that. No one was. She felt the same way as she had when he had killed the wild boar out on the plains.

"Let's move without your light spell for a while," he suggested. "We may need it before the night is through."

"You mean I may need it before the night is through," thought Lena. They walked along the tunnel just as they had before, with Lena holding a little tighter to Malak's hand to make sure she didn't fall or trip on anything. In fact, he was moving faster than he had with the torch. He was sure that without a light, they weren't likely to give themselves away to anyone waiting up ahead. As long as they stayed quiet, they should make it through.

They had made their way upwards through several twists and turns of the tunnel, when Malak thought the light was changing somehow. Up ahead there was a different kind of light. Then the cave walls disappeared, and he could see the light up ahead growing brighter. He looked back at Lena, and couldn't see her anymore. She was just a very vague outline of a head in the dim light coming from up ahead of them.

"Now I see a light," whispered Lena.

Malak slowed their pace.  He almost wished he could see like he had before.  Now that his eyes were back to normal, with the light up ahead, it was hard to tell if there was anything in the tunnel they should be aware of.  They slowed even more as they approached the exit, stopping just back of the circle of light entering the tunnel.  Malak looked and listened for several minutes.  Though he couldn't see anything in the room ahead of them, he had the strange feeling that someone or something was there.  The room was lit up with torches, from inside the tunnel he couldn't tell how many.  The light from them flickered and danced in and out of the tunnel's entrance.  He started moving forward again very slowly, releasing Lena's hand as he did so, and silently drawing his dagger.

Slowly, Malak crept into the lighted room.  His feet apart, knees bent slightly, he was ready to spring at anything.  This room was larger than even the storeroom had been.  There were several doors set into the stone sides of the room.  A large table was set off to one side.  Six high-backed chairs of sturdy wood were set around it as if waiting for the table to be set for a meal.  The other side of the room was empty.  There were also two tunnels leading out of the room.  The room seemed to be deserted, but his mind was yelling at him to be careful.

Malak looked back at Lena to and tilted his head toward the room.  She gave him a questioning look, and then it dawned on her that he wanted her to check for magical tricks.  Once more she called upon the spell that would bring any spots of energy to her attention.  She could tell that she was getting tired.  The part of her that had to sleep after using magic was growing.  She tried to ignore it, knowing that she wouldn't be able to sleep for a long time to come, but also knowing that she would when she reached a certain point.  And there would be nothing she could do about it.

After a minute of watching Lena for any sign of a problem with the room, Malak saw her shake her head that she hadn't detected anything out of the ordinary.  Carefully they both left the relative security of the tunnel, and walked to the table. It was sturdily built, and well worn, like a table that had seen years of service in a large family.

The door across from the table was slightly ajar, and Malak headed around the table to check it out. He carefully opened it a little more, expecting the hinges to creak a little with age. The fact that they didn't make a sound, confirmed to him that someone lived in this place. Not only someone, but someone who cared enough about it keep it maintained. The hinges on the door had been oiled recently. Someone liked it to be quiet.

The room beyond the door had a single torch lighting it. It was obviously where the cooking was done. There was a fireplace with an iron hook suspended over it set into the wall. "There must be a shaft going all the way to the surface," thought Malak. He crossed the room to check if the flew was big enough for a man to climb up, but was disappointed when he saw that it was much too small for that. There was a small fire burning, and coal stacked off to one side. The warmth of the fire seemed to reach out to him, and for just a minute, he wanted to relax by it for a while. The rest of the room was filled with supplies for cooking; a small table, and some food items. Obviously they had been brought up from the lower storage area he and Lena had found earlier.

Lena had her head in the doorway now, and was peering at the food as if she wanted to take some with her. There wasn't really anything more to see in the room, so Malak headed towards the door. He still had the sensation in his head that someone or something was watching them, but he couldn't tell where it was coming from.

Malak slid past Lena in the doorway. "We don't have time for eating food now," he said gently. Lena turned and followed him back into the larger room. As they approached the table, Malak saw a spark of light out of the corner of his eye. It came from one of the tunnels they had yet to explore, but before he could turn his head to look, pain exploded along his entire left side.

The blast of lightning threw him into Lena, and they landed in a heap against the far wall. He tried to get to his feet, but his body was slow to respond. He felt queasy and weak and the room seemed to spin a little.

Malak fought his way clear of Lena, and got to his feet just as another blast of blue lightning exploded from the darkened tunnel. He tried to dodge, but the streaks of energy slammed into him before he could even start to move. Again he felt his body slammed into the wall behind him, and he collapsed in a heap on the floor.

They had walked into a trap. Malak wondered how long they would survive the onslaught, when he saw Lena, still kneeling on the floor extend her hand and whisper something that he couldn't make out. A translucent wall appeared about a foot in front of her hand.

Another crack of lightning exploded from the shadows. This time the energy was aimed at Lena. It slammed into the wall she had put up shattering it into thousands of energy shards that flashed and disappeared. Lena cried out holding her hand close to her body as though it had been burned.

Malak reached out and grabbed Lena by the arm. He pulled her toward the tunnel they had come in. He managed to find some cover behind the table as they crawled over the hard stone floor towards the safety of the darkness. That safety was quickly lost with the next blast from the tunnel behind them. Energy streaked out of the darkened portal and slammed into the heavy wood table. It exploded into hundreds of burning, flying pieces that cut and bruised them.

Malak literally threw Lena into the tunnel ahead of him as he dove for cover. They landed inside its shadows in a single mass of tangled limbs and packs. It took them a few seconds to extricate themselves from each other, and get pointed down the tunnel. They hadn't taken two steps when Malak stopped and started backing up. Lena slammed into him, and they nearly went down again.

"Get back!" Malak yelled.

"Are you crazy?" she yelled back.

"Go!" Malak pushed her in front of him back into the room as hard as he could. He was right behind her, still pushing. Lena started to fall forward, as they re-entered the room. Malak caught sight of a dark-robed figure stepping out of the tunnel where the lightning had flashed from. Its hands were raised, and blue sparks were already leaping from its fingertips.

Malak and Lena had bolted back into the room so quickly that the dark-robes lightning blast missed Lena. Malak unfortunately caught the full force of the blast on his side and was thrown sideways. He didn't let go of Lena in time, and his momentum pulled her backwards off her feet to land on top of him sliding sideways into the pile of coal.

A ball of fire shot out of the tunnel they had just left. It exploded against the far wall of the room, setting fire to the shards of wood on the floor, and cutting the chamber in half. Malak was dazed but struggling to his feet in spite of the pain screaming through his body. He began pulling Lena towards the only tunnel that hadn't launched something deadly at them. He doubted they were going to survive. If there was another wizard down this tunnel... He stumbled with Lena through the flames that seemed to be everywhere in the room now, and into the cool darkness of the tunnel.

As they ran, Malak yanked a dagger out of its sheath at his side, and hurled it down the tunnel ahead of them. If there was another wizard close he might get lucky, and at least hurt him somehow. The only sound he heard was the dagger striking the wall of the tunnel somewhere up ahead. Malak couldn't see a thing in the darkness. After the bright light of the inferno raging behind them, any night vision he once had was long gone. It would be several minutes before he could see anything again.

Lights exploded in his head, and the wind was knocked out of them as they slammed face first into the wall of the tunnel at full speed. Flat on their backs, Malak and Lena tried to breath again.

Malak's face felt like someone had smashed it with a club. Lena was half under him, and he struggled to get off of her. As he struggled to his feet, something sharp on the tunnel floor cut his hand. He felt around carefully, and swore when he recognized the dagger he had just thrown. He paused for just a moment to take stock of their situation.

Malak's side felt like the skin had been flayed off where the blasts of lightning had struck him. His face hurt like crazy, he figured that his nose was probably broken. He could smell burnt hair, whether his own or Lena's he didn't know. His body ached in a hundred different places from all of the falling and crashing about he had done, and to top it all off, his own dagger had cut his fingers.

Lena was trying to get to her feet next to him. She was panting as if she had just run the sprint at the Chistock summer festival. Great gasps of air were sucked into her, and then just as loudly expelled. Still, she wasn't done yet, and was trying to get her feet under her. With the weight of her pack, she was having a hard time of it.

Malak knew that they couldn't stay there. He struggled painfully to his feet, and looked at Lena who had somehow also regained her feet. He put the dagger back in its sheath, and looked up the tunnel. They had run several hundred feet up it before running into this wall, and it looked like the fire in the chamber behind them was starting to burn out. Soon the dark-robes would be hunting them again.

"It's a dead end," Lena said through clenched teeth.

Malak felt the wall. He moved from one side of the tunnel to the other. "No," he said relieved that they didn't have to go back through the wizards. "It's just a sharp bend. Come on."

They started down the tunnel again. This time Lena walked side by side with Malak holding onto his arm for guidance in the blackness. They had taken about five steps together when the ground disappeared in front of them and they fell.

# Chapter 18

The spy watched the daylight hours creep slowly by. He took his meals as normal, with the other wizards in the tower, biding his time. The activities of the day went by as they had for uncounted years. No one but the four knew that the world was about to change. The spy thought that if things went very well tonight, Zartho would be dead, the figurine, would be in the hands of the white-robes, and the kingdom would be safe. If he did things just right, no one would know what had happened, not even the other two of Zartho's helpers.

The years the spy had spent in the dark tower had served him well. He had been sent there as a young apprentice. He had learned from some of the great minds of the dark arts. They always held something back, so he didn't feel bad at all about holding back his true identity. He had shown great promise in the white tower in Thosh when he was very young. That is where his magical studies had begun. He had been able to learn magic much faster than any of the other students in his class. He was well on his way to being the head of the tower. Perhaps the youngest head the world had ever known. Then it had all come crashing down.

In an unusually difficult casting, he had made a slight mistake. It was nothing more than the inexperience of youth, but it had resulted in the deaths of two of his classmates. The rules of the tower were strict. Even stricter was the unwritten code within its walls. He was responsible for their deaths. He knew that even if he were allowed to stay in the tower and continue his studies, he would never be taught anything really important. He would always be an outcast. No professor would help him with anything more than his basic studies, and no student would speak to him.

He was summoned to the tower head's chambers that night. With a heavy heart, he climbed up the steps and knocked on the door. More than loosing his magical career though, he hated himself for having killed two of his friends. Inside those chambers he had been given a glimmer of hope, not only for the future, but that his friends might not have died in vain. It had led him to an intense training on mental hiding, and an embarrassing dismissal from the white tower. They had mocked him and thrown him out. He had born it because of the need for appearances. He had had to feign an attitude of contempt, not only for the friends he had killed, but also for their families. The looks of hurt and betrayal on their faces would haunt him for the rest of his life.

Still, he had to admit it had worked. He had left the white tower, and within a week, had been contacted by the dark tower in Chistock. They had told him that they understood it wasn't his fault. In their hurry to snatch up such a promising young wizard, they had let him in without looking too closely. He had played the part of a hate-filled man for the rest of the intervening years; years of silently learning as much dark magic as he could.

The years had been reasonably good to him. His new teachers had pushed him harder than anyone ever had. Nothing was ever good enough, or learned fast enough. They had kept him on his toes to say the least. But they had also made him a formidable mage. None of his own age could match his power, and only a few of the older ones could. Perhaps only Zartho himself could best him in a duel. Yes, he had to admit to himself that Zartho could take him. He wasn't arrogant enough to think that he could beat Zartho the Great. If he got lucky or cheated he could win, but that was the only way.

The spy intended to cheat tonight. There would be a time when Zartho was so focused on his spell casting, that he would be open to attack. That was the time when he would make his move. It would have to be brutal and fast. He must not fail to kill Zartho immediately, or he himself would die. There was no room for mistakes. Even if he failed to kill Zartho, he mustn't die before he had destroyed the little statue. Then he must make sure that Zartho was forced to kill him quickly.

If Zartho were able to take his time killing him, his death would be one for the scrolls. He was sure that before he was allowed to die, he would tell everything to anyone who wanted to know. His flesh would be pealed and healed in so many ways that it made him want to vomit just thinking about it. The dark robes had indeed learned a lot about taking the human body and mind apart while allowing the whole to stay alive during the process. They would have made incredible surgeons except that they hadn't taken the time to learn how to operate without a great deal of pain to their patient. In fact, they had made a study of how to make their vivisections as painful as possible.

The spy had first hand knowledge of their effectiveness. Once, when he had failed to study enough to appease one of his dark teachers, the instructor had made a lesson of him to the other students. His left hand had been slowly disassembled and reassembled while the class took notes. First the skin had been pealed back. Then the muscles, tendons, blood vessels, and nerves in their turn leaving the bones lying flat on the table for all to see. His arm looked like some kind of macabre flower with his hand blossoming out of the stem of his wrist. The different layers of tissues made the petals, and the skeletal structure protruded from the center like some horrific pistil. Everything was exposed to the scrutiny of anyone who cared to observe, and everything was still wonderfully alive and functioning.

He hadn't screamed during the entire process, although he had vomited twice during it. The instructor had graciously allowed him to finish heaving before he continued the demonstration so that he wouldn't miss a bit of it. He also kept him from fainting when the agony was too great for his mind to endure.

The only thing he had ever experienced more painful than the stripping of his hand was having it reassembled. Tissues forced to reattach and grow together at an accelerated rate without leaving any scarring. It burned, and itched, but mostly screamed in agony. He had screamed then. He had forgotten his pride and shame, and screamed until his throat had bled. Then he had screamed some more. The instructor calmly walked the class through the reassembly in an even more patient manner than he had the disassembly. Making sure that no possible information had been left out of the demonstration.

When it was over, he had slid out of the classroom on his belly, unable to even crawl. He had somehow dragged himself back to his quarters, and studied for the next day. He would never allow himself to be another demonstration like that. He had made an oath to himself that he would die before he allowed it to ever happen to him again. He meant to keep that oath.

He doubted that he would see the sunrise tomorrow, but he knew that if he accomplished nothing else, he would at least have made the deaths of his friends mean something. Then again he might just be able to pull it off. If he could kill Zartho, and perhaps even the other two, and get the figurine out of the tower to Shial, without anyone seeing what happening, then he would be in the clear.

Zartho would have already arranged for the tower to be secured for the night, so they would have no interruptions during their activities. The spy knew that no one would interfere with them until after the spell was cast. Zartho would see to that. He also knew that Zartho must suspect one of them of being a spy, but he didn't think that his identity was known. If it were, he would have been in a lot of pain by now. The others were acting as his shield. They didn't know this of course, but then again, he hoped they would be dead by the time they realized it.

The spy knew that Zartho was planning their deaths. It would probably come after the end of the spell casting when their usefulness, as well as their strength was at an end. What Zartho didn't know was that the spell would never be finished. Whatever it was, he was going to wrap Zartho and the other two into it, and then crash it. He would ride it until the last moment, making sure that no one escaped the blast until the last possible moment. It was a dangerous plan, but if it worked, he might be able to survive the night. He might even be able to ascend to the post of the High Wizard himself. Though he rather thought it would be nicer to have himself transferred to the other dark tower in Thosh. Anyone else who wanted the position would be glad to see him leave, as he would definitely be considered for the post. On his way to the other tower, he could just disappear. As if going for a walk and never coming back.

It was a grand plan, but one that was a long way off. There were a many things to do tonight, and everything would have to go perfectly. The spy knew that things rarely went as planned. He would have to be ready to improvise too.

At the appointed hour, the spy went down to the dinning hall, and sat in his usual place. Zartho and the others were there as well. As normal the meal was consumed in silence. There was nothing out of the ordinary at all. The spy wondered if this might just be his last meal. The fare could have been a little better. The potatoes were all right. The roasted beef was slightly overdone for his taste, but still more than palatable. The vegetables were slightly undercooked as if the cooks had put them on as an afterthought, and they hadn't had enough time to fully cook before it was time to serve them. It was pretty much the usual quality of food. There was a bit more salt in the food than normal, but that sometimes happened when there was a new assistant cook who hadn't been trained in the art of saving money on spices. In fact, the poor idiot was probably in a little bit of trouble.

At the end of the meal, the towers members drifted off to their quarters or laboratories for the evening. There was only a couple of hours left before the lights would be put out, and everyone would be required to be in their quarters. There was no excuse for being outside quarters after lights-out. If someone was caught outside after the curfew, it was assumed that they were trying to steal something or kill someone. There were no trials inside the tower, only punishments.

The spy returned to his room feeling sleepy. He hadn't had much sleep last night, and he thought that he had eaten more than he should have. Well if it was to be his last meal... then again, he might not get to eat for a while. There were always unexpected things that could mess up the best of plans. He wanted to doze off, but his mind was too full of the possibilities of the coming hours, and he was afraid that if he did sleep, he wouldn't wake up in time. Eventually, he did doze off lightly.

The spy awoke suddenly. At first he feared that he had dozed too long, and that things were already happening. But upon checking the stars, he found that he had only been drifting for about half an hour. He had been lucky. He had been able to snatch a little sleep, but not too much. In spite of his nap, he still felt sluggish, almost lethargic. There was still time before he had to meet with the others in Zartho's quarters. Time enough to communicate with Shial.

Carefully he locked the door to his quarters. Then he created several wards and cast spells to conceal what was happening within his quarters. Anyone looking, whether magically or otherwise, would have seen him studying at his desk. Instead, he carefully removed the stone in his floor that hid the crystal ball and its stand. Then he carefully sent out the mental pulse. It was directed out of his window and straight at Shial's farm. No one who wasn't in the direct line of the signal could have detected it.

Almost immediately the globe in front of him began to emit the smoke that coalesced into the familiar form of his contact. Shial had been waiting for him.

"Be ready," whispered the spy to the smoky image before him. "It will be a couple of hours yet, but I'm going to try and stop Zartho."

"What can I do to help?" asked the image.

"I do not know any specifics yet, but it looks like Zartho will be using the top of the tower for at least part of the spells."

"Should I try to be ready to attack there?"

"Yes, if you can."

The image appeared thoughtful for a moment. "I'll be in the woods on the east side of the tower, ready to attack if needed."

"That should work out fine. If I need anything, I'll find you. If you don't hear from me, but you can tell that Zartho has started to succeed, assume that I'm dead, and do what you must."

"I understand," said the figure of smoke as it began to dissolve toward the ceiling.

The spy carefully concealed the ball and its stand back in the floor. He didn't put any spells of concealment on it, because many of the dark-robes inside the tower could easily detect magical spells of hiding. They would be drawn to the spot like moths to a flame if they ever searched his quarters. Instead, there were several other items secreted around the room to draw their attention away from something as mundane as the floor. It had worked for years, and he didn't intend to change the system now.

---

Golan, Harnthiston, and Lorban met at the top of the stairs outside Zartho's quarters. They knocked on the door softly and waited.

"So you three have decided to act together, have you?" boomed a voice on the landing above them.

Zartho descended the stairs with several of the more powerful wizards of the tower close behind him. "Don't try to deny it," he continued, his hands raised ready to lash out with a spell. "I've already told the others in the tower about your intention to murder me, and take over."

"What are you talking about?" asked Lorban putting a hand to his head. He felt a little woozy even as he tried to bring some defensive spells to mind.

"There's no use denying it," yelled a voice from behind the three. "Zartho's told us everything."

The three spun around to see the rest of the instructors of the tower coming up behind them. They were trapped. All three started swaying slightly on their feet now. The room seemed to be spinning.

Golan looked back at Zartho. "What did you drug us with?" he asked Zartho. Things were slowly starting to make sense to him. He felt like his head was filled with cotton. It was hard to think clearly, but he was beginning to figure that Zartho didn't need them anymore. He also realized that no matter what the others in the tower thought, Zartho was going to make sure that there was a fight for them to be killed in. He tried to prepare himself mentally, but it was hard to fight whatever was drugging them.

"What is going on, Zartho?" asked Harnthiston even more under the influence of the drug than the other two.

"Don't play dumb," snarled Zartho, approaching even closer to them. I know you planned to not only take over this tower, but as much of the kingdom as you could. Treason is a capital offense. You'd better give up, you're outnumbered, and we gave you a mild sedative at dinner tonight. There is no way to escape."

Golan knew that the last thing Zartho wanted was the three of them to give up quietly. He felt the affects of the drug even more intensely when he tried to summon any magic to his mind. He staggered slightly towards the wall, away from the other two. He felt woozy, but was acting more drugged than he really felt. Within the folds of his robes, his hands were working furiously to create the spell through the haze of the drug. Lorban and Harnthiston were still clueless as to what was happening. Like two naive fools, they had trusted Zartho to keep up his end of the pact. Golan, on the other hand, had expected some form of treachery. He had thought that it wouldn't come upon them until after Zartho was in power, or at least during the fighting. Not now, before the first spell had even been cast.

The wizards behind them were closing in quickly now.

"Watch out!" yelled Zartho, and a blast of lightning erupted from his hands. It slammed into Harnthiston, throwing him into Lorban. Before they could fall to the floor, more lightning erupted into the two of them from behind, knocking them back up on their feet and towards Zartho and the other wizards.

Magic sparked weakly from Lorban and Harnthiston both up and down the corridor. It sliced into their attackers though, and screams erupted from both sides of the struggle. Zartho slipped backwards through the wizards, to safer ground while the others pressed the attack anew. It wouldn't be long before the three of them were dead. They were simply too outnumbered and overpowered. It was only a matter of time. All to quickly, Harnthiston and Lorban were on the floor writhing under a continuous onslaught of spells from both ends of the corridor.

Just as one of the wizards near Zartho noticed that Golan was standing unharmed by the wall, he stepped toward the center of the landing, and brought out the fireball from within the folds of his robes. The hallway was instantly silent. As wizards stopped their attacks, their half formed spells dispersed back into the nothingness from whence they had been called. The hallway seemed to take a collective breath waiting to see which way the ball would be thrown.

Golan looked around for a heartbeat. Lorban and Harnthiston looked as if they were already dead, or soon would be. He had no love for either of them, and knew that they would kill him if they ever got the chance. Gently he tossed the fireball straight up into the air, and turned to run back down the tower the way he had come. The wizards that blocked his path were paralyzed for half a moment as the fireball reached the apex of its flight. It seemed to hang for just a moment, like it was going to remain suspended in the air. Then it started the short trip back down to the floor of the landing. In the second since Golan had tossed the fireball, he had almost reached the wizards blocking his path. He leapt into the air throwing his arms and legs wide just as the fireball struck the stone floor.

Fire exploded in all directions, but because of the narrow confines of the landing area, the force of the explosion could only go up or down the stairway to either side. Golan caught the brunt of the explosion headed down the stairway, and was thrown through the wizards barring his path like an arrow through a window. He slammed into the wall as it curved downward, and hit the floor spinning and tumbling. He continued tumbling down the stairs and came to a stop on the next landing in a heap of smoking clothes, and singed hair and skin. He was barely conscious, but he fought to get to his feet. The wizards above were battling the inferno he had created. By some miracle he was still alive, and didn't seem to have any broken bones.

It would take only a few moments before the wizards realized where the blast had thrown him. They would come looking then, and they would really be furious when they discovered he had escaped them by nearly burning down their beloved tower. They wouldn't need any of Zartho's tricks to get them to kill him. The phrase *lusting for my blood* ran through Golan's mind as he struggled to stand up through the tangle of his robes. He finally made it, and, after taking a moment to get his bearings, and make sure he wasn't on fire, he ran down the steps towards the lower levels.

On the level above, chaos reigned. Wizards had been thrown from their feet, and flung in every conceivable direction. The landing was a blazing inferno. Smoke quickly filled the air. Lungs burned as they fought to cast spells that would smother the fire. It took several minutes to quench the flames, and clear the air enough to see. All around were signs of the blaze. The walls were blackened, and scorched. Several wizards were lying unmoving on the floor. In the middle of the landing where they had fallen were the bodies of Harnthiston and Lorban. They had been nearest the exploding firestorm, and had nearly been completely incinerated.

Zartho fought his way to the front of the wizards, and looked in disgust at the pile of burned flesh. He looked closer to try and identify who was who, but the bodies were too burned for quick identification. Slowly, he realized that only two of the bodies in the pile were his assistants.

"Where is the other?" he demanded to everyone and no one. "Where is the third?"

As the wizards looked at each other for an explanation, it dawned on them that one had escaped. The body of the one that had had the audacity to drop a fireball at his feet was nowhere to be found. Somehow he had escaped them.

"He went down the tower," yelled a voice.

"Get him!" screamed Zartho, "Get him now, and kill him!"

The dark-robes took up the charge as one. They moved like a wave down the steps to the lower levels looking everywhere as they went. One or two of the younger students carefully poked their heads outside their doors to see what the noise was all about, but they quickly yanked them back and slammed their doors when they saw the looks on the faces of their raging instructors.

All students knew to keep their doors locked at night. It was an unwritten rule of the tower. It just wasn't safe to let others have access to you while you were asleep. They knew this, because they knew what they would do to others that left themselves so unprotected. As a result, the wizards didn't bother wasting any time searching the student's quarters.

Golan ran as fast as he could. The mild sedative that he had been slipped was slowly working through his system. Zartho must have arranged to have the three of them slightly drugged so that they were easier targets. The other wizards would have not been so eager to attack them without an edge. Somehow he managed to keep his feet as he nearly fell down one flight of stairs after another. He could hear them coming down the stairs after him now, and he quickened his pace even more. Twice he fell and rolled, and twice he fought his way back to his feet. He wasn't sure how he kept going, maybe it was the few minutes sleep he'd gotten earlier in the evening. Whatever it was, sleep or sheer willpower, he kept moving as fast as he could.

He didn't waste any time heading for the gate, there were too many guards there to get past. He was running for the portal.

That was his best and only real chance of escape. If they caught him before he could open it, they would kill him before he could stop Zartho. Oh yes, there was no doubt that Zartho was moving ahead with his plans. He was probably on top of the tower now locking the trapdoor so that no one could stop him. Somehow he made it to the tunnels unnoticed.

The pursuing wizards went straight to the gates of the tower. It was soon evident from the guards that he hadn't gone that way. As they searched the kitchen, and storerooms, they soon realized that he had gone lower still. It was insane to think that he had gone down into the tunnels. They knew there was no escape down there, but it was soon evident that that was precisely where he had gone.

As Golan ran down the levels of the underground caverns, he realized that they hadn't followed him. They must have stopped at the ground floor. His heart lightened at the thought that they were searching the upper level for him, and he was gaining a little time. He knew that he would need every bit of it. They would soon figure out where he had gone, and be hot on his trail again. Suddenly his drugged feet tripped on each other, and he went flying. Stars exploded around him as he slammed face first into the wall of the tunnel, and blackness raced into his mind.

The sound of running and confusion brought him slowly back to consciousness. Golan thought that his face must be totally smashed in. He ached all over, and all he wanted to do was sleep. Something in the back of his mind told him that that was a very bad idea. He staggered slowly to his feet, and tried to look around. He realized that he wasn't in his quarters, and he wondered where he was. He saw the faint beginnings of light from one end of the tunnel he was in. There was a lot of yelling and shouting from that end of the tunnel. The commotion was getting closer to him every second.

Suddenly, he remembered where he was, and more importantly what he had to do if he wanted to live. He launched himself down the tunnel away from the light and sound coming for him. He cursed himself silently. All of the time he had gained had been lost the second he had fallen. He had no idea how long he had been lying semi-conscious before he had forced himself up. The only thing he was grateful for was that he had come too before the dark-robes had found him. He thought bitterly that he would be screaming by now if they had caught him, and realized at the same time that he might still die screaming. Arms out in front of him for protection, he raced faster down the dim tunnel.

Even though he ran as fast as he dared, the noise and light behind was getting closer. He was nearly to the door of the portal now. It would only be a few more moments, and he would have the heavy door between him and the raging mob. The doorway to the portal room finally appeared. Relief flooded through him as he leapt for it. He grabbed the handle, tripped the latch, and slammed his body into the door. He bounced off of the solid oak and cursed himself. The wizards were almost to him now.

Grabbing the handle again, he tripped the latch and yanked with all his strength. The door didn't even wiggle in its frame, and his grip failed against the unexpected resistance. He lurched backwards across the tunnel, his back slamming into the far side, almost knocking the wind out of him. He frantically fought his way back to his feet, and leapt at the door. He grabbed the handle again, and alternately pulled and pushed at it furiously. *The Spell!* He thought. In his panic, he had completely forgotten about the locking spell on the door.

The wizards were only feet from the bend behind him in the tunnel now. They would be on Golan in seconds. He took half a second to try and calm himself. He didn't have time to do the spell twice. If he messed it up he was dead. He started the unlocking spell as quickly as he dared. Half way into it, the mob came around the last bend, and saw him not fifty feet away.

"There he is!" someone screamed. Golan didn't hear. He was so focused on finishing the spell that he barely registered they were there at all. Finally, the door swung inward just as the first lightning blasted towards him.

As Golan leapt inside the doorway, his legs were swatted out from under him as if he were a child's toy. He plowed into the doorjamb and fell to the floor half in and half out of the doorway. Energy knifed into his back as he fought to get inside the door. Another blast of energy slammed into his legs as he pulled them inside; they felt like they were broken.

Outside the door, the furious dark-robes were now sprinting at it. Golan fought to pull his useless legs inside and slam the door. Just as the wizards reached it, the latch clicked into place. The door shook as several bodies slammed into it on the other side. Golan spoke the word that would magically lock the door again just as the handle started to shake. Outside he could hear the wizards raging and yelling. It wouldn't take them long to blast their way through the door. He wasn't out of this yet. But he did have a few more seconds now.

If he could cast the spell correctly, the portal would close after he went through. He fought to get to his feet. His legs and back screamed in agony but he finally made it. Time was running out. The raging outside had stopped, and he knew that several of the wizards were even now beginning a spell that would smash through the door. There wasn't any way to reinforce it now. He staggered in front of the portal, and began the spell. He worked as fast as he could by himself. He had never had to open the portal alone before, and he wondered if he still had the strength to do it.

A deep boom sounded from the door as the first blow fell. The sound startled Golan but he kept his concentration enough not to miscast the spell. Another boom sounded from the door, and this time it shook in its frame. Just a few more seconds was all he needed, and he would be out of their reach. The spell this time was different. He had to cast it so that only one person could go through, and then it would close. Otherwise, they would follow him and kill him. Another boom, and the heavy iron bolts cracked loose from the stone.

Finally the spell was finished. The portal lit up with its shimmering image of the grounds to the east of the tower. Golan started forward on shaky legs. Another boom sounded behind him, and the door gave way. It blasted into the room and clipped his side, knocking him to the floor again.

Golan screamed out a spell in pain and frustration, sending red blasts of energy into the wizards now crowding through the doorway. Several fell to the ground and lay where they had fallen. Others were knocked back a few feet only to come on again slightly more cautiously than before. He used the couple of seconds pause to get to his knees and launch himself through the portal. Just as it closed behind him a final blast of blue lightning seared into his back, and threw him to the ground.

He lay on the cold ground trying to get air back into his lungs. It was several minutes before he could take anything more than the shallowest of breaths. His lungs burned for air, but his ribs and back cried out in pain when he breathed too deeply. So he lay on the cold ground trying not to move more than was absolutely necessary. The adrenalin that had kept him going was leaving him now. Pain started to shoot through places he hadn't noticed before. He started to consider just how lucky he was to be alive, and then again maybe not so lucky to still be alive. As the adrenalin subsided in him, the drug took more effect, and he began to doze off.

A hand roughly grabbed him by the shoulder and rolled him over. Shial looked down into the bruised, pain filled face. Slowly he began to recognize the features of the spy. He had only once or twice caught a glimpse of the man in the smoky visage that the ball created, but he was sure from the man's build that this must be the spy.

"Wha..." gasped Golan as he fought to regain consciousness.

"It's me, your contact," whispered Shial to the spy. "How did you get here?" Shial had been a few feet away when he heard what sounded like a body landing on the ground. He didn't think it was possible, but he had to check it out anyway. Impossible as it seemed, there was a body; it turned out to be both alive, and the spy. "What happened?" he demanded.

Golan fought himself back from the edge of sleep, and realized whom it was that was speaking to him. He tried to sit up, but his body wasn't quite ready for that yet and he collapsed back onto the ground.

"Zartho..." he managed to whisper.

"What about him?" asked Shial in a softer tone?

"He... he betrayed us," Golan gasped, his breath starting to come a little easier now. "He lied to the other wizards in the tower, and they ambushed us as we went to meet with him."

"Where is he now?"

"I don't know. He's probably locked himself on top of the tower by now."

Just as Golan gasped the last words out, two beams of red light appeared overhead. They converged on the top of the tower and disappeared over the top of the trees to the west. There was no doubt in Shial's mind, that this was just the start of whatever Zartho had planned.

"What are those lights for?" he asked

"I don't know for sure," was the gasped reply. Golan was beginning to get some of his breath back, and he again tried to sit up. This time, with Shial's help, he made it. "That is a spell that Harnthiston came up with. Zartho wanted to create a straight beam of light to somehow help control whatever comes through the doorway. I don't know why it's aimed out away from the tower. All I know is that whatever is coming will enable him to destroy the forces of the king."

"Any idea why there are two of them going in such different directions?"

"No."

"What can we do to stop him?" asked Shial impatiently.

"Well, we can break the light beams."

"What will that do?"

"I don't know if it will do anything, but it seemed important enough to Zartho so it might mess things up just enough to stop him. Or we could storm the top of the tower, and try to battle it out with him."

"And how," asked Shial exasperated, "do you propose we get up there?"

"You just asked what we could do. You didn't say it had to be practical," said Golan wryly.

"How do you propose to stop the beams?" It wasn't much, but it was better than sitting and doing nothing, or making a suicidal charge into the tower.

---

Dalryms crouched in the underbrush near the dark tower in Thosh. Several of the most powerful white-robed wizards from the tower were with him. They had volunteered to help in any way that they could. They knew that if things went badly tonight, they would be dead, or perhaps banished. Dalryms' Meeting with King Tholan hadn't gone well at all. The king would take no action against the dark-robes until there was a clear threat from them. The act of piracy he said was an isolated incident. The tower head didn't know anything about it, and was investigating. The king was waiting for word from him.

Dalryms was sure that the dark tower's head was telling the truth. He Probably didn't know anything about the attack on the ship. It would take months for the dark-robes to gather together and search the tower in Chistock. It would take even longer to get any answers from the Chistock tower if Zartho was involved. And Dalryms was sure that he was heavily involved. He was also pretty sure that whatever was coming was going to make piracy on the high seas look like a child's tea party. He feared for the entire kingdom. So he had decided to go against the king, and try to stop Zartho himself.

The signal came. The white-robes were all in place. They would wait until something happened, and then take what action seemed best.  It galled Dalryms to no end that in spite of all his efforts, he hadn't any idea what was coming.  Only the word of a spy (that hadn't been in a white tower in years,) and the feeling of power from the tiny statue, made him think there was any danger at all.  There wasn't any other sign of activity from the dark-robes.  He had considered the possibility that it was all a ploy to get the white-robes to do exactly what they were now doing.  Then they could play the part of the martyr to the king, and he would have to take action against the white towers.  It was a trick that Dalryms wouldn't put past the dark-robes.

But what would they gain by doing it?  There wasn't anything he could see that would interest them.  The king would never banish either of the groups entirely, so what was the point?  The more Dalryms thought about it, the more he thought he was missing something: something that from another perspective would be very important, the key to all of this.  That perspective, however, eluded him.  There was nothing to be done except be ready for action.  Last night he had heard about the light beams in the sky.  He had talked to Shial, and still nothing made any sense.  Was it possible for Zartho to be using this tower without the knowledge of the high wizard?  Or did the high wizard see the use of the tower as something benign?  There weren't any answers yet, but he had a feeling that there would be soon.

Suddenly the light beams appeared overhead.  Just as the guard had described them, they converged at the top of the dark tower.  Dalryms wondered what the significance of those lights was.  He watched the top of the tower closely, but there didn't seem to be anything happening.  From his vantage point, he could see around for miles.

The sky beyond the tower was clear and filled with stars.  It was a beautiful early winter's night, and he started to identify the constellations that he knew.  He had always liked looking at the stars.  He didn't get much time to do it anymore, but he tried when he could.  He Looked for several of his favorite, and found them to his satisfaction.  He turned to see if the hunter was up in the southern sky. It was the first constellation he had learned as a boy, and it always comforted his mind when he could pick it out. This time, however, when he looked he forgot all about it.

Way off in the distance, miles from Thosh, was another red line. It was barely discernable on the horizon. Like a spiders web across a garden path: nearly invisible, but there. It disappeared into the eastern horizon, and again into the western. It was separate from the other two beams, but it seemed that they were all on the same level so that they must intersect. In fact he was sure that they did. He was trying to figure out why anyone would want to intersect lines in the sky like that. They, being light would just pass through each other.

Dalryms gasped as the key to this puzzle finally dawned on him. There weren't three separate beams, there was only one. Instead of two shooting out of the tower, there was one that came in and was reflected back out at an angle. The other line in the sky must also be the same line, reflected from other points There must be one vast shape formed by the lines. From the looks of the angle at the top of the tower, it was probably a pentagram. *But what does he want...* Dalryms nearly stumbled with the realization that within this pentagram would be a pentagon of huge proportions. Zartho was going to open a dimensional doorway of horrific size. Even now he was probably casting the spell.

*There's no way he could have the power to open it!* But then Dalryms realized what the full purpose of the little figurine was. Zartho could open the doorway, and control whatever came through too. It would take a phenomenal amount of energy, but it was possible. He remembered the impression of power he had felt weeks ago, and swore. The wizard next to him looked at him reprovingly.

"We have to move now," said Dalryms in a hoarse whisper. "Zartho is opening a dimensional doorway: a big one."

"What?"

"You heard me," said Dalryms. He quickly pointed out the other line across the sky, and explained what was going on.

"But surely he hasn't got the power to open such a door."

"Yes," said Dalryms resignedly, "he does. Send the signal to get ready to attack the tower. We must get to the top before the doorway is opened. I'm going to try and talk to the high wizard. We don't have much time. Who knows what will come through that portal."

Quickly the signal was sent to the white-robes surrounding the tower. They were about to risk open war once again with the dark-robes. Dalryms took a deep breath and stepped out of the foliage. He walked swiftly but purposely towards the main gate of the tower. There was no turning back now. He would try reasoning with the High Wizard, but he doubted it would do any good. They didn't have time to argue, and there was no way the dark-robes would allow white-robes into their tower to look at the roof. They would have to stop one of their own; one who probably had permission from the head wizard to be up there playing with harmless light beams. On the other hand, the High Wizard himself may be in league with Zartho. That would be the worst scenario. They would be ready for the white-robes tonight, and for a fight.

Dalryms doubted very much that the High Wizard would be working with anyone, especially Zartho, on something this dangerous. Zartho was too powerful to be anything but a major player among dark-robes, but he was also not to be trusted. There had never been any real evidence to convict him of anything, but there were cases of mysterious disappearances in his past. No one would trust Zartho with anything as valuable as his or her own lives. Zartho wouldn't want a lot of people knowing about it anyway. The more people who know a secret; the less it is one.

He was challenged before he reached the gate. There was a guard at the gate, and one on the wall just inside. Dalryms stopped short, and spoke loud enough for any others to hear that might be lurking about.

"I must speak to the High Wizard. Please tell him it is an emergency."

The guard just stood staring at Dalryms as if he had gone stark raving mad. He had never heard of a white-robe wanting to speak to a dark-robe, let alone a tower's High Wizard before.

"Now," said Dalryms somewhat louder than before.

The tone in his voice had some affect on the guard, because he seemed to jump into action.

"Wait here," was all he said, and he disappeared into the shadows of the courtyard toward the tower.

Dalryms waited for what seemed like an eternity for the High Wizard, a man known only as Klev to the white-robes. He began to doubt that the wizard was going to come at all. Thinking about it, if the roles were reversed, he doubted that he would have gone out to see what was wanted from a dark-robe, as the request was utterly unheard of. In his long years studying magic, Dalryms had never heard of a request from one tower's member to speak to another's. Perhaps it would be enough to get this Klev to come out. They were running out of time. Soon they would have to make an attack on the tower itself. Then they would probably all die.

Just when Dalryms was about to give up the razor thin hope of solving this without a war, the High Wizard appeared out of the shadows. He didn't seem to have anyone else with him, and he stopped several feet short of the gate. He waited for a moment before he spoke, as if he was deciding that Dalryms really was a white robe.

"To what do we owe this auspicious occasion?" he asked with a hint of sarcasm in his voice. "Speak quickly, I have better things to do with my time than babble with a white-robe."

"I am Dalryms," said Dalryms introducing himself. "I think we need to work together quickly to avoid a catastrophe."

The dark robe seemed a bit taken-aback. This wasn't supposed to happen. When the guard had told him that a white-robe was at the gate, he thought it might be another unhappy youth trying to join with the dark-robes. He was ready to tell the youth to go away, as they chose who they would allow to join them. Now, however he was faced with the white towers High Wizard. This was something else altogether. "Explain yourself."

"The beams of light from your tower," Dalryms said pointing upwards to them. "I don't know what you have been told about them, but they are part of a plot by Zartho the Great."

"What?" Klev asked. "That's impossible."

"Actually it isn't. Zartho has been plotting something for a long time now, and I am sure that those lights have something to do with it."

"Can you prove that?" asked the dark-robe eyeing Dalryms suspiciously. This seemed like a white-robe trick of some kind, and he wanted to walk away from the conversation. There wasn't any way that those useless beams of light had anything dangerous about them. They were the playthings of one of the younger wizards. The youth had asked permission to use them a couple of weeks ago; something about the atmosphere at night. Klev couldn't remember everything about the conversation with the youth. He had given his permission more to be rid of the man, than to advance any knowledge of the tower.

He decided to stay and hear out the white-robe, if there was any chance of getting rid of Zartho, he couldn't afford to let it slip by. In fact, if he could get Zartho into trouble of any kind, he wanted to make the most of it.

"Yes," said Dalryms. "But I don't have time to do it now. Those beams have to be shut down before it's too late," he pointed upwards toward the lights. Klev looked unimpressed.

"So you want me to tell the young man up there that his two beams have the white tower in a panic. How do you think I will look to the rest of this tower if I act in your behalf? At best I would be a traitor. I'm sorry, I'll need more than that."

Dalryms took a deep breath. This wasn't going fast enough. He pointed to the sky behind himself. "If you would care to look towards the south, you will see that there are at least three lines, or more likely one line reflecting from several points forming something like a huge geometric portal."

Klev looked quickly up, and then back at Dalryms. He didn't trust the white-robe before him enough to look away for long, but what registered upon his mind in that brief glimpse forced his glance back into the night sky. Sure enough, there was a third line running east to west. That line had to intersect the two lines from the top of his tower somewhere out of sight. He had been deceived. Rage started to flood his mind. The young wizard would surely pay for this, but not in front of the white-robe. This was not a matter for outsiders.

Dalryms saw the flash of rage cross Klev's face as reality dawned on him. It disappeared even quicker than it had appeared to be replaced with an ingratiating smile.

"So, the white-robes are frightened by a couple of lines in the sky. It doesn't say much for the courage of your wizards," said Klev patronizingly.

"This is not the time for petty bickering," retorted Dalryms. "This is the time to work together to stop Zartho from destroying the kingdom, and taking over everything."

"And what's wrong with a dark-robe being in charge?" asked Klev although he knew he wouldn't want Zartho in charge of anything.

"Let me be blunt," said Dalryms. "I don't want to offend you, but you must understand, and quickly. Right now every wizard from the white tower is hidden around this tower. I am not only willing to kill you and every other dark-robe to stop those lights, but I am willing to die in the attempt. I am even willing to risk open war between the wizards to stop them. Are you willing to die right now or go to war to keep those lights on?"

The question was a trap. On the one hand, it laid out what Dalryms was willing to do, while at the same time it implied a question of the loyalty of the dark-robes to the king. Dalryms knew that there wasn't any real loyalty in the dark tower to anything but the individual wizards. But they had to maintain a semblance of loyalty to the king, or they would have been destroyed long ago.

Rage flashed across Klev's face, but it too was gone quickly, hidden within the man like an underground fault. Dalryms had the reputation of being a man of his word, and the dark-robe knew it. There would be blood tonight. He also suddenly realized the vulnerability of his position.

"I will look into the matter personally, and if there is some substance to your fears, I will let you know," he said trying to defuse the situation. "But if these accusations are unfounded, I assure you that the king will hear about it. Then we will probably see you hang for risking another Wizards War.

"Unfortunately, there is no time for 'looking into this,' we must act immediately..."

"How dare you threaten..." Klev interrupted, when the sky behind Dalryms lit up. The line running east to west seemed to form a boundary, and beyond it was a light almost like daylight. It streamed onto the distant mountains like sunlight through rain clouds. Dalryms saw the bewildered look on Klev's face and spun around to look at the beams.

Within the window of light something unbelievably huge moved. Worse still, what looked like a huge clawed arm began descending from the lighted plane onto the mountains. It was brownish gray, and seemed to be covered with enormous scales as big as houses. At the end of what looked like an arm was a malformed hand, with four short fingers that ended in black, shiny claws hundreds of feet long. From the distance of the two wizards they looked razor sharp.

The two tower heads stood gaping at the monstrosity that was entering their world.

"Oh shit," whispered Klev.

"Zartho's mad," gasped Dalryms. "That thing will destroy the world."

As they watched in horror the clawed hand set on a mountain peak, flattening it down several hundred feet under the enormous weight of the rest of the thing still within the portal. Its claws sank deep into the ground, tearing canyon-sized gashes into the earth.

# Chapter 19

General Leland stood open mouthed at the lights coming from the top of the white tower. There were two beams of red light shooting out into the night. He had been awakened from a deep dreamless sleep by the alarm of the guard, and had jumped out of bed, and ran from his quarters, stopping only long enough to grab his sword. Now he stood feeling the chill night air raise the hairs on his bare chest and back.

"What is it? What's happening?" he demanded from the guard as soon as he reached the gate.

"I don't know sir, those lines just appeared suddenly out of nowhere."

"Tell me exactly what happened."

"General, I was walking my post as normal, when I noticed those lights."

"How long have they been there?"

"They can't have been there more than a couple of minutes, because I always look at the tower, and the area between every time I get to this spot on my post. One time they weren't there, and the next time they were."

"How long does it take to walk your post?"

"Only about two minutes sir,"

The general stared out at the lights, and wondered what this new development could mean. Suddenly the lights disappeared. One second they were there pointing in two different directions towards the southeast mountains, and the next they were gone. The night was as black as before. The only lights visible were the stars twinkling above them.

"What the...?" asked the guard unable to form a complete question.

The last few nights had been quiet ones for the camp. With the destruction of the demon in the pit, they had remained unmolested. The moral of the camp had greatly improved, and they were considering sending out another party to report to the king. Now what was this new development? General Leland didn't know what to think of it.

"We'll send a search party to the top of the tower in the morning," he announced to no one in particular. There didn't seem to be any reason to be alarmed by the lights. That, among other things began to make him uneasy in the back of his mind. Whoever the dark-robes were that had been using the demon to kill everyone for miles around, hadn't gone away. What were they up to? Where were they really? The portal, or doorway, or whatever it was they had been using had another side somewhere. Was it close by? He didn't have an answer to any of these questions. There just wasn't enough to go on yet.

There had to be more to the murders than just the thrill of killing. He had known men that had become battle crazy, and had enjoyed killing for killing's sake, but this didn't fit the dark-robes pattern. Those sorry souls who had loved to kill had been just that. They had been killers. They would never have used a demon, or anyone else for that matter. They loved doing it themselves. When a man went that far down the path of violence, he had to be destroyed. He was as much a threat to his companions as to anyone that was labeled an enemy.

The bottom line, the general knew, was that they hadn't just gone away. They were plotting something else, and the red lines in the sky had to be a part of it. General Leland knew that sooner or later, they were going to fight those wizards. They would be brought to justice for the murders they had committed, and whatever they were up to would have to be stopped. As he stood looking at the tower, it dawned on him that the tower was a major part of this.

They must need it for something. They had killed the wizards in it, and had killed anyone who would have had dealings with it so that they could use it. In fact, now that he thought about it the tower would have been the main economic center here in the mountains. All the food and supplies for the wizards and the soldiers at the fort came from trading with the people of the mountains. If anything happened to the tower or fort, the people would have raised an outcry. Their primary means of cash flow would have dried up. They would have informed the king immediately. That's why they were all killed. The dark-robes wanted to use the tower for something.

But what that was, Leland didn't have a clue. The only thing that came to mind was that it had something to do with the lights they had just seen. A chill went up his spine when he wondered to himself what could be so important to a dark-robe that they were willing to kill so many people to get it. They must know that they would surely face the consequences for their murders, unless somehow that didn't concern them.

General Leland wondered for several minutes how that could be. How could they feel safe killing so many people, and what would they have to gain by it. The only answer was power. The kind of power that only a king could wield. But the general knew that King Nolan would never murder his own people. It had to be something else, unless they figured that *they* would be king at the end of all this. "There's no way," thought Leland. "Could they really be trying to overthrow the kingdom?" The thought stuck in his head. The more he tried to get rid of it, the more it seemed like the only explanation that made sense. Leland shuddered at the thought of a kingdom under the control of the dark-robes. There had to be something else. He had to have missed something in his thinking.

But his instincts were telling him that he had found the answer. He had always trusted his instincts before, and he knew that he was going to trust them this time. He just hated to think that the dark-robes were either so arrogant that they thought they could overthrow the kingdom, or they indeed had so much power that they could. It was a scary thought either way.

The big question in his mind now though was regarding the lights he had just seen. What purpose did they serve? They had to be connected with the dark-robes in some manner, but what was it? They seemed harmless, and they had only been on for a short time, only a couple of minutes. What could they do in so short a time?

Another question that bothered him was; what did they plan to do with the army here at the fort? They had seemed determined to whittle their forces down every night, until the demon had been killed. Since that night, there hadn't been any attacks on the fort, or anyone inside it. It seemed like the soldiers were not interesting anymore. Or, perhaps they were being left alone because they weren't a threat anymore. If the dark-robes felt secure with the army right in the middle of the lands they had so carefully cleared. What did that mean?

The first solution to pop into the general's head again filled him with dread. It could mean that whatever they were planning was going to happen soon, so soon that the army wouldn't be able to do anything about it. And when it did happen they would be able to deal with the army much more efficiently than they could at this time.

Comprehension came to Leland's mind like a shaft of light through dark clouds. The lights had been a test of some kind. They were probably the final step to the plot, and since they were the most visible, and would draw the most attention, they would have to be tested last, when there wouldn't be time for people to wonder what was going on. No time for questions to arise. He realized that they were going to attack tomorrow. *Not tomorrow, but tomorrow night, dark-robes like to work at night.*

The general went back to bed to get what sleep he could. He left orders with the guard that he was to be awakened if the lights appeared again, but he felt sure they wouldn't. He had to think clearly, and prepare his men for the coming battle. He was sure there was going to be one now. The best thing he could do right now was to get some sleep. He knew from many campaigns that sleep was a supply that could turn battles as surely as extra men. Even a little bit went a long way for men sorely deprived of it.

As he lay in his bedroll trying to sleep, his mind was already planning for the battle. He thought about where the best places for his troops would be in most situations, which troops were better suited to which jobs, and which terrain. He didn't leave anything to chance. He considered carefully different scenarios for the battle to follow, and what to do when the unexpected happened. It always happened, and Leland knew that he had to be ready for it.

He awoke with a start at the sound of the breakfast bell. It was still fairly early, but the morning was already under way. Soldiers were milling about trying to look busy at one thing or another. Most of their energy was spent trying to avoid being singled out by an officer as not busy. They were killing time before their turn at chow. There was no point in making their breakfast miserable. They would be working hard for most of the day if they were going to be ready.

During breakfast the officers met to discuss the plans that General Leland had come up with the night before. He told them of his suspicions that the entire kingdom was at stake, and that tonight would decide the matter. They discussed alternative plans, and made specific assignments to the various units of men to make sure they were ready. Then they went to work for the day.

The men ate lunch in shifts, and though they were tired by the evening meal, they were finally ready. Each man was to take an hours rest, and then get ready for the night. There would be men stationed around the tower, as well as a few inside to make the first assault. They had orders to make sure that the dark-robes were on the tower before anyone moved. The signal would be provided by the dark-robes themselves, in the form of the lights they had seen the night before. When those lights appeared, all hell was scheduled to break loose.

The men went to bed and slept for the allotted time. Then slowly, one or two at a time, they would quietly get up, and make their beds as if they were sleeping soundly within them. General

Leland didn't know if they were being watched or not, but he wasn't taking any chances. If some crystal ball was looking into the fort, all they would see was the men idling through the final hours of another boring day.

The men were to make their way out of the fort, by one of several means, and get to their hiding places around the tower before dark. A small force was to remain at the fort to act like the regular guard was posted, and that everything was normal.

By the time the sun had gone down, General Leland's forces were in place. He had made sure that every man knew what to do depending on what was happening. The general was inside the tower hidden with several of the fiercest warriors he had. They would remain hidden, until they heard the forces outside the tower begin their attack. At the sound of battle, they would make sure that the tower doors were opened to allow the others to join in the fight, and make their way up to the top of the tower. It was at the top of the tower that Leland felt sure he would find out the answers to all of his questions.

Darkness soon filled the tower, as well as the grounds outside. Then came the waiting game. Many of the men outside hated this part of the battle the worst. Soon they may be dead, and waiting for it seemed to turn the minutes into hours as the stars made their creeping way across the sky. At the rate they were going, tonight, the dawn might never arrive.

Eventually, General Leland and the men inside the tower heard soft footfalls on the steps coming down from the top of the tower. The dark-robes had used their portal to get to the top of the tower just as Leland had thought they would. The men outside the tower were on orders not to let anyone into the tower just in case they tried to come in the front door. They hadn't, and so Leland knew that they were just looking to see if there was anyone hiding inside the tower.

After several minutes, the footfalls went back up the steps to the levels above. Now they would wait for the lights to appear. If they moved too soon and were discovered, the murderers would have a good chance of getting away. They had to remain hidden until the dark-robes were heavily into whatever magic spell they intended to cast. Leland felt certain that that was when the lights would appear, and that was the best moment to strike.

The general didn't have long to wait. Less than ten minutes after the footsteps had retreated up the stairs, the men outside the tower sounded their battle cry. It echoed through the halls of the old tower, and up the stairs. General Leland sprang from his hiding place and raced for the stairs to the upper levels. Two other men joined him at the foot of the stairs to begin their headlong flight up to the top. The men that had been hiding with them were at the door to the tower. They had left it open, just like they had found it that first day but now it was closed, and the bolts had been thrown. It took the few men only seconds to release the locks, and throw wide the door for the men outside.

General Leland had paused to make sure that the door was open before he and the other two started up the stairs. The last thing he wanted was to get to the top of the tower and find out that no reinforcements were coming. He had learned early in his years of service to the king to lead from the front, but the key to that was to be leading someone that was actually following. The loudest BOOM he had ever heard blasted through the air at the fifth step.

Leland stopped short, and spun around. The two men with him slammed into him, and the three of them went down in a heap of tangled limbs and drawn weapons. By some chance of luck, no one was injured on the swords that all three had in their hands. He fought to be free of the tangle and find out what was happening to his men. Loud booms and flashes of light filled the air. He could hear his men screaming outside.

Leland finally got to his feet and was able to get an idea of the situation. Through the door to the tower he could see lightning flashes striking one man after another. A narrow pillar of fire slammed into the ground, and began to strafe the men trying to get to the door. The realization that the wizards had been expecting them struck him like a blow. A few men were making their way through the withering fire and through the door, but the doorway was filling up fast with dead and dying men. It was obvious that soon the men outside wouldn't be able to help them any more. He had to get to the top of the tower and draw the wizard's fire as soon as possible.

"To the top!" the general yelled at the men who had made it inside the tower. They didn't need to be told twice. As a body they headed up the stairs and into the upper levels. Two of the men even passed the general on the stairs in their haste to get to the top and save the men outside. By the time they had climbed halfway to the top, those two were nearly an entire story ahead of the general and the rest of the men. They ran as if chased by demons. The two were nearly evenly matched in speed; only a few steps separated them from each other.

Suddenly the first man stopped dead in his tracks. It looked like he had run into a brick wall. The man behind him stumbled as he tried to stop and fell at his feet. When the rest of the group reached them, the man on the steps was looking down as if he couldn't endure the sight of his companion. The other was still standing where he had stopped. His arms hung limply at his sides, and he had dropped his sword. His body stood there in a strange relaxed manner, almost as if it would collapse at any moment. Yet it hung there suspended somehow, unmoving.

Then Leland saw the black spike protruding out of the back of the man's head. It was set into the stone of the wall, and the man had run upon it at full speed, forcing it through his face, and out the back of his skull. It was nearly invisible in the darkness, and would have been impossible to see at the rate the two men were running. The hideous sight stunned even the most battle hardened there.

A loud boom echoed through the tower again and roused them from their shocked silence.

"We must get to the top!" yelled the general, and they were off again. A little slower this time, and waving their swords in front of them to check for any more spikes that might be hidden in the gloom. At the next landing the generals blade struck something in the air. It wasn't anything very solid, just a momentary slight resistance gone before the blade could be reversed. A soft twang sounded somewhere up ahead.

General Leland instinctively twisted to the side but not fast enough to avoid the crossbow bolt that slammed into his shoulder. It didn't penetrate far because of his armor, but his sword arm was almost useless now. The impact spun him further around and into the man next to him. They both went down together. There was a moment's confusion among the other warriors, but it quickly vanished as the general ordered them to keep going to the top. They didn't have time to waste on a wounded man right now, general or otherwise. There was no doubt in his mind that his men on the ground were still dying.

Leland fought to extricate himself from the other man and get to his feet. He smiled, only momentarily, to re-assure the fellow that he wasn't in any kind of trouble for being tangled with his commander, and they were off together. Now the general was at the back of the pack of men. They only had two more levels to go and they would be at the top of the tower.

As they continued their climb, General Leland silently cursed himself for falling prey to such a simple trap. They had searched the tower earlier in the day, and not found anything amiss. But now that the dark-robes were back, they should have known that there would be traps of some kind laid for them. The first one had been brutally violent on purpose. It had angered the men that their own strength was used against them in such a gruesome way. They had then played right into the wizard's hands by continuing their headlong charge up the various levels, now swinging swords with reckless abandon to find any other spikes protruding from the walls. The next trap had depended on their swords cutting the tight line holding back the trigger of the crossbow. They were being toyed with, and Leland knew it now.

There wasn't anytime left to warn the men ahead of him. They would simply have to take their chances. He was a little surprised when he heard the first of his men reach the highest level of the tower without springing any more traps. There must be more to it than that. He was now the last man in the charge, the others all having sped past him up the stairs. He heard the doorway to the roof give way, as the men slammed into it. As he made the top landing, the men ahead of him went through the doorway almost as one. He was still twenty feet from the door when the lightning slammed into his men, catching them by surprise.

The wizards had been expecting them all along. They must have been watching them all day. General Leland felt rage and frustration overwhelm him. He didn't have time to think, just act violently and quickly. His years of training came to the front now, and he leapt through the door onto the roof screaming the battle cry of his youth.

Utter chaos reigned on the roof. To the general's relief, all of his men weren't dead. There were a couple lying motionless in front of the door, but most had taken what cover was available. It was only a crate here, and a stone parapet there, but it was enough to shelter them from the withering lightning strikes that blasted at them from the far side of the towers flat roof. Even as he took the situation in, he was diving for what little cover was available. Pain shot through him as he landed on his wounded shoulder, and fought back the waves of nausea as the end of the quarrel pushed and twisted further into him.

In the rush up the last steps, he had forgotten to pull the bolt from his body. Now he did so with a scream. At least it wouldn't go any further into him. The men nearest him looked at him as if he was crazy. He simply smiled back at them, and grabbed his sword again in his good hand.

On the far side of the roof, there were two wizards. The general was sure they were the ones he had seen so briefly in the pit of corpses before they had battled the demon. One of them

343

was throwing the blue wizard's lightning with almost reckless abandon at the men. Obviously he was trying to keep them pinned down while the other one watched a tripod that had something on the end of it. The light beams from the night before were shooting out from the thing on the top of the tripod. From his close vantage point, Leland could see that the beams were a lot thicker than he had thought the night before. They were easily as thick as a strong mans upper arm. Occasionally the wizard protecting the tripod would cast a narrow blast of fire at his men, but it seemed like they were half-hearted attacks, meant more to keep them cowering than to do much harm. At least the men on the ground were safe for the time being. The wizards were determined to keep them from getting to the light source.

As the general looked at the situation, he knew that they were quickly running out of time. They had to shut off that light somehow. Maybe it would be enough just to block the beams. He looked around quickly for something to throw, but found nothing of any use. Then he saw the shield.

Several of the warriors had shields with them. He grabbed the nearest by the shoulder and yelled into his ear.

"We have to block those beams somehow. Throw your shield into one of them, and see if it breaks the spell."

With a nod of agreement the soldier slipped his arm out of the straps, and prepared to throw the shield like a disc. He took aim and launched the shield into the air. It sailed up and away from the roof of the tower, and into the light. There was a bright flash and sparks exploded from the shield, causing the general to blink and turn away for a moment. When he looked back at the beam, he saw two uneven pieces of the shield falling away into the night. The beam had sliced cleanly through the steel, without seeming to have been disrupted in the slightest.

"Well, that isn't what I'd hoped for," he said to the soldier who was now without a shield. "It appears that we'll have to rush them."

344

The soldier looked at him as if he had lost his sanity. He held the general's gaze for several moments, just long enough to verify that he was serious. "Yes, Sir."

They began to signal the other soldiers still hiding from the lightning blasts that were slowly cutting through their small defenses. General Leland held up his hand and started the countdown with his fingers. About two seconds before the charge, the sky was lit up brightly off to the east between the beams of light.

Everyone looked suddenly to the east and the light. It seemed as though somewhere within the mountains something like sunlight had suddenly broken through the night's darkness. All thoughts of attack seemed to vanish as the men stared toward the distant light. They couldn't see it because of the mountain peaks that were in the way. But every man there knew in his heart that it wasn't a good thing. Something was terribly wrong with that light. Even the wizards knew it.

The blasts of lightning suddenly ceased, and the wizards were staring dumbfounded at the light, as if they didn't have any idea what was going on.

"Attack! Now!" yelled General Leland at the top of his lungs. The men started out of their dazed state and into action almost instantly. The wizards were slower to respond to the yell of the charge.

The general and his soldiers leapt out from behind their cover, and sprinted towards the wizards and the strange device between them. Before they could cover half the distance though, the wizards snapped out of their stupor, and counter attacked.

Fire from both wizards blasted into the charging force, shattering its advance, and flinging burned men backwards. The general was hurled back through the air, tumbling until he struck the ground with a couple of other men. His armor was smoking hot, but his thick under garments protected him from most of the heat.

345

"Again!" he yelled to his troops. "This time spread out some. We have to stop them, now!" But even as he spoke, he saw lightning flashing into his men again.

---

Malak fell into the darkness grasping and clawing at the air. In his flailing, he caught hold of Lena with one hand, and held on tight, not wanting to loose her. They fell together another fifteen feet before striking the side of the pit. Pain exploded from his shoulder. His vision began adjusting to the ink around them, and he saw a rocky point coming up within reach. He grabbed at it in desperation.

By some miracle, Malak's grip caught and held. His shoulders felt like they were yanked from their sockets as he and Lena jerked to a stop. Lena was slammed into the side of the outcrop he had grabbed, and was knocked semi-conscious by the impact. Malak checked his grip after a moment, and found that it was not only solid, but luckily he had a good handhold on the stone. It felt like his fingers had caught in a crack in the rock. He couldn't believe his luck.

He rested for a moment hanging there, one hand holding Lena, and the other gripping the rock above them. Finally he began to slowly lift Lena up.

"Lena," he gasped, "get a grip on the wall."

There wasn't any response from her. In her dazed state, she barely registered the sound of his voice. She continued to hang limply in his grip, wondering why it was important for her to fight the sleepiness that was engulfing her. It would be so easy to slip into it, and rest. But something else in her fought it, and wouldn't let her give in.

Malak realized that Lena was out of it for a few minutes, and that he was going to have to do something quickly. Gathering his strength, he heaved her weight upwards toward the outcropping. He was a little surprised when he not only lifted her, but also was able to pull them both up to the ledge with his other hand. He had to struggle, but soon he had them both resting safely on the outcropping. His shoulders weren't hurting as much any more, and Lena seemed to be coming around. With a little luck, they might get out of this hole alive.

He felt around for the crack in the rock that had saved them, but couldn't find it. When he looked closely, he could see four holes in the solid rock the size of his fingers that were glowing softly, as if they were warmer than the surrounding rocks. It was impossible, but somehow his fingers had found the holes in the fall. He decided that there was no way he was that lucky or that good. There had to be another explanation. After looking at the holes for several minutes, the only solution to the puzzle seemed to be that his fingers had mad the holes, but for the life of him he just couldn't accept this as true.

Lena groaned and stirred next to him. "Lena, are you all right?" he asked stooping to help her sit up.

"I think so," she replied shakily. "What happened?"

"We seem to have fallen into a bit of a hole."

"Where are we?" she asked trying to sit up.

"Easy does it," Malak said grabbing her arm to keep her from falling off the side of the outcrop. "There isn't a lot of wiggle room."

Lena gasped as she felt the edge with her legs. "How far did we fall?"

"Only about twenty or thirty feet I think."

"Twenty or thirty feet?"

"I think so, it is hard to tell in the dark."

"Why aren't we dead? I mean some luck both of us landing perfectly on this piece of rock isn't it?"

"Well, to tell you the truth, we just missed it."

"What? What are you saying?"

"How's you leg?" Malak asked trying to change the subject.

"My leg? My legs are fine. Only, only my ankle hurts a little, and my hip too; Malak what's happened?

Malak hesitated for a moment not sure how to proceed. "While we were falling, I felt you in the air, and grabbed your leg to keep from loosing you."

"Yeah, and then what?"

"Well, with my other hand, I managed to snag the edge of the outcropping. Then I swung you up onto it and climbed up myself."

Lena could tell that he was hiding something. "How did you do that? The edge of this rock is too slick and round to get a grip. And you aren't that strong. What aren't you telling me Malak?"

He hesitated again for just a moment. There was no getting around it. Lena would smell a lie, and they needed to trust each other if they were going to survive. "You won't like the answer."

"Tell me, and let me decide."

"Feel here," Malak said guiding her hand to the finger holes in the edge of the outcropping.

She was silent for a moment as she felt the holes, and slid her fingers inside, testing the fit. "I don't get it. How did you catch them in the dark, while we were falling?"

"I don't know. I only know that I did."

"What? How? What are you talking about?" Lena stuttered trying to understand what Malak was telling her.

"Lena, we agreed several days ago that I would tell you if there was anything new about me. I am still the same person on the inside, I'm just not sure what physical limits apply to me now."

"So what else can you do?"

"There are always limits. They may have moved out a bit, but I'm still subject to them. That's the problem. You have to know what you can and can't do. Right now I don't know where that line is, and if I happen to cross it at the wrong time, we could both be killed. We don't have time to experiment, and see what I can really do, or where the edges of my limits are."

"You're right," Lena admitted feeling a little sheepish. She had always known that Malak was a skilled survivor. She had always respected him for his abilities, but now there was another dimension to him. In some ways he didn't seem really human anymore. Where did the old Malak end, and this new creature before her begin? Even now, he was speaking to her as if they could see each other. Obviously he could see her in the darkness, but she could see nothing. How did that change things between them? There were questions in her heart that she didn't have the courage to ask now.

"So what do we do now?" she asked finally.

"Now we keep to the plan. We find a way up to the top of the mountain, and stop the dark-robes."

He was still the determined, focused man that she had known. Once he set his sights on something, he would go after it in spite of any problems or diversions, until he had achieved his objective. It was something she had thought had been ingrained into him from a very early age. Inside she hoped that he would always stay that way. It didn't occur to her at the time what would happen if his will and new strength was ever turned against her. She felt inside that Malak was still the man he always had been.

Malak fumbled around inside his pack for a few moments, and pull out the grappling hook and rope. He carefully tied them together. Taking careful aim, he threw it up into the blackness. It sailed upwards for a couple of seconds, then clanged into the cliff wall. He tried again and again, with the same results. He managed to get the hook over the lip of the cliff, and into the tunnel a couple of times, but there wasn't anything for it to hook on, and the weight of the rope pulled it back over the edge.

Finally, after almost hitting him and Lena with the falling hook Malak gave up and returned the rope to his pack.

"So how do we get out of this pit?" asked Lena. "Down?"

"It's too deep to go down on the rope, and besides, we want to be going up if at all possible. Get behind me, and wrap your arms around my neck."

Lena complied with Malak's instructions. "Now what?" she asked when she was finally settled.

"Now you hold on."

Malak gathered himself for the task ahead. Carefully, feeling for the slightest cracks and crevices, he started to climb. All to soon Malak's fingertips started to hurt. It wasn't really noticeable at first, but soon they started to hurt more and more with every second. He started searching for better finger holds. Soon he was trying to wiggle them into small cracks in the rock. It didn't work though, and he grimaced whenever his fingers couldn't find purchase.

Every now and then, one of Malak's feet would find a small lump or crack that would hold their weight. He would rest there for a few seconds, to take the increasing strain off his arms and hands. Knowing he couldn't stay in any such place for long, he relished each one. If it hadn't been for them, he admitted to himself, they never would have made it.

When they finally did make it to the top, he was shaking from the strain. His fingers were oozing blood out from under the nails. He thought it was a miracle that he still had fingernails at all. They felt like some sadistic torturer had held them in a fire for several minutes. The stinging and burning rendered them almost immobile.

Malak flexed his hands, forcing them to keep moving though. He knew that they would stiffen up quickly if they were allowed to hold still. All he wanted was to bandage them and let them rest. But he knew that he would need them a lot more before the night was over. He wiped the blood off of them, and tested his grip on his short sword. They would do what he asked of them. " My crying little wimpy fingers aren't going to beat me!" He thought.

"We can't go back the way we came can we?" Lena asked massaging her arms and shoulders. The climb had taken its toll on her as well. During it, she had tried to keep her weight off of Malak's neck, and avoid strangling the man. Her chest, shoulders and arms had been shaking so badly when they reached the top that the only reason she had managed to hold on was that her grip was locked almost to the point of her not being able to let go.

"No, they are probably waiting to see if we fell into the pit, or if we are coming back."

"Then where do we go from here?"

"I can see a little ledge around the left side of the pit. We should be able to make it if we hug the wall."

"Then where do we go?"

"The tunnel looks like it slopes upwards, so we'll follow it until it ends, or we come out someplace." Malak reached out and took Lena by the hand. "I'll guide you past the pit."

They made their way carefully around the edge of the cavern. If he hadn't been able to see, they surely would have slipped and plummeted again. As it was, there were only one or two tight spots, where he had to tell Lena where to put her feet. Lena let out a sigh when they were finally past the danger. She wanted to sleep more than anything, but she knew that they had to keep going for a little while longer.

The tunnel did indeed go up, just as Malak had hoped. It wound upwards in a strange twisted spiral. It got steeper and steeper as they went, until the floor of the tunnel became steps, and went up even more steeply. It seemed like they had been going up forever when they felt the first whiff of fresh air. They knew they were close to the outside, and Malak leaned in close to Lena.

"Quiet now." was all he whispered into her ear.

"Like I need to be told," she thought.

They continued upwards at half the speed they had been going. In a few minutes, they could see the stars ahead through a small opening into the night. After being in the absolute darkness of the tunnel for so long, the stars seemed unusually bright to Lena. The air was colder than in the tunnel, and it made them shiver a little as they approached the opening. It was small, just large enough to allow one person at a time to walk through.

Malak cautiously poked his head out of the tunnel into the crisp mountain air. They were almost at the peak. He waited and watched for a moment. His eyes had re-adjusted to the normal light spectrum as they had approached the opening of the tunnel. Now he squinted into the night to see what was around them. He was finally able to make out the forms of two of the wizards at the top of the mountains peak. They were moving around some kind of tripod that had a long center pole sticking up through it.

There was no doubt in Malak's mind that whatever was on top of that pole was the source of the beams of light they had seen the night before. He thought for a moment. Was it really only one night before that they had seen the light? It seemed like a lot longer. It even seemed like a long time since they had entered the tunnels far down the mountain.

"Take off your pack," Malak whispered. "I don't think you'll be needing it in the next few minutes." She did as he asked, and noticed that he was removing his also. Malak drew his short sword with a quiet hiss from its scabbard. He checked to make sure of the location of his knives and daggers.

The two dark-robes were beginning to cast the spell now. Malak and Lena would have to think fast and act faster if they were going to stop them and survive. Malak looked for a few seconds longer trying to see if there were any other dark-robes. He finally gave up, and slipped silently out of the tunnel on his belly.

Lena followed his example, and came out of the tunnel slowly, sliding on her stomach, and trying not to make a sound.

"You're not going up against two dark-robes with that sword and a couple of little knives are you?" asked Lena incredulous that he would even consider such a suicidal course of action.

"I'm sorry, sneered Malak, "I forgot to bring my pocket army."

"We need a plan,"

"I'm trying to think of one, Lena, but at the same time I'm checking to make sure I have everything I need to get myself killed properly."

"You're not going to just charge up the rest of the hill at them are you?"

"No, I'm not that crazy just yet. We need some time and maybe a diversion."

"What kind of diversion?" Lena asked.

"Well, lets look at what we're up against. There are two dark-robes against us. There may be even more, but I haven't seen them yet. We were attacked by two earlier, and I'm hoping that these two are the same ones."

"How many more could there be?"

"I don't know. Two are bad enough. We have to attack them uphill. That means that we have to work a lot harder than they do. We also have to attack without any cover. In fact if they looked at us right now, they would probably see us sitting here with our pants down."

"Maybe they think we're dead."

"I hope so. It's the only thing we have going for us. I'm going to work my way around the hill a little more. When I get where I want to be I'll signal you."

"Then what?"

"I know you wizards don't like to tell anybody all of you abilities, but I need to know what kinds of spells you know."

Lena looked at Malak for a moment. It was true that her father had drilled into her again and again never to let anyone know the full extent of her abilities, but it was also true that if they were going to beat the dark-robes, they would need a real plan. Malak had been honest with what was happening to him, didn't that deserve some honesty in return? If they were going to survive the next few minutes, she was going to have to be honest with Malak, at least mostly honest with him.

"I don't really know any great spells, Malak. The only one that I can think of that might help is a lightning spell," she confessed.

Malak stood aghast. "A lightning spell? Like the one they were using on us earlier?"

"Yes," Lena admitted, "but I can't cast it like they can. I will only get one bolt, and then I'm pretty much done for. I'll probably just fall asleep right here on the mountain. I don't even know if I can get one good strike. I'm already tired, and I might not get more than a spark."

"What if that happens?" asked Malak.

"If that happens, I'll be just as tired as if I had cast a really big one. I'll be pretty much useless to you then."

"If you only get a spark, will they know it?"

"They'll probably sense the spell when I cast it. Unless they are totally absorbed in what they are doing, they are going to know exactly where I am."

"And that you are a threat to them."

"Either way, they'll know that as soon as I release the spell. You can't hide after something like that. The energy marks you. You stand out like a bonfire on a dark night. Then again, if I manage to get a big bolt, and I miss, then the same thing will happen. They'll be all over me. I won't last a second."

"Do you know any protective spells?"

"Only a couple of weak ones. Most of my magical ability is in revealing hidden things, like the traps and the tunnel entrance. I'm also really good at deciphering magical writing. Other than that, I know how to create an illusion, and make it seem real. But even that's a spell I can only work on a mind that isn't ready to protect itself. I'm not powerful enough to make a trained wizard fall for it. Worse yet, they could get access to my mind, and make me start seeing things. I might even attack you."

"All right, that spell's a bad idea," said Malak. "Here's what we'll do. I'm going to work my way over to that boulder," he said indicating a spot where a large boulder seemed to hang precariously to the side of the mountain. It wouldn't take much to send it crashing down hundreds of feet into the tree line below. "When I get there, try to hit one of them with a lightning bolt."

"But…"

"Just try. Send everything you've got. It may take one of them out, but it will surely get their attention. Then I'll attack from the side. They won't know how many wizards are with you now, so they will have to divert their attention between the two of us."

"That's it? That's your plan?" Lena asked incredulously. "Why don't we just kill each other now, and save them the trouble?"

"Look, Lena, there isn't time to call in a cavalry charge. The only thing we have on our side is that they think we fell into that pit and died. They're only half right about that. Fortunately for us it's the half that really matters. Now get ready, and give me everything you've got, if you can kill one of them, great."

Lena didn't think she had it in her to kill one of them. She had never used the spell against anything living before. He father had made her learn it to round out her training, but she had only used it on wooden targets. This was something entirely new. What would she be like if she did manage to kill one of them. Would she be able to live with herself?

Malak was already half way to the boulder. He moved like a shadow among the shadows, smooth and silent, like a panther stalking its prey. Suddenly there was a burst of light from the peak, and Malak dove the rest of the way to cover. He looked up at the summit, and saw the two red beams blazing from the top of the pole.

The wizards had to be close to doing whatever they were really up to. But they were just standing there. Malak knew in his gut that they should have been doing something, anything, but it looked like they were just waiting. *Why are they standing around like idiots?*

Then he realized that that is exactly what they were doing. They were waiting for something to happen. They were only a minor part of whatever was going on, and they were done with their part. Now it was all up to someone else somewhere else. He thought about the different points marked on the map. He didn't know what was coming, but he knew that he had to shut down those lights.

The fact that they weren't doing anything troubled Malak. He and Lena stood a much better chance if they were being distracted by something. It was now or never though, he couldn't wait for whatever was going to happen to land on them. Somewhere else, probably at the top of the dark tower in Chistock, there was going to be some angry dark-robes. He would get that pole down and break those beams no matter what.

He looked at Lena and signaled her to start the spell. She looked hesitant, and then began. It was going to be hard to throw much into the spell. She was exhausted from trying to find traps, the fight and their struggles in the tunnel. She had wanted to sleep then, but hadn't. Now the thought of the effort the spell was going to demand from her almost made her cry. She had come so far, and now she didn't know if she could even get a spark.

Gathering herself, she began the spell. She started as strongly as she could. She felt her strength waning quickly though, and had to push everything she had into it. She felt the spell take hold, and start to pull energy from her. Panicking, she tried to hold back for a moment, but then let the energy flow from within her. Towards the end, she even pushed again, emptying herself into the magic. Letting it flow from her like a torrent.

Lena opened her eyes and looked at Malak. The spell was complete. All that remained was to aim the energy and send it on its way. Malak wasn't looking at her though. He was gazing off into the sky between the two beams. Lena glanced in the same direction, and almost lost the spell. Far off over the distant mountain peaks was a third beam of light. It intersected the two from the mountain. On the other side of this beam, it looked like daylight. A doorway had been opened. Something hadn't been summoned into their world, but a doorway between worlds had opened. Something on the other side of the doorway moved, something bigger than an entire mountain range.

Dread filled her heart, and doubt filled her thoughts. These dark-robes had done something abominable. Worse still, they were trying to bring the destruction of the world. She focused her thoughts on the peak. The wizard on the left, away from Malak would do just fine. She aimed as carefully as she could, and released the energy of the spell with everything she had.

Only at the last second did she wonder if Malak would be ready. She hoped he was watching, and not still staring at the hole that had been ripped in their world. He would have to act fast now. As the lightning left her, she felt the breath forced out of her. A fist of energy blasting its way out of her, that left her stunned, unable to even focus her eyes, she collapsed to the ground and all was blackness.

Malak had never seen anything like this. The night sky had suddenly lit up miles away. He hadn't seen the other beam that was now bordering the other two. The three of them formed a huge triangle in the sky. The light was on the far side of the other beam though. He remembered the map suddenly, and realized that the beams of light from each of the points on the map formed a huge five-pointed star. Within that star would be inscribed a five-sided figure, a pentagon within a pentagram. It was a figure that could go on repeating itself eternally down to the smallest size, or large enough to engulf the stars in the sky.

They had opened a doorway of some kind into another world. There was something within it that was moving. The angle Malak was at made it almost impossible to see into the other world. But there was something moving there, something that was so big he thought he had gone mad just seeing it. *What had they done?*

# Chapter 20

Malak was jolted back from looking at the doorway to the mountain when Lena's blast exploded into the night. He glanced over to where he had left her, and saw her collapse onto the ground. It looked like she had passed out the instant the lightning had left her. She hadn't even had time to lie down. Then he looked up at the peak.

There was only one dark-robe visible from Malak's hiding place behind the boulder. The wizard was looking down at Lena's position. He was standing in a half crouch; rage seemed to infuse every aspect of his being. His hands shot out of his robe's sleeves and pointed at Lena, a spell already spewing from his lips.

Malak stood up without thinking and launched two knives at the dark-robe. They were well balanced, knives, but made of cheap steel. He liked to use them because if he lost them, he knew they weren't worth risking his life to recover. They flew through the air true to their aim. The first one struck the wizard in the ribs just below his arm. It entered at a slight angle, and got caught on his ribs; stopping before it could penetrate into the vital organs.

When the first knife found its mark, the dark-robe's arm dropped reflexively, opening the path for the second knife. It found its mark too. The blade slammed into the dark-robes throat, just below the jaw line. It pierced through skin and tendon, vein and artery, to finally lodge across the windpipe. All of the years Malak had spent practicing had paid off again. The wizard was a dead man, and he fell with the final words of the spell forced out as a gargled hiss.

Malak didn't know how Lena was doing, and he didn't have time to check on her. Somewhere there was another wizard. He might be dead from Lena's spell, or he might just be wounded. *Hell,* thought Malak, *he could just be hiding.* He couldn't take the chance to see about Lena yet. He ran upwards with everything he had. He seemed to fly up the mountain. He didn't know he could move that fast, but somehow he did.

When he got to the top, Malak looked around for the second dark-robe. He couldn't see him for a second, but he had the feeling that he was still there somewhere. Then he saw the black robe lying sprawled out on the ground several feet down from the peak. Lena must have killed him with her lightning blast. The wind was too slight to move the cloth, and it lay there like a shroud over the dead wizard.

Malak looked quickly at the opening in the sky again. It looked like a flat sheet of light extending over the mountains, for as far as he could see. Something had come through it in the far distance. He couldn't see what it was, but he could see that it seemed to reach from the opening to the mountaintops in the distance. Whatever it was, there was no way this world could hold it.

Quickly Malak dashed towards the tripod. He had to destroy the shape in the sky defined by those red beams. He didn't know anything about magical doorways, but he figured that they weren't very stable. If he could destroy the geometry of the shape defining it, it might just be forced closed. He didn't know what would happen to anything in the way of the closure. He didn't know for certain that it would have any effect on the doorway, but he had to try something. If the thing on the other side got entirely into this world, it would be the end of everything. There was no way that he was going to allow that to happen.

Malak dove the last few feet to the tripod. He was going to hit it with everything he had. A blast of pain and fire slammed into the side of him, knocking him sideways. He missed the tripod entirely and was thrown off the peak of the mountain. Screaming in pain, he tumbled town the mountain. Clawing and scraping at anything he could, he managed to stop himself about fifteen feet down the slope. He rolled left and right to put the fire out of his clothes and hair. His skin was charred black anywhere it had been exposed. He felt the pain of it cracking and peeling with his every move.

Malak fought back the waves of dizzying pain, and tried to focus. He quickly gathered himself and lunged back for the peak, every move created an explosion of agony. It felt like his burned skin was being ripped off of him. When he finally reached the summit again, he saw the second wizard. He hadn't died in Lena's blast. He was standing up from behind a boulder. It was almost comical the way his clothing hung in tatters. Lena's spell hadn't killed him, but it had blown most of his clothing off. Even his shoes had holes blown in them. He seemed to be smoking a little too, Malak noticed.

The dark-robe stood looking at Malak for a second. He had hit Malak with a blast of fire that should have burned him to the bone. Yet here he came, screaming his way back onto the peak again. He raised his hands and hot, blue lightning slammed into the charging assassin.

Every bolt of electricity that found Malak knocked him to one side or the other. Sometimes he was thrown backwards, stunned by the force of the shocks. The energy seemed to penetrate under the burned flesh, and tear away at it. Always he kept moving, trying to find cover on the bare peak. He was gradually working his way to the wizard. But he wasn't getting there fast enough. It was taking too much time. He had to destroy the beams, or at least knock them out of alignment, but when he had tried to get to them, he had found it impossible. The wizard was too good with the energy he was blasting into Malak. His only chance was to take out the wizard once and for all. Then he would be able to destroy the portal. All of his attention was on the wizard now.

It seemed to take forever before Malak was anywhere close to his tormentor. He hoped that he would soon be able to kill the wizard, because he was loosing his strength. He just couldn't fight the pain anymore. It had taken over his world. He kept falling towards unconsciousness, and the relief that the blackness would bring. Again, he lunged forward, this time safely. He lunged again, and was spun around by a jolt of lightning striking him in the shoulder. He continued the spin, using his momentum to resume his attack.

Behind Malak, on the other side of the tripod, a thin figure slowly staggered up the hill. Lena had fallen after releasing the energy of the spell, and she was nearly comatose when the fire had struck Malak. His scream had punched its way through her sleep-dulled senses, bringing her back towards consciousness. She had fought then, harder than she had ever fought before. She had to help somehow! She wouldn't give in to the sleep! Not now. Not this time. She had come too far to stop now. She would not let the dark-robes win.

Slowly Lena had crawled up the mountain, to witness the battle on top. Malak was something out of a nightmare. His skin was charred and blackened, and pieces of it were hanging off him. Still he fought on. She couldn't believe what she was seeing. He was leaping from place to place ducking and hiding as best he could, but inevitably being struck by the lightning that the dark-robe cast at him. She couldn't help him. The magic was gone from the place inside where she found it. It would only return with sleep.

Lena looked around with tears stinging her eyes. The tripod stood off to the side of the battle. It was unprotected. At last there was something she could do. She staggered towards it as fast as she could, finally stumbling and falling at its base. The pain of the gravel on the ground cutting into the palm of her hands kept her awake. She reached up with one hand and grabbed a leg of the tripod. It didn't budge. She pulled harder with the same result. She fought to get to her feet, and threw her weight against it. Still she couldn't move it. With her last bit of strength, she stepped back a couple of paces, and flung herself at it.

---

Zartho stood on top of the tower. He laughed to himself. The entire tower was looking for the escaped Golan. Things had worked out better than he had hoped. He had hoped to kill the three fools quickly, get the rest of the tower back to their quarters, and then cast the spell. Now everyone was searching the lower levels of the tower, and wouldn't be able to stop him. Even if they saw what was happening and realized what was going on, they wouldn't be able to get to the top of the tower in time. He would be ruler of the kingdom by this time tomorrow. All he had to do was initiate the light beam, and wait an instant for its return. Then cast the spell that would open the doorway to millions of warriors, all under his control. He quickly set up the beam. It was a magical mirror that had perfect focus, and no loss of light. He spoke the words, and waved his torch in front of it.

Immediately the light of the torch lanced into the night, and returned from all five points back into the mirror to go out again, just as it had worked the night before. Zartho was elated. After all of his work to see everything coming together filled him with a sense of confidence that he had rarely felt before. He removed the figurine from his pocket, and began the spell that would link it to another world. A world outside anything he had ever seen before, a world that would give him its might to use to subject this world to himself. That was what he longed for more than anything else, to rule over everything. Now it was coming to him on a beam of light.

The figurine in his hand began to glow a soft golden light of its own. As Zartho continued the spell, it grew brighter and seemed to focus around itself and then outward. It dimmed, only for a second, and then seemed to grab onto something else and flashed much brighter than before. Zartho was so engrossed in the spell, and the sight of the symbiot that he didn't feel the pain in his hand until it was too late.

Suddenly, Zartho felt the presence of something just beyond his thoughts. It seemed to grow more and more powerful with every second. He realized to his horror that whatever the symbiot was linked to was not millions of tiny minds, but one huge primitive intellect. He tried to drop the symbiot, but found that it was stuck to his hand now. Pain seared into him from the little statue. Then fear gripped him as well. Then something else gripped him inside.

Golden light from the symbiot surrounded Zartho and engulfed him. It shot outward and mixed with the beams of red already in the night sky. Off in the distance, the doorway opened. The golden light stretched across the mountains, lighting the sky there like day. Too late, he realized that the thing on the other side was very powerful indeed. Its will was nearly as strong as his was. It took everything he had not to let it take over his mind. He stood motionless on top of the tower; sweat pouring down his face, in the cool of the night. He fought for his soul and his mind. Finally, slowly he fought the thing back. Then he somehow managed to subject the thing to his will. It was coming through the opening now. One leg was already inside this world, crushing a mountain peak far to the north near Thosh.

The parapet near Zartho suddenly exploded into shards of blasted rock. Pieces of stone cut his face, and knocked him from his feet. The thing on the other side of the doorway sensed the confusion. It tried again to master the will of the one calling to it. Zartho's will was almost crushed then. Somehow he managed to beat the thing back again in his mind.

Alien thoughts of death and hunger almost overwhelmed Zartho for a moment, but only for a moment. He was quickly in control again. The thing, whatever it was, was not very intelligent. Its motivations were based in instinct, survival, and nothing more. If it had had more intelligence, it would have dominated Zartho with its sheer power. He was still not sure what to do with the thing now that he had control of it.

All of Zartho's plans were changing. He could still rule the kingdom, and the world. He would crush the entire city of Thosh, king and all. No one would oppose him with this monster at his command. It could still work. He was determined to make it work.

Another blast of energy came streaking up the side of the tower. It slammed into the parapet next to the first one, and it too exploded with a deep boom. Zartho ran to the edge. Far below he saw two figures preparing another spell to cast at him. He stood there glowing with the power of the symbiot. A target at the top of the tower that was impossible to miss.

Anger welled up inside him. These two puny things were trying to stop him. He threw a blast of energy at them. Somehow, even not clear to him, he mixed the power of the symbiot into the spell. He was becoming entangled with it now, they were becoming one. The blast he launched at the ground lit up the night brighter than the sun at noon. It slammed into one of the men below as if it was a giant boulder cast from that dizzying height. He was crushed instantly, and then his body and the ground around it exploded back into the air. The wizard next to the blast was thrown callously aside by the blast. He slammed into a tree trunk, and lay crumpled on the ground.

Zartho was elated. There was so much power coursing through him now, that nothing seemed impossible. He looked around for someone or something else to destroy. In the back of his mind, he knew that another leg had entered this world.

General Leland watched as the few remaining men rallied themselves to the attack. He knew that they wouldn't stand much of a chance, but they had to do something. If the dark-robes won, a lot more innocent people would die, and everyone else would be enslaved. He gathered himself for one last attempt. Instead of going with the men though, he had a different rout planned.

On Leland's signal, the men charged out from behind whatever cover they had been able to find. He held back, waiting for the blast that he knew was coming. For the first time in his career as a commander, he was leading from the rear. He hated it, but this time there wasn't a choice. The front men were scattered and thrown back like dried leaves in a fall wind. Leland made his charge then.

He knew from working with wizards that he might have a chance right after a spell had been cast, when the wizards were low on the energy that they had built up. Before they could focus on another spell. He ran straight at them, knowing that he wasn't going to make it. He did seem to surprise them for a moment, but they were ready for his attack all too quickly.

Leland had barely covered half the distance to them when one of the dark-robes raised his hands again.

Instantly the general leapt to the side. He ran for the edge of the tower as hard as he could, hoping that they wouldn't detect the angle he was using to get closer to them. An explosion behind him lifted him off his feet, and threw him towards the parapet. They had barely missed him.

General Leland almost smiled as he realized that they had just helped him. He tumbled in the air, and hit the ground sliding feet first into the parapet. Using his momentum, he rocked to his feet faster than any of the soldiers could believe, and sprang sideways off the parapet straight at the tripod. It was only a few feet away now. Both dark-robes were out of his path, and couldn't stop him. He heard one of them start to scream, and then his body slammed into the tripod, knocking it to the side and over the edge of the tower. The general tumbled over the edge with it. Somehow he got a single handhold on the lip of the tower, catching himself just this side of eternity. He watched the poles fall into the darkness below.

A sound of fire filled his head. He looked up to see the beams of light were gone. Energy seemed to be screaming out from the point of failure. It gathered and expanded, until the top of the tower was engulfed in flame, searing his handhold then it shot out into the night towards the light in the mountains. It was gaining intensity as it went, bounded only by where the beams had been. It seemed to fill the sky as it headed east towards Thosh.

Klev looked up at the top of the black tower. He didn't hesitate one second. Lightning roared out of his fingertips towards the top and its damned lights. It screamed through the air and shattered harmlessly as it struck an invisible barrier within a few feet of the top.

Klev spun and shouted at Dalryms, "HELP ME!"

Dalryms didn't need any invitation. He had wanted to attack the dark tower many times in the past, and he did so now with relish. Very soon, the other white robes hiding nearby had come out of their places of concealment, and were lending their powers to the attack. Nothing they did had any affect on the top of the tower. The wizard at the top had placed a shield around the area, and nothing they threw at it was getting through.

Other dark-robes were starting to pour from the tower intent on attacking the white robes. Klev soon had them understanding the situation, and they joined the assault. Though their best efforts were in vain. The protection spell was too strong.

"Look!" yelled a voice, and the blasts of energy trickled to a stop. All eyes were now looking at the doorway. It seemed to be collapsing. Far beyond the clawed thing that had entered their world a line of fire was rushing towards them. Flames engulfed the leg, and continued on towards Thosh. The mountaintops were burning with the heat of the fire.

"Get down!" someone yelled. White and dark-robes dropped to the ground as one. They could already feel the heat of the flames coming. The air seemed to be sucked from their lungs as the inferno passed overhead. It lasted only a few seconds, and then the wave of fire was gone, bearing off to the southeast as if drawn by unseen cords across the sky. The light of the fire slowly disappeared across the ocean, and darkness returned to the land.

Dalryms carefully rolled over, and looked up at the sky. It was dark with only a few stars visible here and there. The top half of the dark-tower was gone, completely melted or blown away. As they got to their feet, the wizards could hear the people of the city coming out of their homes. Screams and yells could be heard far in the distance. Dalryms knew that the king was going to be furious. Someone was going to get pinned with this. He didn't care at the moment though, because his mind was thinking too much about the condition of the white tower. He wondered if half of it was gone as well.

---

Lena was too weak to run, she really only staggered faster and collapsed at the tripod. She didn't even bother to push it with her hands. She just crashed into it with her chest, knocking the wind out of herself. But shifting its position slightly. She fell to the ground as a shattering sound filled the air. The last thing she remembered was a high-pitched scream filling her ears. She couldn't tell whether it was Malak's voice or her own that was screaming when the blackness took her.

Malak heard glass shattering. He had never known such pain in his life. He knew that he was dying, probably already dead, but he kept trying to get to the wizard. His short sword was in his hand, but he couldn't remember drawing it from its sheath. He had fought his way almost within striking distance of the dark-robe, fought his way from running and jumping, to his knees where he knew he would die. He had looked up into the face of the blackest wizard he had ever seen, and knew that the next blast would kill him.

Malak didn't know how he had made it this far. Surely whatever that thing in the swamp had done to him had allowed his body to take more punishment than he had ever imagined possible; and kept him going. But now it was all in vain. The wizard was poised to end it all for him, when the glass had broken. He hadn't known there was any glass around, but the sound was unmistakable. In that instant the wizard had looked away towards the tripod.

Whatever the dark-robe saw changed him. His expression changed suddenly from a gleeful, victorious, hate-filled leer, to panic. Now was Malak's chance. He threw himself from his knees with the blade of his sword leading. The lunge was terribly overextended, he was off balance from the start, but his weight was behind it. Through the searing pain in his legs and body he felt the tip sink deep into the wizard's chest. The sword sliced through the heart, and out the other side. It sank up to the hilt, and Malak collided with the surprised man. He let out a high-pitched death scream that filled Malak's ears.

Malak didn't hear the sound though. As the blade had sunk into the wizard's chest something had pummeled into Malak. He had never felt anything like it. He felt it flow into him through the sword like a tidal wave. Instantly his pain eased. He felt stronger. He was able to stand again. As the dying wizard screamed out his last, he was renewed to nearly his normal strength. When the dark-robe was finally silent, Malak stood looking at an emaciated skeleton skewered on his sword.

With a feeling of revulsion, Malak threw the remains to the ground, and pulled his sword free. Suddenly he remembered the beams, and what he still had to do. He spun around and stopped dead in his tracks. The beams were gone. The tripod still stood, but it was at a different angle than before. Lena's body lay at the foot of the tripod. He didn't know if she was dead or alive, and the question had little meaning to him as he saw the sky beyond her.

A wall of fire was coming right at them. *Not more fire!* Malak raced across the ground. He picked Lena's limp form up, and dove off the peak. They rolled together down the mountain. He wrapped himself around her as best he could, and tried to protect her. They tumbled and rolled down the mountainside several hundred feet, until they finally came to a sliding stop with their heads aiming downhill.

The wave of flames didn't strike the peak with its full fury as it had the other points of the pentagram. It started turning before it was there, and only brushed the top of the peak. Still, everything but the bare rock of the mountain's top was vaporized in the scorching heat.

The captain hated the situation. He had been forced by the black-robes to hove-to in the middle of the Bay of Blood for several days now. Last night they had lifted his ship to an unheard of height, and kept it there while they messed around at the top of the masts. Then two beams of light had seemed to shoot out of the top of the mast, and light up the sky.

He had been furious, when the ship had left the surface of the ocean without a hint of warning. No one said a word to the dark-robes though. Not even he dared to interrupt them. They were paying him well enough, but he hated what was happening. And tonight they were doing it again! It wasn't natural for anything made by man to fly through the air, let alone at such a dizzying height. Even worse was to hang suspended in place, as if by nothing, thousands of feet above the sea. If he opened his mouth, he knew he might not survive to get paid.

A seaman screamed and everyone looked at the horizon. A wall of fire was coming at them. It seemed to move with unreal speed toward the ship. The captain wondered what had happened on land that could cause such a thing, and then he realized that it soon wouldn't matter.

The firestorm swept through the ship and beyond, changing course in a long sweeping arc. The two ends of the wave were being drawn ahead of the center, the whole thing bent on getting back towards the original source of its energy. Far out at sea, the two ends met. One from the north, and the other from the south forming a ring of fire that began to collapse into its center.

---

Zartho stood defiant at the top of the tower. He had obliterated a wizard, and sent another flying like a twig with one single spell. He felt the awesome power of the symbiot swell within him as he looked down. No one could stop him now. He finally knew the power he had craved his entire life. He knew that he could do anything he wanted and no one could stop him. He was everything! The power he felt was even increasing. Was there no end to it?

His leering gaze slowly withdrew from the scene of carnage far below. He didn't care if he had killed the second wizard or not, he didn't even care if they were white-robes or not. All others were contemptible to him now. All was his to destroy or spare on a whim. He looked out over the mountains, and realized that he couldn't feel the entity inside his mind anymore.

Then he saw the fire coming. From within the spell itself there wasn't any way he could have sensed its collapse. Now he saw it. He saw the ring wall of fire closing on him. He knew it was drawn to the symbiot, and he tried in panic to drop the cursed thing. But it had melted its way into his hand. It was now a part of his flesh. Fear leapt into his mind again. How was this possible? How could it have failed?

Zartho turned to run; somewhere; anywhere had to be safer than the top of this tower. He saw the other side of the ring then, and knew that he was trapped. He knew in an instant that there was no way out. The power he felt increasing was, in fact, just being drawn home. He had failed.

A snarl of hatred creased Zartho's features as he and most of the tower underneath him exploded in flames.

---

Malak lay face down on top of Lena for several minutes after the heat had dissipated. She slept under his protective weight unaware of how close death had come to her. The rejuvenating abyss had taken her as she had fallen at the tripod, and wasn't going to let her go anytime soon. He slowly looked up from the mountainside to the peak. The ground was scorched and blackened at the top. There wasn't anything for him to go back up there for. He doubted that there was anything left of the wizards' corpses. He didn't want to think of what had happened when he had stabbed the second wizard.

Carefully, Malak picked Lena up from the ground and made his way to the tunnel they had come out. He entered slowly, half expecting another dark-robe to appear out of the darkness. He didn't really want to go back through the tunnels, but he knew that they didn't stand a chance going down the slope through all of the traps that were still there. When he was in absolute darkness, he stopped to let his eyes adjust to the blackness. They seemed to do it a little faster this time, almost as if they were getting stronger or more accustomed to their new ability.

Cautiously he worked his way back through the tunnel and past the pit. It was a little tight carrying Lena on his shoulder and the two packs, but they made it all right. When he re-entered what must have been the dinning area, he noticed that everything was burned and blackened from the earlier fire. There was still a smell of smoke in the air, but other than that the fire seemed not to have damaged anything. There was no sign of any other wizards.

He laid Lena on the ground, and tried to make her as comfortable as possible. Then he went about trying to prepare some food. He found some in the kitchen area, and ate it quietly as he watched Lena sleep. After the small meal, he left her in the room with a single torch burning in case she woke up, and went to check out the rest of the tunnels.

There wasn't anything of note in most of them. Supplies had been laid up for several months, but they were all of the type that would keep for years. They were hard-tack rations. Nothing fancy, but they would keep men on their feet and fighting, or spell casting as the situation called for. He found a couple of hidden chambers that weren't easy to access, but there wasn't anything of interest in them. In one tunnel, there was a room off to the side that seemed to be some kind of library.

It was dark, and there were shelves of books inside that Malak couldn't make much of. They were spell books, but from the little he could make out they contained only dark magic. The kind of thing that most wizards wouldn't have bothered studying, or admitting they knew anything about. Malak considered burning them, but had an aversion to burning books. One never knew when the knowledge they contained might come in handy for something. He decided, in the end, to hide them inside the chambers he had discovered.

Lena slept for two days. When she awoke, she didn't know where she was at first, but Malak had left a torch burning for light, and some bread and water to eat. She dug into the food with eagerness. It wasn't much, but in her famished state it seemed like a feast. Soon Malak appeared out of one of the tunnels.

"Well, look who decided to wake up," he teased.

"How long was I asleep?"

"Only a couple of days, I thought I would have to drag you all the way back to Chistock so you're dad could wake you up."

With the mention of her father, Lena looked down and ate another bite of bread. When she looked up again, Malak saw a tear glistening in the torchlight.

"We can head for home whenever you feel up to it," he said aware of her homesickness.

"I can leave right now," she said with a smile. The thoughts of home filled her with a happiness that she hadn't felt in a long time. "What time is it anyway?"

"Well, the sun just set, but if you want we can pack up and leave."

"What is there to pack?"

"The wizards who occupied these tunnels were kind enough to leave us some food and other supplies."

"What happened to them," she asked suddenly remembering their former enemies.

"I couldn't find any trace of them after the firestorm."

"What firestorm?" Lena asked confused.

Malak took a few minutes to bring her up to date. The last thing she remembered was throwing herself at the tripod, and he filled her in about the events immediately after. He told her about being healed when he stabbed the wizard with his sword to her obvious distaste, but left out finding the magic books in the tunnels below. He didn't know why he chose to leave them out, but he did. He told himself it was because he didn't want to tempt Lena with dark magic.

They decided to wait for dawn before starting their journey home. They spent a couple of hours deciding what supplies they could take with them, and how best to pack for the trip. They spent the rest of the night sleeping at the entrance to the tunnels they had originally come in. When they woke up the light of day was visible above their heads.

They began the long walk home then. It seemed that their steps were lighter, and they traveled faster than they had before. Their hearts were definitely lighter. Malak didn't worry anymore about what the dark-robes would or wouldn't do if they caught him. He knew somehow that they were worried about a lot more than his theft.

# Chapter 21

Lena caught site of the small cabin through the trees while they were still several hundred yards away. Smoke was rising from the chimney in lazy puffs. At the first sight of her home, she bolted for the door, desperate to see her father again. She ran across the threshold and through the front door of the cabin while Malak was still far behind her. He thought about leaving her and Shial to their reunion, and waited for a couple of minutes. When he thought they had had enough time for an initial embrace, he knocked gently on the door. There wasn't any answer. He stood on the stoop for another minute, then with increasing trepidation he slowly entered.

Lena and Shial were standing in the middle of the floor locked in an embrace that seemed as if it would squeeze the breath from them. Both had tears streaming down their cheeks, and were unable to speak. They just stood there rocking back and forth together, too overcome for words. Malak felt awkward at the sight, and turned to leave.

"No!" said Shial in a hoarse whisper, "don't leave Malak."

It was several moments before he could say more, and Malak couldn't do anything but stand there witnessing the tenderness between the old man and his daughter. They seemed to be reluctant to leave the world of their embrace that they had made for themselves. It was just the two of them. Malak was an outsider. Then Shial spoke again.

"Come here," he beckoned to Malak.

As Malak approached, they parted a little, and embraced him together. The three of them stood that way for a long time. Malak felt as if the father he had found in Shial so many years ago was now, at this moment, truly his father. The moment seemed to last for hours, but it was over in only a few minutes. The three of them finally separated, stepping back to look at each other.

"Well, what have the two of you been up to?" asked Shial smiling from ear to ear.

Malak paused for a breath then he began to recount their adventure. He had to reach back into his memory of months past to the night he had shown Shial the map, and told him about it and the figurine. The smile melted from Shial's face as he remembered all that had occurred since that night. Slowly the story came out. Lena made comments here and there as Malak did most of the telling.

Shial laughed out loud when Malak told of his surprise at finding Lena under the deck of the boat, and stopped him altogether when he recounted landing on the beach in the mists. Before they could continue with the tale, he made them sit down while he made some dinner. Lena helped him despite his protests. Malak attempted to help out as well, but then sat down when the wizard gave him a look that threatened the stuff of nightmares.

Soon the meal was ready, and they continued their tale as they ate. Shial began to intermix his story, so that the entire tale was told at once. Shial grew concerned when he heard of Malak's battle with the thing in the swamps. Most of the details were glossed over. Malak didn't want to be reminded of, or tell about the filth he had gulped so greedily, so he neglected any mention of it.

"I can't believe the two of you are still alive," remarked Shial when all was finally told. "That must have been the thing that killed so many of the men in my expedition. I had hoped that it wouldn't find you, but you defeated it somehow. I have always thought that there was something in you boy, but I never thought it would bring you through like this."

"Well he didn't come out of it the same way he went in," said Lena.

"What do you mean?" asked Shial.

"Go ahead and tell him."

"I'm getting there," scowled Malak.

He continued with the tale of getting out of the swamps, and onto the plains. Shial studied him silently as he told the rest of their tale, and mentioned the strange abilities and strengths he seemed to have gained.

"I don't know what to make of it," said Shial after Malak was finished. "Something passed between you and that thing in the swamp. I'm sure of that. But I don't know what it was. It's probably why you survived. That demon thing wouldn't have given anything willingly to you. You must have taken something from it by force. That's why it left you alone. You hurt it when you took it, and it left."

Malak could see that Shial suspected more to the story than he had told, but he left it alone.

"Many things must have happened at the same time to cause the doorway to collapse the way it did," Shial continued changing the subject. He then told his tale, and tears came to his eyes when he told them of the death of the spy Golan. "His body was literally smashed into the earth. It was crushed into paste. I threw some dirt into the hole the next day to bury him, because there wasn't any way to pick out his body."

Lena turned pale at the description of the poor man. She thought about all that had happened, and knew from Shial that many wizards had died both black- and white-robed. "What happened to the tower in Thosh?" she asked.

"Both of them lost their tops: completely burned off," snorted Shial. "Anybody that was half way up them was vaporized too. The dark tower here was nearly leveled to the ground. All that's left is a bunch of melted stone blocks.

"In fact," continued Shial, "King Nolan is royally pissed off about the whole thing. It's one thing for wizards to try and usurp the kingdom in a nice, quiet, backstabbing sort of way, but scorching most of the mountaintops in the kingdom; that's something else entirely. It makes the population wonder if he is really in charge. Dalryms finally contacted me yesterday afternoon. He has been trying to keep the king from using the army to sweep all magic out of the kingdom forever, both people and records."

"What?" asked Lena incredulous? "He can't do that!"

"He could try. Dalryms has asked me to return to Thosh and help to plead our case."

"We'll come with you, of course," Malak said as Lena nodded in agreement.

"No," said Shial. "The king probably knows that you were involved somehow, but since Dalryms didn't tell me exactly what his plans were when he visited, chances are he didn't tell the king either. Your presence would just be another thorn in the king's side."

"What do you mean?" asked Malak.

"Well, I didn't know that Dalryms was going to use you that night. If I had, I would have tried to stop him, you know that don't you?"

"Yes," admitted Malak. Shial wouldn't have agreed to the spell that would put Malak into such danger.

"That means that the king probably didn't know about it either. You were allowed out of the royal assassins, because Dalryms convinced the king that you could be used in the future if needed: a secret weapon of sorts. It won't sit well with the king that you were used without his permission, or even his knowledge."

"I really hate killing," muttered Malak. "But I think I would like to kill Dalryms."

"I wouldn't suggest trying Malak. He is a very powerful wizard."

"I don't understand something," said Lena. "Malak can perform magical spells, why wasn't he made a wizard when his ability was discovered. A wizard is a lot more of an asset to the king than an assassin. Or at least they were."

At this, Shial chuckled softly. "Can I tell her, Malak?"

"I don't care, I know her weakness, and she might as well know mine."

"Lena, you know that there is always a price for using magic."

"Yes," she responded.

"With everyone capable of magic it is different. Some pay a much heavier price than others."

"You mean like mine."

"Yes," said Shial. "You are used in such a way that you must sleep to restore yourself. By the way, I am very proud of you for the strength you showed through all of this. You have grown a lot in your abilities."

"Get to the point, dad," Lena said blushing and glowing at the compliment.

"Well, Malak pays a high price for the magic; higher than you. He can do small things that deal with sensitivity and be all right."

"You mean like detecting traps?"

"Exactly, but if he tries to put any power into his magic at all, the results are, well, how would you describe it Malak?"

"Excruciating," Malak said with a wry smile, "agonizing, semi-fatal."

"Yes, it was, wasn't it?" Shial said thinking back through the years. "You see, Lena, the first time he tried to light a candle, he failed miserably. Half way through the spell, he doubled over in agony. Later he managed a light spell that flickered weakly for a few seconds. After that small show of power, he couldn't get out of bed for a week."

"I urinated blood for three days," said Malak remembering the experience.

"So you see, Malak may be great at lots of things, but he would never make any kind of wizard at all."

Lena looked at Malak softly. The man had seemed so able to do anything, and now there was a small chink in the iron of his makeup. Strangely he seemed closer to her, and she thought she respected him more because of his inability.

"Besides," said Malak, "I would never have been able to sit still for all those hours of study as a kid."

Lena laughed. Malak thought it was the most carefree laugh he had heard from her during the entire ordeal.

The next morning, Shial broke the news to them.

"You know I am going to Thosh," he began after breakfast. "Neither of you can go with me."

"What do you mean?" asked Lena.

"Well you know why Malak can't already. As for you, Lena, it is because of the magic I have taught you. The kingdom has very strict rules about how it is to be taught and learned, and the strictest is in regard to the towers. Well you have never been taught in a tower. In fact everything I have taught you has been illegal. I think that in Thosh your abilities would be quickly discovered."

"I can hide them, I won't use magic there," she professed.

"Be that as it may, it wouldn't take a wizard to figure out that you had some ability when you're story started to come out. I can keep both of you safe from the king, if I tell a half-truth. I will tell any who ask that I sent you to live with some neighbors when I felt there was some danger to the farm. They are going to continue to educate you, and you are with them still. The fact that Malak was the neighbor shouldn't ever have to come out."

"You want me to stay here on the farm while you're gone?" asked Lena.

"That's not a good idea either. Lots of people know about the farm and us. You can't stay here and be safe. I've already sold most of the animals to whoever I could, and when they are all gone, I will have to leave."

"But what about me? I just got back, and I wanted to spend time with you," Lena said with tears in her eyes.

"Time won't allow that for us now," said Shial. "I want you to go with Malak again, if he doesn't mind."

"With me?" said Malak who had been listening quietly. He had suspected where this was going. "I'm a trained killer with no other real skills."

"You can protect her like no one else in the kingdom can. Besides, it seems that the two of you have learned to work together and survive quite well."

"Dad, what are you saying?" asked Lena.

"Oh, relax. I'm not suggesting that the two of you get married; I'm just asking that you work together for a while until things calm down. I'll contact you when it's safe to get together again."

"How?" asked Lena still hating that they would be apart again.

"The same way I kept in contact with Dalryms and the spy. I'll teach it to you, and give you an orb. That will keep us in touch with each other."

"It's not the same as being with you." said Lena.

"It's a lot better than nothing though. Malak what do you say? I'm entrusting my daughter to you again. Do you accept?"

Malak didn't hesitate. He knew what Shial was asking of him, and he knew that he would die before he would let anything happen to her. "Sure," he said trying to lighten the mood. "But she has to promise not to make her infamous stew."

"After all these months of eating your jerked meat, I would think that anything different would be welcome," said Lena returning the slight.

"Yeah," said Malak smiling, "You'd think that."

"Ha!" scoffed Lena, and she walked off to be alone with her thoughts.

There was silence between the two men for several minutes. Then Shial spoke, "Malak, I'm grateful to you for looking out for her. I know I dumped a lot on you by sending her with you, especially without you knowing."

"You didn't burden me Shial. In fact having her with me saved my life. Several times."

"I'm glad you feel that way. Thank you for bringing her back to me. Even though it's only for a short while."

"How long do you think we'll have to hide," Malak asked changing the subject, and cutting to the heart of the matter at once.

"I don't know. I hope only for a couple of months, but I have never heard Dalryms this worried before."

"Anything else I can do for you?" Malak asked sincerely.

"Encourage her to practice her magic as much as she can. I wish I had time to teach her more. So much more."

"I'll see what I can do," said Malak.

Shial looked up at him suspecting something hidden in Malak's words. Malak looked back with a blank stare that said everything and nothing at once, and then turned away. After that, there wasn't anything more to say.

Within a week, the farm had been cleared out of all the animals. They had used the money from the sale of the land to purchase horses for the three of them, and supplies for their journeys. When the day came to separate, Lena and Shial hugged again tighter and longer than they had when they had been re-united. Neither wanting to let go. Finally they separated and mounted their horses. Shial rode off to the north for a ways, and then turned around to wave one final good-bye. Malak could see the reflection of tear tracks down Shial's cheeks even from the distance. He felt his own tears welling up in his eyes, and quickly looked away. When he looked at Lena he saw that all three of them were afflicted with the same malady. Finally the wave ended, and Shial rode around a bend, and out of sight.

Malak wondered at the strength of the man.

"Well," he finally said after he had control of his voice again. "I think we should head southwest."

"Why?" asked Lena looking through red-rimmed, puffy eyes?

"First, the winter is almost here, and that gives us until the spring before we have to push through the mountains."

"You think we should try to cross the desert too?"

"I know that we can, and I know that there is a lot of risk staying in the kingdom."

"How do you know we can cross the dessert? A lot of people have died trying."

"Because, Lena, I've done it before."

"Lena stared at him thinking that, of all the crazy things he had said he had done in the past, this was the craziest. Everything else he had said had been confirmed by her father, but this time he had to be lying."

"Besides," said Malak, "you'll be too busy to worry about the desert."

"Oh?"

"Yep," said Malak, "You're going to have a lot of homework to do. You're going to school." He turned his mount around to the southwest and clicked it into a walk. Lena stared after him with her mouth slightly ajar as he headed back the way they had come a few days ago. Wondering what he could possibly be talking about, she lightly spurred her horse to catch up with him.

The End.